JAMES HENEAGE

BY BLOOD DIVIDED

Quercus

First published in Great Britain in 2017 by Quercus
This edition published in 2018 by

Quercus Editions Ltd
Carmelite House
50 Victoria Embankment
London EC4Y 0DZ

An Hachette UK company

A CIP catalogue record for this book is available
from the British Library

PB ISBN 978 1 78648 017 0
EBOOK ISBN 978 1 78648 016 3

10 9 8 7 6 5 4 3 2

Typeset by CC Book Production

Printed and bound in Great Britain by Clays Ltd, St Ives plc

To Eliza

CONTENTS

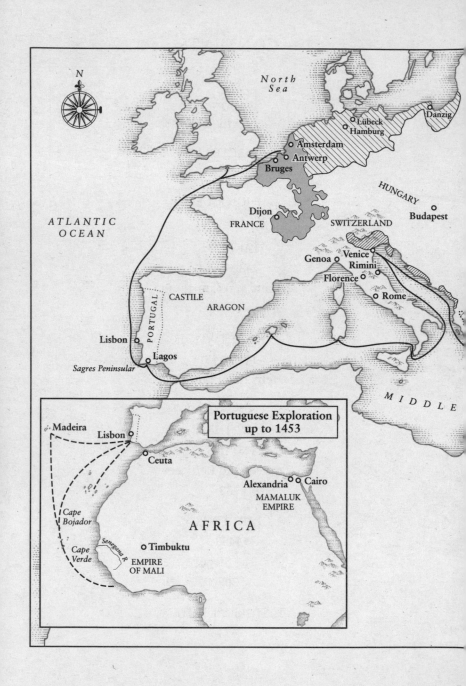

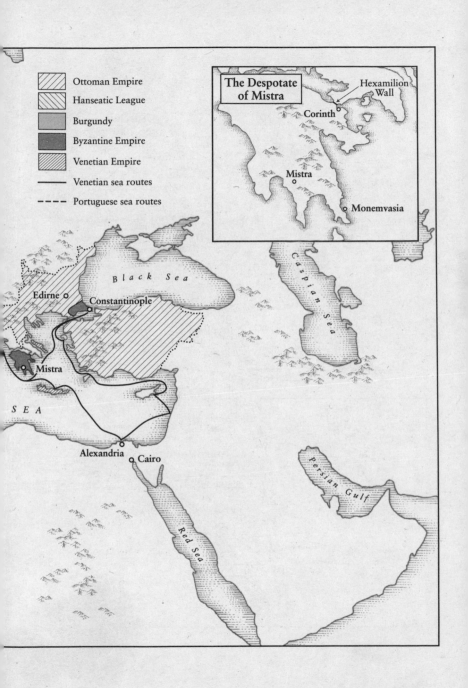

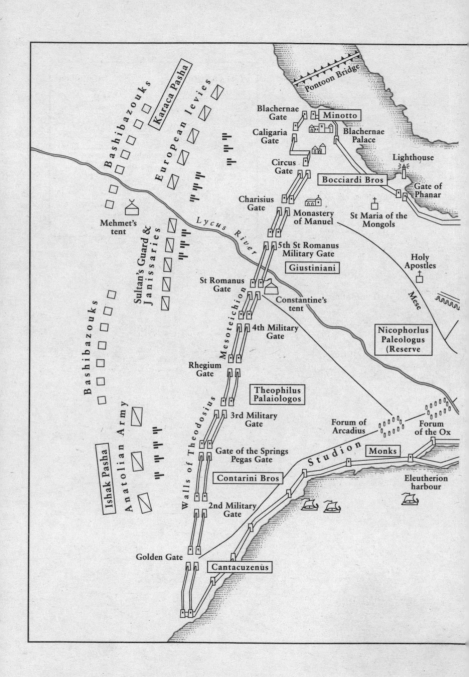

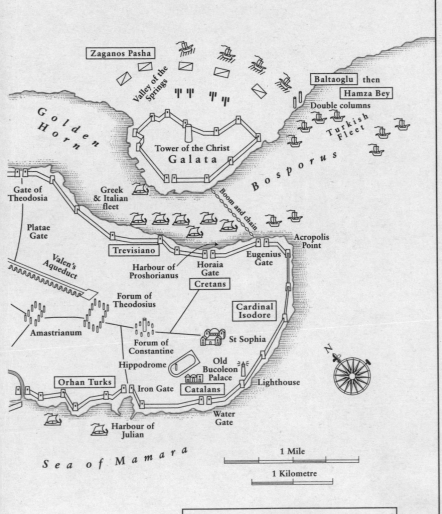

Zaganos Pasha

Valley of the Springs

Baltaoglu then

Hamza Bey

Double columns

G o l d e n
H o r n

Tower of the Christ
G a l a t a

Turkish Fleet

B o s p o r u s

Gate of
Theodosia

Greek
& Italian
fleet

Boom and chain

Plataea
Gate

Trevisiano

Acropolis
Point

Valen's
Aqueduct

Harbour of
Proshorianus

Horaia
Gate

Eugenius
Gate

Cretans

Forum of
Theodosius

Cardinal
Isodore

Amastrianum

Forum of
Constantine

St Sophia

N

Hippodrome

Old
Bucoleon
Palace

Orhan Turks

Iron Gate

Catalans

Lighthouse

Water
Gate

Harbour of
Julian

S e a   o f   M a m a r a

1 Mile

1 Kilometre

Constantinople 1453

CHARACTER LIST

(Where no dates are given, the character is fictional)

GREEK (OR ROMAN)

Constantine XI Palaiologos (b. 1405): last Roman Emperor

Theodore II Palaiologos (b. 1396): Constantine's brother, Despot of Mistra, a holy man

Cleope Malatesta (b. 1400): Renaissance princess and wife to Theodore, famed for her beauty

Demetrios Palaiologos (b. 1407): Constantine's brother, last Despot of Mistra, a weasel

Georgius Gemistus Plethon (b. 1355): philosopher and disciple of Plato, eccentric

Loukas Notaras (b. 1402): last *Megas Doux* of the Byzantine (Roman) Empire

Gennadius Scholarius (b. 1400): philosopher, theologian and first Patriarch of Constantinople under Ottoman rule

Luke Magoris: Protostrator of Mistra (Prime Minister), then banker in Venice

Siward Magoris: Luke's grandson and *Varangopoulos* of the Varangian Guard, reluctant banker in Venice

Petros: Siward's servant, useless but funny

Eugenius: deviant monk, servant to Gennadius, spy for Venice

TURKISH (OR OTTOMAN)

Murad II (b. 1404): Ottoman Sultan, a wise man

Mehmed II 'Fatih' (b. 1432): Ottoman Sultan, son of Murad II, impulsive but astute

Candarli Halil (b. unknown): First Vizier, executed by Mehmed II after siege

Zaganos Bey (b. unknown): Second Vizier, Mehmed's favourite

Baltaoğlu Süleyman Bey (b. unknown): Ottoman admiral of Bulgarian origin

Makkim: Ottoman general, grandson to Luke Magoris

Hasan: *Aga* of the janissaries, indebted to Makkim

VENETIAN

Francesco Foscari (b. 1373): Doge of Venice, wise and good until the exile of his son for treason

Girolamo Minotto (b. unknown): Bailo of Constantinople, died at the siege, probably heroically

Fra Mauro (b. unknown): Camaldolese monk and creator of one of the most important maps in history

Loredan: rich banker

Zoe Mamonas (once Greek): rich banker and courtesan spy-master

Violetta Cavarse (once Bulgarian): Venetian courtesan, famed throughout Christendom

Alessandra Viega: courtesan, her mentor

Prince Henry 'The Navigator' (b. 1394): great sponsor of exploration from his court at Sagres in Portugal

Princess (Infanta) Eleanor (b. 1434): his niece, wife to Holy Roman Emperor Frederick III

Isabella of Burgundy (b. 1397): Duchess of Burgundy, aunt to Eleanor

Joao Gonçalvez Zarco (b. 1390): explorer and first governor of Madeira

Giovanni Giustiniani Longo (b. unknown): Genoese nobleman from Chios who came to the defence of Constantinople

Salazar: sea captain, spirited

HUNGARIAN/GERMAN/POLISH/SCOTTISH

Frederick III, Holy Roman Emperor (b. 1415): husband to Eleanor of Portugal, mean and dull by repute

King Lydislaw of Hungary/Poland (b. 1424): young king who died at Battle of Varna (though the Portuguese believe he went to Madeira)

Christopher Columbus (b. 1451): explorer and Lydislaw's son, if the Portuguese and Spanish historian Manuel Rosa are to be believed

Orban (b. unknown): Hungarian gun-maker who cast 'super-guns' for Mehmed II after Constantine couldn't afford them

Johannes Grant (no dates): Scottish engineer employed by Constantine to help defend Constantinople

PROLOGUE

MISTRA, 1421

In Greece they call it the *maistros*, the winter wind that blows down from the north-west. That night it roared through the forests and chasms of the Taygetos Mountains then up, up over Mistra's citadel to fall upon the little city below like a banshee, snatching souls as it passed.

To one in the room, it was a blessing. The flicker of candle, the explosion of lightning through tall windows – both concealed the shake of a man still too angry to speak. Only two of them could have spoken anyway. The woman on the bed was dead but for the child on top of her, moving to the rhythm of her breathing. An hour into the world, it had yet to open its eyes. The nurse who'd delivered it spoke only when spoken to.

'Will she live?' asked Plethon, his head sunk deep within his ancient frame. Death might not be a hazard to a philosopher in his seventies, but Cleope Malatesta was only twenty-one.

The nurse gave a little shrug, crossing herself twice. 'God willing. It was a hard birth but what I've given her will let her sleep.' She paused. 'The child is strong.'

'Then it must be taken now,' he said softly. 'While she's drugged.' He glanced at the other man. 'As we agreed, Luke.'

Luke Magoris forced his fists still. It had been agreed but it was wrong. Lightning struck and the world was petrified. The horror of it: a bastard child allowed to live, but only if he be taken from his mother.

And what of the father?

Luke summoned the face of Giovanni, his son, exiled four months ago when the truth could no longer be hidden beneath the loosest of Cleope's dresses. Another bastard sent away: *his bastard*. He thought of the man who'd exiled him, the man downstairs whom he'd just spoken to: Theodore Palaiologos, Despot of Mistra and husband to the woman lying on the bed. He thought of a mean, cuckold mouth turned away as it had muttered those awful words.

'She must be told that he died at birth. Giovanni too. Either that or the child dies.'

Above them, the rain rattled the palace roof. 'I will go too,' he whispered. 'I can't stay here.'

Plethon looked up, his long beard suddenly free from the folds of his toga. He was Luke's senior by twenty years and everything about him was old and white. 'To Venice?'

Luke nodded. 'To run the bank. I was tired of being Protostrator anyway. A younger man can do it.'

Protostrator, second only to the Despot in the kingdom. He'd been it for many, many years but not happily since this despot had taken the throne. Theodore II Palaiologos was spare of spirit, pedantic and querulous. No wonder Cleope had been unable to love him. But could she survive her expedient marriage without Luke there to support her? He thought of the only person who might help her to.

2

'I must go to Siward,' he said.

'Not yet.'

Plethon walked over to the bed, lifted the boy and took him over to the nurse, placing him gently in her arms. Luke noticed blood on the sheet where he'd lain. *Whose?* He watched Plethon pause to look into the tiny face, then look back at him.

'Now you can go.'

'And you?'

'I'll see the child off.'

The philosopher turned and led the midwife from the room, taking a candle with him. Luke watched the door close then walked over to the bed. Cleope was almost in darkness.

Lightning struck again and two eyes stared up into his. A hand grasped his wrist.

'Where is he?'

Luke stared back. He'd faced horror in a hundred ways but none like this. Did he have the courage to answer her? He thought of her husband's face turned away.

He did the same. 'The child died,' he said. 'I'm sorry.'

Her cry was as unnatural as the lie. It came from deep, deep within a body already opened to pain. He looked down and saw a face trying to shut out his words, tightened and closed against a monstrous fact that was not a fact. Had his words killed her?

He couldn't stay. One moment more and he'd break an oath sworn by all that was sacred to him. He released her hand, bent and kissed her forehead. He turned.

Outside, in the corridor, all was dark and the only sound was the keening whine of the maistros. He thought he heard her cry out again but it could have been the wind.

His grandson's bedroom was three down. Had he heard her birthing screams? Her more recent cry? He walked to the door

3

and opened it and saw the innocence of a boy asleep, his face lit by candlelight that fingered it with soft shadow. He looked around the room: two windows, both shuttered, an icon of gloomy St Demetrius between, the sword beneath, hung from its hook as it had always been. He stared at the dragon head that was its hilt, the scaled neck, the blade still smooth despite its age. It was the Varangian sword, passed from father to son as long as Varangians had served the emperors of Byzantium. He'd fought many battles with it before giving it to Siward's father, Hilarion, his *natural* son, who'd gone to the plague four years before, along with his wife and baby daughter. The sword had hung there ever since, watching over Siward as he slept; promised to him one day.

He sat down on the bed and placed his hand on the boy's shoulder. For the second time that night, two eyes opened onto his.

'Who were you arguing with downstairs?'

So he'd heard. The boy stared up at him, frightened by what he didn't understand. Luke thought, as he always did, that there was nothing so blue in the world as his grandson's eyes: not the sea, not the robe of the Virgin on the wall of Agios Dimitrios when the sun shone through the cathedral windows. Cleope had told him they were his eyes, and it pleased him.

'It doesn't matter,' he said gently, lifting a curl from the boy's brow.

Siward frowned and sat up. His hair was thatch on fire, his skin as rich as honey. 'Will you tell me a story? A dragon story?'

Luke leant forward and put his nose to the boy's so that his beard tickled his chest. He'd done it every night when he'd put him to bed and it usually made them laugh. Not this time, though.

4

'Not tonight, Siward.'

'Tomorrow, then?'

'Not tomorrow, no.'

'Are you leaving?'

Like everyone else, he thought. Parents, sister, bastard uncle Giovanni ... none had stayed for him. Yes, he was deserting him because there was nothing else he could do. Suddenly he felt old.

'Cleope will be with you,' he said. 'And Plethon, of course.'

He saw tears come into the boy's eyes – unwelcome ones, he knew. Varangians didn't cry, even if they were only five years old. He watched this one shake his head solemnly.

'Not Cleope,' Siward said sadly. 'I heard her die. Just now.'

Luke took his hand. 'No, Siward. She was having her baby, that's all.' He squeezed. 'I want you to look after her for me.'

He watched the boy's face open with relief. He'd still have Cleope's love, even if he didn't have Luke. 'Is it a boy?'

'Yes, but . . .'

He couldn't do it. He couldn't tell the lie again; someone else would have to do it. He looked down.

'Will you come back?' asked the boy.

He tried to smile, cradling the boy's hand in the big cave of his own where it had once been warm and safe.

'Of course I'll come back. I'm only going to Venice. You remember I told you about Venice? It's where our bank is. It's time I went to look after it.'

He could bear it no longer. He released Siward's hand and rose from the bed. He looked up at the sword on the wall, seeing how the blade had turned precious in the soft light. He turned. 'Always remember the dragon, Siward. Wherever you are, it will watch over you.'

5

Siward was nodding gravely, still not understanding. Was the dragon going too? But its place was here, surely. Hadn't it been promised to him? 'Are you taking it with you?'

One more lie, perhaps the worst. He reached up and unhooked the sword from the wall. Two ruby eyes stared up into his and he didn't look away.

'For now, yes. But he'll come back.'

Outside, the maistros was still blowing hard and Luke held his cloak tight around him. There was snow in the air, riding the wind like messenger sprites, as random as fortune. He raised his hood.

He walked up the narrow streets of the little city, seeing the inn signs knock against stones they said had come up from Sparta. He'd miss every part of it: the steep, pebbled streets that echoed with sudden joy or quarrel, the fertile valley beneath, spread out like the feast it was, the dense forest that fringed the upper walls and brought the smell of pine in summer. He'd miss the snow on the mountains behind. He'd spent most of his life here, ruling with what he hoped had been justice. But there was no justice in what he'd been made to do.

He thought of the little boy he'd just left. He'd not looked back to him because his cheeks had been rivers. Would Siward manage the years ahead? He'd have Plethon to guide him, the oldest, wisest friend a man could have. And Cleope, of course.

Cleope. She'd taken his grandson's heart, as she'd once taken Giovanni's, her nature as good and fair as her beauty, and every bit as constant. She'd been mother to Siward since his own had gone. She would continue to be; he could rely on that at least.

If she lives.

He saw the city gate ahead, flames leaping from the braziers either side, soldiers huddled round them warming their hands and stamping their feet. As he approached, they straightened for the man they still thought their Protostrator, loved by all for the long peace he'd brought. He nodded to them as he passed.

He walked under the gate and found Plethon waiting on the other side. He was standing next to a curtained carriage that was harnessed to four horses with a hunched driver up front and mounted guard behind. He was enveloped by furs and only his long beard, stiff with snow, could be seen.

Luke went up to him. 'You shouldn't be out here, old man. It's cold.' He looked beyond him to the carriage. 'Is he in there?'

Plethon nodded. Luke walked over and pulled aside the curtain. Inside was the nurse with a cradle on her lap. She drew back.

'It's alright.'

He reached in and put his hand on the boy's head. Then he lifted the sword and placed it gently beside him in the cradle. He looked at the woman.

'Take this with you,' he said quietly. 'Make sure he has it. Always.'

PART ONE

1432–1444

SOLDIERS AND COURTESANS

CHAPTER ONE

MISTRA, ELEVEN YEARS LATER

Siward was in bed with a servant girl when the message came. It was mid-afternoon and most of the palace was asleep, taking refuge from the unbroken heat that had cauterised the city over the past week. He was watching a cat curled up in the shade of the window and thinking about duty.

'Won't they miss you?'

The girl was called Lela and was, perhaps, ten years older than him. She was plump and pretty and had breasts she'd made sure he'd admired with every bow she'd made.

Siward stretched. They were both naked, he on his back, she on her front, the bedclothes a tangle on the floor. Lela had been loud and energetic and caught unawares by Siward's skill. He hoped they'd not woken anyone.

'Of course they'll miss me,' he said, turning onto his side and letting his palm roam over her bottom. 'But it's my sixteenth birthday. They won't tell anyone. They're family.'

The Varangian Guard were his family in a way. Many had fathers who'd served under his grandfather, Luke, and they'd raised him as one of their own. His charm had worked on them as it had on Lela, and undoubtedly they'd spoilt him. He'd been passed from shoulder to shoulder and petted round the campfire. Now he was their young *Varangopoulos,* as his ancestors had been for four centuries. They were few in number now, these Englishmen who'd fled the Normans to guard the Roman Emperor in Constantinople, and most were in the Peloponnese.

Some of them, the wiser ones, worried about him, Siward knew. They'd watched him become someone very different from Luke: not as tall and not as serious. He was brave, certainly, and could ride better than the best of them, but he was headstrong too, quick to love and quick to fight. It was the result, they thought, of no parents and too many women. Yes, there was Plethon, but the philosopher was old and too busy thinking.

He put his face to Lela's bottom and blew. She giggled and twisted around, taking a handful of his hair and watching it run between her fingers like ears of wheat. His mother had been of Norman stock and it showed.

'You've done this before,' she said with conviction. 'Every girl in the household, I expect. When will they marry you off?'

When indeed? It was what Siward least liked to contemplate. His grandfather had suggested some Venetian match in his last letter: an heiress from the Golden Book. But marriage could wait.

He raised his head to look at her. 'There's no one else, Lela,' he said. 'I'll marry you, I think. Will you have me?'

She leant behind her, found a pillow and threw it at him. He ducked and a vase went to the floor.

'Shhh!' he said. 'You'll wake everyone. Cleope.'

Lela was Cleope's maid and she'd just come from the business of brushing her long hair. A small frown netted her brow. 'I think something's wrong with her.'

Siward sat up, suddenly serious. 'She's ill?'

The girl nodded. 'I've seen blood on her pillow. She coughs it up.' She looked at him. 'She made me swear not to tell.'

A whistle came from the square below and they both turned to the window.

'Petros,' said Siward.

'The cripple? What's he doing out there?'

'Keeping watch. Someone must be looking for me.'

Siward pulled on his shirt and went over to the window. The sun was so bright that he saw nothing at first. Then a toga, whiter than snow, moving fast across the square. Plethon was striding towards the palace.

He pulled back from the window. 'Oh God. Plethon.'

Lela had picked the sheet up from the floor and was holding it to her breasts. 'Is he coming up?'

'Not if I can stop it.' Siward was tucking the shirt into his hose with one hand while trying to close the shutter with the other. He could see Plethon's class over on the other side of the square. They were watching the scene and laughing.

'Siward!'

Plethon was looking up at the window as he strode. He must have seen the shutter close.

'I know you're up there! Your little watchman gave you away. He's the one person in the city I can outrun!'

Petros had been born with twisted legs and lived outside the city where the stinking tannery yards lay. He was poor but he was funny and Siward was his only friend.

Plethon had come up and taken hold of his ear. 'Where is he?'

'With the Varangians, lord,' shouted the boy, loudly in case the whistle hadn't been heard.

'If he's with them, why are you standing guard outside his window?'

Siward had seen enough. 'Alright, stop it!' he shouted. 'I'm coming down, so you can leave him alone.' He ran across the room to the door, still tucking in his shirt. He stopped, remembering something. He ran back to Lela and kissed her hard on the mouth. 'Sorry. Let's do this again.'

Outside, Plethon was watching Petros limp away. He really couldn't approve of the friendship. Siward was grandson to the last Protostrator and might rule this city one day, although it seemed unlikely. But then Luke had been unruly at his age.

'You didn't have to hurt him.'

Siward had emerged from the palace door and was hurrying towards him, his hair standing on end, his buttons only half done up, his blue eyes as blameless as the day he'd been born.

The old man hitched up his toga. 'He lied to me, as you are about to.'

'He was just doing what I asked him to do.'

'And it's somehow right for the grandson of our ex-Protostrator to engage a tanner's son to stand guard while he fornicates?'

Siward did up his remaining buttons. 'Don't be a snob, Plethon. You sound like your pupils.'

Plethon was shaking his head. 'What would Luke say if he were here?'

Sudden anger. 'He's not here, old man. He's in Venice. With the dragon sword.'

They stared at each other for what seemed eternity. Siward was the first to turn his eyes away. 'Anyway, why are you here?'

Plethon recovered himself. 'To tell you to ride to the Hexamilion Wall with your Varangians. Constantine needs you there.'

'Turakhan?'

'Is on his way. You need to leave.'

Turakhan bey, the Turkish general who'd brought an army into Greece the year before. He'd not attempted to breach the wall across the isthmus at Corinth then, but this time? Constantine, the Despot's younger brother, had been up there, strengthening its defences just in case.

But Siward hadn't moved. 'Cleope's ill,' he said. 'She's coughing up blood. It can't be good.'

'Ill? How do you know?'

'It doesn't matter how I know,' said Siward. 'She's never ill. She's the healthiest woman alive and she's only thirty or something. She can't be ill.'

No, she couldn't be, because, in Siward's experience, to be ill was to die. And Cleope mustn't die. He felt a familiar dread steal over him. He'd lost mother, father, uncle and grandfather – all died or gone away. Only Cleope had stayed: Cleope, the Pope's niece who'd come from Italy to marry the Despot of Mistra, an alliance not of love but politics, the first tentative moves towards reconciling the Churches of East and West after four hundred years of schism. She'd mothered and taught Siward the one thing Plethon didn't know: how to live every day like there were no more. He loved her so completely that it frightened him sometimes.

'Can you go and see her?' he asked, taking Plethon's arm. 'Now, with the doctor? Make sure she's doing what he tells her to do? You know what she's like.'

Plethon nodded. 'I will. I'm sure it's nothing.' He patted his hand. 'Now go.'

Siward left immediately. It took five minutes for Petros to put on his armour and another five for the two of them to join the Varangians at the city gate. At their head was Barnabus, a man whose age Siward could only guess at. He'd been monk before Varangian and he'd taught Siward to fight as Cleope had taught him to live: like every battle was his last. Now he was grinning.

'Happy birthday.'

Siward looked behind him at ranks of grinning giants. He was shaking his head as he took his place at their head.

'Is nothing private?'

They rode hard for the wall and got there by dawn the following day.

Constantine came out to meet them on the road. The prince was twelve years Siward's senior and a man he admired almost as much as his grandfather in Venice. He was tall and had the fair, Serbian looks of his mother in Constantinople, Helena Dragaš. Given her backing, he might be emperor one day, his brothers being who they were. Siward wanted to take the Varangian Guard back to Constantinople to guard him there, as his ancestors had done until the money ran out.

Constantine brought his horse to a stop in front of Siward's. 'Turakhan is a day away. He has cannon, but small ones.'

Siward bowed from the saddle. 'And his army?'

'Five thousand at most. *Gazi* raiders but janissaries too. Your Varangians should see them off.'

They both stood and watched the Varangians ride past in silence. Each had a longbow tied to his saddle: the best Spanish yew, capable of felling a rider at five hundred paces.

And so it proved.

Turakhan's *akincis* attacked the following day. They were men of the steppe who swarmed up to the wall on their ponies, unleashing cloud after cloud of arrows that fell harmlessly on stone. Then they retired and the ordered ranks of the janissaries advanced over their corpses while the cannon fired. They didn't get within a hundred paces of the wall.

Afterwards, when it was over, Siward stood with Barnabus and Petros on the wall and looked over a landscape littered with Turkish dead.

'It makes you wonder why they bothered,' said the cripple. He'd not taken part in the battle beyond feeding Siward with arrows. 'We lost two men and they how many? Two hundred?'

Barnabus nodded, his hand up to the sun. 'At least.' He glanced at Siward. 'So what was the point, *generalissimo*?'

It was what they called their teenage Varangopoulos. He wasn't their general but would be one day.

'To warn us, I suppose,' said Siward. There was a cheer behind them and they turned to see Constantine mounting the steps. 'We can ask the prince.'

Constantine was dressed all in white: armour, cloak . . . even the double-headed eagle on the helmet he carried. He looked like a god. He came up to the parapet and peered over. 'Hardly bruised,' he pointed. 'Look.'

Siward looked. There were little dents all along the wall where the cannon had hit. He shook his head. 'Did they ever hope to win?'

Constantine straightened. 'Perhaps. They were testing their cannon and their slave soldiers against us, but neither passed. Did you see the janissaries break? They'll need some work before they're any match for your Varangians.'

'So why did he come?'

'To send me a message.' Constantine pushed his long hair from his eyes. 'Murad knows my plan so he sent Turakhan with his message.'

Siward also knew of Constantine's plan. He'd been Constantine's lieutenant before he'd taken command of the Varangians six months ago. They'd discussed the plan often enough with Cleope.

'You've had news from the Emperor?'

Constantine nodded. 'He's heard from the Pope. There's to be a council in Italy where the issue of Church Union will be finally decided. After Rome and Constantinople are reunited, a crusade will be launched from the west while I come up from the south: a pincer to drive the Turk from Europe.' He smiled. 'Cleope has brought us a miracle.'

Cleope, niece to the Pope, whose marriage to Theodore had been as important as it was unhappy. Catholic had been joined to Orthodox, the precursor of a bigger union. She'd not wanted the marriage, but at least there'd been Giovanni to love, then Siward when he'd left. He thought of what Lela had told him.

'She may be ill,' he said carefully. 'I'd like to return to Mistra, if you'll allow it.'

A week later, Mistra was still prostrate under the heat. Men only left their houses to work and dogs guarded their shade like butcher's bones. Beneath the walls, the plain stretched out in shimmering waves of field and farm and dried riverbed, glowering up at the city like the hard Spartans it had once fed.

Cleope was very ill. She lay on her bed with her almost-white hair splayed out across the pillow and her skin, usually pink with health, pale and stippled with sweat. Lela did what she could to improve her comfort, tying wet muslin to the windows to cool whatever draught might enter, fanning and sponging her as fever set in. But whatever was afflicting Cleope had dug its claws in deep.

Siward hardly left her side. With Lela, he nursed her as best he could, keeping vigil through the night in case she woke. He tried to coax food into her mouth as she'd once done to him, long ago in a different life when she'd been well and strong and always there. He felt sick with anxiety, numb with dread, and the short periods not in her room were spent in the palace church.

He supposed his prayers were low on God's list for attention. His life so far had not been virtuous in any way he could think of, and his latest adventure with Lela, let alone the others, weighed heavily on his mind. So he ran up to the Pantanasia and Perileptos monasteries to get the monks there to pray as well. He even asked Petros to attend his first mass, thinking his condition might bestir God's pity. The boy needed little encouragement. He'd only ever received kindness from Cleope.

The Varangians returned from the wall and kept their own kind of vigil in the square outside, speaking in low voices from the shade. They loved Cleope almost as much as they loved Siward and, like all soldiers, they admired courage. They'd marvelled at the way this young girl had come from Italy to marry a man who preferred God to women, then used her beauty and charm to subdue this foreign land more completely than the Turk could ever hope to.

A week after returning, Siward sat alone with Cleope on her balcony, looking out over the plain. It was early and a breeze had come down from the mountains to spread some coolness, and he'd lifted her gently from her bed and set her down on a daybed in the shade. They'd not spoken for a long time, the silence only broken by the soft cough that came from deep within her chest. Siward had turned away every time it sounded, not wanting to see the blood.

'It's just a cough,' she said at last, noticing him turn. 'Colds bring forth coughs, Siward. It's usual.' She hid the kerchief beneath her sheet.

Siward didn't answer, preferring to let the lie settle gently between them, undisturbed by breeze or argument. He knew she was watching him.

'I'm sorry I was ill for your birthday,' she said. 'But you got your present. Did you like it?'

He'd hardly looked at the mare that had been waiting for him on his return from the wall. It had been brought up from the Magoris stud near Monemvasia and was a magnificent creature. In normal circumstances, he'd have spent every minute on its back. Now he'd almost forgotten it.

'It's descended from Eskalon, Luke's horse,' she said. 'Giovanni used to ride her mother.'

They'd never spoken about Giovanni and he wasn't sure he wanted to now. 'I won't ride her until you can come too.'

They'd ridden out together almost every day of his life, leaving the city before dawn to watch the sun rise over the mountains and turn the Evrotas River to shimmering silver. They'd galloped across the plain, scattering birds before them, resting on the riverbank to watch the heron spread their wings out to the sun. She'd told him about other birds that would be rising over her home by the sea: Rimini, seat of the Malatesta clan.

'And Lela's present to you,' she said, 'did you like that?'

He looked up. The illness had not taken the mischief from her eyes. 'How did you know?'

Cleope turned back to the view, smoothing the sheet to her legs. 'She told me, of course.'

'Told you? Why would she do that?'

'Because I asked her. Did you think I hadn't noticed?' She looked back at him, smiling. 'I'm glad she gave you her present. Though I doubt it was the first time.'

With anyone else, Siward would have felt embarrassed. He

took her hand. 'I'm not going to discuss such things with you, Cleope. Not now,' he said. 'You won't get better thinking about my disgusting habits.'

She turned, frowning. 'That's true. But we should probably talk about them nonetheless, shouldn't we?' She squeezed his hand, the frown now moving beads of sweat on her brow. 'You do need to change,' she said firmly. 'You know that. Everyone knows that except you. And perhaps Petros.'

Siward was shaking his head. 'Please can we not talk about me? I'm not the one who's ill.'

Her frown spread. 'That's why we *must* talk about you, Siward. I may not be here for much longer.'

'Don't say that.'

They sat in silence for a long while. Then she said very quietly, 'You need to grow up, Siward. Listen to Plethon. He will teach you what you need to know, if only you'll listen.'

Her cough came again and Siward looked at her this time.

'You were born to do more than be Varangopoulos,' she continued. 'You have destiny beyond Mistra, Siward.'

'I know. I'll go to Constantinople when the time comes.'

'To do what?' She coughed and wiped her lips with the cloth. 'Die on its walls? Has it occurred to you that Rome's time might be over, finally? That there might be something better to fight for?'

He'd never heard her speak like this. He'd seen her serious, of course, when he'd done something more than ordinarily wrong. But not like this.

'The Roman Empire gets smaller every year,' she continued. 'What do we have left? Constantinople and the Peloponnese. That's what the Empire of Marcus Aurelius has come to.' She looked up. 'Not a great inheritance for Constantine, is it?'

21

'But the Sultan has left us in peace since he failed to take Constantinople ten years ago. What's just happened at the wall was a feint, nothing more. Constantinople won't fall so easily. The Pope won't let it fall. Constantine said it himself.'

'Ah, Constantine's plan,' sighed Cleope. 'The one that began with my marriage to poor Theodore. Will it survive my death, do you think?' She looked at him in silence for a long time, her eyes infinitely sad. 'Will you promise me to change, Siward? Now, on my deathbed?'

Siward shook his head. 'Cleope,' he said, turning his whole body to her and leaning forward so that his blue eyes held hers. 'You are not going to die.'

Five days later, Cleope was lying in Siward's arms but thinking she was with someone else.

She'd talked of Giovanni more and more as the fever had taken hold of her mind, calling out his name and reaching out for him in the night as if he were in the room, as if he'd come back to her. Siward had watched it all and, at last, he'd known what, perhaps, he'd always known.

Plethon, finally accepting what was to come, retired to his study to write Cleope's eulogy, while Theodore joined the monks at the Pantanasia in saying masses for her soul. This left Siward, Lela and the doctor to care for her.

Lela took infinite care with her mistress, cooling her with wet towels, changing her gowns and sheets, bringing flowers and herbs to mask the many smells of decay in the room. But Siward hardly noticed her come and go. He sat by Cleope's bedside, sometimes talking, sometimes reading to her, sometimes just listening to the world outside, going about its business as if unaware that it was about to lose its greatest ornament.

One day the Patriarch came but Siward sent him away, summoning instead the Catholic priest who looked after the Norman flock still present in the Peloponnese. He and Siward alone knew that Cleope had only pretended to convert to the Orthodox Church five years ago to please her husband. He gave her extreme unction and wept as he left, for he had loved her too.

Then one evening, Cleope slipped into her last dream. Lela had just come to change her sheets and close the shutters, one by one, against the fading day. She'd looked at Cleope, lying with her eyes closed, a sheen of sweat clinging to her pale skin, and run crying from the room. Siward was alone with her.

She'd not spoken for many hours and Siward wondered if she was asleep. But then she opened her eyes.

'Giovanni.'

He saw that she'd moved her hand very slightly. She was trying to reach out to him. He took her fingers and bent to kiss them, one by one, feeling how cold they were against his lips.

'Yes,' he said. 'I'm here.'

She didn't speak for a while but stared up at the ceiling with her lips slightly apart. He saw that her eyes weren't seeing anything beyond what was in her head. He thought she might be smiling.

'Lie with me.'

He rose and climbed onto the bed and laid himself next to her, his head beside hers, feeling the soft ripple of her hair all around him, smelling the roses that Lela had plaited in it earlier. He moved his cheek to hers and felt its chill.

'I'm here,' he said again, taking her hand.

'And you won't go this time. Will you?'

He shut his eyes to stop the tears from coming, shut them hard, but they came anyway. He forced his voice to stay even.

'No, I won't go.'

She laughed then, the softest laugh he'd ever heard from her, lighter and more distant than mist.

'No, not this time,' she whispered. 'Not this time.'

They were silent for a while and Siward listened to the soft cadence of her breathing and prayed for the miracle that might let it stay just a week longer. But her cough had turned to a rattle and he heard it now, not so deep.

'You'll want to know why I didn't come to you,' she murmured. 'It wasn't Theodore, it was the boy. I couldn't leave Siward after everyone else had.' She sighed. 'I'm sorry.' He felt tiny pressure on his hand. 'Where is Luke?'

Where had she gone to in this dream? Was it before or after Luke had exiled himself to Venice, before or after Giovanni had gone to wherever he'd gone to? He bit into his lip to stop the tears.

'He's . . . he's coming,' he whispered, not sure if it was what she wanted to hear. 'Soon.'

'Good. We'll make him godfather to the child.'

Then she let out a long sigh and he knew that she'd fallen asleep. Was she happier in her dream now? He moved his head very slowly and saw that her eyes were closed. For a long while, he lay looking at her, remembering rides to the Evrotas River and a laugh so faint that it might have been a dream itself. At last he fell asleep.

Siward awoke to a soft breeze against his skin. It was everywhere in the room and had her laughter somewhere within it. He lay perfectly still, listening for her breathing. But it was in the breeze with her laughter and it was drifting out through the window and up over the Taygetos Mountains and across the sea, taking her soul back to Rimini.

Cleope Malatesta was dead.

CHAPTER TWO

VENICE

Violetta was born in Venice on a morning of sunshine and oranges.

'From Seville,' said the tall woman as she came into the room, setting the fruit down by her bedside and opening the shutters one by one to the sounds of the canal outside. Violetta blinked, nodded and put her teeth to the orange. She'd heard her new name and liked it.

The woman who'd given it to her was Venice's greatest courtesan, Alessandra Viega, and she was dressed in a silk day-gown that looked like milk had been poured from above. She had tiny arches over her eyes and a spot painted on her cheek. She was thirty years old and hoping to retire.

'I will call you Violetta from now on,' she said, walking over to the bed. 'You are born again as my daughter. I will teach you and you will replace me.'

It was at Ragusa that she'd first felt the pull of Venice, letting it draw her in to its scented bosom on invisible cords. She'd walked up the coast to Split, then Trogir, finding tantalising hints of what was to come in the pillared lions that looked down on every square, in the huge, pennanted galleys that rode the swell in every harbour. She was eighteen and already experienced in the many ways of survival.

Once in the city, her strange, dark beauty seemed to suit the melancholy of the place and she found work at an inn off the *Piazza San Marco*, serving drinks, distracting drunkards and listening to the gossip of travellers. One night, she learnt how to benefit from it all.

'There's beauty beneath that apron,' said the man with moustaches as she passed his table. 'Come here and sit.'

He was a rich merchant and sober, so she sat and he talked to her of the Rialto and the money to be made there. She'd listened so hard that she'd missed the inn-owner when he'd come over to complain, and then again when he'd come back to dismiss her. An hour later, she'd risen calmly, removed her apron and left the inn. She'd walked out with the merchant.

She was not surprised by the terms he'd offered: live with him and learn the business of Venice. Her body would help her survive as it had before, many times. The priest had anaesthetised her to men's lust.

Sometimes, as she lay awake beside her benefactor at night, she remembered a time when perhaps she might have changed things. She'd been eight or nine years old and lying in a field beneath a big blue sky and a sun too bright to look at. Beside her lay her brother and they were holding hands.

They'd finished building stories in the sky, told by clouds that changed shape as the wind moved them. She'd turned and looked at eyes much bluer than any sky and felt the same fear she'd felt for as long as she could remember.

'They won't take you, will they, Illy? When they come?'

'They might, yes. I'll be old enough next year.'

'But who can stop it?'

'Only the priest. He has the list.'

Silence then.

'He touches me sometimes,' she'd whispered.

'That's what priests do. It's their way.'

Of course he was right, she'd thought. Ilya was wise and kind and strong and she couldn't imagine a world without him. She wouldn't let anyone take him. Not ever.

'I will do anything to stop you going,' she'd said. And she had.

It was the merchant who'd shown her her future. He'd taught her everything he knew, including the most important: who in Venice got the best information. He'd pointed them out beneath the arches of the Rialto.

'It's the courtesans who get all the news,' he'd said. 'The *cortigiane di lume* ply their trade here and can tell you the changing price of bread. But it's their grander sisters, the *cortigiane oneste*, who are clever as well as beautiful, who can tell you the minds of princes.'

So she decided to become one. She left the merchant and gained employment with the best cortigiane oneste in Venice, Alessandra Viega, and for a year was one of scores of servants who tended her palace. Then her beauty promoted her to the weekly salon where the *signore* met to talk. She was dressed in silks, cut low at the bosom, and her black hair was lifted and sculpted and filled with scented flowers and little jewels. She served drinks and was noticed.

But she wanted more than notice. Opportunity came to her one hot summer evening when the windows of the palace were thrown open to breeze from the Grand Canal and she was serving chilled wine in a dress of canary yellow that turned to flame as the sun went down outside. In the vast drawing room were Loredans, Mocinegos, Stenos, Grimanis, Veniers and other men of consequence who'd arrived that evening by liveried gondola.

First the signore talked of Venice. Its fleets commanded the Middle Sea and its wealth was beyond counting. It was the bullion centre of the world, taking gold from Africa and turning it into coin for the rich nations of the East with whom it had a monopoly of trade. It had a martial Doge in Francesco Foscari and its enemies were in retreat. Only two clouds darkened the signores' horizon: the immediate threat of Islam and the more distant one of Portugal. It was this that they talked of most. And a map.

'Fra Mauro of the Camaldolese has the commission,' said a Steno, 'and it's ambitious: to collect every known fact about our world and turn it into a great map. It will take ten years to complete.'

'And our Doge gave the commission?' asked a Venier.

'Yes, but it is shared with Prince Henry of Portugal. It will be expensive in the making.'

'And in consequence perhaps,' said a Grimani. 'What if it shows a way round Africa to the East? Portugal will steal our trade, then Spain. No wonder Prince Henry wants to share it.'

Alessandra Viega had been sitting amongst these men with her head a little to one side, her bright eyes moving from speaker to speaker. Now she spoke. 'But can Ptolemy have been so wrong? For centuries we've known the way round Africa closed. Why have things changed?'

'Perhaps our Greek friend can help?'

The question had come from a man Violetta hadn't seen

before, a dark man of pointed nose and beard whose face held no warmth. He was addressing another, older man with striking blue eyes.

Alessandra Viega clapped her hands. 'Ah, the bailo speaks of the Chinese rumour.' She turned to the Greek. 'Can it be true, Luke?'

But the older man only smiled.

'Are you talking of the Chinese junk?' asked Venier of the bailo. 'The one they say sailed round Africa and came to Mistra twenty years past?'

'I am.' The bailo was persistent. 'And we have a man here tonight who can confirm or deny it.' His smile was thinner than Parma ham. 'Luke Magoris, you were Protostrator of Mistra then. Tell us, can Africa be rounded?'

But Luke Magoris would not be drawn. 'Let us wait and see what the map says, Minotto.'

'But I am bailo of Constantinople,' cried Minotto, already a little drunk. 'If the city falls, our trade route to the East will be cut. Venice might survive that calamity but not Africa as well.' He lowered his voice. 'You are Venetian now, Magoris. You should tell us what you know.'

The room had fallen silent and all eyes were on the Greek.

Luke rose. 'It is late and I am a man who tires easily these days.' He took Alessandra Viega's hand and bowed. 'Thank you, Alessandra.'

He left. With such a question left unanswered, it seemed that no other could rise to the occasion. One by one the party rose and went down to meet their gondolas at the canal gate. At last, only Minotto remained and he was now very drunk.

'I'll stay, if you please,' he said.

Alessandra smiled. 'But your new wife,' she said. 'She will be waiting for you.'

He shrugged unevenly. 'Let her wait. I want to stay.'

'It is not convenient,' she said. 'It is my time.'

'And mine,' said Minotto, rising without balance. 'I've seen blood before.'

No movement of Alessandra's body indicated any measure of offence. There was silence for a while. 'Very well,' she said, rising too. 'But afterwards you must leave.'

She turned and walked to the door, her scents drifting in her wake. Minotto followed her, his walk erratic, his wine-breath insulting her fragrance. At the door, he stopped and looked back. His heavy eyes fell to Violetta's breasts and stayed there. He smiled his wafer smile, then shook his head. He turned and went.

She began to clear away the glasses, placing them on a tray and admiring each as she did so. She lifted one against the last candle's flame, turning it by its stem: the miracle of Murano glass – sand, heat and a sprinkling of arsenic. She'd have to visit the island one day. Wasn't that also where the Camaldolese monastery lay? Might Fra Mauro even show her his map?

She heard a noise from upstairs: the closing of a door. She put down the glass and bent to blow out the candle. She turned and went out into the hall.

A cry came: involuntary, choked back. She stopped and listened. It came from Alessandra Viega's bedroom.

She went over to the wide, sweeping staircase and began to mount it, step by careful step.

Another noise: harder, sharper. Was it a slap?

She quickened her pace, taking the stairs two at a time. She came to the top, then walked over to Alessandra's door. She heard the sound of voices from beyond: one male, raised.

The door opened. Alessandra Viega was standing in her night-clothes. 'I need your help,' she said.

'What can I do?'

'Take my place,' she whispered. 'He has agreed to it. You want to be a courtesan? Well, this is your chance.'

So began an education.

The night with Minotto had been painful but mercifully short. Afterwards, he'd fallen asleep quickly and servants had arrived to lift him down to his gondola. She'd tried to rise too, but they'd told her to stay. So she'd fallen asleep, bruised but happy, to awake to sunshine and oranges.

The education took less than a year. Alessandra Viega had underestimated how much her student had already taught herself on the road. She was amazed by her grasp of languages, of world affairs, of the business of making money. Within a month Violetta was reading Plato, within two the poetry of Catullus. In four months she'd mastered the lute and a dozen *ballate*, in six she was making riddles and epigrams that Plutarch might have admired. In ten months, Alessandra could teach her no more.

'You're ready,' the courtesan announced one morning. 'Violetta Cavarse is ready to take on the world.' She smiled. 'Have pity on it.'

She was used to the name by now, liking its subtle colours, its curves. *Violetta Cavarse.*

'Where do I live?' she asked.

'Here for now, then your own palace. You've made money on the Rialto, I know.'

'And my patrons?'

'You will take mine. I'm too old for this profession. I want to retire.'

'But you're only thirty!'

Alessandra Viega smiled. 'I'm tired and I can afford to retire. Zoe has seen to that.' She paused. 'It is time to tell you about Zoe Mamonas, I think.'

CHAPTER THREE

EDIRNE

Makkim lay in bed and listened to the beating of the rain on the roof tiles. Dawn had crept into the room not long ago and he'd not heard the call to prayer for the noise. He wondered if he'd been missed at the palace mosque.

He looked around the room, unused to such luxury. There were tapestries and thick carpets, candalabra above with enough candles to keep slaves at work for an hour. Hasan had said it had belonged to some *Megas Doux* when he'd shown him in last night. That had been when Edirne had been called Adrianople and the Roman Empire included Thrace.

He closed his eyes and thought of the barracks outside: rows of hard beds, a wooden floor that would glow from hard polishing and a smell so clean you might be in the mountains. Did he miss it? *Of course.*

He thought of another place where he'd slept long, long ago: another lifetime it seemed sometimes. They'd loved storms, the two of them burrowing deep beneath the blankets to make a cave of cosy warmth, telling stories in excited whispers, letting their imaginations fly out on the wind, out into the violent darkness. Another family, before the janissary one.

He opened his eyes. The rain was stopping, which was good. The Sultan should inspect the men in sunshine, not rain. Murad should walk down the janissary ranks and see himself mirrored in their magnificence. He heard splashes outside.

He got up and went over to the window, passing his new armour hung like fleece from its frame, his reflection in its gold: the big face beneath cropped fair hair, the blue eyes, the scar that ran from eye to chin. *Not a Turkish face.*

In the courtyard below, the men were forming up between puddles, looking up beneath their tall *bork* hats to see if more rain was coming. Some were flattening moustaches to their cheeks with their palms. Officers in their tall boots were carrying cauldrons to the front of each unit.

'Spoons!'

Hasan, *aga* of the janissaries, was walking along the first rank where each man held up a spoon for inspection. Makkim smiled. That had been his idea: the men using spoons to feed from their unit's cauldron that they'd carry with them and be proud of. They'd be the *kaşik kardeşliği*, the brotherhood of the spoon: a new family to replace the one they'd lost.

A shout came from below. The Aga had found a blemished spoon. A man was being dragged away to some punishment and the janissaries didn't move a whisker of moustache for the shame of it all. Makkim watched and remembered and felt some nostalgia. He turned and began to dress.

There were footsteps on the stairs and a knock on the door. He looked up from his laces to find Hasan entering the room. He rose and bowed. 'Aga.'

Hasan was in his thirties, ten years older than Makkim, and

every inch as tall. He'd been made for a more titanic age when a man could stand between temple pillars and break them in two. He ducked as he came through the door.

'I think I should be bowing to you, strictly speaking,' he said. 'Or I will be after you've seen the Sultan, I suspect.' He went to the window and leant out. 'The rain has stopped, the streets will be washed of offal and the dogs will bark.' He turned. 'I hope not too loudly during the parade.'

Makkim put both hands to his friend's arms. 'I will always bow to you, aga,' he said. 'You've taught me everything I know.'

'Not so,' said Hasan, meeting his eyes and giving a rare smile. They'd known each other since Makkim had come to Edirne to learn how to be a janissary. 'What you've become, you've earned yourself, Makkim. Murad knows it. That's why he wants to see you.'

'And will you tell me what he's likely to say?'

Hasan shrugged and looked back at the view. 'You can guess, I daresay: that he never wants to suffer another defeat like Kunovica, that the janissaries must make every battle a victory from now.'

'Was it very terrible?'

'Kunovica? A battle fought at night and in deep snow is always terrible, even under a full moon. It was a massacre.' The Aga shook his head. 'You should be thankful that Murad left you behind.'

'And he's put Turakhan in prison?'

'In Tokat, yes. So there's a vacancy for general. One with a scar on his cheek, perhaps?' Hasan lowered his voice. 'This is your chance, Makkim.'

There was the sound of trumpets outside and they both looked towards it.

35

'Murad is coming,' said the Aga. 'Finish your dressing. We should go out.'

They went down to a silent world. The janissaries in their ranks stood to rigid attention, officers and cauldrons to their front, the high, white hats on their heads the only things disturbed by the gentle breeze. Hasan and Makkim walked past them to take up position by the gate through which the Sultan would arrive.

Murad had not come alone. With him were his twelve-year-old son, Mehmed, and the vizier Candarli Halil. Mehmed was taller than his father already and his thin face looked up into the watery sun, his eyes closed. All three of them wore furs against the cold and their hands were thrust into muffs of squirrel-fur.

Hasan stepped forward and bowed deeply, Makkim behind him.

'The janissaries await your pleasure, serene highness, and their aga and captain are here to present them for your inspection.'

Makkim rose from the bow to both Murad and Mehmed's gaze. They were looking at him quite differently: the father with an interested smile, the son with some curiosity amidst the scowl. Candarli, meanwhile, was exchanging glances with Hasan.

'We've heard good things of you, Makkim,' said Murad, 'over these past few years. First, at the *enderun* palace school, you proved yourself the best of the best. In study alone, you surpassed the janissary requirement of three languages: you mastered six. Is Greek among them?'

'Yes, majesty,' said Makkim.

'And Italian, for speaking to Venice?'

'Yes, majesty.'

36

Murad glanced at Candarli and back. 'That is good. Take my hand.' They walked over to where the janissaries stood waiting, Mehmed, Candarli and Hasan behind. Every man was a giant next to Murad but he didn't seem to mind. He nodded as he passed them, lifting a spoon or sword for a closer look, even putting his fingers to a moustache. He came to the end of the front rank and turned.

'Things might have been different if such men had been at Kunovica. I suppose they were still being trained.'

Makkim bowed. 'Indeed, majesty. But they are ready now.'

'Yes,' said Murad. 'They are.' His gaze drifted over the janissary ranks and he sighed deeply. 'You've done well. I would speak to you with the vizier.' He turned to Mehmed. 'Not you.'

Mehmed's scowl hadn't left him for any part of the inspection. Now it deepened.

'Why not?' he asked.

'Because I say it,' said Murad sternly. 'Now go. Hasan, take him.'

The Aga placed a hand on the boy's shoulder. It was immediately shaken off. Mehmed swung round to face him.

'You dare touch me?'

Hasan took a step backwards. 'I . . .' He fell to his knees. 'Forgive me, master.'

Murad had taken Makkim's arm and was leading him away with Candarli. Makkim glanced behind them. Hasan was still on his knees but Murad was staring after him with his head to one side.

They entered the palace and walked down a corridor and came to a door with guards outside who prostrated themselves. Inside was a small room without windows, a secret room built for secret talk. It had a carpet with three chairs on it: simple, uncushioned seats devoid of ornament. Murad sat in one and gestured to the others.

'Please.'

They were silent for a while, facing each other. Murad arranged the folds of his day-gown at the sleeves, then smoothed it to his knees. Makkim watched him, noticing the slight tremor beyond the thin wrists, the rapid tap of his heel on the carpet. *How well is this sultan?*

Murad looked at him. 'I am tired of ruling,' he said, as if in answer. 'You see a tired man before you, Makkim.'

The silence lasted longer this time and Makkim considered what he'd heard. How old was Murad? Forty? Were the pressures of rule so exhausting? He thought of a tall boy outside, excluded from the meeting. Angry.

Again, Murad answered him. 'My son is spoilt, impulsive . . .' he glanced at Candarli, 'yes, perhaps even dangerous. But I am considering letting him rule. Am I mad?'

Why was he hearing this? Since graduating from the enderun five years ago, Makkim had risen to second in command of the janissaries, propelled by an aga who'd recognised a genius for leadership and planning. He'd been given the task of reorganising the janissary corps, a process that had kept it, and him, from the battlefield of Kunovica. But he'd never been engaged in high politics, nor met his sultan before this. Why was he hearing this now?

Murad continued. 'My janissaries were humiliated at the Hexamilion Wall twelve years ago. These past few years, you have recruited thousands more and created corps for everything from road-building to bread-making. Before, we sultans had too often been betrayed by our gazi troops. Now we have a professional,

38

standing army: well-armed and possessed of unquestioning loyalty.' He nodded. 'We owe you much.'

Makkim dipped his head. All of it was true but it had been no more than his duty. To his sultan. To his God.

'So I ask myself,' said Murad, 'why would a man wrenched from his family do so much for those who had wrenched him? Is it love for what you've come to, or hatred for what you've left behind?'

Makkim considered this. What was it? Was it the quiet logic of Islam learnt every day for six years amidst five daily prayers? Was it the love of the new, janissary family he'd entered into? Or was it, in fact, a deep hatred of Christianity? Had the actions of one man made him hate a whole religion? He remembered a trapdoor shutting above him in a crypt that still reeked of the man's breath. He remembered the shame of being down there while others were taken above. *For your mother and sister's sake,* he'd said. *Who else will look after them if you go?*

Why hadn't he seen it then?

'I have done it for Islam, highness,' he said, 'for Allah and His Prophet Mohammed, may peace be upon him.'

Murad was nodding. 'And is what I do also for Islam, do you think? All this *jihad* against our Christian enemies who worship the same God? All this fighting to provoke the Pope into sending another crusade against us? All this *blood*?'

Was he talking about the disaster at Kunovica? Makkim supposed so. 'What has happened was one defeat amongst many victories, highness. The janissaries are now ready to reverse it.'

Murad looked down at his hands that were gathered in his lap like an open book. He might have been reading from his palms. 'I expect they are,' he said quietly. 'But I have another plan. I will make peace with this crusade before it comes against us again.

I have written to Pope Eugene, to King Lydislaw of Hungary. It is time to think of my soul.'

Makkim tried hard not to allow the shock into his face. 'Peace, highness?' He glanced at Candarli. He'd heard that the vizier's brother had been captured in the battle. Had Candarli persuaded him to make peace with the infidel?

Murad had seen the glance. 'You are right. Much of my thinking comes from Candarli Pasha. He can explain.'

Makkim looked at the vizier. He was middle-aged and tall and had heavy eyebrows above eyes that were dark pools of intelligence. It was said that Murad depended on him more and more these days.

Candarli had turned his full attention to Makkim, his long beard resting on his chest like a bib. His gaze was unwavering.

'We live in important times, Makkim,' he said. 'Consider the world: half of it obeys the laws of the Prophet, the rest is in darkness. Over the past hundred years we've conquered more and more in the west, with Constantinople always the greatest prize to come. We've assumed the East all within the Abode of Peace, but it's not. The Mongol empire of Tamerlane is disintegrating and in Persia new Shi'a sects are challenging the unity of Islam.'

The vizier was nodding, his beard dipping as far as his knees. He spread his hands. 'Meanwhile, what do we find further to the west? We find the only place where Islam is in retreat. The Spanish kings have nearly driven us back to Africa while in Portugal . . .' now he was shaking his head, 'in Portugal this new House of Aviz is producing princes who want to turn the flank of Islam by sailing round Africa to the East.' He gestured. 'While we build fleets to take Constantinople and claim the Mediterranean, they look to the wealth of the Indian Ocean.

And why wouldn't they? Since the Chinese left, it is there for the taking.'

Makkim didn't understand. He'd not learnt much about China during his years at the enderun. 'China, lord?'

'The Ming emperors, yes. They sent seven expeditions out under their Admiral Zheng to claim the whole Indian Ocean, to dominate the trade of the East. They say one ship might even have rounded Africa. But Zheng died ten years ago and there have been none since. The trade of the East is suddenly available.'

Makkim searched his memory for what he'd learnt of Portugal. 'But the Portuguese number less than a million, lord. They're not a powerful or rich people. Their geography locks them out of the trade of the Mediterranean.'

'Precisely, which is why they are looking to Africa. Thirty years ago they took the fortress of Ceuta from our brothers in Morocco. It is the gateway to Africa and every year since they've ventured further and further south. One day they'll find a way round Africa, if it exists.'

Makkim remembered something else from his lessons. 'But Ptolemy . . .'

'Yes, yes, I know. Ptolemy told us there's no way around,' said the vizier. 'But what if he was wrong? The Venetians and Portuguese have commissioned a map that will tell us one way or the other. If India can be reached from the west, Christians will surround us, instead of us them. Much is at stake.'

Murad had been watching the exchange. Now he raised his hand. 'All of which explains why I must now turn my attention to the East,' he said. 'We must forget Constantinople and instead recreate the strong Islamic Caliphate the Abbassids once had. We must forget the Mediterranean and return to the Indian Ocean, before the West takes it from us.'

Makkim saw the logic but still wondered why it was being shared with him. He thought of how he might put the question.

'Which takes us back to my son,' said Murad, obliging. He had his hands flat to his knees, sitting upright as if preparing to rise. 'I will abdicate and I will make peace with the West to give Mehmed time to learn how to rule, to learn the logic of turning to the East. You will teach him.'

'Me, majesty? But . . .'

Murad had raised his hand again. 'My son admires you, Makkim. He knows what you've done for the army. He may listen to you as he does no one else.' He straightened. 'I hope so, for at present he is obsessed with taking Constantinople. You must persuade him otherwise.'

Makkim had imagined some sort of military promotion, not appointment as tutor to a spoilt prince. But if what Candarli believed was true, then the future of Islam was at stake. Then again, what he knew of Mehmed he didn't like. He was said to be cruel, vindictive and given to sudden rages – hardly the temperament for learning.

He protested, 'I am a soldier, highness, I have no skill . . .'

'And you will remain a soldier,' said Murad. 'In fact, I am promoting you to general, but you will keep Mehmed by your side always.' He rose. 'As to other things you might want, I will leave you to discuss these with my vizier.'

Murad left. What did Makkim want? Nothing but to serve his Sultan and God. Except . . . there was something the janissary training had not obliterated: his memories.

Candarli knew it. 'Your family,' he said, leaning forward in his chair, 'were from a village in Bulgaria. You would like them brought here, no?'

'I . . .' Makkim stared at the vizier. Of course, his agents would

42

have told him. What else did he know? Did he know about the murdered priest?

'But you were rescued more than taken, I think,' Candarli said softly, his head to one side. 'Is it not so?'

Makkim remembered a lightning flash that revealed a body on the floor, a girl standing next to him, wide-eyed in horror.

'Ilya, what have you done?'

What had he done? A priest lay with his cheek to the ground, blood spilling out across the stone. *He touches me sometimes.*

He'd closed his eyes without knowing it. Candarli was speaking again.

'Your family . . . well, there is a problem,' he said. 'All that's left there is your mother.' Candarli looked down at his hands, the first time his eyes had left Makkim's. He looked up again. 'But she never wants to see you again.'

CHAPTER FOUR

BATTLEFIELD OF VARNA, BULGARIA

Across the plain, between Lake Varna and the sea, the dead
lay thick on the ground and the very earth wept blood. Birds
skipped and slipped between the armour like clumsy bathers
finding balance. The stench would stay until the soil was turned
in the spring.

'Did you find him?'

Murad leant forward in his saddle. He wore boots above his
knees and rested a fist on his thigh. He held a cloth to his face.

Makkim replied, 'We found a body, lord. It was his armour
but there was no head.'

The Sultan frowned. 'So we need a head.'

Prince Mehmed sat on a horse next to Murad's. He pointed
his whip at the man kneeling next to Makkim, his head bowed.
'Take Hasan's, then find Lydislaw's.'

Makkim glanced down at Hasan. His neck seemed hard to
sever. He looked back. 'Hasan fought hard, prince, as hard as I.
He doesn't deserve to die.'

Makkim's face told of how hard he'd fought. There was blood
on every part of it so that, for once, the scar was hidden. When

44

King Lydislaw had made his last, desperate charge, he'd saved the battle and the Sultan's life. But he hadn't found the thing that mattered most: King Lydislaw's head.

The head of the man who'd broken the treaty.

Prince Mehmed said to his father, 'You marched to this battle with Lydislaw's peace treaty nailed to your standard. The battle isn't won until we have his head.' He turned to Makkim. 'And Lydislaw would have won if you hadn't rallied the janissaries, yet it is Hasan who commands them.'

'He was wounded, lord.'

'Because of him, Lydislaw may have got away. He should die.'

Mehmed's eyes were a furnace of hate. But for whom? Hasan? Lydislaw? Murad? It was hard to see into such fire. Mehmed hated his father for coming out of retirement to fight this battle, but he hated Lydislaw more for being the reason he'd had to do it.

Makkim looked at Murad. The Sultan seemed so much older, his skin as patched and grey as the sky above. He hoped it was nothing beyond exhaustion. He met the eyes of the vizier beside him. They both knew that Mehmed couldn't have ruled for any longer. He'd proved himself too dangerous in the few short months he'd tried. *And I was supposed to restrain him.*

Murad dismounted slowly. He approached Makkim and put his hands on his shoulders, looking up, for his general was tall. 'You have won a great battle, Makkim. And you saved my life.'

It was true. It had been Lydislaw's last, reckless gamble: to charge Murad's bodyguard with five hundred of his Hungarian knights, to try and cut the head from this monster that was devouring the flower of Christendom. It had nearly worked. Hasan had fallen but Makkim had rallied the janissaries and they'd held. The janissaries, *his* janissaries, had defended Murad.

The Sultan turned to Hasan. He took his hand and raised him up. 'Makkim saved me and now he saves you, aga. You owe him a life.'

Hasan got slowly to his feet, his hand to his side where the blade had struck. He looked at Makkim and held his eye. 'I will repay the debt,' he said. 'Be sure of it.'

Makkim was dizzy with exhaustion. The day was fading fast, low cloud hovering over the distant hills. He felt rain on his forehead and looked up. 'I will look again, majesty. Before it gets dark.'

He walked towards the marshlands where the Cardinal had died, swallowed up on his horse as he'd tried to escape. It was he who'd persuaded King Lydislaw that no oath given to a Muslim was one you had to keep, that the ten-year peace treaty might be broken by a surprise attack before the crusade went back to its homes. He stopped and looked down at a young knight still holding his shield, Wallachian judging by the arms. He wore no helmet and his face was calm. How old was he? Sixteen? A black crucifix hung from his neck.

Makkim looked down at the dragon sword at his side, finding his fingers curled tight around its scaled, curving neck. He tried to relax them.

A shout.

'Makkim!'

Prince Mehmed was walking towards him, picking his way through the corpses, his arms thrown wide like a scarecrow's, the birds rising grudgingly before him, pulling at things.

Makkim rose. 'Highness, it's dangerous. Some may still be alive.'

The prince stumbled, kneeling on a breastplate with his hand pressed to a face. 'Help me then.'

Makkim gave him a hand and pulled him to his feet. The boy shook him away, then looked down at his glove with disgust. 'Christian blood.' He wiped it on his sleeve. 'Enough to fill the Bosporos, do you think?' He looked at Makkim. 'Hasan has a good friend in you.'

'The Aga did all that was asked of him.'

'He should still die.'

It always shocked him how much blood Mehmed wanted to spill. There was enough of it on this field to slake even his thirst, so why must he have more? He knew why. Mehmed hadn't forgotten Hasan's hand of restraint eight months before.

Was it really only eight months? It seemed a lifetime that he'd been mentor to the boy, a task he'd failed at. Despite his best arguments, Mehmed still wanted to lay siege to Constantinople. At least now, with his father's return, he'd have to wait. Perhaps there was still time to change his mind.

He sighed. 'If you are ever to take Constantinople, you'll need Hasan.'

Mehmed took his arm. 'Have you spoken to my father about it, as I asked you?'

Makkim shook his head. 'The prince should ask the Sultan himself. Have you considered a little deference?'

Mehmed spat and watched the spittle land, saw it mingle with the blood on the ground. He glanced back towards where Murad still stood, too far to hear. 'To you, perhaps, sometimes. Not him. The old fool won't speak to me. You know that.'

'Because you revile him.' Makkim spoke quietly. He studied the boy awhile. Mehmed's hatred surrounded him like a fog, blinding him to the world. 'We'll not lay siege to the city,' he said. 'Your father wants to turn east and Constantinople has the strongest walls in the world. It will take cannon of a size not yet seen to break them.'

'It will take courage to break them,' said Mehmed. 'Courage my father lacks.' His grip tightened on Makkim's arm so that his mail pitted his skin. 'I will break those walls when my father is dead.' He looked up at the sky and held out his other hand to the rain, watching the blood of his enemies wash through his fingers. 'I *will* be Caesar, Makkim.'

CHAPTER FIVE

VENICE

Murad's great victory at Varna threw Venice's Rialto into a frenzy of speculation. With so much at stake, the Doge had placed agents at the battlefield and fast riders over the thousand miles between. It took only four days for news of the catastrophe to reach the city.

For nearly everyone, it was bad. The last Christian crusade had been annihilated. It was only a matter of time before Constantinople was put to the siege and, if it fell, all Europe might go to Islam.

They didn't know that Murad had other plans.

For the courtesan Violetta Cavarse, it was better news. She'd learnt of the complacency of the Christian leadership and bet on a victory for Murad. Only afterwards did she learn how close it had been and how much had depended on a man of only twenty-two who all Europe was talking about: Makkim.

She was thinking about him when Alessandra Viega came to visit her in her new palace on the Grand Canal. The older courtesan was retired by now and most of her patrons had transferred gracefully, even gratefully, to Violetta. But there was one piece of business remaining.

She met Alessandra in a garden full of citrus trees to remind them both, perhaps, of how their friendship had started. They sat down on a bench to talk.

'You judged Varna well,' said Alessandra, sipping her wine. 'Though no one could have predicted this Makkim.'

'I was thinking of him when you arrived,' said Violetta. 'Will he be the one to take Constantinople, do you think? We need to learn more about him.'

'Which is why I'm here.' Alessandra put down her glass. 'Zoe Mamonas thinks as you do. She wants to meet you. Tonight.'

They came after dark and by gondola. They took the Grand Canal first, then smaller channels with low bridges and sudden corners. They carried a lantern at their prow but the boatman shouted his warning at every turn. There was no moon and the water was heard but not seen. At length they arrived at some steps. Violetta looked up at a tall building.

'No lights.'

Alessandra had stood up to disembark. 'She prefers darkness. There will be few candles inside.'

The boatman lifted the lantern and helped them ashore. He'd not spoken a word on the way there and now glanced up at the palace. Alessandra took the lamp and they mounted the steps. The doors were of blackened wood with brass lion-heads for knobs. She pushed at one and it opened. There were no servants to greet them.

'Where is everyone?' whispered Violetta. 'Does she live alone?'

'At night, yes.'

'She is strange.'

Alessandra stopped and turned to her. 'Perhaps. But she is also the most extraordinary person I have ever met. You'll see.'

They came to a wide staircase of marble with candles too dispersed to see beyond. There was no carpet and their footsteps were loud; the volume of the building could only be guessed at. They climbed to the top and stood facing two large doors. Alessandra knocked.

If someone had answered, Violetta didn't hear it. But Alessandra opened the door and led her in.

The room was better lit than outside, but only just. It was large and high and arched on one side. On the other were windows that stretched from floor to ceiling where stout candles stood before closed shutters, unlit. A long table with a map on it, secured by more candles, stood in front of them. Opposite, in the shadows beneath the arches, were dark figures that became statues. The floor was marble and it shone with pale lustre from the light of a single, suspended lantern. At the end of the room stood a chair facing them. On it sat a veiled woman dressed entirely in black. She didn't move.

Alessandra seemed at her ease. 'I've brought her.'

'Good, then light some candles.'

While Violetta watched, the room slowly revealed itself. Alessandra took a candlelighter from the shadows, applied it to another lantern and went from window to window lighting the candles, each one throwing its shadow onto the next. She went back and reappeared with a chair, then another, which she placed in front of Zoe. She and Violetta sat.

The woman in front of them did not move in her high-backed chair. Her dress was of black silk unadorned with tracery. It had a raised neck that disappeared beneath the veil and its sleeves fell either side of the chair-arms, on which her gloved hands held lion-heads.

She asked: 'How old are you?'

51

'I am twenty.'

They were silent again. The woman still hadn't moved but they could just hear her breathing. There was a rasp to it.

'Would you like to see me?' she asked.

Violetta glanced at Alessandra and back. 'Yes,' she said. 'I would.'

Zoe raised a gloved hand and lifted the veil. Violetta looked into a face whose past beauty was hidden deep, deep beneath the erosion of years. It was as cracked and fissured as a desert landscape and there were brown islands among its sands. Her eyes were the colour of crimson.

'The effect of the *teriaca*,' she said. 'You know of it?'

Violetta shook her head, too shocked to speak.

'Prepared with powdered viper, opium and the horn of a narwhal, and made only in Venice. It's said to prevent aging.' She gave a little grunt. 'It doesn't.'

'But your eyes,' Violetta whispered. 'Can you . . . ?'

'That's the opium. And no, I can't stop it. Hence the veil.'

They were silent for a while.

'Would you like me to replace it?'

Violetta looked into bloodshot eyes that gleamed in the candlelight like open wounds. She saw that little veins ran out from them, bloody channels to irrigate her tortured face. She felt sudden pity and shook her head. 'No.'

'Good. You're not squeamish. Sensible in your profession.'

Violetta thought of Minotto whom she'd refused to take as patron and who'd minded the insult. It wasn't squeamishness that had prompted it; she simply didn't trust him.

Zoe coughed twice. She raised a kerchief to her lips and dabbed. She let her hands settle in her lap before speaking again. 'Alessandra's patrons have all gone to you without a murmur. You must be good.' She looked at her. 'Should I have the same faith in you?'

Violetta didn't answer. Zoe Mamonas would make up her own mind. She glanced around the room. The arches were filigreed and the statues beneath were Greek and mainly female. In front of Artemis stood a table with a clock on it that had the sun at its centre and zodiacal signs around. Beside it sat a Bible and a Koran, side by side.

Zoe had followed her gaze. 'I'm not taking chances with eternity,' she said. 'The Koran was given to me by Tamerlane. Did you know that I was his mistress?' The candlelight made patterns on the old woman's dress. It was her only movement. 'But that is my past. Tell me about yours.'

Violetta shifted in her seat. The question made her uneasy. 'There is little to tell,' she said. 'I was born to a peasant family in Bulgaria and ran away. I came to Venice and here I am.'

'What age did you flee your village?'

'Eleven,' she said.

'And you came here at eighteen, I'm told. What happened in between?'

What happened? *I survived, that's all.* How much should she tell this woman with the teriaca eyes? Should she tell her that she'd fled without telling her mother? That she'd dressed as a boy and found work scaring crows from fields and rats from barns? That she'd become feral, trusting her instincts more than her brain? That most nights, she'd harnessed her young body to the business of staying alive?

Or should she talk of kindness? Of the village where she'd been taken in to mind children, of a woman of some education who'd taught her to read and write? Or of the pilgrims who'd

53

shared their food with her and told her of Venice, a place so rich that its very cats wore collars of gold?

'I survived,' she said.

'Which is why you're so good a courtesan,' said Zoe. 'You see things clearly.'

'Perhaps,' she said. 'I don't know.'

Zoe studied her awhile, her eyes too ruined for any reading of them. 'Well, I will have faith in you, if only because she does.' She jabbed a sudden finger at Alessandra. 'You know my terms?'

'I spy for you and retire in luxury.'

'And why shouldn't you have luxury?' asked Zoe. 'You'll have worked for it.' She wiped her lips again. 'Whores age early,' she said, 'however beautiful they are. It's not nice to be poor when you're not used to it.'

Violetta nodded slowly. *How would you know?* She asked, 'What do you want me to find out?'

Zoe tried to sigh but the cough took over. 'Everything,' she muttered into her fist, recovering. She looked up. 'But especially things specific to these strange times. The Varna battle has changed much.'

Violetta glanced at Alessandra who was watching Zoe as a pupil might her teacher, a slight smile lifting her lips at each end where there were tiny lines. The light did not flatter her. *Whores age early.*

'The Rialto believes Constantinople will fall,' Zoe continued softly. 'But are they right? There will be money to be made if they're not, be sure of it.' She coughed and dabbed, leaning forward slightly, her bony hands on the chair's arms. 'And what does our competitor the Magoris Bank believe? Why has Luke Magoris been seen on Murano where Fra Mauro's map is being made? Will the monk show Africa open to the south and, if so, will the Portuguese round it? And if they do, isn't there a bigger problem for Venice than Constantinople's fall?' She took a breath. 'A lot of questions.'

'And who has the answers?' asked Violetta.

'The most interesting men have them,' answered Zoe, 'and a few women too. I can name the men for you: Prince Henry of Portugal, King Lydislaw – if he survived Varna, Fra Mauro who is making the map, and Mehmed, who will one day replace Murad as sultan and is said to be fixated on taking Constantinople.' She was counting on her fingers. 'And the most interesting of all? This new one, Makkim.'

'Except for the monk, none of them are in Venice,' said Violetta. 'Am I to go so far for my patrons?'

Zoe raised a finger. 'Ah, but they all *speak* to Venice, you may be sure. Someone in this city will know their mind.'

'The Doge?'

'Well, he may be interesting too. This Foscari Doge started wise and prudent but what will happen when the Council of Ten tries his son Jacopo for corruption as it intends to? What if they exile that son? Foscari loves Jacopo beyond reason. Will he *stay* wise and prudent after that? When so much is at stake?'

'If Luke Magoris has been seen on Murano,' said Violetta, 'might he know what this map says?'

Zoe shook her head slowly. 'Perhaps, but he is discreet. I have known Luke all my life and still don't know him. He won't sleep with you and he hardly drinks so it's difficult to learn much from him.' She considered. 'There's Nikolas, of course, his best friend and once his fellow Varangian. But he's just as impossible.'

Violetta stared at the woman before her. She thought about all that she'd said. It seemed that the world was on the cusp of momentous change and it excited her. She asked quietly, 'So what does it all amount to?'

Zoe stayed silent for so long that Violetta wondered if she'd fallen asleep. After all, it was late and the meeting had been thorough. She'd just glanced at Alessandra for guidance when the old women spoke again. She spoke softly and Violetta knew it was the final thing she'd hear from her that night. 'We in Venice have always seen ourselves at the centre of things. We fear irrelevance more than wars or plague. But the future of the world may be determined not by us, but by a young sultan's obsession with Constantinople.'

She was nodding very slowly as she leant back in her chair. 'Or perhaps by this Makkim. We shall see.'

PART TWO

1449–1451

HEIRS TO AN EMPIRE

CHAPTER SIX

MISTRA, GREEK PELOPONNESE

The torture of cold marble. Siward Magoris's knees had felt over thirty winter marbles but none so cold as this.

Perhaps he'd just forgotten them all, just as he'd forgotten the words of this interminable service. It wasn't as if he could even hear it. Outside was chaos, the wind hurling snow against the cathedral walls, roaring through the steep, mazed streets of Mistra like a minotaur.

The Patriarch had stopped talking and his hands fluttered over the new Emperor's head like doves. Far above, a shutter was rattling and Siward looked up. He saw its doors straining against their hinges as if a fist was trying to push through.

His eyes fell from the shutter to a vision in golden mosaic: Cleope Malatesta, once queen of his city, now immortalised on that wall. Her face was solemn but he didn't remember it like that. Her laughter was with him most days. He remembered her funeral in this very cathedral, the sea of people outside to hear Plethon's long and brilliant eulogy. It was sixteen years ago that she'd begged him to change. He had, and he'd learnt fast and well, pleasing Plethon but not Petros. Then Constantine had taken him off to fight.

He looked at a figure beside her on the wall, one of many bearing her skywards. Lela, surely. She'd died giving birth to a guardsman's child five years after Cleope had gone. Two angels taken back to heaven. *What sort of God destroys His own?*

He glanced around. The cathedral was very small. There were perhaps twenty of them inside it, mostly old men wearing the heavy robes of ancient empire, the insignia of titles no longer with any meaning: Protostrator, *Megas Doux* . . . even his own: Varangopoulos. Once, men such as these had led armies and navies to guard half the world. Now the Roman Empire was Constantinople and this little Despotate of Mistra in the Greek Peloponnese. Most of the nobles had moved to Mistra where they felt safe from the Turk and Constantinople was left a place of orchards and fields and empty churches: a city of echoes, too many for a coronation.

'Hear our prayer, Lord, and those of your servant . . .'

No echoes here. The snow muffled and wrapped the little city in its embrace. He caught the eye of the oldest man there: Plethon, philosopher or heretic, depending on where you lived. He saw how stooped he'd become of late. He'd hate this service but for different reasons, preferring the new Emperor to look elsewhere for his inspiration. Plato, for instance.

Siward looked at the new Emperor. A galley was waiting at Monemvasia to take Constantine to the city he'd been named for, to rule over what was left of his empire. Was he to go with him? They'd fought together, nearly achieving what Constantine had said he'd do all those years ago: catch the Turks in a pincer and throw them out of Europe. But then Lydislaw had

60

broken his oath and the northern pincer had been destroyed at Varna. Now the Turks were stronger than ever.

He looked up.

The sound was more urgent this time. Not a fist but something sharper. Could snow do that? His mind swept up and out to the Taygetos Mountains that cradled this little city in their comfortable lap. The Melingoi tribe was up there somewhere, sheltering in their caves. Did they know they had a new emperor? Did they care? Did anyone care?

There were two gunshots and the shutters gave way in an explosion of snow. A black bird came in, shrieking and flapping. It circled above the nave, round and round like something held by a string.

The congregation stood as one and looked up, twenty mouths agape, twenty hands to their hats. For a time, the bird was borne up by the snow's withered fingers. Then they opened and it came down hard to the ground, shrieking its pain. It lay still. What had killed it?

Siward pushed past the Patriarch, saw the bird resting on the heart of a bigger bird: the Palaiologos double-headed eagle carved into the stone. He saw blood spread its crimson tide across the eagle's face. An omen.

He stooped and picked up the bird, wrapping it in the folds of his cloak. He turned to a guard: 'Wipe it up.' To the Patriarch: 'Finish.' To Constantine, a whisper: 'Majesty, forgive me.'

He turned and walked through the congregation to the door, then outside. Petros was by the door, where he'd left him.

'Take this and throw it over the walls. Make sure the people see you do it.'

*

Much later, after the last courtier had kissed the new Emperor's ring, Siward was waiting in his grandfather's study in the Magoris house. It was a small room, a place of work and contemplation, unused since Luke had left for Venice over a quarter of a century ago. He looked around at the panelled walls, hard woods to make the features of hard Romans: Augustus, Trajan, Diocletian who'd cut the Empire in two, Stilicho who'd tried to save it, Justinian who'd so nearly won it all back. There was a map on one of the panels: the Roman world as it had been a thousand years ago, a Pax Romana gathered round the trade of the Mediterranean, guarded by invincible armies at every frontier. He'd always seen Rome as eternal. It would endure because it stood for civilisation and peace in a barbaric world. His destiny was simple: to preserve it.

He could see his face in the polished wood: the beard above the square jaw, the high cheeks, the nose squashed in some forgotten battle. It was a face imperfect but strong. They said he had the same height as his grandfather, the same fairness and blue eyes that spoke of northern forests and lakes. He laughed like Luke, they said: loud, like you might across a lake. *Why didn't you come to the coronation?*

He turned away to the desk. It had the head of Luke's first-born on it, Giovanni shaped in agate: his illegitimate uncle, banished from Mistra for getting Cleope with child, a child who had died.

The door opened and he looked up. Constantine entered, then Plethon. The Emperor still wore his robes, snow lining his shoulders like epaulettes. Plethon was in his customary toga, a vest beneath it. They sat.

There was silence, unusual between the three. Since Constantine had become despot on his brother Theodore's death, they'd been a triumvirate, bound by friendship and argument, especially over Siward's destiny. Plethon had seen a future Protostrator of Mistra, practising sound, humanist government. Constantine had seen a soldier to take north to fight. Constantine had had his way and Siward had campaigned with him until five years ago, when Varna had stopped everything.

The Emperor looked solemn. He turned to him. 'The reason that your grandfather isn't here, Siward, is because he died three weeks ago in Venice. The news came yesterday but we thought it best to wait.'

Siward was shocked but not surprised. Luke had been old and only visited Mistra twice since Theodore's death. The second time Siward had been away fighting with Constantine. He knew he'd been close to him once – even remembered bedtime stories beneath a dragon sword hung on the wall. But that was long ago.

And the dragon didn't come back as he said it would.

Plethon said, 'He was a great man and he was my friend. I missed him when he went to Venice.'

Siward was nodding slowly. 'I should go there to bring back his body.'

'He wishes to be buried in Chios,' said Constantine. 'You will take the body there, then return to Venice. Luke has asked that you take over the bank.' He hesitated. 'I have seen his will.'

Now Siward was surprised. 'But I know nothing about banking.'

'So you'll learn. Nikolas will teach you.'

'But what about Constantinople?' he asked. 'You'll need me there.'

'Constantinople can manage without you for now,' said Plethon. 'We've been expecting Murad to besiege it ever since

Varna, but he seems to have other plans. He may be turning to the East, despite Varna.' He paused. 'And Demetrios has asked for the Varangians to be kept here in Mistra. Our new despot fears another attack on the Hexamilion Wall.'

Or on his person, thought Siward. Demetrios was not popular since he'd tried to usurp the imperial throne, an act only prevented by the brothers' mother, Helena Dragaš, who'd known Constantine to be the better man.

Siward tried again. 'Murad is ill and we know who'll succeed him. I should go with Constantine to prepare Constantinople against Mehmed.'

Constantine shook his head. 'You're more use to me in Venice, Siward. I need money to rebuild its walls.'

Plethon leant forward across the table. 'There is a banker there called Zoe Mamonas who is Greek and may be able to help. She knew your grandfather and knows Nikolas.'

'But why can't Nikolas do all this? You must know by now that I'm a soldier, surely?'

Plethon looked at him for a long time, seeing deep into a character he'd helped shape more than anyone, a character he'd seen change since Cleope's death. 'I don't know that, Siward,' he said gently. 'You were my pupil once, then Constantine's until Varna brought you back. I've seen greatness in you and the times require great men.' He smiled. 'Perhaps you were always meant to be more than a soldier.'

Constantine placed his hand on his shoulder. He rose.

'I also need your uncle Giovanni back from exile,' he said. 'He became an expert on siege warfare after he was banished, improving the defences of the Portuguese fortress at Ceuta. I want him back in Constantinople.'

CHAPTER SEVEN

MADEIRA, COLONY OF PORTUGAL

Giovanni Giustiniani Longo leant forward from the prow of the boat and smelt fennel. He raised his nose to it like the whiskered monk seals he'd passed on the *Camara de Lobos*, lying thick as mangrove on the beach. He breathed in and smiled. No burning.

He'd smelt burning for seven years and now it was over. The forest of laurel and juniper that had once covered this island of Madeira was in the air, drifting out to the edge of the world on a breeze from Africa, making way for fields of sugar.

Before him lay Funchal, thatched *palheiros* climbing the amphitheatre of its little bay to the stone church at the top like early worshippers. On either side were tall red cliffs with birds swarming their surfaces: swifts, wagtails and kestrels nesting in the cracks. Behind were mountains capped by cloud, their forests too steep for burning. He'd hunted pigeon in them once, amidst clouds of copper butterflies axed by sunlight. That had been in the early days when the silence of this Eden had been broken only by the whisper of scented wind.

Three stocky square-rigged coasters rocked in the bay like fat ducks. Around them were skiffs and supply barges with men standing and shouting: Portuguese mostly, for the island had been empty when they came.

'That's it.'

Giovanni glanced to where the sailor was pointing. One ship was anchored apart, the only one not flying the arms of Portugal from its mast. A single figure was leaning over its side, drawing water from a bucket on a rope.

'How long has it been here?'

The man shrugged, one hand on the tiller, the other shielding his eyes from the sun. 'A month? They say he's building a house on the *Cabo Girao*. Calls himself Henry the German.'

Giovanni smiled. *Henry the German*. Was he German, this Lydislaw? Zarco hadn't said much about him in his letter, except that he was a fugitive. Cabo Girao was a sensible place for a fugitive to hide. Lydislaw would see for miles from up there.

He felt in his pocket for the letter. He'd not read it but then he'd not opened any of the letters that had come from his father in Venice over the years. So why had he kept this one? Did it have something to do with the man he was about to meet?

They were approaching the jetty and someone was waiting to take their rope, someone with one eye patched beneath a straw hat. The man performed a little curtsey, hat in hand. 'Welcome to my capital, now with cathedral.'

Giovanni glanced at Zarco, then up at the little church at the top. Santa Caterina's foundation stone had been laid two years earlier.

Zarco caught the rope. 'At least the Franciscans will shut up now. Have they reached Calheta yet?'

Giovanni jumped onto the jetty, taking Zarco's hand, his satchel clamped to his front. He took a moment to regain his balance. 'They've built hermitages in the caves.'

Zarco rolled his eyes. 'Hermitages! Who are they saving us from? We've no women!' Zarco drew back. 'Well, maybe a few. Do you need one?'

Giovanni laughed. 'I'm over fifty, Zarco, as are you. We should be setting an example.'

'Yes, but abstinence is not good for a man. Humours build up, bad ones.' Zarco had turned and was walking him down the jetty, one arm through his, the other fanning the air with his hat. 'But then . . .' He glanced sideways.

It was what they never talked about: why Giovanni was on the island at all. Zarco knew most of it: his love for a queen that had ended in a child that couldn't possibly be her husband's, a child that had died. And he knew that letters had come constantly from Venice, none of which had been answered. He changed the subject.

'How does your sugar?'

The effort of forgetting had been channelled into the production of sugarcane on the walled terraces above Calheta Bay. It had made Giovanni rich, but not happy.

'We've built bamboo walls. For the wind.' He looked out at a sea mottled with cloud. Would this incessant wind blow them all over the edge one day?

They'd reached the dirt track that ran up between the houses to the church, little eddies of dust spiralling in front of them. Zarco stopped and pointed at a wooden building with piles of ropes outside.

'Our first chandler. And we're building a dry dock below. A hostel too.'

Giovanni whistled. 'Who's paying for it all?'

'Prince Henry,' said Zarco, wiping his brow, 'through his Order of Christ. Did you know he runs the Order now?'

'I'm told they're also calling him "The Navigator". How far down Africa have we got?'

'"We"? Are you Portuguese now?' Zarco laughed. 'He's sent ships past the gold coast they call Guinea. They've gone inland too. They think the Senegana River joins to the Nile. They want to find Prester John.' He looked at him. 'Did Henry tell you this?'

Giovanni shook his head. 'Just the way to Ceuta. It was only after that he started trusting me.' He looked away. 'And sent me here, of course.'

Zarco had started walking again. 'Well, Madeira will become the main staging post for the fleets sailing down from Ceuta. They'll find everything they need here: fruit, cordage, women.' He winked with his good eye and Giovanni remembered that the other had been lost taking Ceuta thirty years ago.

'Is King Lydislaw staying with you?'

Zarco nodded. 'While his house is being built. He, his wife Anna, and a new son who they've called Christopher.'

Christopher. It was an odd name for a prince but perhaps not for one who was to grow up disguised as something else, he supposed. *Christopher the German.*

They'd reached the little square in front of the church lined with dragon trees, their branches scaly like serpents' flesh, little cups tied to their bark to collect the blood-red sap. Giovanni thought about a dragon sword he'd once known. He supposed his nephew would have it now. His father's letters might have told him, if he'd ever opened them. He thought again about the one in his pocket.

They started walking again, slower now for the way was steep. The track was lined with geraniums, orchids and giant buttercups turned towards the sun. Everything grew in this rich island garden, especially sugar.

Zarco's home came into view, its tower clustered by vines. There were chickens and pigs in the road and a child squatting by the side talking to a monkey. The smell of wood smoke was in the air. They walked through the gate and into a courtyard with a tiny chapel to one side. A large millstone, pitted and holed at its centre, lay on the ground. A young man dressed in black sat at a table beneath an umbrella. He had a book propped before him but was looking over it into a cradle that he rocked with his foot.

'There he is.'

The man stopped rocking and rose. He looked younger than Giovanni had expected, but then, he remembered, King Lydislaw had only been twenty at Varna. His face was unbearded and his thick black hair fell straight to broad shoulders. Giovanni bowed, straightening to see sad eyes looking into his.

'King Lydislaw,' said Zarco, 'may I present Giovanni Giustiniani Longo, once of Chios, now of Madeira?'

The king made a little bow. 'But were you not also once of Mistra?'

Giustiniani dipped his head. 'Long ago, majesty. Tutored by Plethon.'

'Ah, Plethon. And his tutoring extended to sugar?'

'No, majesty. That was the *Cornaro* men from Cyprus.'

Lydislaw continued, 'Zarco has told me all. The Cornaro men brought sugar beet cuttings to an island with more sun than Cyprus or Sicily, but it was you who brought water from the mountains by hewing channels from the rock. That must have been hard.'

Giovanni brought his satchel round to his front and unstrapped it. He took out three small cones of sugar wrapped tightly in vine leaves and placed them on the table.

Lydislaw picked one up and studied it. 'The price per pound is the same as nutmeg, which is why it's called "white gold". The Arabs refine it in Syria, the Venetians are starting to in Tyre.' He looked up. 'Would you be able to refine it here?'

'We have wind and water so we can work the mills. We're building them at Calheta. We'll soon be exporting white and muscavado. More than Cyprus.'

'Then Venice will suffer.' The king smiled and turned to Zarco. 'Shall we take wine to celebrate?'

A woman appeared at the door of the house. She wore an apron hemmed with red dust and held a jug in one hand, brass cups in the other. The men moved into the shade and sat while she poured wine the colour of honey. They drank.

Giovanni asked, 'Venice's discomfort pleases you, majesty?'

The king didn't answer at first, turning his cup slowly in his hand. Then: 'At Varna, they could have made the difference.'

Varna. For the rest of his life, Lydislaw would be on a Bulgarian plain strewn with Christian dead, caparisoned horses wandering aimlessly among the bodies like awkward guests. The smell would always be with him. Always the smell. He took a deep breath. 'Since Varna, I've been among the monasteries of Christendom, trying to repent, trying to find some forgiveness – some reason even – for breaking my oath. God has not forgiven me.'

'You lost a battle, It happens.'

'No.' Lydislaw turned to him. 'I broke an oath, an oath sworn before God and His Angels. I broke it and God punished me. Constantinople will fall and Madeira will be my home for the rest of my life.'

Zarco frowned. 'Well, there are worse places to hide; Murad's agents won't find you here. Christopher will be safe.'

Lydislaw was watching Giovanni closely. 'We're both exiles, I suppose. Why did you choose here?'

Giovanni looked down at his hands. He spoke quietly. 'Because it was as far from Mistra as I could find.'

Lydislaw glanced around the courtyard. It was empty of life beyond goats. He turned to Giovanni. 'I met your father in Venice. I was staying at the Camaldolese monastery on Murano and he visited me.'

Giovanni thought of the letter in his pocket. 'Is he well?' he asked.

'He is dead,' said Lydislaw. 'Which you would know if you'd opened the letter that came with my ship.'

Giovanni felt a sudden surge of something unexpected. Luke Magoris was dead. His father was gone and he suddenly felt unmoored, adrift on this island at the edge of the world. Why did it matter so much to him?

'You misjudged him, I think,' continued Lydislaw. 'He had no choice but to banish you.' He was fingering his crucifix, which Giovanni noticed he did quite often. A bead of sweat fell into his wine and he wiped his brow with his sleeve. 'He told me to tell you something.' He hesitated. 'In case you hadn't received his letters.'

Giovanni waited.

'Your son born by Cleope,' he said. 'He is alive.'

Much later, after Giovanni had recovered from the rage that had driven him from the courtyard, he found King Lydislaw praying in the little chapel.

He'd spent the afternoon lying on Zarco's bed and the others had left him alone, knowing he'd need time to absorb such a revelation. He'd stared up at the ceiling, unable to speak, his fists clenched with fury. For thirty years, he'd believed his son to be dead. For thirty years his father had let him believe it.

He found Lydislaw kneeling on the altar steps, his head bowed, a single suspended candle above his head. He came to sit in the pew behind him. He waited for Lydislaw to cross himself.

'How did my father die?' he asked, watching Lydislaw rise. It was evening and the chapel was very quiet.

The king came and sat beside him. 'I don't know,' he said. 'News of his death reached me on the road. I only know what he told me.'

'Which was what?'

'What he tried to tell you in his letters, Giovanni,' said the king. 'That he'd been sworn to say the child had died in exchange for its life. Theodore had wanted to kill it but it was sent away instead with its nurse.'

'To where?'

'She'd come from Bulgaria,' said the king, 'so perhaps there. Luke had tried to find her over the years, but then the Turks invaded the country and it was no longer possible to look.'

Giovanni closed his eyes. The pain of discovery had made a lattice of his brow. Lydislaw glanced at him and took his hand.

'Why didn't you open the letters?' he asked gently.

Giovanni shook his head slowly. 'Because I didn't want to read anything from him,' he said bleakly. 'When I was exiled, Cleope wanted to come with me but he wouldn't let her.' He opened his eyes and looked at the king. 'I never forgave him for it.'

For a long time they were both silent. Giovanni's mind, so long trammelled by anger and misery, was suddenly remembering things he'd chosen to forget. He thought about rests by the side of the Evrotas River, watching dragonflies skim the water with their busy wings. He thought of what had happened during one longer rest as the sun had dipped over the mountains. He thought of that moment of ecstasy, a glimpse of heaven granted to them both for a love that could only have come from God. The son that had come from that ecstasy was alive and somewhere in the world.

Then he thought of his father, a man he'd once loved too, but chosen to hate instead. If only he'd opened the letters.

He turned to the younger man beside him. 'How do I find him?'

The king was watching him closely. 'Well, the boy may have something still. Your father told me that he put a sword into his cradle when he left Mistra, a sword you know well.' He leant forward. 'Perhaps you should look for that sword.'

CHAPTER EIGHT

VENICE

It took longer for Siward to arrive in Venice than the Emperor Constantine might have liked and much longer than Nikolas had hoped for. Nikolas had been his grandfather's closest friend and, on Luke's death, suddenly felt mortal. He longed to retire to Mistra.

He came by round ship with his servant, Petros, who was seasick throughout the voyage and unable to perform his duties. The ship weighed anchor outside the lido until skiffs arrived to haul it through the treacherous waters that protected the city. They got into one and travelled through air hazy from evaporation, watching the *briccole* emerge like sentries to mark the channels. The sky was the colour of pearl, its uncertain light drawn from the horizon. All around, the sea churned thick as milk.

The pilot was informative, describing the islands they passed.

'A cemetery.' He pointed at one. 'Two in three lost to the plague and all buried there.' He was shaking his head. 'Heaped between the earth like lasagne.'

Siward looked across to an island pricked by crosses. A solitary dog, chained to a gatepost, barked as they passed. He smelt the fugitive scent of jasmine and banksia roses.

'What's that?' asked Petros, pointing to another island.

'The *Isole del dolore*. Where they put the mad,' answered the pilot. 'Though it's hard to tell these days.' He spat over the side. 'Venice has gone mad. You'll see.'

Siward heard the bells first, carried over the water in little eddies of sound. He saw a hedge of shimmering crenellation that slowly became buildings. He'd come only once before to the city, ten years ago, to meet his grandfather's partner, Nikolas, who'd just returned from China, and some rich daughter of the city that Luke had thought might make a suitable match. Siward had not missed the city, or its daughter.

They dropped anchor again in St Mark's Basin and the pilot left to find another tow. Siward and Petros transferred themselves to the ship's tender and were rowed into the city, Petros vomiting over the side. The sun shone from a watery autumn sky and the *palazzos* of merchant princes presented themselves in gaudy procession, each a stage property, each sited for the eye. All were encrusted with ornament, as fine below as above, shimmering like shells at the bottom of a rock pool. This, thought Siward, was a city locked in its own reflection, like Narcissus.

The boat was turning into the jetties fronting the Piazza San Marco where a man was waiting, too young to be Nikolas. He wore a tabard and a beret on his head. A seagull stood beside him, looking up.

Then they were ashore, being greeted and pushing their way through the crowds in the square, Petros with the luggage. There were pilgrims everywhere, some at booths where galley-owners spread maps on tables, some at stalls buying a last indulgence.

At the base of the *campanile*, money-changers had their boards and a puppet theatre made diversion for the pickpockets.

They came to a street lined with expensive shops and busy with traffic, most of it male and dressed in sober black, the colour of gravity. These were the merchants of Venice, priests of Mammon with their sallow skins, long noses and high cheek-bones. A woman stood talking to a man in front of a shop. She was dressed in peacock blue, her gown mantled in velvet, flowers in her hair. A dwarf stood behind her glowering at passers-by. Siward stopped.

'Violetta Cavarse,' said the liveried servant. 'Venice's greatest courtesan.'

'Greatest?'

The man nodded. 'They bring her out to entertain kings and ambassadors. For her wit.'

'Not just her wit,' said Petros.

Siward stared at her. She'd turned from the man and the dwarf was pulling at her hand to leave. She had the dark, rich look of the gypsy, unaltered by powder or paint, and her black hair fell in ringlets to her shoulders. She wore little stilts against the mud.

But the man she was with wouldn't let her go. He was holding her arm, talking into her ear.

'Who is the man?' asked Siward.

'He is the bailo of Constantinople, Girolamo Minotto. He is here to prepare the fleet.'

'The fleet?'

'For Constantinople, should the city be besieged.'

'He is hurting her.'

They watched in silence for a moment. Violetta Cavarse seemed unworried by the man's insistence. She listened to him

76

patiently, then calmly removed his hand from her arm, one finger at a time. She turned and walked towards them. She saw Siward and, in an instant, her eyes travelled from his head to his toes. She smiled and walked on.

Siward smiled back. He was used to female attention. In Mistra, women had admired and sometimes succumbed but few had stayed. He'd seemed unlikely to marry.

'Where does Violetta Cavarse live?' he asked.

The man shook his head. 'Sir, she has few patrons. She is not to be bought.'

They walked on and passed a nunnery where women in black sat behind grating on little stools while slaves poured drinks. They giggled and nudged each other as Siward passed. Petros stopped and stared at them. Siward pulled him on.

'I can introduce you to others if you like,' continued the man, 'including some in nunneries.'

Siward glanced back. Violetta Cavarse had gone.

They came to the Rialto, the beating heart of Venice where the bankers plied their trade and slaves were sold amidst the fish. A man with a bell stood in front of a group of chained Tartars who watched him impassively. The place smelt of fear and fish and they hurried on, Petros limping behind. At last they came to the Magoris fondaco, arriving at its back door since the front took goods from the canal. Nikolas was there, waiting for them.

'You took your time.'

Nikolas had aged since Siward had last seen him. His face had new lines stretched over a gaunter frame. He was dressed, as usual, in the style of the Ming, a rich silk tunic scattered with dragons, but the body beneath was bent. He leant on a stick but straightened to receive Siward.

'I'd thought you here for the spring,' he continued, taking Siward's hand. 'I want to leave this swamp. Who is this?'

Nikolas had pointed at Petros who was sitting on the luggage.

'My servant. Petros, get up.'

'He is impertinent.'

Petros rose and performed an awkward bow. Venice seemed more formal than Mistra.

Siward kissed Nikolas on both cheeks. 'You look well.'

'I doubt it. It's impossible to be well here with all the mosquitoes and intrigue. I don't know which is worse.'

It had always been thus. Nikolas had complained unceasingly since returning from China. But he'd stayed in Venice, perhaps seeing some adequate reflection of what he'd left behind in its inscrutable face. He'd been married once to a Ming concubine, they said, whom he'd loved beyond reason. Siward had often wondered if it was her death that had driven him west.

Nikolas put his arm round Siward's shoulders as they walked. The two men were tall and had to dip their heads to enter the fondaco's door. They kept them dipped through a passage that led into a colonnaded square, open to the sky, with pebbles sloping down to a central drain. The ground was wet. 'We've been cleaning up for your arrival.' He prodded the stone with his stick. 'Careful you don't slip.'

Siward heard movement above and looked up to see the stairs crowded with people, all staring down at him. They were, perhaps, the entire staff of the bank. They looked anxious.

'You can see them later,' said Nikolas, turning him to a side door. 'We need to talk first. Your servant can stay here.'

They left Petros and went into a room lined with bookshelves crammed with ledgers. A wide desk stood in the middle with papers piled on it. On one wall was a large map with coloured pins in it. The room smelt of ancient leather and parchment and the faintest veil of dust hung in the air. Nikolas sat heavily at one end of the table and gestured to the other.

'Sit.'

Siward sat. Something was wrong, he knew, beyond the death of a friend.

'I know you don't want to be here,' said Nikolas gently. 'You want to be in Constantinople with your Varangians.' He leant his stick against the table. 'But Luke has left you the bank and there are serious matters to attend to. Firstly, the Songhai have invaded the Empire of Mali. They've closed the trade route to the gold.'

This was bad news indeed. Luke Magoris had long ago travelled to Mali and set up the trade route for their gold. Caravans had left Timbuktu every year for three decades. Some of the gold had gone to Nikolas in China and some to Alexandria, bound for the bullion centre of the world: Venice. It was a trade that had made the Magoris Bank rich. And it was a trade Venice depended on.

They were silent for a while. Then Nikolas continued, 'The news has led to a run on the bank. We've lost all our deposits and can't pay those who still want to withdraw their money.'

'There's no other route to the gold?'

'Only by sea. As Luke discovered, the Senegana River can take it west to the coast, but only the Portuguese have the ships to get there.'

'Perhaps I should go there.'

'Will the Portuguese lend you a caravel? I don't think so. There's something more.'

Siward waited while he arranged his hands before him.

'I think your grandfather was murdered.'

Siward recoiled. 'Murdered? By whom?'

'No one knows. He was found in a canal, apparently drunk. But Luke hardly drank,' Nikolas continued. 'At first I thought it might be to do with losing the Mali gold. But it must be something bigger. Something he knew, perhaps, that others didn't want him to.'

Siward was surprised at how angry he felt suddenly. He half-rose. 'Well, we must find out who did it, Nikolas. Whoever it was must pay for it.'

Nikolas raised a hand. 'Yes, yes, of course, but we need to show caution. Something is happening in Venice. Francesco Foscari's son Jacopo was convicted of treason and exiled to Crete. Ever since, the Doge has become a recluse, some say mad. The city has become dangerous.' He gestured for him to take his seat. 'And I have your grandfather's will.'

Siward had almost forgotten Luke's will in this torrent of bad news. He'd not thought much about it, beyond looking forward to owning the dragon sword. He knew he'd be heir to the bank and trading company but it sounded as if that was more burden than benefit. He'd been looking forward to seeing the sword again, though.

'Oh yes, the will,' he said, sitting again. 'What does it say?'

Nikolas was no longer meeting his eye. He was staring down at a parchment on the table that Siward hadn't noticed before.

'What does it say, Nikolas?' he asked again, more quietly. 'Is the trading company in trouble as well?'

Nikolas looked up. 'No, it's not. In fact it's in rude health. Only it's been left to someone else.'

Siward didn't understand. 'Someone else? Who?'

'It appears that Luke had another grandson.'

Siward didn't understand. Then he did. 'Giovanni's child? But he died at birth.'

Nikolas shook his head. 'It appears he didn't. He was sent away and Luke was sworn to give out that he'd died. It was Theodore's price for letting the child live.'

Siward felt a drumming in his temples. He thought of Cleope. All those years of thinking her son dead. He remembered the night that Luke had left, the night of the storm. He remembered him at the end of his bed, wearing a cloak. *Of course. That's why you left.*

Then he remembered something more: the sword hanging on the wall of a bedroom, lit up by lightning. He remembered Luke taking it down. *You never brought it back, as you'd promised.*

'Who is he?' he asked slowly.

'His whereabouts weren't known until recently. But he had one identifying feature: the dragon sword. Luke put it into his cradle when he went away.'

Siward felt numb. 'So again, who is he?'

'That is the problem, Siward.' He paused. 'He is Sultan Murad's greatest general, the victor of Varna. He is Makkim.'

He stared at Nikolas. He'd just told him that the Empire's greatest enemy was heir to one of the greatest trading companies in Europe. If Nikolas hadn't looked so serious, it might have been a joke.

'How . . . ?'

'The *devshirme*, or the kul, as it's known. It must have been that. He did well.'

'But who's to say Makkim didn't come by the sword by some other means?'

'Possibly, but we've checked. Makkim is exactly the right age, the right height, the right looks to be Giovanni and Cleope's son.

Anyway, it doesn't matter what we think. Luke was convinced enough to leave him half his fortune.' He looked down. 'It's all written down here. You can read it for yourself.'

Siward didn't need to. He knew Nikolas was telling the truth. 'Did Luke try and make contact with him?'

'No, I don't think so.' He paused. 'He seems to have left that to you. Perhaps on purpose.'

'On purpose?'

'He always blamed himself for Giovanni's banishment. Perhaps he wanted some sort of reconciliation between you.'

Siward grunted. 'That's unlikely. Makkim is my enemy. He's about to besiege Constantinople.' Something dawned on him. 'Oh God,' he said softly, 'the bank.'

Nikolas was nodding gloomily now. 'You've realised. The only way the bank can be solvent is through the trading company's assets.'

Siward's frown deepened. He was shaking his head. 'Why would Luke have done such a thing?'

Nikolas shrugged. 'I suppose he never could have foreseen the end of the Mali gold.' He stopped and considered. 'Perhaps it's as I said: he wanted to bring two grandsons together, to reunite his family.'

'Well, he got that wrong. If Makkim was my enemy, he's even more that now.'

Nikolas rose and walked slowly to the window where he stood looking out at the canal. The sunlight danced up and down his face, and he narrowed his eyes against it. 'Except that Makkim mustn't be your enemy,' he said carefully. 'He is the only way we can keep the bank solvent, the only way we can get money for the Emperor. We need him.'

'So how do we persuade him? He's been trained as a janissary.

He's not interested in money, just serving Allah and his sultan.' Siward pushed his chair back. 'He's not going to be swayable.'

'Probably not. So we'll have to meet him somehow.'

'How do we do that?'

'I don't know, Siward,' said Nikolas. 'I'd hoped you might think of a way. Plethon said you were clever.'

Siward wondered, briefly, what else Plethon might have said by way of preparation for his arrival. 'Let's concentrate on one thing at a time, Nikolas. Isn't Luke's murder the first thing we should tackle? You need to tell me how to set about it. After all, you know Venice.'

Nikolas nodded. He returned to the table, took Siward's arm and led him back to the window. Outside was a scene of transaction, uncaring of events outside the lagoon. The air was alive with the cries of traders and gondoliers steering their curtained cocoons through the traffic. The sun seemed to melt everything above the water, leaving slippery traces on the walls of the buildings, making them glow like flesh.

'I don't think Luke ever realised quite how much I hate this place,' he murmured. 'I came here because he was here, and because this city suits those acquainted with sorrow, and I'd lost a wife.' He was silent for a while. Then he turned. 'Did you know that the whores here dye their hair with their own piss? Venice is a city of swindlers, fraudsters, shamed women and quacks: the rootless drawn to the city without roots.' He warmed to his theme. 'It's a place of masks and whispers where every wall has a crack. It's ruled by old men and everyone is their spy. Especially the whores.'

Siward hadn't seen Nikolas like this before. He'd always been cynical, but never bitter. He remembered a peacock-blue dress. 'But not every whore is the same, surely?'

Nikolas shook his head. 'They're all whores whether they change their undergarments or not. I'm told the tax they raise pays for twelve galleys.'

He walked over to a cupboard, opened it and took out a pitcher and glasses. He brought them over to the table and poured wine. He passed a glass to Siward and raised his to the light, turning it. It was threaded with copper crystals that dappled his hand.

'On Murano,' he said, 'they can make glass so fine that it shatters on contact with poison. I've just bought some.'

'Nikolas, you're scaring me. Just tell me how to solve Luke's murder.'

Nikolas turned his head to him. 'Well, we need information and the whores have that. The more expensive the whore, the better the information.'

'Like Violetta Cavarse.'

Nikolas looked at him. 'You've heard of her?'

'I've seen her.'

'Well, she is not just Venice's greatest courtesan. She also works for Zoe Mamonas.'

'Ah yes. Plethon mentioned Zoe Mamonas. What does she do for her?'

'She runs a network of courtesan spies. It employs only the cleverest and most beautiful of women. Zoe gets information for her bank and gives them a pension in return: something for them to rely on when their looks have faded.' He examined Siward. 'You should infiltrate the network.'

'How?'

'By meeting them. I'll find a suitable occasion, then it's up to you.' Nikolas returned to the table and retrieved his stick.

Then he walked to the door and opened it. 'Now, you should talk to the staff.'

Later, on the top floor of the fondaco, Petros was kneeling beside the bed with Siward's foot between his knees.

'Sit still. If you move, I can't pull.'

'Can't pull, *sir*,' said Siward. 'In Venice, you should call me "sir", Petros. As if you respected me. It was embarrassing earlier, with the luggage.'

'I do respect you,' said Petros, yanking the boot off and sitting back on his heels, looking at it. 'Otherwise I wouldn't be your servant.'

'Do you have other career opportunitites?'

Petros pushed himself to his feet and hobbled over to the wardrobe. 'Now that's not fair,' he said, opening it and putting the boots inside, 'and, if I may say so, beneath you.'

Siward lay back on the bed. It was late in the evening and they'd both fed well from the Magoris kitchens: Siward above, Petros below.

'So what are they all saying about me?' he asked, closing his eyes. He was exhausted by wave after wave of shock. In one afternoon he'd been told that his grandfather had been murdered, his bank was broke, and his cousin an Ottoman general.

'Downstairs or at the bank?' asked Petros, closing the wardrobe door. 'I have both versions.'

Siward smiled. Yes, Petros would have both versions. It was why he was Siward's servant, really. He certainly failed in every other respect. 'Let's start with the bank.'

Petros sat at the end of the bed. 'The bank's staff are scared,' he said. 'They know there's been a run but they trust Nikolas.'

'Not me?'

'They don't know you. You'll have to earn their trust.' He sighed. 'At least they know you were taught by Plethon. You have that on your side.'

'And what do the servants say?'

'Ah, now, they like you more. Something to do with the match Luke arranged for you when you last came.' He wiped his nose with the back of his hand, a habit Siward would have to correct. 'Whoever she was, they didn't like her.'

Siward remembered it as if it had happened yesterday. Julia da Vale had been the daughter of one of Venice's richest merchants. The family was old and Julia was beautiful, educated and witty. But she wasn't Cleope. Cleope had ruined, forever, his version of perfection. The closer women got to it, the less he could think of marrying them.

'What happened to make them dislike her so much?' asked Petros.

'She was cruel,' Siward answered. 'To anyone she thought beneath her, she was cruel.'

Petros knew about cruelty. He'd been its victim too often. It still baffled him, though. 'Why? What was the point?'

Siward had often wondered this. He'd thought of one possible answer. 'I think she was scared,' he said. 'Venetian women must marry or they're put into a convent. Neither is pleasant.' He scratched his chin. 'I think she took her fear out on people who couldn't fight back.'

'Where is she now?'

Siward shrugged. 'Married, I expect. She was beautiful, after all. She'll be shut up in some grand palace watching the cortigiane oneste have all the fun.'

'The what?'

'The courtesans,' said Siward, stretching.

86

'Like the woman we saw today? The one in the blue dress?'

Siward thought back to Violetta Cavarse. She was close to Cleope's perfection, but she was a whore. Only in Venice could you find such a creature.

'Yes,' he said. 'Like Violetta Cavarse.'

CHAPTER NINE

VENICE

'Dip your head.'

The bridge was low and the call just in time. Siward returned quickly to the gondola's cushions. He'd been standing, looking up at the moon.

'I was worried for the bridge,' said Nikolas, who'd recovered most of his humour since their talk the day before. He was sitting in the boat's little cabin, looking out, his turban on the seat beside him.

The moon disappeared and the smell of wet stone closed in around them. Then there was light again and Nikolas was looking behind him at the canal.

'My horsetails are in the water,' he said, pointing at the floating pole. 'I had three of them on it.'

Siward was amused. The previous afternoon's news had changed a great deal but there was a life to live. 'Three? Are you going as a general?'

They were floating down a narrow waterway on their way to a *masque* where the theme was *turca*. There were tall buildings on either side that made their voices the only ones in Venice. Even whispers travelled far in this city. Siward looked up at the gap above, where the moon poured through like mercury. Venice, lunar city subject to tide and two kinds of gravity. A church bell struck the hour of ten.

'Why do the Loredan not have their palace on the Grand Canal?' asked Siward, standing again. There was a corner ahead, but no bridge.

'They have many palaces,' replied Nikolas. 'This one has a garden. We are to be entertained *all'aperto* tonight.'

Siward looked down at his cloak. The night was warm but it would be cold later. How late should he stay? Certainly until he'd seen Violetta. But the party was masked. How would he know her?

He was dressed as a *sipahi* and had small wings on his back that made sitting a formal affair. He looked attentive, however tired he was. Sleep hadn't stayed long with him the night before, and he'd lain awake most of the night brooding about his grandfather's murder. And his actions. Why had Makkim been so favoured? The hurt had kept him awake.

The gondola rounded the corner and the canal widened and was joined by another. The sound of revelry came to them suddenly and there were lights ahead. Quite soon, they saw steps framed by braziers with men in livery between, helping Turks from their gondolas. They joined the queue waiting to dock.

'That's not a Turk, that's Tamerlane,' said Siward.

Nikolas peered out from the cabin. 'Both eat babies and steal Venetian trade. What's the difference?'

Siward watched an exquisite creature alight. In her hair were flowers and little birds that moved when she laughed, almost taking wing. Not Violetta.

'Is she a courtesan?'

'Of course, no wives or daughters will be present tonight. The men mean to enjoy themselves.' Nikolas came to stand beside him. 'You see the mole on her nose? It means she's an adventuress. If it's on the chin, something else. I forget what.'

They arrived, put on their masks and were helped from the boat. The steps were empty, the guests having hurried into the garden beyond lest they be recognised. Nikolas adjusted his mask, then led Siward by the arm.

'Let's get a drink. It's not fun being the Magoris factor these days. And you've had bad news.'

'But they won't recognise us. You'll be a tall pasha tonight who knows nothing of banking, and I a fierce sipahi knight.'

They reached a loggia beneath which was a long table where dwarves dressed as janissaries served wine. Each had a white bork on his head, so tall that it doubled his size. Siward glanced around.

'I can't see her.'

Nikolas turned, two glasses in his hands. 'Violetta? Of course not. She'll be in disguise.'

The garden was full of men in turbans, moustaches and curling slippers beneath trees hung with scented candles. The women were more varied, none knowing quite what the female Turk wore. Some were dressed for the harem in pantaloons caught at the ankle and short jackets that exposed their breasts.

Siward sipped his wine. It was *malvasie*, dark and sweet and bearing the scent of Greece and a memory. It was evening in Monemvasia and Cleope was sitting opposite him over a game of chess. The Mirtoon Sea was far below, flat as beaten brass, and she was offering him the glass and laughing. *Go on, you're old enough.*

He shook it off. The Sultan was approaching, his hand fixed

to a gigantic turban that swayed like luggage. He wore a wide sash with a scimitar inside. His moustaches curled more than his shoes.

'Nikolas.'

Nikolas bowed and sighed at the same time. 'I had hoped not to be recognised.' He turned to Siward. 'May I present your host, Giacomo Loredan, who is the Sultan Murad tonight.' He turned back. 'And Mehmed? Who here is frightening enough to be his son?'

'Antonio, of course.' Loredan looked around the garden. 'I can't see him now.'

'Your son? Is he old enough to be at such a party? The women are almost bare.'

Loredan laughed. 'Nikolas, Nikolas! It's to be regretted that your Chinese concubine never gave you a son. He'd have been the biggest libertine in Venice. Antonio old enough indeed!' He put his hand on Nikolas's shoulder and lowered his voice. 'Not everyone here will be so friendly to you, but then you don't owe me money.' He glanced at Siward. 'Is your friend who I think he is? If so, I should advise him to keep his mask on.'

Loredan walked away, catching a branch with his turban as he went. Siward watched him go. 'He was friendly to you.'

'He knows me. We gamble together. He is a good man, trustworthy, one of the Council of Ten.'

'So, he meets with the Doge?'

Nikolas shook his head. 'No one from the council has met the Doge since they exiled his son. Foscari is going his own way and no one knows where.' Nikolas glanced away. 'Do you play?'

There were tables set out to one side where men sat with women at their shoulders playing baccarat around single candles. Piles of *grosso* and *ducats* were heaped in front of them.

'No, but you must. I'll mix with the company.'

'If you're sure. We won't stay long.'

He moved away and Siward was left with his malvasia, drawing some comfort from the anonymity of his mask. He wished it were larger.

He walked past low hedges with bushes trimmed into cones and came to a plinth with a giant wrestling a lion on it. Next to it was a smaller man roasting chestnuts on a grill, a good smell after the cloying artifice of spice. He took a plate and ate, blowing on each before putting it in his mouth. There was music coming from somewhere and he wanted to find it. He walked over to where a quartet played in a grotto framed with pillars of green-veined marble: a reminder of leaf and sap in this most unnatural of cities. There was an open tent to his left where women sat on men's laps around a table. One was laughing too loudly.

'Not a good courtesan. She shouldn't drink.'

Siward turned to see a boy beside him wearing a turban almost as big as Giacomo Loredan's. He guessed who he was.

'I've just met your father,' he said, giving a small bow, 'the Sultan.'

The turban nodded. 'He drinks too much, like that courtesan. He won't recognise me soon. Shall we sit?'

Antonio Loredan took Siward over to a bench beside the grotto where the music was quieter but the view just as good. In front of them was a wide pool with a rock in the middle. On it sat a mermaid with wings, paddling her fin in the water. Little shells covered her nipples and long fair hair fell to her waist.

'You're not from Venice, I think,' said the boy. 'Where?'

Siward drank his wine. 'Greece.'

'Ah, then I know you, sipahi,' he said. 'We've been expecting you. Siward Magoris come to save his grandfather's bank. You took your time.'

'Well, I'm here now.'

They were silent for a while. Siward asked, 'Is Violetta Cavarse here tonight, do you know?'

Antonio looked around. He was dressed in a long, unbelted tunic with the widest of sleeves. His mask had a thin beard at its bottom: Mehmed's beard. 'No, not yet. You'll know when she arrives.'

'How so?'

'Because my father will be strutting like a peacock. He is one of the few.'

'The few?'

'Who can afford her. She's very expensive.'

Siward turned to the boy. 'Is it just money for her?'

Antonio nodded. 'Of course. What else?'

In front of them the mermaid was throwing grapes into the mouths of two bravos lying prostrate in the pool, glasses of wine in their unstable hands. Their turbans floated on the water beside them.

'The Muslim doesn't drink wine,' said Antonio. 'What we fear, we mock. Isn't it so?'

'Or treat with.' Siward glanced at the boy. 'Your Doge will be talking to the Turk.'

'Well, the stakes are high. Constantinople may fall this time.'

'And if it does?'

'Then our main trading route to the East will be cut. You've not learnt much since you've been here.'

The boy was impertinent. He may have been Loredan's son but he was half his age and suddenly Siward felt tired. He needed another drink to keep him awake. He got up.

93

'Wait. I can introduce you to her.'

'I want a drink.'

'Have mine.' Loredan offered his glass. 'I have a bottle somewhere.'

Siward sat down again. He took the glass and drained it in one swallow. The tiredness was going but the garden was not the shape it had been. Neither of them spoke for a while.

'Why do you want to meet Violetta Cavarse anyway?' asked Antonio.

He was unprepared for this. 'I saw her,' he said. 'In the street.' He hesitated. 'She smiled at me.'

Antonio laughed. 'She smiles a lot. It's her work.'

Siward nodded. 'I'm sure. Well, anyway, she's famous. I'd like to see why.'

'She's also curious.' Antonio was silent for a while. 'If you meet her, she'll want to know things.'

'Such as?'

'Perhaps what you're going to do about your grandfather's death?'

Siward looked at the boy. He wanted to talk about something else.

'You said you had a bottle?'

He watched Antonio reach down and bring one up from beneath the bench. He'd heard nothing but bad news since his arrival in Venice, he was tired and he needed a drink. Anyway, he was hidden by a mask. He looked at Antonio. His mask was very fine but a little hazy round the edges. He thought he saw amusement in its eyes.

A throat cleared above them and they looked up. The man Siward had seen in the street with Violetta was standing there, his mask lowered to his neck. He was dressed as Lucifer, which left no doubt as to how he saw the Turk. Siward's mind searched clumsily for the man's name. Nothing.

'Not convincing,' said the man to Antonio. 'Mehmed indeed. Why a man?'

This seemed rude to Siward. Antonio was almost a man, after all, though he was, perhaps, small for his age. He retorted, 'Why a goat? Isn't that what you've come as?'

Antonio and the man stared at him, one through a mask. The boy rose. 'Perhaps a mistake,' he said nimbly. 'Siward Magoris, may I present Girolamo Minotto, the *serenissima's* bailo in Constantinople?'

The bailo was not amused. 'You're drunk,' he said to Siward. 'Which is, perhaps, to be expected. Your bank is ruined and you owe money everywhere. Better to be drunk, I suppose.'

Siward had risen too. The garden swayed around him. The Venetians were said to add things to your drink. He wanted to be more sober. He thought of Plethon.

'I think I should be going,' he said. He was suddenly conscious of the wings on his back.

'Wait,' said Minotto, taking his arm. 'You insult a man, then expect to leave?'

'Girolamo . . .' Antonio's voice had changed.

Minotto turned to the boy. 'And you have encouraged him, no doubt. Will you sleep with him later?'

Siward took a deep breath. 'You are rude,' he said. 'Even for a goat.'

Minotto reached for his sword but it had been taken at the gate. Instead he drew back his hand and slapped Siward.

Antonio intervened. He stepped between them and turned to Minotto. 'Girolamo,' he whispered, 'please. If this is about me, then we'll talk elsewhere.'

Siward shook his head to try and clear it. Why would it be about Antonio? He hadn't called him a goat. He put his hand to his cheek. It stung from the slap. He pushed his way past the boy and brought his face close to Minotto's.

'That was a mistake, goat,' he said. 'Take yourself somewhere else before I throw you into the canal.'

Minotto glanced up at the man in front of him. Siward was taller than him and looked strong. With his sword, he wouldn't have hesitated, but he didn't have it, and the garden was full of people he knew. He was brave but he knew how to calculate risk. He took Antonio's arm.

'Come on. We'll go somewhere else.'

Antonio resisted. 'No.'

Minotto looked thunderous. He reached up and tore off Antonio's mask. Beneath it was Violetta Cavarse.

Siward stared at her. Her hair was tied back and this close, her face was even more arresting than it had been in the street. Her rich, dark skin was framed by high cheekbones that lifted her olive eyes. If they'd been amused before, now they flashed with anger.

This time Violetta slapped Minotto. It was hard and he reeled from it. He lifted his arm.

'No.' Siward caught it mid-swing. He twisted it so that Minotto had to face him. 'Don't do that. I advise leaving. Now, before I hurt you.'

The bailo blinked at him. One cheek was the colour of malvasie and there was more hatred in his eyes than Siward thought possible in things so narrow. He pulled his arm away and rubbed it and looked around. No one seemed to have noticed the altercation.

He stepped forward. 'You are fortunate I don't have my sword, Greek. Next time I will have it, be sure of it.'

He glanced at Violetta, gave the merest of nods, then turned and walked away.

They both stared after him for a moment in silence. Violetta broke it first.

'Well, there's an enemy you don't need. You were foolish.'

Siward rubbed his jaw, suddenly quite sober. 'You deceived me. I think you owe me an apology.'

She turned to him, frowning. 'An apology? How so?' He noticed that she'd lifted her head, as if speaking to a maid who hadn't swept the porch properly. 'Were you not the drunk one who insulted the bailo of Constantinople, or was it all my imagining?'

'He was dressed as Lucifer: that is, as a goat. I was accurate. And none of it would have happened if you hadn't pretended to be who you're not.'

Violetta put her hands on her hips. 'You are attending a masque, Signor Magoris.' She waved her hand around the garden. 'The general point is to pretend to be what you're not. Or are you, in fact, a sipahi knight with ridiculous wings on your back?'

He stared at her, unable to think of what to say next. He'd suspected for some time that one of his wings might be slipping and cursed Petros for his incompetence. He wished he'd come as a ghazi.

Then she threw back her head and laughed. It was as different from Cleope's laugh as two sounds could be. It was loud and belonged entirely to the tavern. It was not the laugh of a courtesan.

'I'm sorry,' she said, bringing her palm to her lips. 'It's just that . . .' But she couldn't finish the sentence. She bent forward at the waist and slapped both hands to her pantaloons, the laughter overwhelming her.

He waited until she'd stopped.

'I'm sorry,' she said at last, choking back the last of it, raising one hand to her nose and dabbing her eyes with the other. 'I'm sorry.' She straightened and sniffed. 'There. You have your apology. Can we talk now?'

Siward hesitated. He was not given to taking himself too seriously, even after Plethon telling him to learn more *gravitas*. But he'd never been laughed at like that. He wasn't sure how to react.

She offered her hand. 'Please?'

He took it and she led him past battened gardens of different scents. The people came and went, laughing and whispering and peeping behind each other's masks. They met a dwarf janissary with a tray and she took two glasses of wine from it, handing one to him. They came to a bench facing the canal and sat. It was deep in shadow and Siward removed his mask.

She put her head to one side and smiled. 'You show yourself to me at last. More handsome than in the street.'

Was she flirting with him? 'I was hot.'

'But that's not the face of a banker. What are you if you're not that, Siward Magoris? Are you a soldier?'

'Perhaps,' he said. 'But for now, I'm a banker.'

'With nothing to bank. You must have time on your hands. Time, perhaps, to solve a murder?'

He looked at her. The eyes were still amused, the mouth suppressing a bigger smile, as if the joke was not really over.

'Tell me about Minotto,' he said.

She shrugged. 'He's rich, he's powerful and he's dangerous. What else would you like to know?'

'What he is to you. I saw you arguing in the street.'

'What he is to me is none of your business.' She sipped her wine. 'But I'll tell you all the same. For some time he's wanted to be a *patrone* to me. Do you know what that is?'

He could guess. 'Why not, if he's rich?'

She frowned and her eyes darted to his, no longer amused. 'Because I don't like him. Worse, I don't trust him.' She shook her head. 'Nor should you.'

Siward nodded. 'And you must like your lovers, must you?'

'It helps, Siward.' She lifted her head as she'd done before and he saw the fine curve of her neck. 'Don't you find?'

He thought back to Lela. She was right, but then she was a courtesan. 'Do you like me?' he asked.

She smiled. 'Of course I like you. Otherwise we wouldn't be sitting on this bench. But will I sleep with you? No.'

Siward felt like his other cheek had been slapped. 'Why not? I can pay.'

She shook her head, her ringlets coming loose from their tie and dancing at her shoulders like little toys. 'Because I don't feel like it, Siward Magoris. I am here to talk and dance and wear my mask to watch people do funny things. I'm sure you're a very accomplished lover but I have other plans tonight.' She rose and patted his head. 'You should go home. You're tired and you shouldn't drink any more.'

She gathered her hair, re-tied it, then lifted her mask to her face, fastening it at the sides. She gave a little wave, turned and walked away.

He stared at her retreating back. He watched a man approach her and take her hand. He saw her disappear into a throng of laughing Ottomans.

He felt bewildered as well as angry, his tiredness forgotten.

If he'd not been laughed at before like that, he'd certainly not been rejected so completely. There had been a few refusals, yes, but he'd found his charm had usually won the day. But tonight? His proposal may have been clumsy, but he'd just saved her from a man she despised. He felt a fool.

The anonymity of the mask suddenly seemed pointless. He rose without it and walked over to the canal steps where dwarves were delivering people to gondolas. One turned to him as he approached.

'Would you like a gondola, sir?'

Siward shook his head. 'I'll walk. I'm sure I can find the way.'

He went into the backstreets, walking with only a vague sense of direction. It was ten minutes later that he stopped. He'd thought himself going towards the Grand Canal but it seemed to be getting no nearer. The alleys were dark and narrow and the gap between the rooftops only allowed a ribbon of moonlight through. Thank God for the moon.

He looked up. The tops of the houses seemed to nuzzle each other. You could hold hands between them, or jump from roof to roof like a cat. He tilted his head, listening for footsteps, someone to ask. He heard a cry from somewhere. Pain or pleasure? He smelt earth and piss and the rank smell of canal. He felt muddled and shook his head. Too much wine.

He heard something. He opened his mouth; sometimes it helped. Nothing beyond the beating of his heart. And his breathing.

Nikolas. He'd not thought to tell him he was leaving. Had he suffered for Siward's idiocy?

There. Footsteps, certainly. But whose? Minotto's, with a sword this time? He looked up and down the alley. Should he shout?

He walked on, turned a corner, then another, then a third. He met a dead end with a door with a red cross on it, terrible under the moon.

He quickly retraced his footsteps. Go right here. Then left. No, right, surely. He came to a courtyard with a well, on its side a lion with wings. Big shadows covered half the area, where anyone might hide. He hurried through.

He came to a tiny bridge, heard the slap of water on stone, the sudden extension of sound as his breathing came back to him. Something scurried past him, too small for a cat. He thought of the cross on the door.

He walked faster now, feeling the sweat on his brow and salt on his lips. His shoulder scraped stone and something brushed the top of his head. Only washing hung out to dry. He heard something. Conversation? Was that light up ahead?

He nearly collided with them. Four men, carrying torches. The relief swept over him and he felt weak with it. He gathered himself. 'I was lost.'

He'd spoken in Greek. 'Lost,' he repeated in Italian, laughing. The men smiled.

He pointed all around. 'Fondaco Magoris?'

One of the men nodded. 'Follow us.' He turned and led the way. Two of them were in front, two behind.

Siward glanced behind him. The two men were shoulder to shoulder between the walls, their torches held high. Their faces were in darkness but their bodies bathed in light. They weren't wearing anyone's livery.

They came to a bridge, then a street too narrow for the men to walk abreast. Siward looked up to see nothing beyond the torchlight.

They turned a corner. It was a dead end. The men in front

were turning as those behind grabbed his arms. One pulled a gag over his mouth. Their torches were lying on the ground.

'Hold him fast.'

The first blow was to the stomach, so that he'd have doubled up if he hadn't been held. It was hard and he felt something crack. Then his legs were kicked from behind so that he fell forward onto his knees. The next two punches came to the face and his head rocked back to take them. He tasted blood in his mouth and felt it run from his nose.

One of the men picked up a torch and stamped it into the earth. He waved it slowly in front of Siward's half-closed eyes, then thrust it into his chest. The smell of burning wool came up to him, then the agony. As he opened his mouth to scream, the gag tightened.

Then the kicks came: one after another, to all parts of his body. He tried to rise, to shield himself, but they were too many, too fast, and they came from every direction. In the end, the pain was too great. He felt himself fade into unconsciousness. The last thing he heard may have been in a dream.

'Enough. He doesn't want him dead.'

CHAPTER TEN

VENICE

He woke to lavender and silk and utter darkness. He could smell, he could feel, but he couldn't see. He could hear too: soft rain on leaves and the rattle of wind on a window. And he could taste: old blood amidst the broken teeth.

He tried to open his eyes and managed one. Still darkness. His head was bandaged. He raised a hand to it and almost cried out from the pain in his chest. He remembered the first blow and crack of ribs.

He lifted the bandage and saw luxury. He was in a room the size of a *piazza*. The ceiling was a riot of Bacchae and wood-nymph, too distant to follow the story. There were tall windows smeared with rain between velvet curtains held back with gold cord. The branches outside parted and joined as water cascaded down more glass than he'd ever seen. One thing was certain: Siward was in the house of a rich man.

Man? He looked more closely round the room. The walls were hung with tapestries of lovemaking amidst the landscapes of Flanders. Between them, chubby cupids held up wall-sconces entwined with flowers. There was a fire in the grate and the room was warm. This was a place of rich, unhurried love, expertly applied. This was the room of a courtesan.

And the smell. Was it on his pillow? No, it was on him. He put a finger to his neck and felt oil. He traced it down to his chest and stopped. Another bandage. He was a mummy.

'I should lie still.'

The voice came from a chair he'd not seen, too painful to turn to. He managed it. It was Violetta Cavarse and she was smiling. Without Mehmed's clothes, she was even more remarkable. She was softer, warmer than the night before, her skin the colour of Greek honey, uncreased until the eye, where laughter had made its estuaries. What age was she? Not far off his, he guessed. In her prime.

'Was it Minotto's men?' he asked.

She rose in one movement, drawing her gown to her and walking over to the fire. He saw that the body beneath the silk moved with precision.

'Who hurt you? Perhaps.' She spoke to the fire. 'It would be like him to get others to do his work.'

'My factor, Nikolas. Is he safe?'

She nodded, her ringlets moving against her back like springs. 'He's actually just left, with Petros who brought you some clothes. Your servant is funny.'

Siward was relieved, and surprised. Petros seemed funny to few outside of him and Plethon. But then much was beginning to surprise him about this woman. 'How did I get here?'

She stretched out her hands to the fire. 'I sent men to follow you,' she said. 'They arrived too late.'

'But they brought me back here.'

She glanced back at him. 'How else would you have come? Your wings weren't big enough.'

He thought suddenly of a moon-river, banked by house tops, of a cat jumping across. Another thought came to him. 'And the bandages?'

'Applied by my doctor. The oils I did myself.'

He felt some embarrassment, but some excitement too. She'd touched his body, his bruises. She'd rubbed oil into his skin. He murmured, 'Thank you.'

She turned. It was the same smile he'd seen last night. She dipped her head and the ringlets bounced. 'It was a pleasure.'

They were silent for a while. She walked over to a window and traced rain on the glass with her fingertips, her back to him. He set his teeth and pulled himself up to sit. He lifted the sheet and looked down at his body. He was bandaged from chest to navel; below that, he was naked. He saw bruises quite high on his thighs, yellow and purple and shining with oil. He tried not to think of what she'd done there.

He said, 'I'm told that you spy for the Mamonas Bank.'

Her hands moved to the velvet curtains, stroking the folds between finger and thumb. 'I did once. If everyone knows you're a spy, they don't say anything. Life becomes dull.' She ran her hand down the length of a pleat. 'Others do it now.'

'Who you control.'

'Who I . . . *organise*. The best courtesans don't need controlling. They get information for Zoe Mamonas and she gives them a pension when they retire.'

Siward thought of what he knew. Zoe Mamonas was invisible. Her courtesans were her eyes and they saw everything, in Venice and the world. She was the woman Plethon thought might help him get money for the Emperor and this surprising courtesan was his route to her.

'Can I meet her?'

She turned. 'Perhaps. When you're better.' She moved to a chair and sat down. She was wearing a gown of white silk and the skin that emerged at her neck, wrists and ankles glowed like satinwood.

'What would we talk about?'

She rose again, seeming to prefer movement. She went to a table and picked up a marble egg from others in a basket. She examined it, holding it away from her, turning it in her hand. It was red and veined and could have been an organ plucked from a body.

'I don't know,' she said, turning. 'Perhaps about your grand-father's death? She knew him.' She put the egg down carefully so that there was no sound. 'Perhaps the map that's being made on Murano?' She considered. 'Perhaps you'd talk about Venice. I know she worries this Doge may be planning something bad for Venice, bad for the world.' She looked at him. 'I've not seen her like this before.'

'Like what?'

'Uncertain,' she said quietly. 'I've never seen Zoe Mamonas uncertain.'

Siward stared at her. Her intelligent eyes were fixed on his and there was no tease in them. It occurred to him that she was uncertain too. 'So when can I see her?'

'As I said. When you're healed.'

'I am healed.'

'No, you're not. Most of your ribs are broken. You will stay here until they are mended. Then you'll see her.'

'And the bank?'

'I expect Nikolas can manage. He has so far.'

*

He stayed with Violetta for a month, never venturing from her house.

The rain stopped and a mild autumn sun turned the leaves outside his window to red, then gold. They crisped and curled and gradually left branches that bared themselves to wind gusting in from the sea. The birds went too, leaving like pilgrims for warmer climes, and he missed their song. Venice became a place of melancholy and departure. Except for him.

Every day, the fire in his grate was stoked higher by people he never heard enter or leave. Delicious meals of fish and fowl from the lagoon were left beside him while he slept, with sweet wine from Cyprus. He lacked for nothing.

Nikolas visited again, with Petros. He was pessimistic. 'You'll have to leave Venice,' he said. 'As soon as you're better, you must go. It was a warning.'

But Siward shook his head. 'It was punishment, Nikolas. I insulted a proud man.'

'But are you sure it was him?'

Nikolas left but Petros stayed for a while. He sat on the bed and patted Siward's knee. He looked over his shoulder, then leant forward. 'It was well done,' he whispered, winking. 'I've not seen you do better. You're even in her bed.'

But Siward, for once, didn't laugh. And finding his friend too serious, Petros soon left as well.

Violetta came to him every evening to tell him news of the city outside. She talked of a world he didn't know: picnics afloat on the Grand Canal or bull-baiting in the Campo San Polo, where mastiffs bit the animals' ears. In the evenings they'd talk, he from his bed, she from a chair where a little dog sat in her lap. When she was interested, she would lean over the animal, pointing her joined fingers towards him, her olive eyes wide to him, perched on the edge of her chair.

They talked most about Venice.

'It has its faults,' she said one evening, 'but dullness isn't one of them. It's where the world comes to trade and play and it's never dull.'

'To scheme also?'

'Sometimes. But more often to exchange what they know. If people are sharing knowledge, they're less likely to fight.'

'You sound like Plethon. He'd say that trade can replace war, that busy people don't fight.'

She pointed her fingers. 'Luke said that too. He came to see the point of Venice, I think.'

He nodded slowly. He'd often wondered why Luke had chosen to stay in Venice after Cleope had died. After all, Nikolas could have run the bank.

'And Lydislaw, he saw its point too.' She looked at him. 'Did you know that he came here after Varna?'

Siward lifted his glass carefully to his lips. His ribs were still bandaged.

'Not to play, though,' she continued. 'He went to live with the Camaldolese brothers on the island of Murano. Your grandfather used to visit him there. Perhaps they talked of such things.'

Siward remained silent for a while, wondering why Luke might have visited the man who'd lost at Varna.

Perhaps she'd read his thoughts. 'They might have talked of the map Fra Mauro's making out there,' she said, stroking the dog. 'I remember Minotto once asking him about it, whether he could confirm that it was possible to sail around Africa.' She scratched its ears. 'Something about a Chinese junk coming to Mistra. It was long ago.'

Siward knew the story from Luke. It was true and it was secret. He chose not to accept the bait. 'Did you know him?'

'Lydislaw? Yes, but not as I know Loredan, you understand.' She frowned. 'He was a sad man. He suited Venice where people are like the tide: six hours up and six down. Luke would have cheered him up.' She tipped her head to one side. 'I liked your grandfather. He was good and noble and reminded me of someone I used to know.' She thought. 'You look like him. Not as tall, but you look like him.'

Siward was pleased. It always pleased him when people told him that he looked like Luke. Especially her. 'And you?' he asked. 'Do you see the point of Venice?'

She looked puzzled. 'Of course! Why else would I be here? It's a theatre, the very best, and I am a performer.'

'Performer?'

She brushed a ringlet from a cheek. 'A courtesan is a performer. She is whore, mother, healer, confessor and sparring partner, all in one. You need a good theatre to perform well.'

'And there's no shame in it?'

She looked surprised. 'Shame? Never.'

Sometimes he wondered what she wanted from him. Not the sharing of her bed, that was for certain. She'd given no sign that she'd changed her mind in that quarter.

What then was it? He found her as baffling as he did intriguing. She was strange yet brilliant, brittle yet soft, calculating yet open. But what did she want?

One day he asked her.

She laughed. 'I'm nursing you, aren't I? I like to see a project through.' She was sitting at the end of his bed eating a peach, her head bent, her hand cupped for the juice. She looked up at him. 'Besides, I enjoy your company. Is that so odd?'

She rose and put the peach stone into a saucer. Without turning, she said, 'I asked you once which you were: soldier or merchant. Have you decided? Are you going to stay in Venice?'

He was lying back on his pillows, his arms behind his head, enjoying fresh air on his skin. The bandages had been removed the day before and Petros had brought him the clothes to leave. He wasn't sure he wanted to.

'I want to find out who killed my grandfather, and I want to save my bank. Both require me to be in Venice.'

'And then where?' she asked. 'Will you go to save Constantinople?'

'If it is attacked, of course. My duty is to the Roman Empire.'

'Then you're a soldier,' she said simply. 'But a rich one.'

He didn't answer. She was watching him closely. Could she possibly know about Luke's will along with everything else? His grandfather had been friends with Zoe Mamonas, after all.

She said, too carelessly, 'I suppose nothing was left to the bastard son.'

'Giovanni chose not to be forgiven,' he said carefully. 'He went to the furthest place he could find to spend his exile. I don't believe they spoke to each other after that.'

She nodded as if he was merely confirming what she already knew. 'You came here, ten years ago. Why was that?'

'I was Luke's heir,' he said, 'and Nikolas had just returned from China. He wanted me to meet him.'

'No other reason?'

How much did she know? 'There was a match,' he said.

'Julia da Vale. A good one. Why didn't you take it?'

He felt mildly irritated. 'We turned out to be ill-suited,' he replied shortly. 'I'm sure she found someone more appropriate.'

'She did. Minotto.'

Now Siward stared at her. 'Does he know?'

She shrugged. 'Perhaps not, but she does, and she is his equal for revenge.' She smiled and leant back in her chair. 'She might have quite liked being married to the heir to the Magoris Bank.' She laughed. 'Oh, and the trading company, of course. You'll need its assets now, I suppose.' She studied him. 'And now you are single. Why?'

He shrugged. 'I'm not the sort women choose to stay with, I suppose.'

She shook her head. 'I don't think so.' She examined him. 'No, it's something to do with *you*. Something inside.'

She seemed to know him better than he did himself. It was unnerving. He turned it back to her. 'And you? Why haven't you?'

'Me?' she asked, surprised. 'What man wants to marry a courtesan? We are everybody's and nobody's.' She repeated the words he'd said: 'We are not the sort men choose to stay with.' Then she laughed. 'Unless, of course, they have to because their ribs are broken.'

That night he woke to hear singing. It was late and he thought he might be dreaming but the tune continued, so he got up, lit a candle, put on a day-gown and went downstairs. The music was coming from the other side of the door to the *piano nobile* and there was candlelight flickering at its edges. He opened the door.

Inside, Violetta stood before a lectern, while a man sat at a long instrument with its top opened to the ceiling. They were circled by a ring of low candles on the floor as if some ancient rite was being enacted. The rest of the room was in darkness.

He stood in the doorway and listened. Her voice, normally deep, was high and clear and carried a melody of some complexity and great beauty. When the song had finished, the man at the instrument rose and left. She turned to him.

'It's a harpsichord,' she said, following his stare.

He nodded. 'The song was beautiful.' He noticed she was dressed for the day, not night. 'But why practise so late?'

She looked surprised. 'Practise? No, this was a performance.'

He glanced into the darkness. 'To no audience?'

'I am the audience.'

The voice came from the other end of the room, where the darkness was complete. It was the voice of an old woman and he knew who she was.

'Zoe Mamonas.'

'The same.' Two coughs came out of the dark. 'Violetta, please help me.'

Violetta left the lectern, stooped to pick up a candle and walked over to where the voice had come from. As she moved, the room partly revealed itself and Siward saw that it was empty of furniture. She came to the only thing it contained: a chair on wheels with a woman seated on it. She gave the candle to Zoe, walked to the back of the chair and pushed it towards him, stopping just outside the circle of light. Zoe was wearing a long black veil over a black dress and the hands that held the candle were gloved.

'You look like your grandfather,' said a voice beneath the veil. It was softer than he'd imagined it would be, perhaps muffled by the gauze. 'Or perhaps Giovanni. Not as tall.'

She coughed again and Siward thought of another who'd done that. Long ago.

'We all shrink with age,' she went on, 'but at least Luke kept his looks. They were strong enough to withstand time. Are you his heir?'

Siward looked at the veil. It moved slightly with every word. It was the only part of her that did. 'My father is dead, so yes.'

'And your uncle, the bastard?'

He didn't reply.

'Do you have the sword?'

Siward looked down at his hands. 'No, I don't have the sword.'

'Then Giovanni must have it.' She watched him for a while in silence. 'I suppose you were reared by Cleope. You'd have reminded her of him.'

Silence.

'Did you know that your grandfather saved the Empire? He brought Tamerlane to fight Bayezid to stop him taking Constantinople.' She paused. 'He was modest, so he might not have told you that. He must be a hard example to follow.'

Siward knew that Luke had saved the Empire. That was something he could follow.

'So, your bank has no money,' she continued, 'and Constantine needs so much. What will you do?'

Siward felt irritated. Too many questions. 'I don't know,' he said. 'What would you suggest?'

'You need to find new opportunities for it. The west of Europe is where you should be,' she said. 'Portugal, Flanders, Burgundy. Perhaps England: that's where the money will be in the future. Your uncle knew that, which is why he went to Portugal. Did you know he is coming here?'

Siward frowned. 'Giovanni's coming to Venice?'

'Well, perhaps not to Venice. He's coming east, anyway.' The old woman looked up at him. 'He's coming to find the son who turns out to be alive, who turns out to be inheriting the trading company instead of you. Who turns out to be your enemy.' She turned to look at him. 'He doesn't know this yet. But you do.'

As had Violetta all this time. He felt a flash of anger.

'So what will you do?' she asked again. 'Whatever it is, you'll have to do it fast. Your depositors who haven't removed their money are assuming that the trading company's assets will come to their rescue.'

'I'll find a way,' he said, still angry.

'Perhaps persuade Makkim to help? A man you already hate, I expect. Not easy to persuade a man you hate to lend you a hand.'

They were silent for a while and Zoe's breathing filled the silence like worn bellows. He watched her cough for a while, her head bowed, her shoulders shaking. Violetta gave her water which she drank.

He breathed in slowly to restore some calm. 'As you said, I know all this,' he said deliberately. 'And you know that I do. You both do.'

'Yes, you do,' she said, looking up. 'So I'll tell you something you don't know: why your grandfather was murdered.'

'You know that?'

'I can guess,' she said. 'Do you know what they're doing on Murano? Apart from making glass, that is?'

Siward waited.

'They are making a map that will change the world. The man doing it is Fra Mauro. Luke visited him before he died. He gave him the map that the Chinese had given him when they came to Mistra all those years ago, the one they used to come round the bottom of Africa.' She gazed at him. 'You know this already, of course.'

Siward did. The Ming had arrived in the biggest ship afloat,

114

with dragons on its sails. It was why Nikolas had gone to China to trade.

'I think Luke's death had something to do with that map.'

'Why?'

'Because the only Europeans who know that Africa can be rounded are in this room, or dead.' She nodded slowly. 'Because if it can be rounded, then Venice's days of glory are over.' She reflected. 'Telling Fra Mauro what he knew was the bravest thing Luke did in a lifetime of bravery. He must have guessed what it might lead to. He wanted a better world to follow the fall of Rome and he sacrificed his life for it. We must make sure it wasn't in vain.'

Siward stared at her. For a long time nobody spoke. At last, he asked, 'So what must we do?'

She leant forward, the veil brushing her knees. 'We must discover what this mad Doge is contemplating. Help me and I will help you. I will support your bank in the West and I will pay for an army to go to Constantinople when Mehmed lays siege to it.'

'How do I help you?'

She sat back and placed her hands on the arms of the wheel-chair. 'Go to Murano. Talk to Fra Mauro at the Camaldolese monastery and discover what he knows. We cannot because of our sex.' She lifted a hand and pointed. 'Help me find out why Luke was murdered, then leave Venice and go west. As I suggested.'

CHAPTER ELEVEN

EDIRNE, THEN VENICE

Murad, Sultan of the Ottomans, was dead. Across an empire that stretched from the desert to the Danube, many mourned: some for a man who'd restored the Empire after Tamerlane's destruction, some because they feared for what would come next. Makkim mourned for both reasons. Prince Mehmed didn't mourn at all.

The Sultan had died at the palace in Edirne on a night too cold to snow. Fires had been lit in his bedroom and curtains were drawn against the draught. Murad was less than fifty but the burden of ruling had broken him. He'd tried to retire to a monastery once, had given the throne to Mehmed when he was just twelve. But when Lydislaw had broken his oath, his vizier Candarli had begged him to return and he'd had little choice. His son had never forgiven him or the vizier.

Murad had spent his last days on a bed surrounded by candles, at its head a mahogany board etched with the words of the Prophet. Murad had met with his Imams and was ready to die.

Two men were with him at the end, one of whom didn't expect to live long afterwards.

'Makkim will protect you,' Murad had said to him.

Candarli Halil had dipped his beard to his stomach. '*Inshallah*. I have had a good life.'

Murad had turned to Makkim. 'Protect the vizier and restrain my son. You are the only one he listens to.'

Makkim had held Murad's hand in both of his, feeling the last tides of his life tremble through them as he breathed his final words. He'd nodded but known that what Murad said was no longer true. Mehmed didn't listen to him as he once had. He listened to Zaganos bey now.

'Tell him to forget Constantinople,' Murad had said. 'Tell him to turn to the East, rebuild the Caliphate, keep the Indian Ocean a Muslim sea.' He gripped Makkim's hand. 'Before the Europeans take it from us. Before it's too late.'

In Venice it was hot. The sun scalded the city by day, only lifting its iron at sunset. The streets became ovens and children fried fish on the stones of St Mark's when they weren't impeding traffic in the canals. The smells of the city became a nuisance, then intolerable. No amount of Eastern spice could disguise the smell of burning, unwashed flesh.

The heat brought bad temper to the city. Sudden arguments erupted without warning, some leading to the drawing of swords. People shrank to the edges of streets, where shade and anonymity might be found. Siward and Nikolas chose to stay indoors. They worked in the Magoris fondaco office, the windows flung open, and tried to make sense of the bank's predicament.

When he wasn't thinking about Violetta, Siward thought about his grandfather's murder. When he wasn't thinking about that, he thought about Nikolas, who'd spent a lifetime in the service of the company and now wanted to go home. Since he meant that to happen as early as possible, Siward would learn the business of banking before finding Luke's killer. He'd also work out how to save the Magoris Bank without involving Makkim. He had no wish to meet his cousin, except on the battlefield.

As for Violetta, she'd used him, trading her company for information. He tried his hardest to forget her, reminding himself that, for all her charm, she was still a whore. But she clung on in his mind.

Then there was Zoe. The old woman had set out the terms for her help. He would consider them in his own time, but not before he'd persuaded Nikolas to go home.

So the days were spent with Nikolas patiently explaining the art of banking, or how Venice did it, at least. The Medici of Florence had pioneered accommodation with the Church, making a loan into a gift and interest into something else, usury being a cardinal sin. The Venetians were less worried, seeing themselves as having a more commercial relationship with God. They cared more about currencies and exchange rates: the lubricating oils of trade. And they cared most about the comfort of gold to anchor it all. Or the lack of it.

A month went by and the bank remained in business, but only because no further calls had been made on its deposits. Siward asked Nikolas why this was.

'Because no one wants to be the one to pull out the brick that brings the whole edifice down,' Nikolas answered, 'in case their brick gets buried under all the rest.'

'And because they still think their deposits have the trading company's assets behind them?' asked Siward.

'Precisely.' Nikolas rose and went to the map on the wall. 'And what assets they are. Look at them all: wine from Monemvasia, sugar from Cyprus, horses from Spain, mastic from Chios . . . Makkim has a handsome inheritance, if only he knew.'

Siward frowned. 'So, assuming he's not to be persuaded to help us, which seems likely, how are we to repair things?'

'By looking for new opportunities.' Nikolas pointed to the map. 'We need to look to the West. People are getting richer there and they'll need bankers.'

It was what Zoe had said. Almost the exact same words.

The heat brought enforced siesta, and with siesta came reflection. Siward's annoyance with Violetta gradually departed and all he thought of was her sitting at the end of his bed, gypsy head pushed forward and cupped by a hand, a ringlet curled round her finger, the little dog in her lap.

So he found himself pleased when she entered his office one morning.

It was early and the blinds were still drawn. Siward was bent over a manifest of goods from the Levant and didn't hear her come in. He was dressed for the heat in a long linen shirt and little else. He had a quill placed above an ear and ink was in his hair. He was whistling, as he did when trying to concentrate.

'Does it add up?'

He looked up, startled, upsetting ink onto the table. She was dressed as if the heat was occurring somewhere else. She wore a black dress beneath a hooded cloak and held a scented kerchief to her nose. He rose, buttoning the front of his shirt. He was too surprised to answer.

She walked over to a cabinet where Luke had put his store of curiosities: coins from Persia, prayer beads from Timbuktu, a toy elephant from Calicut, printed paper from China – the last, presumably, sent by Nikolas. She bent and peered into it, then straightened and turned.

'You do not greet me?'

'I'm sorry. Will you sit?' He gestured. 'I can call for wine.'

She shook her head. There was something indefinable in her face, something that had hardened its soft contours. She sat, reached over to the inkstand and righted it, using her kerchief to dab the papers. Everything was done precisely. He realised that she was nervous. 'You are sensibly dressed,' she said, glancing at him. 'It will be hot.'

'I wasn't planning to leave the fondaco.'

'You never do. It's wise. Venice is in bad humour. It must be the news.'

'The news?'

'Hadn't you heard? Mehmed is building a castle on the Bosporos. Constantinople will be closed from the north. The bailo Minotto has been shut up with the Doge these past days.'

He hadn't heard. The news was indeed bad. Much of Constantinople's food came from the Black Sea. Mehmed was preparing to lay siege.

She continued. 'So the ducat has fallen against the florin and the city is worse-tempered than on the first day of Lent.' She lifted the kerchief back to her nose. 'Then there's the smell.'

'I'm sorry. I can bring herbs.'

She waved the suggestion away. 'Do you stay inside to escape the heat or your creditors? What about Luke's murder? Are you not interested in solving that?'

He didn't answer. His ribs still hurt and the ridge of his nose was forever diverted. He asked his own question. 'Were you sent by Zoe?'

120

She leant back in her chair. 'Here? No.' She hesitated. 'She doesn't know I came.'

'So why did you?'

'I want to help you.'

Siward had been standing for this exchange. He saw her glance down at his bare knees. He went to the chair on the other side of the table and sat.

Violetta leant across the table suddenly, her curls bobbing. 'You think that if you just get on with your banking, the threat will pass. It won't. They'll kill you in the end.'

'And that matters to you?'

She looked down, for a moment uncertain. 'You are more likely to get to the truth if you're alive.'

'And why is the truth so important? You Venetians seem to get along quite well without it.'

'I'm not Venetian,' she said. She got up and returned to the cabinet, placing her hands flat on its top, gazing down. 'I've made Venice my home because it has a place for capable women. The same goes for Zoe, who is Greek. Now it feels cornered and is turning on its own.' She glanced back at him. 'Perhaps we want to save it from itself.'

'Are they still making ships for the Turk?'

Violetta looked surprised. 'They've been doing that for years. They tow them out into the lagoon at night to stop us noticing. Everyone knows.' She tapped the cabinet top with her fingers. 'No, it's as Zoe fears: the Doge is planning something more than that, something to do with Fra Mauro's map.'

Siward felt the familiar prick of irritation.

'I'll go to Murano when I'm ready to,' he said. 'I have a bank to save first.' He rose. 'The day's already hot, Violetta, and I wouldn't have you suffer on the streets. Do you feel that our interview is over?'

She turned and fixed her eyes on him. 'Will you at least consider what I've said?'

He moved to the door and opened it. 'I'll talk to Nikolas.'

Three days later, Siward was with Nikolas and Petros on a boat to Murano. The heat had given way to a fierce storm that had lasted for two days and the lagoon was still choppy, its waves fleeced with white.

They smelt the island from halfway there, the noxious fumes from its glass factories blown to them by the last of the storm. They alighted on steps slippery with seaweed and held onto each other for balance in the wind.

They were met by a man in a cloak that he fought to keep under control. His long hair was blown across his face.

'I am Andrea Bianco,' he said, taking Nikolas's hand and bringing him ashore. 'I work with Fra Mauro.'

Siward bowed to the man. His face was pale and pocked, his chin unshaven. There were flakes on his skin that spoke of ill-health and his breath was sour. He was dressed for the laity. He seemed unenthused by their arrival.

They walked through gardens of hedged beds, some with poles tied together at their tops. There were rows of cabbage and lettuce and a monk on his knees amongst them, putting up netting against the birds, his hood flapping against the side of his face. Smaller beds held herbs and Siward smelt mint, rosemary and thyme. He felt in his pocket for a coin, fell back and gave it to Petros who was limping behind.

'Buy some vegetables while we're with the monk,' he murmured. 'They'll be cheaper here than in Venice.'

'I don't like him,' whispered Petros, nodding at Bianco who was striding on ahead with Nikolas. 'Do you?'

'I don't know him, Petros.'

'He doesn't want us here.' He looked around him. 'Be careful.'

The monastery was a low, walled building with a church and campanile at one end. The wall was of red brick and had holes in it for firing; every part of every island in this lagoon was a fort. They entered through a door with a grille and a box for charity. Inside was a courtyard with a well at its centre and cloisters at its edge. A sheep was tethered to a millstone trimming the grass. Bianco hadn't spoken since meeting them. Now he turned and waited for Siward and Petros to join them.

'Fra Mauro will meet you in the chapter house,' he said, not looking at them. 'The room where he makes the map cannot be visited.'

He turned and led them through an arch into another court-yard with a hexagonal building at its centre. Nikolas, catching up with him, asked, 'For what reason can we not see the map?'

'It was commissioned by the *Signoria* of Venice and the King of Portugal. It is for them to decide who should see it.'

At the door of the chapter house, Bianco stopped and knocked on a door. He opened it and stood to one side. 'You admired our garden,' he said to Siward as he passed. 'I will arrange for some vegetables to be dug for you. There will be no need to pay.'

Leaving Petros to collect the vegetables, Siward and Nikolas entered a room with bare stone walls, chairs set against them and rush matting on the floor. At its centre was an altar with a lectern beside it. The room seemed to be empty.

'Grandson to Luke Magoris, you are most welcome.'

The voice came from a chair partially hidden by the altar. They looked over and saw an elderly monk rising from it. He

123

walked over and stood looking at them. He was a head shorter than Nikolas and stooped. His skin was yellow and his tonsure white, so that his bald scalp looked like an egg fried in oil. He wore a simple white habit, worn and patched and stained with different-coloured inks. He smelt faintly of linseed.

'Luke Magoris's grandson,' he repeated, his arms spread in welcome. 'I am honoured.' He turned. 'And Nikolas, who I met before with Luke. You were a good friend to him.'

They each took one the monk's hands. Siward bowed. 'It's we who are honoured, father. Your fame is universal.'

'Is it? And yet I cannot go out to meet it. I am cloistered here for eternity and happy to be so. I'm old and prefer the company of monks.' He squeezed Siward's hand. 'But I miss your grandfather. His death is a tragedy. He will be in heaven, be sure of it.'

Siward looked around him. 'Do you prefer to sit to speak, father?'

'No, no. I sit all day. I have to, to see the maps. My eyes are failing, I fear. What is it you wish to speak of?'

'My grandfather came here and showed you a map.'

'He did, and it changed everything,' said the monk, smiling. 'Since I cannot leave here, I rely on the reports of brave men who've travelled: men like Marco Polo, Nicolo di Conti and your grandfather. His map was more valuable than any other.'

'Because it showed that Africa can be sailed around.'

The monk looked uncomfortable. 'I am not permitted to talk of the map,' he said. 'Signor Bianco is most insistent.'

'But we know this,' said Nikolas gently. 'I was there when the Chinese treasure ship came to Mistra forty years ago. I have seen the map they gave to Luke.'

'Then you are one of the few,' said the monk. 'And perhaps you should keep your knowledge to yourself.'

The monk released their hands and went over to the door. He opened it, looked out, then closed it. He put his finger to his lips and walked back to them.

'Bianco sometimes listens at the door,' he whispered. 'We should talk quietly. Are you aware of what this new map will mean?'

'It will not be good for Venice.'

'No, because they have a virtual monopoly of the land trade routes east that they'd like to keep. But for Portugal?' The monk spread his arms again. 'For Portugal, it is the future. They are at the right end of the Middle Sea and have built a ship that can voyage down Africa and beyond. Their little caravels will change the world, you'll see.'

Siward had seen something else. 'Which means they can also get to the gold,' he said. 'My grandfather took it west to the coast down the Senegana River all those years ago. It could be done again.'

Nikolas was nodding. 'Exactly. So we can understand why the Portuguese were as interested to commission this map as Venice.' He turned to Fra Mauro. 'But, father, the truth is the truth. Sooner or later it must be out.'

Fra Mauro glanced at the door. 'You would think so,' he said sadly. 'But we have a strange Doge in Venice at present. It was he who sent me Signor Bianco.'

Siward suddenly had a burning ambition to see the map. He thought of something. He said, 'Father, did you know that my grandfather was murdered?'

The monk looked shocked. 'No! It cannot be,' he whispered. 'Luke murdered?'

Siward nodded. 'Thrown into the canal like a diseased dog.' He watched the monk, seeing the news take effect. 'Perhaps someone feared that he would not keep his knowledge to himself. As you said.'

The monk was silent. He stared at Siward with eyes so sad that Siward thought he might cry. Here was a good man in a bad city. He'd chosen to live away from it, but the city had come to him. He took Siward's arm. 'You poor child.'

'I'd like to see the map,' said Siward gently. 'If my grandfather died for it, I'd like to know why, or at least if it was worth it. Will you show it to us?'

The monk looked at Siward, then Nikolas. He looked back at the door, then nodded. 'I've long wanted to show it to someone. It is truly fine. Come quickly, before Bianco returns.'

He led them out of the chapter house, across a lawn and into the cloisters, their stones still washed with rain. They came to a door that Fra Mauro unlocked and pushed open. They walked into a room full of light. There were windows everywhere, big with panelled glass. Even the ceiling had windows propped open with poles. Against one wall were busts of travellers and geographers: Ptolemy, Strabo, Ibn Battuta. There were tables cluttered with drawings and measuring instruments. In the centre of the room was an enormous easel and stretched out on it, Fra Mauro's unfinished map.

'It's almost finished,' said the monk, 'just some notations to do. The work was delayed when Bianco took the draft to the Doge. He didn't return it for many months, I don't know why. Now, it's all hurry. It has to be ready for next spring when King Frederick of Germany will be crowned Holy Roman Emperor in Rome and wed to the *Infanta* of Portugal. The Doge wishes to present her with the first copy as her wedding gift.' He turned, his hands pressed together. 'And the abbot has given me special dispensation to go to Rome.' There was pure joy in his eyes. 'I am to meet the Pope!'

Siward stared at the parchment before him, his breath suspended. There were mountains and deserts and rivers between oceans full of ships. There were cities and turreted castles across every continent. Beside each was script describing the land and its people, and how the information had been derived. His eye travelled down Africa, to the Senegana River, and down, down, racing past tiny caravels, to the very bottom. There it was: the way round. For a thousand years, men had looked at Ptolemy's map and seen the Indian Ocean imprisoned. Now it was free.

Fra Mauro's head was next to his. He was pointing at two tiny islands off the tip of Africa. 'Those are the Islands of Men and Women,' he said. 'The Arabs have it that one island has just men, the other women. They meet once a year to procreate. Extraordinary.'

Siward pointed at what looked like a junk. 'Is this ship Chinese?'

'It signifies Admiral Zheng's treasure ship that went round Africa, the one that came to Mistra. They say his fleets had junks ten times the size of our largest ship.' He propped the spectacles up his nose and leant forward so that he was almost touching the parchment. He read out the notation.

'Around 1420, a junk crossed the Sea of India towards the Island of Men and the Island of Women, off Cape Diab, between the Green Islands and the shadows. It sailed for forty days in a south-westerly direction without ever finding anything but wind and water . . .'

Siward asked quietly, 'Do the Portuguese have any notion of what this map says?'

Fra Mauro leant back. 'Oh no. Bianco says the Doge wants

127

it to be a surprise. It's important they're not told.' He turned, smiling. 'You must mark that.'

'And King Lydislaw,' said Siward. 'Did he not visit you here?'

The monk was about to reply when there was a sound behind them. All three looked towards the door. A key was turning in the lock.

The door opened. Bianco stood there, his hand on the door handle and disbelief on his face. He looked from Fra Mauro to Siward to Nikolas.

'I'm sorry,' said Fra Mauro, walking towards him, 'but I owe so much to this man's grandfather.' He stopped. 'Don't concern yourself – they already knew what this map shows. They'll be discreet. I've told them about the Infanta's surprise at Rome.'

Bianco nodded his head slowly, his eyes fixed on Siward. 'Of course, father,' he said softly. 'Signore, your servant has vegetables and some herbs from our gardens. He is waiting for you on your boat.'

The vegetables were consumed that evening. Siward, Nikolas and Petros returned to Venice in a different boat on a different sea. The wind had died and the water was still. By evening, only the last, bruised knuckles of cloud clung onto the horizon.

Siward and Nikolas sat down to a dinner of mullet, pasta and buttered cabbage from the monastery garden. The dining room had its windows open for every breath of air and there were new bowls of herbs in front of each, should it be noxious. The evening sun shone in and turned the long, polished table into a river of fire, catching the Murano glass and exploding it into a hundred splinters of colour.

Siward raised his glass. 'To Fra Mauro. What an extraordinary man. How did you like Bianco?'

'He is a cartographer but also the Doge's spy,' said Nikolas. 'The question is: why did the Doge take the draft of the map and sit on it for so long?'

'To delay giving it to the Portuguese,' said Siward, sipping his wine. 'Which is understandable if it shows a way round Africa.'

Nikolas nodded slowly. 'Yes, but the truth will out. Why delay it?'

They both ate in silence for a while, listening to the evening bells. Siward looked out of the windows. The sun was about to go behind the palazzos opposite and the canal was already in shadow. He heard the call of the night watch echo through the streets.

There was a knock on the door and a servant entered.

'There is a woman here,' said the man. 'A courtesan.'

'And one who would like wine.'

Violetta Cavarse came into the room, dressed as she had been that morning but carrying a parasol. Nikolas nodded to the man, who left.

'Well, at least you're still alive,' she said, tucking her hair behind her ear and putting the parasol on the table. She looked hot. 'Is there a chair for me?'

Nikolas rose and brought one from the wall. 'Why shouldn't we be alive?'

'Because there were mushrooms among your vegetables,' she said, sitting. 'Bad ones.'

'Bad mushrooms?'

'From the monastery. The boatman was mine. He removed them from Petros just in time and checked them when he got back. They'll be poisoning fish in the lagoon now.'

Siward stared at her. 'We owe him our lives. You, as well.'

She looked back at him, her olive eyes catching the dying sun.

129

She was sitting as if a ruler had been placed down her spine. Her head was high and her long black hair framed her beauty in an intricate border. 'So perhaps now you'll see how much danger you're in,' she said simply. 'What did you discover at the monastery?'

'That Fra Mauro's map may well be the reason for Luke's murder. He showed it to us.'

'And?'

'It shows the way round Africa.'

'Which you already knew and soon everyone will know.'

'Very soon,' said Nikolas. 'The finished version is to be presented to the Infanta of Portugal in Rome when she goes there next spring to be married to the Holy Roman Emperor.'

They considered this for a spell, sipping their wine as the sun's rays surrounded them all with tiny dancing motes.

'But why would they want to kill us if everyone will eventually know what we know, anyway?'

'You,' corrected Violetta. 'If they'd wanted to kill Nikolas, they would have done it long ago.'

Siward nodded slowly. 'So you'll say I should leave,' he said. He turned to Nikolas. 'But what about you? What will you do if I leave?'

Nikolas leant forward. 'Siward, Siward. What kind of a retirement would I have if you're killed in Venice? The bank is finished here and we need to do our business in Flanders and Burgundy, where the world is moving to, if we're to survive. You know you must go.'

It made sense. He had to save the bank without the assets of the trading company and that meant finding new prospects. It was time, anyway, to distance himself from this woman who'd charmed him and used him. Yes, he had to go.

He looked from one to the other of them and his eyes stayed on Violetta.

'Two conditions,' he said, 'and I'll go. The first is that your spies continue to search for the man who killed my grandfather. The second is that you protect Nikolas as you have me. When I come back, I want to find him alive.' He looked at Nikolas. 'Then he can retire.'

PART THREE

1451–1453

CAPTIVES AND REFUGEES

CHAPTER TWELVE

PORTUGAL

Giovanni was at the end of the world. Everything and Jerusalem lay to the east; to the west: nothing but sea. Then Asia, if the Arabs were to be believed.

The wind hurled itself against the cliffs and roared through the grass; no trees could survive on the Sagres peninsula. In the tiny village of *Vila do Infante*, the tallest building was the palace tower from which Prince Henry watched his ships come in. That night, its walls trembled under the onslaught.

Giovanni had watched the storm come in earlier, lying on the grass above the cliffs. He'd seen boats scurry in to take shelter in the lee, leaving the journey round Cape St Vincent to another day. He'd watched black clouds mass on the horizon, thicken and roll in like the apocalypse. He'd seen lightning flash from their bruised bellies and heard the thunder grow loud and felt the first rain part his hair. And he'd thought about the Romans who believed that the sun sank hissing into the sea here. At the edge of their Roman world.

Now it was night and, at the top of the tower, Giovanni was sitting with Prince Henry in his study. It was late and they were

135

both a little drunk, the wine fortifying their voices against the storm. It was four months since Giovanni had arrived from Madeira but only a week since the prince had returned from the shipyards at Lagos. They'd met before, of course, when Prince Henry had commissioned him to repair the defences at Ceuta, and again when the land in Madeira had been given as his reward.

First, they'd spent an hour studying the design of a new caravel. This one was bigger, able to take more crew, more cargo. But the idea was the same: square sails to ride with the wind, lateen to sail into it. For the first time, a ship could beat upwind to come home, and it was Prince Henry and Portugal's secret.

The prince was tall and thin and unbearded and he spat when he spoke, more when he drank. He wanted to talk about a map.

'Venice has delayed and delayed and now won't even tell me what it says,' he complained. 'And it's never Fra Mauro who answers my letters but some assistant called Bianco. He won't tell me whether the way round Africa is open or not.'

'But you'll know next spring, majesty,' said Giovanni, 'when it's presented to the Infanta. Why the hurry?'

'Because I need more funds from the Order of Christ to build this new caravel,' said Henry. 'I need them before they're spent on churches and relics and other nonsense. The Church doesn't like its riches spent on discovery.' He drank and pulled a face. 'They think if God had meant us to know more of the world, He wouldn't have put oceans in our way. And didn't the serpent in Eden show us the sin of curiosity?' The prince shook his head at the idiocy of it all. 'If I'm to build more caravels and send them further south, I need proof of what they'll find.'

Giovanni knew that Prince Henry's court was riven by two factions: those who believed the way open, and those who thought that Ptolemy had had it right. The proof couldn't come soon enough. Especially since bad news had arrived: a fleet had failed to return from beyond Cape Bojador. Suddenly all the doubters of Prince Henry's court were whispering louder into his ear. The merchants and ship-owners and men from the treasury were warning him not to waste more money on pointless expeditions. They told him to exploit what he'd already found: the gold from Guinea that could make Portugal as rich as Venice.

'We live in an age of science, Giovanni,' Prince Henry continued, 'but the forces of reaction are strong: especially from our Holy Mother Church, and perhaps now from Venice too. So I want you to go to Rome and make sure we get this map. As you know, my niece, the Infanta Eleanor, is to be married there next spring. I'd like you to accompany her on her journey: it will be by sea and might be dangerous. And you can teach her things that may be useful for her new position on the way.'

Giovanni frowned. He'd waited four months to see this prince when he could have been on his way to find a son. Now this.

'Majesty, it is a great honour . . .'

But Henry had raised his hand. 'I know why you're leaving Madeira. King Lydislaw told me. You are more likely to find your son with a prince's help.' He gestured. 'Do this, and I'll give you men to scour Bulgaria. It's your best chance.'

Giovanni looked up at the map on the wall. The sea route from Portugal to Rome was a dangerous way for a seventeen-year-old girl to travel, but it was the quickest way, perhaps quicker than leaving now to go overland. And he'd not properly considered how he was to make contact with his son. What the prince said made sense.

He decided. 'I accept,' he said.

'Good,' said Prince Henry, rising. 'The Infanta will be arriving here for Christmas. You can meet her then.'

Later, Giovanni lay in bed in the room above Prince Henry's study. It was really storage space but he'd asked for a cot to be put up there because he liked the view. He lay with his hands behind his head thinking of the ships trying to ride this storm. Their sails would be shredded by now, even if their masts were still upright. He turned onto his side. What if it was his sugar aboard?

There was a shutter banging downstairs in the study. He thought they'd closed them all before retiring. Perhaps the wind?

It came again. Should he go down and close it? But the bed was so warm. He thought of the ship's designs, spread out on the table for him and Prince Henry to pore over. Had the Prince locked them away before retiring? He couldn't remember. He rose and put on his gown. He went to the door and opened it as another bang came from below. He took a candle from a sconce and descended the stairs.

He unlocked the door to the study and went in, shielding the flame. Big cabinets lined the walls with maps pinned above them that moved in the draught. In the cabinets were the paraphernalia of measurement: compasses, rulers, sextants and rolled parchment, some used, some waiting to be scraped clean.

He looked over to the other side of the room where the big shutters were swinging on their hinges. They crashed into the stone outside and swung forward again. He looked at the table in front of them: empty. Thank God.

He walked across the room to fasten the shutters, pulling them towards him against the wind. He could hear the explosion of the sea on the rocks below. He reached for the latch and felt pain. Splinters. He looked down and saw that the shutter had been forced. By the wind? Not possible. No wind could make a steel bolt leave its channel. A rope was bridging the windowsill, tied to a ring in the floor. Someone had climbed down it, down the wall of the tower.

He went over to the cabinets. There was a gap. It was where the designs for the new caravel would have been stored. He looked around the floor, then searched the other shelves.

Giovanni sat down, staring at the windows. Someone had climbed through them to steal Portugal's greatest secret. *Who?*

CHAPTER THIRTEEN

EDIRNE

Hasan turned from the window. He needed a favour. 'He has taken another of the boys,' he said.

Makkim had tied the sash around his waist and the dragon sword was in his hand, waiting to be put beneath it. He was still the only man allowed to wear a weapon in Mehmed's presence, though he imagined Zaganos would soon get the honour. He looked up.

'From the enderun?'

The Aga nodded. 'The last one killed himself for the shame. He was only twelve.'

Sultan Mehmed's predation on the janissary recruits was beginning to affect their training. They were the Sultan's slaves, taught to obey his every command, but what he wanted from them was unnatural. Makkim thought suddenly of a man he'd murdered many years ago. *He touches me sometimes.*

'I'll speak to him. Is the Venetian here?'

Hasan nodded again. 'The bailo of Constantinople, Girolamo Minotto.'

'And the Sultan?'

'Is admiring the model galley given to him last time Venice came to call.' Hasan watched Makkim's sword disappear beneath the sash, only the dragon-head visible. 'The bailo doesn't smile.'

'Well, he hasn't much to smile about,' said Makkim, walking over and putting a hand on the aga's shoulder. 'They've had bad news from Africa.'

One of Makkim's initiatives had been to build an efficient spy service. He'd got Candarli to place ambassadors in every important city and include spying among their tasks. He knew most of what went on in the world.

'What news?' asked Hasan. Their friendship had waned somewhat since Makkim's promotion, but they still talked about most things. And Hasan hadn't forgotten what Makkim had done for him at Varna.

Makkim went over to the door and opened it. 'They've lost the Mali gold trade. The Doge will be worried.' He looked back. 'And I suppose the building of that castle on the Bosporos must make our intentions there pretty clear. I'll join you in a minute.'

Hasan left and Makkim glanced down at his sword, seeing the dragon's ruby eyes look up into his.

He remembered standing in the shadow of the parade ground with Hasan. Long ago. It was the first time he'd seen it.

'It arrived this morning from your father,' Hasan had said. 'The message said that it was yours.'

He remembered looking into those eyes then. 'Mine? I've never seen it before.' He'd lifted and turned the sword. 'It's beautiful. May I keep it?'

He'd been allowed to. It was the finest sword anyone had ever seen and he still had no idea why it was his. He frowned. *Another reason to go back to the village.*

He walked through the door and down the stairs. Mehmed

was waiting for him at the bottom with Candarli and Zaganos bey. They were standing around a model galley.

Mehmed glanced up. 'I've been looking at the galley's *rembata*,' he said. He was wearing a turban of a size that made his face look thin.

'For guns?' asked Makkim, joining them.

'We can fit two ribaudkins on it, one either side.'

Makkim bent to inspect the galley. 'They'd not do any damage to walls, highness. Too small. The Italians use them to scatter an attack.'

'But against sea walls? Wasn't that how the Venetians got in two centuries ago?'

'They used platforms thrown out from the mastheads. And they had catapults on the decks below, throwing stones.'

'So you'll say we need to wait for bigger cannon,' said Mehmed. 'Zaganos believes we should attack now, while Constantine is still getting used to being emperor. He hardly has an army, after all.'

Makkim glanced at Zaganos, whose face was expresionless. He was tall like Mehmed, and not much older. He was bald, had long moustaches and the physique of a wrestler. There was a small jewelled dagger at his waist. *So, it's happened.*

He had to be careful. 'He may be right, but should we risk it? We ought to besiege Constantinople only when we're certain we can take it. That requires cannon of a size we don't have.'

Zaganos bey cleared his throat. His voice was high for a man of such size. 'And how do you suggest we get them?' he asked. 'Respectfully.'

Makkim studied him. The respect was still there, but only just. He'd have to watch him more closely.

'That is why we have agreed to meet the bailo,' he said. He turned to Mehmed. 'He is waiting for us. Shall we join him?'

They arrived at the audience hall where the doors were open. Inside they could see four Venetians examining the ceiling. They wore short cloaks above black doublets.

'Gentlemen.'

Makkim and Candarli had stopped at the door to let Mehmed pass. Zaganos had been left behind. The Venetians fell to their knees.

Mehmed entered and went to the throne where he sat, his angry, suspicious eyes darting from one Venetian to the next. 'You asked to see me. Why?' He spoke to the man in front. 'Get up to answer.'

The bailo rose, managing to look calm, deferential and insolent all at once.

'My name is Minotto,' he said, his lips invisible through his beard. 'I am the bailo of Constantinople.'

'That is not an answer. I asked why you wanted to see me.'

'Because we come to talk about Constantinople, magnificence,' said Minotto, his voice softer than breeze through silk.

'Which you've calculated I'll take this time. Very sensible.'

The bailo made a little reverence. 'Which our galleys will help you to take,' he said. 'When they're finished.'

'Which is soon, I hope?'

'The *arsenale* is working at full capacity. The King of France is made to wait for his ships.'

'So I can have them within the year?'

Minotto cleared his throat. It was the sound of water on pebbles. 'We would like to talk about trade, magnificence. Specifically, trade through Constantinople, should it fall.'

Mehmed lost his temper. Makkim and Candarli had seen it often but the Venetians hadn't. It was a lightning bolt without storm cloud for warning. Only Minotto remained perfectly still.

Mehmed rose from the throne. 'You dare *bargain* with me, Venetian? The bailo of Constantinople dares to discuss *trade* with the Sultan of the Turks?' He took two strides to face Minotto so that their noses were inches apart. '*You dare?*'

The Venetian stared back at him, his head slightly raised. He said nothing.

'You will deliver the ships to me in six months,' hissed Mehmed, 'all of them. And you will fit them with the ribaudkin that I know your arsenale makes. If you fail to do this, there will be no *trade* negotiations. There will be no Venice.'

Silence. No one in the room moved. Mehmed returned to his throne, his eyes not leaving Minotto. He sat.

Now Makkim spoke. His sultan's performance had been all that he'd hoped for and if the Venetians weren't frightened, they were stupid.

He asked, 'Tell me, bailo, are you aware of what is meant by the *dar el-salaam*?'

Minotto dipped his head. The movement was far short of obsequious. 'The "abode of peace",' he said. 'Yes, I am aware of it.'

'Well, it is what Venice will soon be part of. Your city will be able to trade, pray, love as you have always done. The rule of Islam is the rule of peace.' Makkim smiled. 'Better than any *Pax Romana*, you can be sure.'

'No enslavement?' Minotto asked softly, looking straight at him. 'Can I be sure of that too, Makkim Pasha?'

Makkim stared back at him, the smile still there. 'There is something you can do for us, bailo. A gesture of goodwill.'

Minotto bowed slightly. 'If it is in my power.'

'Your arsenale made cannon for the Sultan's great-grandfather, Bayezid. Do you still have the moulds?'

'They were sold to Hungary.'

'Ah, Hungary.' Makkim's mind travelled the map. Hungary was next to Bulgaria where he wanted to go. 'To whom were they sold in Hungary?'

Minotto seemed to be weighing up something. He said, 'Venice is a Christian republic. We'll not give you the means to make that size of cannon.'

Mehmed began to speak but Makkim got there first. His smile was intact, his voice low but calm. 'Venice has been excommunicated more times than a Hussite, usually because it put its welfare before God. I ask again: who were they sold to in Hungary?'

Minotto's face remained impassive. 'I don't know.'

'Yes, you do. And if you don't tell us now, then you may inform your Doge that all existing trade with ourselves is at an end.' Makkim raised an eyebrow. 'Quite apart from any that may arise through our taking of Constantinople.'

Minotto glanced at Mehmed. 'You will need to speak to the gunsmith Orban of Budapest. He may be able to help.'

Makkim nodded. 'Thank you. You may leave.'

Minotto frowned. His mission had gone as badly as it could have gone. He'd not look forward to his meeting with the Doge. He remained where he was for a minute, looking from Sultan to vizier to general. Then he turned.

'Wait,' said Makkim. 'One further thing. King Lydislaw. My agents tell me he was seen in Venice.'

Minotto didn't blink. 'King Lydislaw is dead, pasha, slain at Varna as everyone knows. Your agents are mistaken.'

The two studied each other for some time before Makkim looked away. 'Very well. You may go.'

When they'd left, Makkim said to Mehmed, 'I should go to Hungary to meet this Orban.'

'You? But I need you here.'

He glanced at Candarli. The vizier said, 'The cannon are important, majesty, and Orban will need to be persuaded. Makkim should go.'

Mehmed was frowning now. It was the frown that Makkim knew meant he'd get his way. But he still needed something else from this prince. He nodded discreetly to the vizier.

Candarli Halil bowed. 'Majesty, allow me to depart.'

He left and Makkim went and stood opposite his sultan. 'Highness,' he said quietly, 'may we talk about the janissaries?'

For once, Mehmed took vizier Candarli Halil's advice and Makkim was sent to Budapest in Hungary, where the gunsmith Orban lived and worked. The given reason was that he was to meet King Frederick, soon to be Holy Roman Emperor, and discuss a peace that Mehmed had no intention of keeping. After that, Makkim was to go and find cannon to bring down the walls of Constantinople.

What Mehmed didn't know was what he planned to do then.

He rode up through Thrace, Macedonia and Serbia and, in a week, crossed the border into Hungary. He rode beneath spring sunshine and branches rippled with new buds. The fields around were softening and men were beginning to put them to the plough. He was happier than he'd been in months and knew why. He was free of Mehmed. He no longer had to witness his capricious cruelties, or suffer his dangerous affection. He was free.

At last he had time to think, and he had much to think about. It was seven years ago that Murad had asked him to prepare Mehmed for rule and he'd failed spectacularly. He'd tried his best to present him with a vision of a new Caliphate, spreading from Edirne to Baghdad, a land united under the peace of the Prophet. He'd tried to warn him of the dangers of neglecting the Muslim trade of the Indian Ocean, telling him of a map and the new Portuguese ship that would take them there. He'd done everything in his power to shift Mehmed's gaze to the East, but he'd failed. Constantinople remained his obsession.

Inshallah.

His janissary training had taught him that no outcome other than Islam was possible for mankind. The message of the Prophet was universal, absolute, undeniable. But was it a message of war or peace? For the first time since leaving the enderun, he found himself questioning the will of his master.

He came with an escort, as befitted the Sultan's general: a company of sipahi knights with tall plumes and little bows at their sides. They wore silver mail and their horses were caparisoned. They had wings on their backs and they sang as they rode. Villagers came to their doors and their children ran after them. At night they camped beside streams filled by winter snows whose music lulled them to sleep.

At Budapest, Hunyadi was on the road to meet him. Makkim had last seen him at Varna, escaping with his army, perhaps with Lydislaw.

'If he's not dead, then he's far away,' was all Hunyadi would say when asked about the king. 'Too far for your assassins to find.'

They entered the city to trumpets and two flags set out above the gates: double-headed eagles and a crescent moon.

'I thought the Palaiologi emperors in Constantinople claimed that bird,' said Makkim, looking up. 'Isn't your emperor premature?'

'It binds us to them,' replied Hunyadi, smiling. 'In case you were in any doubt.'

King Frederick had no doubt. Constantinople would not be allowed to fall. He told this to Makkim in the great castle hall in Budapest. There were shields on its pillars bearing the arms of the most ancient families in the land and, between them, members of those families, there to bear witness to Europe's pledge to Constantinople. Whatever Mehmed's talk of peace.

Afterwards there was a banquet at which Makkim sat beside Frederick and they talked of marriage.

'I am thirty-five and will be crowned Emperor next year in Rome,' said Frederick. 'I am to marry as well.'

'I will be there to see it, highness,' said Makkim. 'I am to be the Sultan's representative.'

'Then you will meet my bride: Eleanor, Infanta of Portugal. She is seventeen and beautiful.'

And rich, thought Makkim as he bit into chicken. The man beside him had made the dinner dull. This was the first interesting thing he'd said.

'A sensible choice,' he said.

Frederick turned to him. His face was long and pale and bearded to his soup. He had a long, waxen nose, thin lips and eyes that were permanently doleful, as if the world owed him money. He was, Makkim knew, reputed to be miserly.

'Sensible indeed,' said the king. 'Eleanor has a genius for an uncle. Prince Henry is rich because he is master of the Order of Christ and he spends his money on ships. The Portuguese call him "The Navigator" with good reason. He will discover the world.'

'Your majesty has an interest in discovery?' asked Makkim, with hope.

'I have an interest in gold, Makkim: gold from Africa.' Frederick paused to eat a grape, balancing the fruit between his thin lips before tilting his head and swallowing it whole. 'So she comes with a good dowry.'

Escaping the entertainment now became Makkim's mission. The days were full of jousting and hunting, the nights of banqueting and avoiding the eye of beautiful women. He noticed that ever more lovely creatures were placed opposite him at the feasts. But he'd guessed the game: the oldest in diplomacy's sordid repertoire. Get the janissary drunk and bedded as his oath forbids. Then negotiate.

So he decided to retire to his bed with a cold. He'd brought a doctor among his retinue and the sipahi guards stationed at his bedroom door were instructed to permit entry to no one, not even King Frederick himself. Makkim was to be infectious.

Then he disappeared into Budapest.

He dressed himself as a Franciscan monk since there seemed to be many about the streets. He went out after dark, his hood pulled forward, to visit the various janissary spies he'd sent into the city beforehand. They'd done their work well. On the second night of his illness, Makkim was knocking on Orban the gunsmith's door.

It was opened by a woman with a pan in her hand containing thin meat soaked in oil. The woman was stout and her face shiny with sweat. She made the sign of the cross when she saw him.

'Father.'

'May I come in?'

The woman nodded and he stepped inside. The room was small with a low ceiling of darkened beams, its only furnishing a table, two chairs and a range beneath a chimney. It smelt of smoke and onions. A curtain on one wall suggested another room beyond.

'Is this the home of Orban the gun-maker?' Makkim asked, lowering his hood and turning to the woman. 'May I speak with him?'

There was a growl from behind the curtain. 'It's late. Is it about money?' There was the sound of a chair being scraped back and the curtain parted. 'Oh. Father.'

Makkim looked at a man of middle years who'd spent too long at the foundry. His face was burnt and the little hair above it looked like grass after a forest fire. His eyes were large between eyelids with no lashes. His teeth were black.

'May we talk?'

Orban lifted the curtain and waved him into a room with another single table and two chairs, much like the first. A small bed stood in the corner. On the table was a Madonna half-carved out of wood, and beside it, wood-shavings, a knife and a candle. Makkim stared at the Virgin.

'It's beautiful.'

'For the friary. I will present it next week.'

Makkim nodded. He knew nothing of Budapest's friary. 'The brothers will be pleased. You have other work?'

Orban's home suggested that the gun-maker's orders were few. The house was modest and seemed to contain no servants.

'Very little, father. There's not been much call for big cannon since Varna.'

Makkim was encouraged. Before him was a man in need of money. 'Do you still have the Venetian moulds?' he asked.

Surprise came to Orban's face. Why would a Franciscan monk be interested in cannon moulds? He glanced at the heavy crucifix at Makkim's front.

'Why do you ask, father?'

150

Makkim decided on candour. The smoke from the other room was drifting through the curtains and stinging his eyes.

'I'm not a monk,' he said. 'I speak for a master who will pay you well to make cannon of a size not yet seen.' He reached inside his habit, bringing out a small sack of coin that he opened. Gold florins glittered in the candlelight. 'There will be more.'

Orban stared at the coins. Then he looked up at Makkim, something new in his eyes. 'Who sent you?' he asked softly.

There was silence between them.

'The Sultan,' said Makkim. 'Mehmed the second, Emperor of the Ottomans.'

Orban glanced down at the crucifix. 'And you are his slave?'

Makkim gave the smallest of nods. 'I am his general, the one they call Makkim.'

'And you, a Muslim, dare to dress like that, to wear a crucifix?' Orban's voice had dropped to a whisper.

Makkim thought quickly. 'We worship the same God,' he said. 'And I wasn't always a Muslim.' He stood and lifted the habit over his head, the crucifix with it, and draped it over the chair. He was now dressed in a simple cotton tunic. He sat. 'There. Can we talk now?'

Orban didn't answer.

Makkim said, 'I was born a Christian. I grew up not far from here. I was taken by the Sultan's men when I was eleven.'

'You are a slave.'

'A willing slave, one who wishes to bring the peace of Islam to the world.'

'Peace? You want to drench Europe in blood. Is that peace?'

There was silence again.

'I have seen both sides,' said Makkim, his elbows on the

151

table. 'The Ottoman rule is fair and just, and the taxation less. Everyone is permitted their own religion.'

'You weren't permitted yours.'

'But I was given opportunity I never could have found had I stayed a Christian.' He leant forward. 'This is what you're being offered, Orban.'

'You want me to convert?'

Makkim shook his head. 'We just want you to make cannon. We will pay well.'

'To bring down the walls of Constantinople.'

There. It had been said.

'Yes,' said Makkim.

Orban rose and went to the curtain. He spoke softly to his wife for a while in a language Makkim didn't understand. He returned to the table and sat. He put his palms to the table and looked down at them.

'I won't do it,' he said at last. 'I won't do it not only because I will not betray my faith but because I don't like what I see of yours.' He spoke quietly to his hands, not looking up. 'Christianity will change. We have new thinking in Italy that will promote science and end superstition. Christianity will absorb this change but Islam won't.' He looked up. 'The word of God is no way to run a world.'

Makkim stared at the man. He'd not expected such an argument, but then he remembered that Orban was, more than anything, a man of science. To him, the cannon were a means to an end. He nodded his respect, even attempting a smile. He rose.

'Then I will leave your house,' he said, collecting the coin and turning to the habit on the chair. 'May I be permitted to resume my disguise?'

CHAPTER FOURTEEN

BULGARIA

Three days later, Makkim left Budapest with his sipahis. Miraculously recovered, he'd graciously declined a farewell banquet, not wishing to spread any illness that might linger. He'd also declined an escort to the border. Once there, he sent his sipahis on and turned left for Bulgaria.

This time, he travelled as a Christian knight, a common sight in Ottoman vassal lands. He wore padded doublet and woollen hose with leathers for chaps against the chafing. His armour was strapped behind his saddle, his dragon sword on top. As the days grew hotter, he abandoned the doublet.

The disguise was for his learning as much as safety. The country was full of janissaries discreetly recruiting for Mehmed's new army and Makkim would be known, his passage noted from village to village. He wanted to see how the Empire was preparing for war and whether any news of it was likely to cross the frontier.

It seemed likely that it would. He travelled on roads busy with soldiers on the move, their verges thick with pollen and buzzed by bees. In the villages, he found the forges working at full blast and new buildings rising everywhere: warehouses to store the harvest, barracks for the soldiers. At inns, the talk was of Constantinople and little else, whether Mehmed would finally take it after a thousand years of trying by Arab, Bulgar and Turk. Many wanted it to happen. The Byzantines were lazy and corrupt and their end was overdue.

It seemed likely that it would all be noticed, but would Europe come to Constantinople's aid?

At night he didn't sleep. He lay awake and remembered the last time he'd spoken to her. It had been in the barn by the side of the road. It was the morning after and she was cleaning his wound.

'You'll carry a scar,' she'd said, 'a big one. The priest's knife went deep.'

She'd sat back on her ankles to pour more water and he'd watched her then with more love than he'd ever felt.

'Thank you.'

'It kept you safe,' she'd said, misunderstanding. 'I'd do it again.'

They'd stared at each other, their young minds confused by feelings they didn't really understand.

'I'll have to leave. You should go back.'

'No, Ilya. I'm coming with you.'

He'd tried to dissuade her. There was no reason for her to go too: it wasn't her who'd killed the priest and their parents would need one of them to stay. But she'd not listened and he'd been glad.

Which was why the memory of the janissaries, four of them waiting for him when he'd come out to piss, had been the one that had stayed with him above all others, causing him sleepless nights, becoming more vivid with every passing mile. *I left you alone.*

154

So he came tired to the village to find that it was much the same as when he'd left: the church, the cluster of hovels that had once seemed a city, the graveyard beside the bubbling stream. No Muslim graves there; the village was still quietly Christian for all the Sufis' work.

He dismounted and walked his horse over to what had been his home, the same chickens outside, pigs amongst them. He remembered finding truffles with her in the forests once, the pigs rooting amongst the autumn leaves. He remembered her laughing at the noise they made.

He looked at the house. It was still early and the shutters were closed. It seemed so small but to them it had been a mansion, a theatre for a hundred fantasies. He remembered their bed, the world beneath blankets when the storm raged outside, the whispered conversation, brow to brow.

He turned and walked into the field, across earth that would soon be thick with wheat for a new generation of children to play in. Something made him turn. A woman was standing at the door, watching him. His mother? It was too far to see her face. Did she recognise him?

He began to walk towards her, feeling the thump of his heart as his feet trod each furrow. She looked small, so bent; the right size for the house. He was closer now. She must recognise him.

'Mother.'

She hadn't moved. There was no smile or wave or any sign that she knew him. He approached her slowly.

'Mother, it's me. I am Makkim now.'

He took her hands in his and looked down into eyes narrowed by the morning sun. There was no expression on her face, no feeling in her hands. Did she even have her wits?

'Mother, I'm here.'

She shook her head then. 'No.'

He frowned.

'Can we sit?' he asked, gesturing towards the well. He led her across to it and gently set her down, her back to the sun. He sat opposite her, feeling the stone against his legs, still cold from the night. He looked around. He'd thought so long about this meeting but now he didn't know what to say.

'Did Father die in peace?' he asked.

Something flashed in her eye. 'Peace? We knew no peace after you left.'

There was expression in her face now. Was it anger? She wasn't mad, at least. She was a fraction closer to the woman who'd hugged him so hard that he'd felt her laughter through his chest. But there was no laughter now. She'd not wanted him to come.

'The priest?'

'He made us suffer.' She shook her head. 'We were shunned. Even by the Jew.'

He stared at her. 'The priest lived?'

'After what you did to him, it was a miracle.' She looked away. 'You took our daughter from us.'

Makkim was shaking his head slowly. He'd thought the priest dead for twenty years. Suddenly he longed to tell her the truth about him, about everything. But the truth would destroy every small thing she had left in her life. The truth, he knew, would kill her.

'Is he here?' he asked.

She shook her head. 'He went away, to Constantinople. He was clever, I suppose.'

He found his fists clenched. *Clever.* He remembered the face looking down from the pulpit, always looking down. He could see the thin finger pressed to the vellum as he read out the Latin that no one but him would understand. *I'd understand you now.* He nearly laughed.

'Do you know where she went?' he asked.

His mother shook her head. 'She wrote to us, but she didn't want us to know where she'd gone.'

His mother looked so sad then that he thought his heart would break. She'd been deserted by everyone in her life: her husband, her son, her daughter.

He reached out. 'Mother, I can take you back with me to Edirne. You can live in comfort, have everything you want. We can be together. Perhaps we can find her.'

But she shook her head. 'You should go,' she said. 'I don't want you here. I am not your mother.'

He misunderstood. 'You will always be my mother.'

'No,' she said. 'I never was. I brought you into life but you were someone else's child. I was the midwife.'

He stared at her. 'But . . .'

'The sword.' She pointed to it by his side. 'It came with you in the cradle. All the way from Greece.' She frowned. 'You are not my son.'

He was shaking his head now, slowly, his eyes looking past her, wide, as if seeing something strange emerging from the distance. *Of course.* It was perhaps not such a surprise. It explained so much: their different heights, looks . . . *Of course. I've always known.*

He suddenly felt a dizzying joy. If she was not his sister, then what he'd felt . . . all the guilt . . . He found himself smiling.

His mother had risen. 'Please go. Now.'

He looked at the woman who was not his mother. 'You'll not see me again,' he said softly. 'I can give you money.'

157

She shook her head. 'No. Just go.'

He felt the sun's heat on his head, heard the chatter of chickens around him. 'And will you tell me who my true mother is? Now that I am leaving?'

'Never.'

He'd known that would be the answer. She turned away, not wanting to meet his eye. This woman who'd raised him with more love than he'd thought the world could hold, with the same love she'd shown to her own daughter, wouldn't look at him. She blamed him for everything. But it had been God's will, hadn't it?

Inshallah.

He felt despair like he never had before.

'Goodbye.'

He turned and walked away. He was the only one who said it.

It took a week to get back to Edirne. He hardly felt the days pass. He didn't see the people sowing the fields either side of the road or the scarecrows going up. He didn't hear the creak of sap rising in the forests or the first birds return to resume their song. His thoughts were on a sister forced to flee because he hadn't killed the priest after all, on a sister who was not a sister, on a crucifix lying shattered on a church floor.

He'd left his mother and gone to the church. He'd walked through a graveyard where generations of villagers lay, put to rest with the eternal lie crossed into their foreheads: don't protest in this life and you'll be given it all in the next. He'd looked down at them. *Do you have it now?*

He'd opened the church door. Inside were the rows of worn benches, the baptismal font at the end, the rope hanging from the bell, the walls bare except for candle-holders, blackened stone around them. He'd looked at the pulpit, at the lectern at its front. He'd seen him up there, beneath the big crucifix, speaking from above and from below: the space for hypocrisy to thrive.

He'd walked to the pulpit and mounted the steps. He'd reached out to touch the feet of the Christ. He'd pulled and the crucifix had smashed to pieces on the stone.

Then he'd closed his eyes to remember what he wanted to remember: banging on the door with the branch he'd picked up from the storm, the priest opening it with a knife in his hand, expecting him.

'You should not be here. This is sanctuary.'

The priest had lunged as he'd ducked, feeling the blade open his cheek. He'd brought the wood down with every ounce of his strength and the man had fallen, lain still. Dead for sure.

'Ilya, what have you done?'

Now he was in Edirne and there was comfort in the muezzin calling the faithful to prayer: a language and message that everyone could understand. Rules for this life and hope for the next. *Better*. The gun-maker had been wrong.

He found Mehmed in the throne room, pretending to examine a galley on a plinth. Standing next to him were his old vizier and a new one: Zaganos bey.

'It's bigger,' said the Sultan, not turning, 'to fit the cannon.' He pointed to a platform at the front. 'Baltaoğlu has suggested mounting towers onto those.'

'Baltaoğlu, lord?'

Baltaoğlu and Makkim had done their janissary training together. As far as Makkim knew, he had no experience of ships.

'Yes, Baltaoğlu,' Mehmed said to the galley. 'I've made him my new admiral. It was Zaganos's idea.'

Makkim exchanged glances with Candarli Halil. 'An excellent choice, lord,' he said mildly. 'Who better?'

Mehmed frowned a little, then finally turned. He walked up to Makkim, embraced him, kissed him on each cheek. 'I've missed you.'

'And I, you, lord.'

He wondered how much Zaganos would have told him. Certainly he'd have spoken to his sipahi guard. He decided to be direct. 'I have failed you,' he said. 'Orban won't make us cannon. But I have another plan.'

Mehmed glanced at Zaganos bey, then back. 'I hope so.' He studied him. 'Where did you go?'

'To Bulgaria to see how we prepare for war. To my village to see my mother.'

'But we are your family now, surely?' Mehmed challenged. 'Did you ask her to come here?'

Makkim nodded. 'She does not want to.' He turned to the galley. 'Now, my plan. It will involve the Venetians.'

'You'll persuade them to make the cannon?'

Makkim shook his head. 'Not make, highness. Buy.'

CHAPTER FIFTEEN

MEDITERRANEAN SEA

The storm had been terrible and they weren't going to outrun anything in their state. Giovanni turned from the approaching galley and saw the torn sails, the loose ropes trailing in the sea, the smashed deck washed by water. It was just after dawn.

'Are they pirates?' asked Eleanor, her hand lifted to the sun, her eyes on the galley.

'Probably, Infanta. Berber corsairs, I imagine.'

Giovanni looked at the other caravels, all lying low in the water, all trying to do what they were: summon what was left of their sails to catch the wind, to get away. 'Captain?'

Diego Costa had sailed the African coast and back a dozen times, beating up to the Azores under lateen sails to collect the trade winds home. He was built for the caravel: small, quick and agile. He'd weathered many storms, but few to match the one they'd just sailed through. 'Corsairs, certainly,' he said. 'They've judged it well.'

'Can we run?'

Costa looked up at the pennant on the masthead. 'There's

not much wind and we're still square-rigged. The Infanta should go to her cabin.'

'No.'

It had been a month before Christmas that Eleanor, Infanta of Portugal, had come to Sagres.

Giovanni had been there to welcome her, along with the mix of nobles and academics that made up the eccentric court of her uncle, Prince Henry the Navigator. Over the following weeks he'd watched, amazed, as a seventeen-year-old girl had turned the place on its head.

It had been always been on its head really. Put the cleverest people in Europe together in a village at the end of the world and you were likely to create something strange. Add a teenage incendiary to the mix and it would be mayhem.

She'd decided on a Christmas play, and it was at its casting that Giovanni had first spoken to her.

'You'll be St George,' she'd said, her wide eyes on his, the quill stroking her chin. 'You're old but then who knows what age St George was? Anyway, you're big and fair.'

Giovanni was sitting opposite her in Prince Henry's study in the tower and they were alone. He was impatient to leave for Rome.

'And I want the boat-builders to build me Siena, which can be Bethlehem,' she continued brightly. 'The painters can do the windows and doors. It'll make a change from Madonnas.'

'And the lords, highness? Won't they expect roles?'

She'd shaken her head vigorously. 'No, they'll only mess it up. You know what they're like over precedence. No one will ever get onto the stage. We want this to be *fun*.'

Fun was new to the court. After the disaster of the unreturned

162

fleet, its mood had stayed sour. Two factions had drawn up on either side of their king: aristocrats and merchants arguing for trade, artisans and academics for discovery. Eleanor had made it plain whose side she was on.

'The nobles throw their weight about and talk too loudly,' she'd said. 'It'll do them good to be an audience for a change.'

Certainly Henry won't mind, Giovanni had thought. He'd always preferred the company of thinkers.

'I wanted to ask you,' she'd said, the quill now scratching her ear, 'are the nobles winning, do you think?'

Were they? Giovanni had sat back and examined the marvel in front of him. They had been, certainly. But now? Eleanor was energy in miniature; everything about her was neat and abrupt and going somewhere. She had pale skin, a high forehead and the pointed nose of an inquisitor. Her small head was always held aloft, alert to any learning or entertainment, whichever was on offer. Her eyes were never at peace. From the moment he'd met her, Giovanni had been enraptured.

But were the nobles winning? That would depend on a map.

'They don't like losing to me,' she'd said. 'Have you noticed?'

Giovanni had. Eleanor had brought gambling into the court's evenings, introducing a series of card games taught to her by her aunt in Burgundy. She'd not given the nobles permission to leave the table until she'd won most of their money. They grumbled that she'd hardly explained the rules, then spoken to the friars.

'The cardinal tried to talk to me,' she'd said. 'But I reminded him that he keeps the Duchess of Pombal for his mistress. I want to teach the mathematicians to play. They'll fleece the nobles. Will your son play, do you think?'

He'd been taken aback. He'd supposed she'd been told by her uncle.

'I have no idea,' he'd said.

Three weeks later, they'd sailed out of Lisbon. They'd left in four caravels, square-rigged before the wind, passing the straits of Gibraltar in a week. They'd been becalmed off Minorca and fished tuna from the side. Then the storm had come and everything had been blown from his mind.

It had risen from nowhere. One moment the sea had been as calm as evensong, the next it was chaos and they'd barely had time to trim the sails. Even Captain Costa hadn't seen it coming.

'We'll run for Africa!' he'd yelled as the first waves had crashed over the decks. 'We need to find shelter!'

But the storm had made that impossible. For two days the little fleet had turned and tossed like corks in a fountain. Two of the crew had been swept into the sea from Giovanni's ship alone.

Eleanor had gone to her cabin, then emerged in trousers and oilskin. If they were short of crew, she'd play her part. Giovanni had tried to stop her.

'I am Infanta of Portugal!' she'd shouted, standing on tiptoes to be heard above the roar. 'Almost equal to Neptune!'

She'd learnt how to sail the boat over the time they'd been at sea, her curiosity too great to keep her indoors. Now she put it to use, helping haul on the ropes and batten the sails. Then it had happened.

It was night and she hadn't seen the wave coming. It had flung her across the deck like a doll but she'd not screamed. Giovanni had thrown himself after her and just managed to grab her hair before she was swept overboard.

'That hurt,' she'd said afterwards as they sat panting against the rail. 'What was wrong with my arm?'

'You'll be tied from now on,' shouted Giovanni, helping her to the crouch. 'To me.'

It hadn't stopped her working. She was everywhere she was needed and some places she wasn't, Giovanni always behind her at the end of a rope. He was exhausted by the time the storm had died.

And now they were sitting together against the ship's side with corsairs on their bow. Eleanor turned to him. 'I never thanked you,' she said quietly. 'For saving my life.'

'It was nothing.'

'It wasn't nothing. The Holy Roman Emperor would have minded, for one.' They heard the crack of cannon, the whoosh of ball in the air, the splash beyond them. 'Anyway, since I'm now to be sold into the harem, I thought I should say that.'

Giovanni nodded slowly. 'Do you dread it very much?' he asked.

'The marriage?' She seemed surprised. 'Not really. I was bred for slaughter, after all.' She let out a little laugh. 'At least I'll have jewels in the afterlife.' She nudged him gently. 'What about you? I never asked.'

He inhaled deeply. Another cannon ball passed above them. 'I have loved once, someone as royal as you. Someone also bred for slaughter. She died.'

Eleanor was silent for a while. 'Which is why you went to the end of the earth,' she said softly. 'Of course.' She put her head on his shoulder, put her hand in his. 'So why are you going to Rome?' she asked softly. 'It can't just be to bring me there.'

'To find my son,' he said, smelling the salt in her hair. 'As you know.' He patted her hand. 'Come.'

He rose and scanned the horizon. The galley was drawing closer, moving fast, and its decks were crowded with men.

Costa shouted to him. 'How are the other ships?'

He looked at the caravels. 'They're turning.'

'Good. They must have some wind over there.' Costa leant forward over the rail. 'Take it out a yard!' He lifted his nose to the wind. 'It's coming – I can smell it!' He gripped the wood. 'Come *on*!'

There was a bang from across the sea and a puff of smoke. A splash broke the surface not far from them.

'Cannon!' yelled Costa. 'They're ranging! Bring her about!'

'Cannon?'

'Don't worry, I doubt they want to hit us. And they can only fire from the front.'

'Which means?'

Costa rolled his eyes. 'Which means we can evade them. But we need some wind and the sail's ripped.'

Giovanni looked over to the other caravels and saw they were slowly drawing away.

'Isn't silk strong?' asked Eleanor, looking up at the sail. 'I have dresses.' She turned to the captain. 'The one I'm to be wed in is enormous.'

Another bang and this time they saw the cannon ball pass over the ship.

'Get it, highness,' said Costa. 'And any others.' He swung round to the crew. 'You two get rope, as much as you can find.'

Eleanor ran to her cabin, Giovanni behind her. Her maidservant was inside sitting on the cot, ashen-faced, staring into a bucket before her. She'd been seasick since Lisbon.

'Giovanni, help me open the trunk.'

They lifted the lid and Eleanor rummaged inside, throwing

one, then another, exquisite dress onto the floor. Last came a white one of heavy brocaded silk that seemed to go on forever. 'Ah, this is it. I actually like it for the first time.'

She gathered it in her arms and ran back to the deck, Giovanni following with the other dresses. Costa was waiting on his knees with rope.

'Help me tie them together by the arms and hems, the white one in the middle. Rip them where you need to.' Costa looked at Giovanni. 'Tell me what the corsairs are doing. I want to know every move they make.'

Giovanni went to the side as another shot rang out. The ball fell fifty paces to their front. The pirate ship was closing fast and he could make out the men on board. They were half-naked and waving weapons and every mouth was open. He glanced up at the masthead, then down at the deck. 'Where are our cannon?'

Costa was pulling a knot tight. 'Below decks for the storm.'

'Why aren't they here now?'

'Because we're trying to run. They'll get in the way.' He rose with the dress. 'Anyway, their range is too short.'

Giovanni looked up at the masthead again, saw the pennant lift. 'There's wind now. I'm no expert but wouldn't it be easier to turn that way?' He pointed.

'*Towards* the galley? Are you mad?'

'No. You said it yourself. Their guns are at the front. If we wait and turn into their side, we can come up and fire, then turn away. Isn't that the point of these caravels? That they can turn quickly?'

'Only under lateen sail, but then . . .' Costa thought for a second, turning his head from the masthead to the galleys. He decided. 'You're right. It's our only chance.' He shouted to the crew. 'Lower the skiff, we're going to tow her round. You,' he

167

pointed to Giovanni, 'help me lay these across the canvas. We'll rope them on as a jury-rig.' He picked up the joined dresses and dragged them over to the mast.

Two more shots rang out and Giovanni heard the crack of wood. The bowsprit had been blown away. He tied one end of the silk to his waist and lifted himself up the mast like a monkey, hands then feet. At the top, he hung over and let the dresses fall, the ropes with them. Costa pulled on the ropes until the silk covered the hole, then he lashed them to the side-rail. Giovanni looked out over to the galleys which were now no more than five hundred paces away. He could see the skiff in the water with ropes attached to the caravel's bow. Slowly the ship was coming round.

'Why don't they fire?' he yelled. 'They can't miss!'

'They want our boat.'

'And us, presumably,' said Eleanor. 'Come down. They'll shoot you.'

Giovanni dropped to the deck. All eyes were on the sail and he could see that it was slowly filling with wind. Very gently, the ship was getting under way. Two men were knelt either side of a cannon set before a firing port, its shutter closed. A barrel of gunpowder and cannon balls lay on the deck beside them.

Costa called to the men. 'Keep low. Don't let them see you.'

They could hear the galley now. Giovanni looked over to see hundreds on its deck, all shouting. Its oars were beating the sea in perfect rhythm. It was nearly on top of them.

But the caravel was picking up speed, leaving the skiff behind. It was sailing straight at the galley's bow and the corsairs' two cannon were pointing at its prow. Giovanni held his breath. *Surely they'll fire.*

They didn't. The prize was so close: a cargo and slaves to sell in the markets of Morocco. They'd not send it to the bottom.

'Wait . . .' said Costa, his arm raised, watching the sail above him. 'Steady . . . steady . . . what are we now – thirty paces?' He dropped his arm. 'Now!'

Two of the crew leapt up and yanked the ropes holding the dresses to the mast and they fell away. The ship turned onto the galley's beam. 'Now!'

The port hatch was flung open and the cannon pushed through. The fuse was lit and the cannon roared.

At twenty paces, the carnage was terrible. The cannon ball tore through the hull and into a dozen oarsmen. Blood and limbs exploded into the air.

'Reload and fire!' shouted Costa. 'Here!' He'd jumped to the deck and was helping pull the cannon round. Giovanni joined him.

'They're turning,' shouted Eleanor from the stern deck. 'And they've handguns. Oh.'

Shots sounded and Giovanni saw the Infanta hurl herself to the deck. She grinned at him. 'Missed.'

He looked up at the mast. They'd shifted the dresses so that the rip was closed again. The ship was picking up speed. He heard wood hit wood and saw the cannon being pushed through the port again. He saw the skiff hauled aboard.

'*Now!*'

Another roar and the cannon spat flame. This time the ball hit the galley at an angle and three ranks of rowers were blown apart. Screams of agony joined cries of rage. Giovanni could see that the galley was listing badly. The second hole was on the waterline and sea was pouring through it.

'She's sinking!' yelled Eleanor, up on her knees.

'Get down!'

Too late. Giovanni heard the crack of a handgun, saw the Infanta fall. He leapt to his feet. He took the steps to the upper deck in one bound. She was lying still, blood all around her head. He knelt beside her. She was covered in splinters and he couldn't see the wound. He turned to find Costa at the rudder. 'Get us out of here. Now.'

The captain nodded grimly. 'We're leaving.'

CHAPTER SIXTEEN

GERMANY, THEN FLANDERS

Siward left Venice on St Stephen's Day, the day that Giovanni sailed out of Lisbon, in a mood of general, unfocussed unhappiness. He went with Petros, going north into the Alps, keeping to the main roads for safety. He slept at inns, not always alone, and woke each morning not much happier.

He knew it had to do with leaving Venice, but he wasn't sure why. Was it that he'd failed to find his grandfather's murderer, or because he'd not been able to send Nikolas home? Or was it Makkim . . . his inheritance, his very existence?

Or was it simply that he was distancing himself from Violetta, however much she'd used him? His mind always came back to her and when it did, his head would fall, his fists clenched against his thighs, and Petros would deem it wise to keep silent.

At least the days were clear and the sunshine constant, making the Alpine passes sticky underfoot and their glaciers bright with diamonds. They rode down into Germany in their shirts, not a single snowflake disturbing their hair. At Augsberg, they fell in with some musicians who sang beneath blue skies as they made their way up to Nürnberg. They shared inns with them.

'She wanted to *protect* me!' he said one evening to the company. 'As if I can't look after myself!'

He was sitting with Petros and the musicians around a tavern table and they were mainly drunk. None but Petros knew what he was talking about. So far they'd been discussing German beer.

Siward drank some of it, frowning. 'I can take care of myself.'

A viol-player nodded. 'You're strong. I've seen few stronger.'

Siward nodded emphatically. 'Quite.'

She was a courtesan, for God's sake, however refined. *A courtesan.* She'd said it herself: *Courtesans are not the sort men choose to stay with.*

With such thoughts percussing through his head, Siward rode into Lübeck with Petros on an evening that promised snow. Nikolas had produced an itinerary that would take him to places not yet explored by the Magoris Bank. Lübeck was capital of the Hanseatic League of cities that dominated northern Europe. They'd got rich through trade with Scandinavia and the Rus of Kiev: trade in furs, resin, timber and flax. It seemed a good place to start restoring the bank's fortunes. And, with the news of Mehmed's new castle on the Bosporos, there was no time to lose. The Emperor needed money.

At first, things seemed to go well. Armed with a letter of introduction from Zoe, Siward met the head of the Medici Bank branch in Lübeck, Antonio Levantino.

'Your grandfather was friend to Cosimo de Medici,' said Levantino, as they sat over a lunch of mussels. 'He has instructed that all help should be given you with the city's merchants. I shall see to it personally.'

Levantino was as good as his word but Venice was not the only place to get news. The merchants of Lübeck knew of the Magoris Bank's problems and were wary of making arrangements with a party that might not be able to honour its commitments. After all, they could keep their money with the Fugger Bank. It was expensive perhaps, but at least safe. He stayed a month, then moved on. At Danzig, he spent an afternoon with men from the Company of Merchant Adventurers of London and discovered that the news had reached even England. By Rostock he felt frustration, by Hamburg, despair.

One night, as snow fell thickly outside his bedroom window, he poured out his misery to Petros.

'What's wrong with me? Why won't people talk to me? Do I smell?'

'No, that's me, remember,' said Petros, putting down his mug of beer. 'Your problem is you're not used to people saying no to you. German bankers or Venetian courtesans, you don't like it.'

Siward scowled at him. 'Nonsense.'

'You're too proud,' continued Petros, just warming up. 'There's an obvious thing you must do, but you're too proud to do it.'

'And what's that?'

'Ask Zoe for more than letters of introduction. Write and ask her for money. If you've got money behind you, people will talk to you. Perhaps even courtesans.'

'Nonsense,' he said again.

'Really?' Petros poured himself more beer from the jug. 'You've been like a cat on coals since she turned you down. You just need to face it: not everyone likes you.' He drank. 'Present company excepted, of course.'

'That's a relief,' said Siward. 'I'm going to bed.'

*

An hour later, he rose, sat down and wrote to Nikolas.

He wrote of what he now knew, and Zoe had told him: that western Europe was where the bank's future lay. The Hanseatic cities weren't just trading with the north. Flanders and England were booming from the trade in cloth; France was uniting; Spain was finally throwing out the Moors; and Portugal . . . well, Nikolas knew about Portugal. If he could just have some money to invest. Could Nikolas ask Zoe Mamonas for a loan, perhaps?

From Hamburg, they went south into Flanders, stopping at Antwerp on the way. At Bruges, he received Nikolas's reply.

The letter astonished him. An interview had been arranged with none less than the wife of the man who ruled Flanders: the Duchess of Burgundy. He was to buy new clothes and present himself at her court, currently residing in Bruges. He was expected in a week.

He re-read the letter, then saw there was another attached to it, sealed. On it, in Nikolas's handwriting, was written: 'From Luke for Giovanni. Should you meet him.'

Why should he meet his uncle, and why did he need to? With a loan from Zoe, he could repair the bank's fortunes without the trading company's assets. And if he didn't need those, there'd be no need to meet Giovanni. Or Makkim.

Except that Constantine had said that he wanted his uncle at Constantinople.

Siward arrived at the bricked, turreted Prinsenhof in clothes he'd spent some time choosing with Petros's help. He wanted to look prosperous, but not so prosperous that he needed for nothing. He wanted to look handsome, but not vain. He wanted to look cultured, but not so cultured that he didn't know a ship's manifest. He knew that Philip the Good's court was renowned for its wealth and splendour, that it set the taste and fashion for the rest of Europe. How, he wondered, could he make an impression in such a place?

In the end, he presented himself at the palace in black. He'd come from Venice, after all, and a little of the devil might suit the situation well. But it was no normal black. His doublet was of the richest silk, traced with embroidery so fine that it was almost invisible. His hat was of black velvet edged with fur. Its feather was a blackbird's.

'Good luck,' said Petros as they parted. 'Remember to watch your pride. You need money.'

Siward was shown into a room where black was the only colour absent. As he made his reverences, doffing his hat as he'd been shown by the man who'd sold it to him, he became aware of many women in rich reds and blues and yellows, all with elaborate headdresses shaped as hearts, butterflies, steeples and turbans. Which of them, he wondered, was Isabella of Burgundy?

She helped him by stepping forward.

'Siward Magoris: banker and one-time Varangian. You are most welcome.' She looked him up and down. 'The black suits you.'

He was looking at a smiling woman in her fifties, if he was any judge. She was small, dark and compact in every way, her body perfectly measured for her size. She wore a long-sleeved gown of green and gold with fur at its collar. On her head was a tall steeple-hat with veil. She looked like a rich wet-nurse.

She clapped her hands and women everywhere picked up skirts and needlework and took their colours somewhere else. Only one stayed, one standing alone in a corner.

Violetta.

His first sensation was bewilderment. He'd just left her in Venice, for God's sake. His second was familiar. It was the same mix of joy and anger he'd felt last time he'd seen her. Now he had to work to maintain his composure. 'I see we'll not be alone.'

'No, but then you are old friends, I'm told.' She turned to Violetta. 'Join us, please.'

She walked over to a small table where three chairs had been set. There were sweetmeats on it and flowers that didn't look real. They were scented.

As they sat, Siward watched Violetta. She seemed serious and deferential, not as he'd seen her in Venice. She didn't meet his eye.

'I want to talk about banking,' said Isabella, offering sweet-meats, 'which is what I think you're here for?'

Siward nodded. 'I have a bank.'

'One that is finding doors closed, am I right?'

Her voice was clipped, precise. Here, he thought, was a woman who liked things straightforward. He decided to be likewise.

'More closed than I would prefer, yes, majesty.'

'And you would like them opened. Well, you should.' She gathered her small hands into her lap. He noticed they wore rings of some weight. 'The world is shifting and you have noticed it.' She tilted her head. 'Tell me what you see.'

Siward glanced at Violetta. She had hardly moved and sat straight-backed, as if she were in attendance. She was dressed for the Burgundian court, not Venetian. He was reminded of an animal he'd heard of in India that changed its colour to suit its surroundings.

It didn't take long to collect his thoughts. He'd been thinking of little else since his arrival in Lübeck. 'Venice is at the height of its wealth and power,' he began, 'but two things may change that: the loss of its gold supply from Africa, which has already happened, and the fall of Constantinople to the Turk. If the Ottomans control Constantinople and Asia Minor, then the trade routes east by land, and north to the Black Sea, may be cut.'

The Duchess was watching him intently, a little smile putting dimples in her cheeks. He glanced at Violetta, who was doing the same without the smile, or the dimples.

'Meanwhile, Portugal and Spain are getting rich from the trade in sugar, slaves and gold from Africa. The English and French are about to end a hundred years of war and the cities of the Hansa are creating new trade with the north. As you said, majesty, the world is shifting. To the west.'

'Good so far. Go on.'

'But something else is happening that could change everything more significantly. And it could ruin Venice. For the first time, men are daring to believe that a way can be found round Africa to the East.'

'Men *and* women,' said the Duchess tartly.

'Yes, of course. Men and women,' Siward said quickly. 'And with the Chinese withdrawing from trade, the Indian Ocean is open. A way to the East, free of danger and levy, could at last be open. By sea. That is why Portugal is more interesting than anywhere else.'

'Bravo.' Isabella clapped her hands together. 'Well said, no?' She looked at Violetta.

'Well said, indeed,' said the courtesan, smiling for the first time.

'And I can add to that,' said Isabella. 'Who senses these things first, do you think? Greedy kings. It's not for my beauty that I'm married to Burgundy. Nor is it for hers that my niece is to be

177

married to the Holy Roman Emperor. Little Portugal is suddenly important, and its Infantas to be desired.' She leant forward a little. 'Do you know the most profitable industry in Bruges?' she asked. 'Making art for the grandees of Madeira. They send us drawings of themselves and we put them into a Nativity and send them back. Usually as the Magi.'

She sat back. 'There's something else, of course. This thing they're calling the *rinascimento* in Italy. It's perhaps Europe's greatest advantage: being allowed to explore things without fear of damnation. Not something the Muslims of the East will enjoy for a very long time, you can be sure. And the further from Rome, the greater the enquiry. My brother Prince Henry has a court stuffed full of merchants and scientists, and they call him "The Navigator". Can you imagine that happening fifty years ago?'

Siward was wondering where this was leading. He'd learnt of the new thinking from Plethon and Cleope, and he'd discussed it with Violetta.

'So,' she went on, 'the fall of Constantinople, if it happens, may not be the end of the world after all, and dying on its walls should not be the destiny of great men who want to change the world.'

He stayed silent. She spoke as Zoe had spoken, Violetta too, even Cleope. But however much his circumstances had changed, his duty hadn't.

'Then there is this map,' she continued, 'the one my brother and the Doge commissioned, the one you have seen.'

He waited.

'It is to be presented to my niece the Infanta who is currently on her way to Rome to be married to the Holy Roman Emperor. Do you know who is with her?'

He waited.

'Your uncle.'

'Giovanni?'

'The same. The one who grows sugar for the Portuguese in Madeira.' She glanced at Violetta. 'I want you to go to Rome and meet him and give him the letter that Nikolas gave you.' She leant over and picked up a letter from the table. 'And this from me.'

Siward frowned. He didn't want to go to Rome. He wanted to stay here and rescue his bank. He asked, 'And why would I do this, majesty? We have just agreed that my opportunity lies here in the West.'

'Because it will open doors for you. You may be surprised by how many. Everyone will be in Rome. You will go as my envoy,' said Isabella. 'You will have all the letters you need.'

Siward stared at her. Petros had told him to forget his pride, but it was there, throbbing in his temples, part of him. He was tired of women promoting him, making him do things he'd rather not.

'No,' he said. 'I'm sorry. No.'

She looked at him, her head tilted to one side, her eyes narrowed, the letter to her chin. There was a long moment of silence. Then she asked, 'What is it you *want*, Siward Magoris? What is your *purpose*, exactly?'

He expected she was about to tell him. She did.

'You want to find out who murdered your grandfather, and why. You want to save your bank so that you can get Constantine his money. You want to save the Roman Empire. But you've been surprised by how much you've enjoyed the business of trade. Am I right?'

He stared at her.

'Yes, I am,' she said, nodding and jabbing the letter at him. 'All roads lead to Rome, as they say. Luke's death had something to do with Fra Mauro's map. Rome is where the map is. Your bank can only be saved, in the time needed, with Zoe's and my help. That help depends on you going to Rome and giving Giovanni the letters.'

Siward knew he was trapped. The Varangian response to entrapment was to fight your way out. But what if she was right? What if he was changing as she said? He tried one more time.

'Why is Rome so important? If you can convince me of that, then I'll go.'

Isabella rose and came over to him. She looked down into his face, pushing his long hair to one side as if she was his mother. 'You are handsome,' she said gently, 'and you are brave and you are clever. Once you were wild and untrainable. Then a woman died who was more to you than your mother and you made a vow to change. You have changed and you've become remarkable, but perhaps not great yet.' She took his hand. 'Great men look beyond their own selfish priorities, is it not so? Is it not why they are great?'

She turned from him and went to the window. She opened it and breathed in the air. 'Venice is planning something terrible,' she said quietly. 'Zoe suspects it and so do I.' She glanced at Violetta. 'We need your help to find out what it is: for Constantinople, perhaps for the world.'

'I am a soldier,' said Siward softly, 'not a great deal more.'

'You are too modest,' said Isabella. She looked at him hard. 'You should go to Rome.'

He knew he was beaten. He looked at his feet for a moment to pretend the victory still in the balance. Then he raised his eyes. 'Alright,' he said. 'I'll go.'

Isabella smiled and nodded at the same time. She was all business again. 'Good. Here is the letter. You can go with Violetta.'

Siward stared at her as he took the letter, uncertain whether this was the best or worst of news. He glanced at Violetta. He was to be spied on and there was the spy.

'And if I choose to go alone?'

'Don't be silly.' Isabella had gathered her skirts and was walking towards the door. 'You'll have fun. I have enjoyed Violetta's company these past weeks. Now it's your turn.'

CHAPTER SEVENTEEN

THE ROAD TO ROME

Violetta and Siward left Bruges for Rome on a February morning of sunshine and bluster that made the horses of their retinue skittish. If Siward had, until then, travelled discreetly, he did so now with all the pomp and luxury of a Burgundian envoy. Violetta rode side-saddle beside him and they led a long cavalcade of soldiers, scribes and servants, all bearing the lions and *fleur-de-lys* of the richest man in Christendom. Petros rode somewhere within it.

The party would keep to Ducal lands most of the way to Savoy, passing from Flanders to Namur, then Luxemburg and into rich, ancestral Burgundy that had been held since Roman times. They would rest at palaces and castles and their pace would be leisurely. Violetta was looking forward to it; she'd have time to think.

Certainly she had much to think about, not least why she was making this journey at all. She was, after all, a courtesan of Venice with important clients who would miss her. Might they move away? Probably not for a while, but it wouldn't do to be away too long.

She also wanted to think about Venice. Since Siward's departure, something about the city seemed to have changed. Its splendour had become gaudy, its wealth ostentatious, its glamour pretentious. The perpetual noise of the place: the shouts, song, laughter of the Grand Canal – the essential lubrications of trade – irritated her as it never had before. Even her clients were tiresome. She longed to get away and she longed, once again, to talk to Siward.

But her companion was silent and she knew the reason. Here was a man not used to being beholden, especially to women. He'd moved from commanding men to what seemed like being commanded by women. Worse still, what the women said made sense. No wonder he was cross. She wanted him to be less so; she remembered their conversations and she missed them.

The road was busy with traders coming north for the spring fairs of Champagne, and pilgrims going south to Rome. Pope Nicholas had declared a special jubilee to mark the coronation and marriage of the Holy Roman Emperor. There would be a full remittance of sins for those who made the pilgrimage.

It was as they were leaving the palace at Dijon that Violetta decided to try for a thaw. They'd been entertained by Duke Philip, who'd arrived unexpectedly to meet the famous courtesan. They'd dined with him alone in a hall the size of a caravanserai. At ten o'clock, Siward had been shown politely to his room and Violetta had been obliged to stay on.

'Did you sleep well?' she asked.

'Better than you, I daresay.'

She bit her lip. He wouldn't look at her but stared straight ahead. She heard the clink of bridle and mumble of conversation behind them. They were far enough ahead not to be heard.

'I am a courtesan,' she replied in a low voice. 'And we travel at the Duke's pleasure.'

Siward made a sound. He leant forward to pat his horse.

She tried again. 'How do you like being a banker? You make a good one.'

He glanced at her. 'How could you know?'

'Because you attack it like a soldier. You don't give up. The Hanseatic merchants were impressed by you, even if they couldn't help you. Zoe Mamonas wouldn't trust you if she didn't think you capable, nor Isabella of Burgundy.'

Siward remained silent and Violetta looked out over the landscape. It had been a hard winter and there was relief that it was over. The fields might be bare but the soil was good and the season for sowing a month away. The people in the villages smiled and, when they saw the retinue, knelt. The good Duke had kept them out of the war with the English that had so ruined the rest of France. His envoy was popular.

'I used to enjoy talking to you,' she said. 'Is it to be a thing of the past?'

He leant back in his saddle, stretching his legs. 'What would you like to talk about?'

What indeed? They'd spoken so much of what was on this earth and beyond. She'd seen a mind shaped by the greatest thinker of the age, Georgius Gemistus Plethon, and he'd done his work well. But she'd seen something more: a curiosity and candour that was rare in her city of cynics. Cynicism was the currency of Venice, the bitter residue of greed and avarice. Siward had no idea how different he was.

'We could talk of Rome,' she suggested.

He turned to her. 'Have you been there?'

'I've never left Venice until now. I've met men from every continent but not seen beyond our lagoon.'

'But you weren't born in Venice. You said so.'

'That is true.'

'So where were you born?'

'Somewhere to the east. A village.'

'And why did you come to Venice?'

Why? Could she speak of a man who'd done things to her so terrible that there was only one godless place on earth she could flee to, only one profession where her shame could be buried beneath a carapace of pretence? She closed her eyes and thought back to the night before, to a Duke too drunk to perform. In the past she'd prided herself in coaxing pleasure from the most unpromising of subjects, but not last night. Was she losing her skill? Or was it something else? *Shame?* She heard him speak.

'I'm sorry.'

She opened her eyes. He was watching her, a small frown creasing his brow.

She suddenly felt angry. What right did he have to pity her, if that's what he felt? 'Why sorry?' she asked. 'My past has nothing to do with you.'

He nodded and looked away. 'Of course. But there's pain there, I feel.'

Pain? What was her pain? Was it that the one person who'd understand how she felt had been forced to leave her long ago? Was it that she'd never find another to replace him? She wanted to talk of something else.

'Did you like the Duchess?'

Siward considered this. 'She is clever. The Duke is fortunate.'

'You're right. When he first married Isabella, Philip ignored her. But she refused to be the invisible Duchess. Now she conducts all of the Duke's trade negotiations and arranges most of the royal matches of Europe. Eleanor and Frederick was her work.'

'And how did she come to be so shrewd?'

'Education. Her mother was Philippa of England. She insisted her daughter be educated alongside her brothers.' Violetta nodded. 'If I'd had a daughter, I'd have done the same.'

'Would she have become a courtesan?' he asked.

She looked at him sharply. 'Possibly. Venetian husbands are the worst in the world, and as fathers they're cruel. Do you know how many convents there are in Venice? Better a courtesan.'

'Who gave you your education?'

A butterfly had landed on her arm and she studied it for some time, her head to one side. 'Two extraordinary women. Alessandra Viega taught me how to be a courtesan; Zoe, everything else.'

They were now in a forest where sun broke in patterns, making verdigris of the ground. As they passed, birds rustled the branches and rose suddenly in clouds.

'You said Zoe wants to save Venice from itself,' said Siward. 'Why would she care? She's Greek.'

'She is old,' Violetta said, 'and age brings regret. She wants to leave a better world and she has the money to do it.' She looked thoughtful. 'I think your grandfather had much to do with it.'

Siward glanced at her. 'They were friends?'

'Not always. But at the end, when it mattered, yes.'

They rode on in silence through columns of light, passing a cardinal shouting from a carriage held up by pilgrims while its wheel was changed. They passed more pilgrims taunting Jews at the side of the road while women tempted them from the trees.

She asked, 'Was the Duchess right, do you think, about you changing?'

He shrugged. 'I don't know. What do you think?'

'Well, you are certainly different from the man who propositioned me at the party.'

'It worked. I ended up in your bed.'

She laughed. 'A painful way to get there.' She reflected. 'You never tried again. Why not?'

'Because you'd have said no. I am not fond of rejection.'

She looked at him. 'You weren't then, no. But now? After you've had so much? I wonder.'

He frowned. 'So it's failure that defines a man. Am I the better for it?'

'Possibly. You listen more, for a start.'

They came into Rome on a fine day in March, entering under walls caparisoned with flags. The arms of Burgundy swung above them as the Pope's soldiers politely asked for their arms. No fighting would be permitted to mar the celebrations. Siward, as envoy, was allowed to keep his.

Rome was being rebuilt by a Pope who believed in this *renascimento* and they came into a jungle of scaffolding. They rode through crowded streets to a square where a magnificent palace occupied the whole of one side. From its balconies hung lions rampant and fleur-de-lys in cloth of gold. A man was waiting for them on the steps. Seigneur Ferry de Clugny was the youngest ambassador in the service of Philip the Good and had been admitted to the bed of Violetta Cavarse while studying in Bologna. She hoped he'd make no reference to it.

But he was all business. 'You've come at an interesting time,' he said as he walked them into the courtyard of the palace, their horses having gone to the stables. 'You saw all the construction? This pope spends too much money.'

'But surely the pilgrims fill the Curia's coffers?'

De Clugny nodded. 'Yes, but everyone must be housed and kept safe. Two years ago, two hundred were crushed at the Pont Sant'Angelo. We must hope they'd already bought their indulgences.'

'Has the Emperor Frederick arrived?' asked Siward.

'And the Infanta of Portugal. Giovanni Giustiniani Longo escorted her here. They say she nearly died on the voyage but he accounted for himself well.'

So Giovanni had arrived. The image of the agate head on Luke's desk came to his mind. The beloved uncle. *I'll have to meet him.*

'How so?'

'Storms a-plenty and corsairs. The Infanta owes much to him.'

They had come into colonnaded shade and before them were servants with cool drinks. De Clugny gave one to each of them, ignoring Petros who'd come up to stand beside his master. 'The coronation will take place next week and afterwards there will be a ball. This is when Venice will present Fra Mauro's map to the Infanta. The Imperial couple will meet envoys after that.'

Violetta remembered Duchess Isabella's concerns for her niece. 'How was their first meeting?' she asked.

'Bad. He finds her too small and her entourage too large. They served him a Portuguese dish at the banquet that he fed to his dogs.'

'Ah. And where is she now?'

'She stays with her uncle, the King of Naples. I'm told you can hear her unhappiness two squares away.'

*

Two mornings later, Siward woke to find his servant staring down at him.

'What is it, Petros?' he yawned, stretching.

'When will you see your uncle?' He sat down on the bed. 'You have two letters to give him.'

'And do you know where he is?'

Petros nodded. 'The same place as the Infanta: the King of Naples' palace. I've been up there.'

'Then I'll know the way. Thank you.' He turned onto his side.

Petros nodded, still frowning. 'So you'll go.' He pressed. 'Today?'

Siward sighed, looking up. 'Why are you so anxious for me to meet my uncle, Petros?'

'I've spoken to the servants up there. He has the ear of Prince Henry of Portugal.'

'Which makes him fortunate. Why is this of interest to me?'

Petros smoothed the bedclothes with his palm. 'Well, he might be helpful to the bank. The duchess's letter may be about it.'

Siward was becoming irritated. Had Violetta spoken to Petros? He moved to rise. 'I will ask him when I see fit to ask him. I don't want to get much involved with my uncle, beyond delivering letters.'

But Petros hadn't moved. 'But don't you want to know what's inside them?'

'I know what's inside one of them,' he said. 'It will be the news that his son has inherited a great fortune. To go with the sword he took earlier.'

'Did you know he is here?'

'Who's here?' He stared at Petros. 'Makkim is in Rome?'

Petros nodded. 'As the Sultan's envoy.'

Siward sat up. He found his heart beating faster. He nudged his servant from the bed and got up. 'I'll visit Giovanni this evening. You can show me the way.'

Giovanni was in the bath when the message came up to him.

'My nephew?'

'So he says.' The servant left.

Giovanni lay and studied the dolphin whose mouth had brought forth such luxury. His nephew was downstairs. Hilarion's son. Hilarion his half-brother whom he'd loved when he'd lived and mourned bitterly when he'd died. He remembered the boy. He'd been wilful, intelligent and charming. He'd come to live at the palace so that Cleope could mother him. Sometimes, in secret, they'd imagined him as their own. Why was he here?

He rose from the bath and dried himself, noticing the vivid sunburn of his arms against the white of his chest. The years in Madeira would stay with him for the rest of his life. *Exile.*

He dressed and came down the staircase. He opened the door of the grand salon and found a man in fine clothes with long, fair hair. It was as if he was looking at himself. He stopped and stared.

'Siward.'

'Uncle.'

He found he could not embrace this nephew but then Siward showed no interest in embracing him either. In fact, he looked uncomfortable.

Giovanni walked over to where the wine was. 'I hope you got here safely,' he said. 'I'm told the gangs are under leash. The Orsini and Colonnas were made to shake hands before the Holy Father.'

'But your journey was less easy,' said the nephew behind him. 'Is the Infanta recovered?'

He nodded. 'The corsairs' shot was wild and she suffered a graze, nothing more.' He poured and brought a glass over to Siward. 'But the introduction to King Frederick did not go well.'

'No?'

His feigned surprise was badly done. All of Rome knew of the disastrous meeting. He tried to bring warmth to his smile. 'But ours might go better. Uncle and nephew meet.' He raised his glass. 'To speaking at last. Was that why you came?'

'I come to deliver letters. One from Luke, the other from Isabella of Burgundy.'

'I am indebted.' He sipped the wine. So that was why Siward was here: as Luke's envoy. He glanced at him. He could so easily be his own son. He remembered Siward on Cleope's lap, both of them listening to his first stumbling words.

But how did he know he'd be in Rome? And why did he have a letter from Burgundy? He asked, 'Do you know what my father's letter says?'

Siward shook his head. 'I can guess. It will be about Makkim, I expect.'

Giovanni frowned. 'The Sultan's general? Why?'

Siward stared at his uncle. 'His inheritance. The trading company.'

Giovanni didn't understand. 'What has the trading company to do with Makkim?'

His nephew sat back and studied him for a while. He seemed to be deciding something. At last he said, 'Luke has left the trading company to your son. Your son who is Makkim.'

Giovanni shook his head. 'But . . .' He looked down at his glass. *Makkim?* What did he know of Makkim? He was the

Sultan's general, the victor of Varna. *But hadn't he been a janissary first, taken from Bulgaria in the devshirme?* 'My God,' he said softly.

Siward leant forward. 'You didn't know?'

But Giovanni didn't answer. He stared into his wine.

Siward watched him for a while. He knew that whatever he said would not be heard. At last he rose and took the letters from his doublet. He gently laid them on the table and left, closing the door quietly behind him.

Much later, Giovanni read the letters. He opened the one from Isabella first. It was polite but clear: help your nephew's bank and expect to please the wife of the richest man in Europe. *They eat a lot of sugar there.* He wondered how Siward had made such a powerful friend.

Next, he broke the seal of the letter from Luke.

Giovanni,

If you are reading this, then I am dead. I wanted so much to see you once more before I died, but it was not God's will.

I suspect you received the many letters I sent you over the years, but chose not to read them. Why would you? You thought me cruel and unjust for not allowing you to take Cleope with you into exile. You'll now think me cruel for not telling you that your son, my grandson, lived all that time.

But you must know this: I did what I did to save the life of that son. It was the Despot's condition for letting him live. I was made to swear that no one, including you and Cleope, should know it. I spent the years trying to find him; the sword told me where he was.

You will ask why I did not let my own son find happiness with the woman he loved, and who loved him, in exile. That question

192

is more difficult and I have asked it of myself every day. But its answer is this: Theodore's union with Cleope was a political match, perhaps the most important in history. It was meant to lead to the union of the Churches of East and West. It was meant, one day, to save Constantinople and the Roman Empire. It was, in terrible truth, more important than the love I had for you. Perhaps now, when you are older, you will understand that.

But to the point: by now you will know that your son lives. He is called Makkim and he is a man of great importance, someone to be proud of. But he is also our enemy. I am leaving half my fortune to him, and half to Siward. The trading company will go to him, the bank to Siward. My hope is that, with time and persuasion, he'll choose to leave his master and be reunited with his father. My equal hope is that he will join Siward in running both businesses as they are meant to be run: side by side.

Thus, perhaps, may the past be rectified. I may pray so.

Know this, Giovanni. I have never stopped loving you from the moment you were born to me. I have missed you every hour of every day. You will never know how much.

Forgive me.

Your father, Luke.

For a long time, Giovanni stared at the letter. He wanted to re-read it but he couldn't. His eyes were filled with tears.

CHAPTER EIGHTEEN

ROME

'Look, Almighty God, with a serene gaze upon this, your glorious servant.'

Another coronation, another Roman Emperor, this one 'Holy', whatever that meant. The church might be bigger but the stone beneath Siward's knees felt just as hard. He glanced at the roof. There was netting above the pillars lest the congregation be hit by masonry. The Basilica of St Peters was falling down and even the saints in their alcoves looked up. But this Pope had his plans. Siward had seen the Colosseum being dismantled.

'Remember of whom the Psalmist prophesied, saying, *"Gird the sword upon thy thigh . . ."*'

What must Constantine be thinking on this day, he wondered? The man in front of him, kneeling beneath the Crown of Charlemagne, claimed the legacy of Rome and was about to swear to defend all Christendom. But would that extend to Constantinople when the time came?

But whatever Frederick did, Siward would go and defend its walls. Zoe was wrong. Rome was not the past.

He could see the Emperor quite clearly. He'd already seen

him crowned and presented with a sword that he'd brandished thrice while Eleanor looked on like his daughter. The Duke of Burgundy stood to the side with the German Electors.

He looked up at the stained glass window above the nave.

Violetta. She was as changeable as the day that shone through it, like that animal in India. At first she'd seemed opaque to him, like a pearl, absorbing the light shone onto her by others. Now she seemed a kaleidoscope: she both dazzled and puzzled. Why should it matter to him that she did what she was meant to do? She was a *courtesan*, for God's sake.

The gospel ended and the Pope lifted his hands.

'Imperator Electus Romanorum.'

Caesar.

Even Mehmed wanted the title and, with his new castle on the Bosporos, seemed closer to getting it. Siward rose with the congregation and saw the incense form clouds above their heads. A thousand voices answered.

'*Imperator Electus Romanorum!*'

There she was, three pews away, looking at him, her gaze settled, secure. Was that *trust* in it? He smiled at her.

He thought of his meeting with Giovanni. She'd wanted to know what the meeting had produced.

'Nothing.'

'You've not arranged to meet again?'

'No.'

'Perhaps I should go.'

He'd stopped pouring the wine. 'To seduce him? I don't think so.'

'I didn't mean that.' She'd taken the wine and watched him over its rim, angry now.

He'd felt regret. 'What would you say?'

'That in helping you, he can help himself, perhaps even the world.'

Siward had drunk the wine, nodding. 'Constantine wants him at Constantinople. You could tell him that. I forgot to.'

'You could go there to fight with him,' she'd said casually. 'You'll be a soldier at last, as you always intended to be.'

He'd shaken his head then. 'Fighting is not my vocation. Constantinople is my duty.'

'You're probably right. It's likely to be suicide, but then you'll have realised that.'

'But you agree I should go?'

'It doesn't matter what I think. You'll go anyway.'

Now he found himself wondering. *Does she care if I die?*

The Mass was ending and the congregation was rising to leave. The Pope would lead, the imperial couple following. Then would come the Electors and the great powers. After that it might get amusing. The jostle for precedence was never dull.

Siward watched them all process past him, led by a middle-aged man of mean and bearded face who'd taken the hand of a girl twenty years his junior and not looked at her once. Eleanor's face was a mask of grim purpose.

He saw turbans among the dignitaries waiting their turn, one higher than the rest. They said that Makkim was the tallest among the Ottoman party. Siward wanted to see him.

They came out in twos, like the ark: lion with ox, peacock with grinning hyena. There he was, walking beside the King of Cyprus and as tall as promised. He wore a turban that would have shielded many from masonry, above a tunic of richly-worked gold. He was fair and unbearded and bore a scar. All eyes were on him. Siward looked for Violetta. She was some way behind in deep conversation with a man. She did not catch his eye as she passed, but another did: Andrea Bianco.

Where was Fra Mauro?

Makkim and his retinue had been housed in a cardinal's palace of an opulence reminiscent of Edirne. There were fountains and statues and tapestries of the hunt and more servants than he could count. One had just brought sherbet to his bath.

He lay there and thought of how free he felt here in Rome, as he had in Hungary. He was free from Mehmed's dubious love, from his obsession with Constantinople. But he'd not done enough to protect the janissary boys and Zaganos bey's influence was growing . . .

He'd think of other things. The Venetians would be waiting downstairs and that bailo would be among them. How to bend him to his purpose? Minotto was cunning.

He thought of the woman he'd glimpsed talking to Minotto on the steps of the cathedral. He'd only seen her profile but it had so reminded him of someone that he'd found himself staring. Then she'd gone. If she was from Venice, she'd be a wife or courtesan, probably the latter. He'd heard that the Venetians used them in negotiations.

There was a knock on the door.

'Yes, yes, I'm coming.'

He was, he thought, always rising from his bath to see Venetians. Was it best to meet them clean? He stood, arms raised, as servants stood on stools to drop a simple kaftan over his long body. He enjoyed the brush of fine linen against his skin. They tied a sash around his waist and sprayed a light scent. He was ready.

Downstairs, Minotto was alone. He was dressed, as usual, in black and wore a cape on his shoulders.

'Does the Venetian wear black for every occasion?' asked Makkim as he closed the door behind him. 'How can you tell if it's a ball or a funeral?'

The bailo's thin lips forced a smile. 'We drink at balls, and sometimes dance. At funerals we just dance.'

'As you won't at Constantinople's, I fear. All that trade lost.' Makkim watched the Venetian absorb the threat.

Minotto shrugged. 'Venice has suffered setbacks before and survived. Our city is based on survival.'

'Ah, but from Goths whom you outsmarted by placing yourself in a lagoon. We are better than the Goths.' Makkim smiled. 'And much stronger.'

'You forget we have the sea.'

'For now, but for how long? You are building a navy for us.'

Minotto was silent, his head held slightly back as he studied the tall man before him, seemingly dressed for the bath. There was, thought Makkim, advantage in presenting yourself simply, as the Prophet from Nazareth had known.

'You summoned me,' said Minotto quietly. 'What do you want?'

'I've told you – cannon.'

'And I've told you we can't do it.' The bailo's voice was harder. 'You know why. Did you talk to Orban?'

'And was refused. He'll only cast for Christians, it seems.' Makkim placed his hands to his front. 'So I have an idea.'

Minotto waited.

'You'll buy them for Constantinople as your gift to the Emperor in the city's defence. They'll be built and delivered by ship. But they'll be waylaid.'

'Waylaid?'

'The seas around Greece are lawless, I've heard. Pirates everywhere.'

Minotto narrowed his eyes. 'You want us to pay for cannon, then let you steal them? No. The Doge won't allow it.'

Makkim frowned. 'But he's allowed so much, this Doge. I'm sure he'll see the sense in this, just as one day he'll enjoy the dar el-salaam.'

Minotto shook his head. 'We'll not buy cannon for you. We'll make ships, yes, but cannon of the size you want? No.'

Makkim turned. 'That is a pity. The Sultan is young and unpredictable. I don't know how he'll take the news.' He shook his head. 'He already suspects you of harbouring King Lydislaw. I'm told he stayed on Murano.'

Minotto remained silent.

'I think your Doge will come to regret not getting us our cannon.' He smiled. 'Perhaps you already do.'

The coronation ball, hosted by Pope Nicholas, was held at the Palazzo Colonna on the Quirinal Hill, no other palace in Rome deemed big enough for the occasion. It had once been the home of Pope Martin, Cleope's uncle. It still housed Pope Martin's chef, Bockenheym, who was thought to be the best in Europe.

Siward was standing looking at Bockenheym's creations, set out on white-clothed tables. There were swans and peacocks and boar-heads and exotic fish cooked in ginger and almonds between bowls of Castellina Chianti. There was a unicorn's head with a sugar cone for its horn. It was art to match the rich tapestries on the walls.

He was dressed as Duke Philip had directed. Burgundy led Europe's fashion and its envoys were to be its advertisement. He wore a doublet of double-cut velvet, slashed with two shades of silk, above a hose striped in the Venetian way. He felt conspicuous.

He looked again at the doors. Violetta had not arrived. He'd already seen Giovanni come in with the Portuguese, dark men above their gold, but not Violetta.

He looked around the room. No turbans to be seen. The Turks would neither drink nor dance but their presence would add to the splendour. He studied the row of black slave-statues, all motionless, their torches held aloft. He looked up and saw more netting than he'd seen at St Peters. It held flower petals that would snow on them later.

He moved over to the food table. He might try the pheasant. He picked up a plate and fork and heard a throat clear by his side.

'Had you read the letter before you gave it to me?'

Giovanni was standing next to him in clothes more sober than his.

'Of course not. It was sealed.'

'None of it is good news for you,' he said in a low voice. 'I'm sorry. I know what has happened to the bank.'

Siward grunted.

'But Luke would have written the letter when he thought the gold route from Mali secure,' Giovanni continued, 'when the bank would have been more valuable than the trading company.'

Siward looked up at his uncle. 'He had already given him the sword.'

Giovanni nodded. 'I was given it first, because I was the eldest son,' he said, 'though a bastard.' He gestured. 'And it made my son known to us, as it was meant to.'

'Yet it is used against us.'

'Not me,' said Giovanni.

'You don't care if Constantinople falls?'

Giovanni put down his glass. He'd stopped caring about what remained of the Roman Empire when he'd left Mistra. 'Constantinople is not my fight, Siward,' he said firmly. 'It is yours and it is Makkim's, but it is not mine.'

'And if the Emperor asked you to return, to bring what you learnt at Ceuta?'

'Then I would refuse.' Giovanni looked down. 'The Roman Empire, the Ottoman . . . they are the old world. I have lived in Madeira and Portugal. I have seen the new.' He brought his eyes back to Siward's. 'You should consider that too.'

Siward looked at him, something undefinable in his eye. 'How will you tell Makkim?'

'That he is my son? He is to have an audience alone with the Infanta Eleanor after the presentation of the map. I will join it.'

'And will you tell him then about his inheritance?'

'I will. You could be there too. If you want to, that is.'

But Siward was already shaking his head. 'There will be no need,' he said. 'You will have told him already everything he needs to know.' He put some pheasant on his plate. 'Anyway, why would I want to meet my enemy?'

'And if he turns out not to be?'

Siward turned to him. His uncle's face, sunburnt and lined, was serious. 'Then you will tell me.'

Giovanni picked up a plate of his own. He looked at Siward. 'I would be your friend, if you'd allow it. I can help the bank.'

Siward was suddenly aware of silence around them. He looked over to the doors where trumpeters had assembled. 'The Emperor and Empress are arriving.'

But before the trumpeters could lift the instruments to their lips, someone slipped into the room. Violetta skipped down the steps with her skirts held high, flashing diamonds from her shoes. She wore a high-collared *houppelande* of figured silk in the same peacock blue that he'd first seen her in. Her sleeves swept the steps as she descended. A murmur of surprise broke the silence.

The trumpets sounded: three notes, the third held. The Emperor and Empress appeared at the top of the steps, hand in hand, Pope Nicholas behind them. There was the sound of silk sweeping across marble as the room made its reverences. Frederick watched it all and looked bored, but Eleanor looked magnificent. She wore a high-waisted *verdugado* of pomegranate chased in gold, its skirts stiffened with reeds, ermine at its sleeves. On her head was a hennin topped by a floating veil. There were no clothes richer in the room. Isabella of Burgundy had dressed her niece well.

As the imperial couple joined the gathering, the music began. First came *chansons* from a choir of French castrati. Siward saw Violetta look around. She met his eye and started to come towards him. But Ferry de Clugny was there in front of her, claiming the dance. The choir finished, the dancers took their place and the players struck up a lively *lavolta*. He watched as handsome de Clugny lifted her into the air in the three-quarter turn.

The dance came to an end and he saw de Grugny bow as Violetta presented her hand to be kissed. *Was that part of the dance?*

She came up to them with de Grugny on her arm. She was flushed and her dark eyes shone with exertion. She fixed them on Giovanni as she fanned herself. 'I know who you are, sir. You look too much like your nephew. Giovanni Giustiniani Longo.'

'Your servant.'

'And yours. This is Seigneur de Grugny from Burgundy.' She turned to Siward. 'Fra Mauro isn't here, which was why I was late. I was looking for him.'

De Grugny looked surprised. 'Fra Mauro was to come in person?'

'He was given special dispensation,' said Violetta. 'He wanted to meet the Pope. I had thought him here, at his devotions somewhere. But he never came to Rome.' She looked at Siward. 'Apparently, he fell ill before the party left.'

'But Andrea Bianco is here.' Siward put down the plate of unfinished pheasant. He became aware of commotion in the room. The Ottoman envoys had arrived at the top of the steps and all heads were turned. All except Violetta's, who was unaware of anything but her theme.

'So what does it all mean?' she continued. 'Are we to expect that the map was left behind?'

Siward watched Makkim look around the room. He was dressed as the Sultan's special envoy in a tunic of dazzling silver with a heavy gold pendant at his chest. His turban was vast and scattered with jewels. At its front, a tall red plume spouted from a ruby like blood from a wound. He saw the scar that ran from his eye to his chin.

De Grugny had seen him too. 'Now that,' he said, 'is an argument for the devshirme. The best specimens rise to the top.'

Violetta turned to look. Giovanni hadn't spoken. Siward glanced at his uncle and saw him staring with his lips apart as if he wanted to say something. He saw the minute shake of his head, the wonder of a father who was looking at his son for the first time.

He looked over at Makkim. He was staring back, but not at Giovanni. He was beginning to walk in their direction.

'Violetta?' Siward asked. Her gaze was fixed and she didn't answer. She was moving her head slowly from side to side.

'*Violetta?*'

203

She hadn't heard him. She'd removed her hand from his and begun to walk towards the approaching Makkim.

'Violetta . . .'

But she didn't turn back. She went on walking, threading her way through the people, who parted for her in surprise. He saw her reach Makkim. He saw her put her hand on his arm.

For what seemed an eternity, they stared at each other. Then Makkim took her hand and led her away.

Siward watched them go. He saw them, as others saw them, walk over to a window seat and sit. And when others turned back to their conversations, he looked on, seeing them take each other's hands. He felt desolate.

'Do they know each other?' he heard Giovanni ask, beside him.

Siward turned away. He needed wine. He reached for the Chianti and poured a glass, then another.

'Does this matter to you?' His uncle was looking at him strangely. 'Are you . . . ?'

Three drumbeats sounded and the music stopped. Two men in black had appeared at the top of the steps with something they were setting up: an easel. Two more carried an object draped in black that they placed on the easel. Minotto and Bianco flanked it and the bailo raised his hands.

'I would beg your Imperial Majesties, Royal Highnesses, Eminences, Graces, Lords and Ladies,' here he spread his arms as if to encompass the whole world in his embrace, 'to witness a miracle.'

He brought his hands together and bowed to the imperial couple who had walked to the bottom of the steps. He continued. 'Ten years ago, the most serene Republic of Venice and the King of Portugal commissioned Fra Mauro of the Camaldolese Order to make a map of the world. It was to replace Ptolemy of Egypt's, produced twelve centuries ago.' He smiled. 'It was to be the greatest map ever created.'

Minotto gestured towards the easel. 'Now it is finished. And, to mark Venice's joy at the union of the Infanta of Portugal with our Holy Roman Emperor Frederick, we wish to present the first of the maps to the Empress Eleanor as our wedding gift.'

He turned, raising his hand like a magician, and the men lifted the black cloth. It was too far away for Siward to see the map.

'Fra Mauro was to be here to present this himself but, regrettably, fell ill before we left. However, his noble assistant Andrea Bianco is here to describe what has been achieved.'

Bianco stepped forward. He wore the black robes of academia. He cleared his throat, then turned to the map and pointed.

'We see here the three continents of Europe, Asia and Africa. We have known Europe well since Roman times but Fra Mauro has gathered new information about the coastline of Africa from the Portuguese, and about Asia from the travels of Arabs and our own Marco Polo, among others.'

Siward saw movement at the bottom of the steps. Eleanor of Portugal had left her husband's side and was mounting them, one by one, her skirts held in her hands. She reached the top and leant forward, peering at the map. Then she straightened.

'You show the Indian Ocean closed, no way past Africa to the East,' she said, loud enough for the room to hear.

'As it always has been,' said Bianco smoothly. 'As Ptolemy had it.'

Siward stared in disbelief. It did not seem possible that such a monstrous lie could be told. How did Venice believe they could commit such a crime? Something needed to be said. He started to walk forward.

'No.'

Giovanni had caught hold of his arm. 'Not here.'

Siward turned. 'Then where? This lie must be exposed.'

'Your word against Bianco's?' whispered Giovanni. 'Against Fra Mauro's?'

'But the monk isn't here. That's why they left him behind!'

'Exactly. Think, Siward.' He looked intently into his face. 'This is not the way.'

Siward glanced back at Bianco, then at the window seat where Violetta had sat down with Makkim. It was empty. He looked around the room, rising on tiptoes to see better. She wasn't in it. Nor was Makkim.

'I need to find Violetta,' he said. 'She's not here.'

He began to move away. Giovanni pulled him back. 'They will be here somewhere. Makkim has his audience with the Infanta later. Perhaps they're in the garden.'

'Then come.'

The two excused themselves as they moved through the crowd. They heard Bianco's voice grow fainter as they reached the doors to the garden. Siward opened them and they slipped out. The light from the palace windows washed everything with amber. There was no sign of them – of anyone.

They moved further in, smelling the scents of roses and jasmine.

'It doesn't make sense,' Giovanni said beside him. 'It's only a matter of time before the world knows the truth about the map. What have they to gain?'

'Time,' said Siward. They'd turned left between tall hedges with statues between. Suddenly, it was darker. He could hear Giovanni's heavy breathing. There were shadows up ahead: men standing, waiting for them with things in their hands. Clubs.

'Oh no.' Siward had stopped. He looked back. There were more shadows behind them.

'Who are they?' asked Giovanni.

'Venetians. They must have been waiting for me. This is not your fight. Go.'

But Giovanni hadn't moved. 'I count six,' he said. 'Do you have a weapon hidden somewhere?'

'No.' Siward saw a wheel leaning against a statue. The men were walking slowly towards them from both directions, trapping them.

'The wheel,' muttered Siward. 'Do you see it? We pick it up and charge, get it between us and their clubs.'

Giovanni nodded. 'I see it. On my count?'

Siward readied himself.

'One . . . two . . .'

The men were no more than twenty paces away now, drawing together. They wore masks and their cloaks were thrown back. They lifted their clubs. Ten paces.

'*Three!*'

Uncle and nephew ran over to the wheel. It was big and heavy and had a metal rim but they were strong. They lifted it by its spokes and steadied it. Then they charged.

The men in front of them had no time to split. They felt the full force of the wheel and went over on their backs, one into the hedge. Their clubs scattered on the ground.

'Now run!'

They dropped the wheel and Siward leapt forward but he was alone. He looked back and saw Giovanni picking up a club. Was he too old to run?

'What . . . ?'

'I want to know why they were waiting for you,' shouted

Giovanni. He picked up one of the felled clubs and swung it twice with precision. The two men on the ground lay still. The other rose cautiously from the hedge and backed away towards the men behind.

'I *know* why they were waiting for me,' shouted Siward. 'It was the map! They know I know it's a lie.' He picked up another club and stood by his uncle's side.

But the attack never came. The four remaining men saw their broken comrades on the ground and they turned and ran. Siward and Giovanni watched them go in silence.

'Cowards,' said Giovanni, setting down the club. He glanced at Siward. 'I must go back for the audience. You won't come?'

But Siward was shaking his head.

CHAPTER NINETEEN

ROME

Makkim's audience with the Infanta did not take place.

He'd forgotten about it, as he had everything else, in the wonder of seeing her again. Half a lifetime had passed, but to him she hadn't changed. He'd looked across the room at a Venetian courtesan in silks and high-hooped hair and seen a sister with ringlets and fire in her eye. He'd felt the breath escape his body and held onto a man's arm to stop from falling.

Then he'd begun to walk towards her, deaf to the surprise of his companions, blind to everything but the person also walking towards him. He'd watched her approach as if in a dream, seeing the same look on her face as when he'd left her at the barn. Then she was in front of him, her hand on his arm, and she was speaking.

'Ilya.'

He'd not been able to reply. There was too much to say and it couldn't be said here. He'd taken her hand.

'Come with me.'

Now, as the Infanta waited in her audience room, and Giovanni waited outside it, the man who'd once been Ilya lay next to

209

his sister as they had many years ago, in a field. They'd hardly spoken on the way there, perhaps not wanting to break through the soft membrane of their dream. They'd passed benches and hedges and statues of Roman gods and come to an area of wild flowers, its grasses brushed by moonlight. Makkim had cleared a space for them. Now they lay side by side in silence and looked up at the stars. The years fell away. They were together again, holding hands in a field.

It was Makkim who spoke first. She heard the rustle of grass as he turned his head to her.

'How?'

How? Violetta pressed his hand, wondering what to answer. She'd waited so many years for this meeting, rehearsed it time and time again in her mind, anticipated the elation that would accompany their reunion. She was too dazed to feel it yet, but it would come.

'There are stories to tell,' she said, looking back at him. 'Who'll go first?'

She did in the end. She told him everything, from her arrival in Venice to her coming to Rome. She told him how she'd been picked up by the courtesan Alessandra Viega. She told him how she'd become her apprentice.

He frowned then. 'But . . . a *courtesan*?'

'Why not? At least I'm free. I have no master, as you have Mehmed. I can do as I please. That is rare for a woman.' She was looking at him beside her, seeing the contour of his shaved head, the shadow of his scar in the moonlight, remembering how he'd got it. She reached over and touched it, her fingers following its line. 'I'm Violetta Cavarse now,' she said gently, 'and proud to be.'

'You took no husband?'

'Husband? No. Lovers? Many.' She laughed. 'But then it is my profession.' She lifted her bottom to arrange her dress for more comfort. The ground was hard and she suddenly felt over-dressed for a field. It had not been like this when they were young. Should she let down her hair? She didn't believe she knew how. Servants had always done it. She asked, 'And you?'

'Lovers? None. But then it was my profession.'

She sensed the fall of shadow. Did he mind what she'd become? But she'd had to survive and he'd been somewhere else. In any case, she wasn't ashamed.

'So tell me about you,' she said. 'All of it, even the bits I might not like.'

Makkim told her about how the Sultan's men had taken him to Edirne, how he'd been sent for a year to live with a family in Anatolia, learning Turkish and the Koran by heart. He told her of his return to Edirne where he'd been put into the janis-sary school to learn warfare, languages and the art of blind obedience. He told her how he'd been singled out and given an education permitted to the very few, how he'd risen from janissary to general in eight short years. At last, he told her about Varna.

'It was a terrible battle of chaos and slaughter. But we won and the Sultan honoured me.'

'And you became famous throughout the world.'

'Inshallah.'

She looked at him. Of course, he was a Muslim. But it was strange, nonetheless.

'The Ilya I knew has become Makkim Pasha, the Sultan's general,' she said wonderingly. 'Imagine.'

He laughed. 'And you have become Violetta Cavarse, the most famous courtesan in the world. Imagine.' He rolled onto his side and brushed a stray ringlet from her cheek. 'I visited our mother to find out if she knew where you'd gone. She sent me away.'

Violetta shook her head. 'She never knew what happened.'

'Not from you, not from me. It would have killed her.' He smoothed her hair with his palm. 'You know, I suppose, that the priest lived?'

It had been the first time they'd mentioned the priest. She'd tried to forget the priest in every way that she could over the years, perhaps knowing, somewhere, that much of what she did was because of him. Now he was back.

'It was why I left,' she said quietly. 'After the janissaries took you, I went back to the village with a story of how he'd died. But when I saw that he hadn't, I knew I had to leave.' She nodded, remembering. 'I think I wanted to go anyway. Life there without you . . .' She stopped herself.

'Well, he's in Constantinople now,' said Makkim. 'And when it falls, I will find him and kill him.'

She nodded slowly. 'What he did was terrible,' she said softly. 'But its consequences weren't so bad. I have been happy in Venice, Makkim.'

'But you can come with me now. As you were always going to.'

Violetta laughed. 'But you are the Sultan's general, a Muslim, the man who'll conquer Constantinople. Am I to be one of your janissaries?' She propped herself up on her elbow, her palm to her chin. 'Are you even *allowed* women in your retinue?'

'I am permitted a harem. You would be its only member.'

'Your harem? I don't think so!' She felt suddenly awkward and glanced down at the ground. They'd never talked of such things.

He looked away, thinking awhile, then back at her. 'She told me something else.'

'I know.'

Makkim frowned. 'What do you know?'

'What she told you. That she is not your mother. That I am not your sister.'

He stared at her. 'How long have you known?'

She smiled and shook her head slowly. 'For ever, I think. But she confirmed it for me, when I asked her.'

'And you never told me?'

'Why would I do that? What good would it have done?'

They were silent for a long time, the past suddenly altered, recalibrated.

She said, 'You could come to Venice. I have a palazzo. There are many Moors in Venice.'

He smiled. 'I'm not a Moor. I am just Muslim.'

'Are you devout?'

He seemed to consider this. 'Devout enough. I can recite the Koran. But I've been known to miss prayers.'

'But you believe in the will of Allah?'

He nodded slowly. 'I believe that the world will be a better place under the peace of Islam.'

She frowned. 'We've become very different, haven't we?' She paused. 'Wouldn't you say?'

He shook his head. 'No. No, *no*! The differences are nothing beside what binds us, what has always bound us.'

'But we may want different things now,' she said, 'different lives even.' She hesitated. 'What do *you* want, Makkim? Apart from Islam, that is.'

He was silent for a moment. 'I want what I once had. Family. You.'

She looked at him. 'Aren't the janissaries your family? You've said so.'

'Yes, but now that I'm distant from them . . .' He turned and met her eyes. 'You are the only family I have.'

She thought then of what she knew but he didn't. But it wasn't for her to tell him, it was for Giovanni, who she'd met that evening. She took his other hand. 'Shall we remember it then, that family?'

So they lay back on the ground and remembered it.

For both of them, the past was a country without allegiance, as far from Rome or Constantinople or Popes or Prophets as any country could be. Above all, it was safe. They talked so much that they didn't notice the creeping light of dawn, nor the distant shouts of those looking for them. Only when the sun broke the horizon and turned the Tiber below into a ribbon of copper, did they stop.

They sat up and looked out at the view in silence, their hands still joined. She thought she knew what Makkim might be thinking. He'd spent the last part of their conversation talking about it: how he might find a way to come and live in Venice.

She was thinking something different. She was wondering where the elation was that she'd supposed would come to her.

CHAPTER TWENTY

BOSPOROS

It was dawn on the Bosporos and the Venetian galley had just passed through the Ottoman fleet. Its captain was Antonio Erizzo and he was well known to the Turkish admiral. His ship had been bringing grain down from the Black Sea every month since the Turkish fleet had been stationed off the entrance to the straits.

Erizzo looked up at the masts. Both flew Lions of St Mark's big enough to carpet a small *campo*. They did nothing for the galley's speed but were necessary, he knew. The galley was approaching the point where the new castle had been built: Rumelihisari, or 'throat-cutter', as it was aptly called. Its commander, Firuz Aga, had been clear: make sure we know who you are.

The ship was a *galere de mercato*, only a year out of the arsenal. At four hundred tons, it was the biggest merchant vessel the Venetians possessed. The grain it carried would fetch a good price in the markets of Constantinople. The city was preparing itself for siege.

Erizzo looked down the length of the galley, watching the silent rowers, three to a bench, work their oars to the low beat of the drum. The silence, the drumbeat and the mist on the water made the scene mythic: Jason and his Argonauts on their quest. Any moment they'd see the Halil Pasha tower.

'Castle coming up, sir,' said a man by his side.

Erizzo looked up at the mast again. The mist was clearing and the flags were snapping in the morning breeze. They'd be quite visible from the castle. He remembered the first time he'd stopped there to meet Firuz Aga. They'd drunk sherbet on a pile of stones and watched the Byzantine fleet scuttle back to the safety of the Golden Horn. He heard they'd put a chain across its mouth now. He smiled. As the siege drew nearer, the price of grain would soar ever higher.

'There it is.'

They were approaching the narrowest part of the channel, no more than six hundred yards across. The mist swirled and glowed as if the water was alight. Greek fire, thought Erizzo; Greek fire must have looked something like this. Did they have it still? It might be useful now. He watched the shoreline as it closed in to their right. The Halil Pasha tower suddenly rose up from the mist, glowing in the hard dawn light. He saw the flash of metal at its top.

'Slow the tempo,' said Erizzo. 'We don't want to seem in a hurry.'

The drumbeat slowed and the oars rose and fell to a lesser rhythm. Erizzo never grew bored of watching them touch the water with such exactitude. He'd sailed in cogs and carracks that lumbered over the sea like fat turtles. Give him the speed and agility of a sleek galley any day. He looked up into the new sun, closing his eyes and lifting his face to its warmth. He wondered how many more of these trips he'd be allowed to make before the Ottoman navy finally blocked the entrance to the straits. When would this siege begin?

The crash of cannon opened his eyes, then his bowels. The ball hit the galley at an angle that caused carnage in the rowing bays. He saw it tear through twenty bodies, sending limbs into the air, spraying rowers with blood and splinters. Their oars hovered in mid-air as men cowered from the rain, cowered from the screams of their shattered comrades.

'What . . . ?'

Erizzo was not a fighting man; he was a merchant and a coward. He backed towards the end-rail, his arms flailing. 'No!' he shouted. 'NO! *NO!*' He looked up at the lion at the top of the mast, still winged and flying. 'We're Venetian! *We're Venetian, for God's sake!*'

But God wasn't watching. A second crash sounded across the straits, echoing off the twin castle opposite. Their mast fell.

Erizzo ran to the side of the ship, listing now as water came through the hole in the galley's side. Men were jumping into the sea, some without arms. 'Firuz Aga!' he yelled, knowing that his voice wouldn't carry over the men's screams. 'Firuz Aga . . . *what are you doing?*'

He looked down at his ship. It was sinking fast as water now streamed over its side. They'd be underwater in a few minutes.

'Sir!' The man beside him fell to his knees as the galley lurched. 'Sir, we have to go. We can swim. It's not far to the shore.'

Erizzo looked wildly from side to side. 'Which shore?'

'It doesn't matter. They've both got Turks. Come on!'

Erizzo looked over the side. He waited for empty sea beneath. He jumped.

The water had the cold Black Sea current beneath its surface and it took Erizzo's breath away. When he came up, he found the surface warmer. His doublet was heavy and he wrenched it open, then pulled it off. He began to swim to the bank, closing his eyes against the spray.

He drew nearer and heard shouts. He opened his eyes.

The bank was lined with janissaries. Each man had an axe.

'Impaled?'

Makkim was standing in the hall of the Orsini Palace in Rome. A messenger had just brought him the news from Constantinople.

'The captain only, sir,' said the man. He was wearing boots covered with dust. 'The rest were beheaded. Their heads are on poles all along the banks of the Bosporos.'

Makkim shook his head slowly. Impaling a man was the cruelest way to make him die. Mehmed had made his point in a new, more savage way. Was this Zaganos bey's work? Was this the dar el-salaam he'd boasted of to Minotto? He felt revulsion.

Minotto. Had he heard?

'When did it happen?'

'Five days ago, lord. I have ridden fast.'

He had, thought Makkim, as he gave the man gold. It was eight hundred miles from Constantinople to Rome. A servant appeared at the door.

'The Venetian bailo of Constantinople is here, lord.'

So Minotto had heard. He cursed Mehmed for his cruelty. The timing couldn't be worse. He'd planned to establish a new relationship with the bailo, one that might lead to the serenissima asking the Sultan for a new ambassador after the fall of Constantinople: a man to live in Venice who they could trust . . .

He'd not thought about much else since seeing her again. He'd stood for hours every day, staring through various Orsini palace windows, going over every word of their conversation, every nuance of her look and movement. They'd arranged to meet that evening in the same garden. It was seven long hours away. But there was something he must deal with first. He turned to the servant.

'I will see him.'

He walked into the room to find Minotto alone and serious. He didn't bow when Makkim entered.

'It was unecessary,' he said, not moving his head, his voice barely controlled.

'I agree,' said Makkim, walking up to stand in front of him. Their eyes met and he gestured to a chair but was refused. 'I told you Mehmed is unpredictable. I had no idea he would do that.'

Minotto was staring at him with even more anger than he'd expected. His fists were clenched and twitching, as if they held coals. Had he been related to this Erizzo perhaps? They said that every grand family in Venice was related somewhere.

'The Doge has instructed me to say that we will buy the cannon as you suggested. I am to travel from here to Budapest. We will expect full protection of Venetian property when the city is taken. We will expect a monopoly of European trade through Constantinople: trade with the Black Sea, all of the East.'

Makkim was taken aback. It had all been said in a rush but the tone was very different.

'The Sultan will not give away so much for a few cannon,' he said carefully.

'We can do more. Even with the cannon, Constantinople will be difficult to take. Its walls are impregnable. And it is protected by the Blessed Virgin.'

Makkim saw only seriousness in the man's face. 'But you managed to take it.'

219

'Perhaps she favoured other Christians that day. She's unlikely to favour you, wherever you were born.'

Makkim wondered how much this man knew about him. Could he also know about Violetta? Was it possible that she'd told Minotto about him? For a second, he closed his eyes. No, that wasn't possible. No. Never. He opened them. 'What more will you offer?'

'When the time comes, we will let you into the city.'

'How?'

Minotto shrugged. 'There are many gates and we are likely to be part of the garrison. It will be a question of knowing which gate to be at, when.'

Makkim nodded slowly. It was a glittering prospect. And how much bloodshed might it avoid? But there was something else, something he needed that was personal to him.

'I will put this to my sultan.' His tone was conciliatory. 'How I put it will have great influence on his answer. It usually does.' He leant forward. 'There is something you can do for me that will ensure my words land well.'

Later, Makkim made his way up to the garden of the Colonna Palace. The sun had recently set and the day was still warm. An orange halo hung over the city, smudged with the smoke of a thousand cooking fires. He walked slowly for he was early. He thought again of what she'd said to him.

'Its consequences weren't so bad. I have been happy in Venice.'

He shook his head. A courtesan was different from the sluts in the back streets of Edirne. She had more freedom than any other woman alive, more power as well perhaps. Violetta was educated, refined. *But still a whore.*

The priest. He'd made her that. He'd deadened her to any

love outside the transactional kind, though it was love for him that had made her first take that path. He felt an old burning inside. *You'll pay for that when I take Constantinople.*

He was halfway up the Quirinal Hill by now, passing new and old palaces, barely aware of the evening traffic of Rome's rich as it stopped to look at him, bowing warily, wondering why such a magnificent specimen should be out on his own at such an hour. He smiled and nodded and walked on.

It was long ago and people change with their circumstances, do what they have to to survive. He had, after all. But whatever his circumstances, he'd never once changed his feelings towards her. He'd accepted the janissary proscription on marriage because he'd never wanted anyone else. Now he'd found her, how could he make sure they never parted again?

He'd thought it through carefully. He'd come up with an idea that would work, an idea he'd just put to a man who'd promised to help. *Ambassador to the Serenissima.* It sounded like a fitting job for a pasha. After Constantinople had been taken, the Doge would ask for him as a sign of the new alliance. And Mehmed? How would he react? Well, he had Zaganos bey now.

He'd reached the gates of the garden to the side of the palace. He went into a symmetry of nature that, however tamed, couldn't prevent its scent from escaping. He filled his lungs with the smell of early roses. He looked around. There were the busts of the Caesars; there was the bench, empty. He was early. He went and sat.

Violetta was late to the garden. Despite the long cloak, Minotto had recognised her in the street. He'd wanted to talk about her and Makkim. He'd seemed unusually interested, but then all Rome was talking about little else.

'It is my job,' she'd said calmly. 'I am a courtesan and my task is to charm. So I charmed him.'

'Where are you going now?'

'Somewhere you are not. Let go of my arm.'

He'd done so reluctantly and she'd left. He knew she was lying to him, she could see that. She hoped he wouldn't follow her.

She walked up the Quirinal Hill without any more encumbrance and entered the garden. She saw Makkim standing with his back to her between the Caesars, his palms on the parapet, leaning out over Rome. She stopped and looked over her shoulder. No one seemed to have followed her.

He looked enormous against the russet sky, big enough to lift up the city below in his two hands: a colossus. He'd always been such in their childhood: her big, gentle, protective older brother. Whether it was from storms or dragons or older children in the village, he'd always taken care of her. He'd do so now, if she'd only let him.

So why wouldn't she? She had spent the past days asking herself that question. Why could she not submit to the love she'd always known she had for him . . . would have for him if he ever came back? Well, he had come back and it hadn't been there, or not as she'd expected to feel it. Exhilaration hadn't come to her, just unease. She looked at the broad expanse of his shoulders silhouetted against the sky. He was a good man – surely he'd understand.

She came to stand beside him.

'They plunder the ruins to build their palaces and churches,' she said quietly. 'They have no thought for the past.'

He glanced at her. 'But we do.'

She took his hand, met his eye with hers, ran them down the line of his scar. It was both comfort and threat, a frontier for the past and the future. It could so easily be crossed in either direction, if only she dared.

'We do, Makkim,' she agreed, 'but the past must know its place, especially with you and me. We are brother and sister.'

He shook his head. 'No, we're not. We never were.'

She put both hands over his now, turning to do so. 'Yes, we were. We shared a bed as brother and sister. We loved each other as brother and sister.' She made her words precise. She wanted them understood, each in its turn. 'We've changed, grown up, but we'll always be brother and sister.'

He shook his head slowly. 'What is this?' he asked. 'Is it that you think I'll make you change? Try to stop you being a courtesan?'

'No, Makkim,' she said plainly. 'You couldn't stop me even if you wanted to. That's the point.'

He was still shaking his head. 'Is it the priest? Has he made any honest love impossible for you?'

Honest love? Was there such a thing in the world? Certainly not in Venice where everything was a lie. She shook her head.

'Perhaps. But I don't *care* about honest love, whatever that is. I'm happy as I am.'

He released her hand and they stood side by side and looked at the view like two tourists. The city below was very different from the stars they'd looked up to not long ago. It was a hard, glittering sea of artifice and, had they been any closer, they'd have smelt it for the cistern it was.

He spoke into the night. 'It's very simple, really,' he said. 'I want to be with you. I never want to leave you again. I can come to Venice after Constantinople falls, as ambassador. It can be arranged.'

She knew, then, what he'd talked about with the bailo. But

it was not what she wanted. 'I don't know that that would be a good idea,' she said quietly. 'For either of us.'

'But we can be together,' he said. 'We don't have to marry. We can live in the same city, meet every day.' He reached for her. 'I love you. I have always loved you.'

She closed her eyes. 'No,' she said softly. 'We were children and we are something else now.' She sighed. 'Can't you see?' She leant forward. 'I *choose* to be a courtesan because no man can ever own me.' She placed her hand on his shoulder. 'I have never once been ashamed of what I do, Makkim.'

It wasn't true. With a suddenness that almost choked her, she remembered how she'd felt with Siward after her night with Philip of Burgundy.

Makkim was staring at her with such misery on his face that she almost said something more. But there was no need. She'd been precise so that there'd be no misunderstanding. There was only one more thing to say.

'I'm sorry.'

He turned away, a faint frown on his brow, his eyes unfocused. She watched him shake his head slowly, perhaps to absorb, perhaps to deny. She couldn't tell.

She left the wall, then the garden, praying he wouldn't follow her. She thought of what she'd just said, of the hurt she'd just caused a man who'd only ever tried to save her from hurt. She thought of the lie she'd told about her shame. She'd felt it as much with Makkim as she had with Siward, but only with Siward had she minded feeling it. That was what had decided her, really.

Suddenly she wanted to see Siward again. She'd left him at the ball standing with Giovanni and De Grugny, not giving them a backward glance as she'd walked away. She'd not seen him since. What must he have thought? She would go to him and she would tell him everything. She needed to tell somebody.

She stopped. No, she couldn't do that. How could she be sure he'd tell no one else? How would people judge a man who'd tried to kill a priest? Makkim was his enemy, after all. She'd go to him but not tell him *that*.

It was not long after dawn on the following day that Makkim took his leave of Rome. Rising that early was not difficult since he hadn't slept.

His business in Rome was done anyway. He'd attended the marriage and coronation of the Holy Roman Emperor on behalf of his sultan, and at least part of the celebrations afterwards. He'd been there when the *Dum Diversas* bull had been read out by Pope Nicholas V, granting Papal blessing to King Alfonso of Portugal for the enslavement of Saracens, and duly registered his master's outrage. And he'd agreed the supply of cannon.

He hadn't attended the audience with the Empress Eleanor but it wasn't the most important of meetings.

He'd been surprised when Zaganos bey had arrived in Rome, but not especially. His mind had been on other things. It was only as they'd ridden towards the *Porta del Popola* that he thought to ask him why he'd come.

'To take you home,' said the new vizier. They were moving slowly through the traffic of pilgrims and merchants leaving the Holy City, their escort of sipahis doing their best to clear a path. 'To prevent any more . . . *incidents*.'

'Incidents?' They were riding side by side in a busy street and Makkim was having to speak louder than he cared to.

'Such as that reported from the Colonna Palace. Were you drunk?'

Makkim hadn't considered any interpretation of his actions at the ball. But he was noticing a new confidence in Zaganos's tone.

'No, I wasn't drunk.' He turned to the vizier. 'She was a courtesan of Venice. She charmed me. It is over.'

'It is said she is also a spy,' said Zaganos. 'It seems careless to be charmed by such a person.'

It had occurred to Makkim, at that point, that the truth might be told: he'd been reunited with his long-lost sister. But then the story would be told and the priest lived and might hear of it. No word must get to him that Makkim was the boy who'd once struck him. He wanted to find him when Constantinople fell.

'And I hope the Empress wasn't offended,' continued the vizier. 'You failed to attend an audience with her.'

They were approaching the city gate, still half-ruined from the days of the Emperor Aurelius. There was congestion there as the guards delivered weapons to those who'd given them up. There were stalls for last-minute indulgences with friars ringing bells. The noise was tremendous. Makkim looked down at his own sword, its dragon head resting against his thigh. He placed his cloak over its hilt.

There was a procession converging from another street, guards in imperial livery opening the way, shooing away dogs with their halberds, while servants with other dogs came on behind. He saw the Holy Roman Empress riding behind.

'We should give way. We have Eleanor of Portugal going to the hunt.'

'Will you apologise to her?'

Makkim ignored him. He reined in his horse and told the sipahis to do the same. But the Empress saw him and turned her horse, detaching herself from the party. She rode up to him.

226

Makkim bowed from the saddle.

She stared at him for some time, the critical appraisal of one who'd been told to expect something. She was dressed for the hunt in jerkin, cloak and leather skirts above boots, and she sat her horse better than most of Makkim's cavalry. She nodded.

'You were meant to have audience with me,' she said. 'Did you forget?'

Makkim felt the blood rise in his cheeks. 'Highness, forgive me.'

'Oh, I don't mind,' she smiled. 'It's just that there was someone who wanted to meet you. Someone important.'

Makkim frowned. Was she speaking of her husband? But he'd gone to bed surely.

'Are you leaving?' she asked.

Zaganos chose to speak. 'The pasha has been called back to Edirne, highness. I am to escort him there.'

Eleanor looked at him without much interest. 'And you are?'

'Zaganos bey, second vizier,' he said, bowing.

'Ah yes. I've heard of you.' She frowned and looked at Makkim. She seemed to be deciding something. 'I hope we meet again,' she said delicately. She glanced at Zaganos and back. 'In the meantime, I hope you'll choose your friends with care.'

She turned her horse.

Siward was sitting upstairs in the Duke of Burgundy's palazzo writing a letter to the Duchess. It was evening and hot and he was in his shirt-sleeves with the windows wide open. Through them he could hear the usual sounds of construction. It didn't seem to stop in this city. He wondered if the pilgrims saw enough of God's glory among the scaffolding to make their journeys worthwhile.

His had certainly been worthwhile, commercially at least. He'd been busy on the Duchess's behalf, and his own. He'd found that her patronage had indeed opened doors for the Magoris Bank and he'd met with merchant bankers from Flanders to Portugal, all of whom had branches in the Eternal City. And help had come from Giovanni, unbidden but timely. His reputation as a trader in sugar had made him many friends among the bankers and he'd put it about that Siward was the man to trust. The Magoris Bank was in business again.

He'd been pleased to keep busy. What had happened at the ball had decided him that any further interest in Violetta Cavarse was a vain pursuit. Her behaviour with Makkim had shown that she was, after all, what she was: a courtesan. And Makkim's reaction to her had demonstrated how good she was at it. The fact that it was Makkim she'd chosen to seduce – whom she knew to be heir to a fortune much greater than his – had been particularly galling. He'd resolved to forget her completely.

So her arrival at the palace was not welcome. He'd lied at first, telling the servants to say he was out. But she'd not believed it and was now crossing his threshold.

'You work late,' she said, passing a servant.

He rose and pushed his hand through his long hair, damp with sweat. The heat didn't seem to be affecting her. She was dressed for occasion in a long gown of intricate motif, cut low to the bosom. He wondered where she might be on her way to.

'I am busy,' he said. 'I have to work late.'

She sat down in the chair opposite his desk and began to fan herself with her hand. 'So doors are opening. That is good.'

He didn't say anything. If she expected some credit for the bank's success, he wouldn't oblige. But she didn't seem her usual self. She seemed unsure. He reminded himself that courtesans deployed different strategems to get their way.

'Is there something I can help you with, Violetta?' he asked, after some silence. 'As you see . . .'

She stopped fanning and looked at him. She leant forward. 'I just wanted to say I'm sorry,' she said simply. He saw that she was serious. 'I'm sorry for what happened at the ball. I . . .'

He raised his hand. 'You don't have to explain. You are a courtesan, as you keep telling me. Please.'

She began to say something but stopped. She looked down at the desk. 'Will you be coming back to Venice?' she asked quietly.

He got up and went to the window. 'I thought you considered Venice too dangerous for me, Violetta. Certainly Rome seems to be.' He shook his head. 'I'm going to Constantinople. The Emperor wishes to see me.'

She kept her gaze fixed on the desk. 'Of course.' She looked up. 'I heard about the attack. Well, at least we now know why Luke was murdered.'

Siward nodded. 'The map. The same reason I will be, if I stay here. After all, I know the truth.' He frowned. 'They may well think you do, too. You should consider that.'

There was more silence. The evening had brought breeze and Siward lifted his face to it, closing his eyes. Her scent came to him and he realised she was standing next to him.

'When will you return to Venice?' she asked softly.

He opened his eyes and found her staring up at him. He knew that if he reached for her now, she'd come to him. He felt suddenly dizzy with the possibility. But she'd not mean it any more than she had with Makkim.

There was a knock on the door. A servant appeared.

'The lord Longo, sir.'

Giovanni entered the room. He showed no surprise at seeing Violetta there. He just looked annoyed. He nodded to Siward behind the desk, then turned to her.

'I have been looking for you,' he said. 'The Empress did not have her audience with Makkim, so neither did I. Now he's left Rome.' He sighed in frustration. 'What happened?'

Violetta glanced at Siward. She moved away. 'Nothing happened,' she said. 'We talked and he forgot. I'm sorry.'

'Had you known him before?' Giovanni asked. 'You were strange.'

'I . . .' She seemed to be struggling with something. She shook her head and looked out of the window. 'No, of course not. How could I?'

'Did you tell him about me, about the inheritance?'

She looked back at him. 'No,' she said. 'That's not my business, it's yours.'

'So why . . . ?'

Siward rose suddenly. He wanted this meeting to be over. 'She is a courtesan, Uncle,' he said. 'It is her instinct. Just as a dog goes to a bone.'

Violetta turned from the window. Her anger was in her eyes and the stretch of her neck and every muscle of her body. She stared at Siward. 'It is, yes, just as yours is to go and get yourself killed at Constantinople. I wish you luck there. You will not see me again.'

She walked to the door, opened it, and left the room.

They both stared after her. Siward fought down the impulse to go after her.

'She'll not be safe in Venice,' Giovanni said at last. 'They'll know that she arrived here with you and may think she knows about the map. Shouldn't you go there with her? For a little while, at least? To make sure she's safe?'

Siward brought his fingers to his temples and closed his eyes. His head had begun to ache. He shook his head slowly as if to gauge the pain. 'She is not my responsibility, Uncle.'

Giovanni frowned. He was silent for a while. 'So where will you go?'

Siward looked at him. 'Constantinople.' He lowered his hands. 'I had hoped to persuade you to come with me.'

But Giovanni was shaking his head. 'It is not my fight, I told you. I am the bastard child, Genoese more than Greek. Besides, I want to find my son, not kill him.'

Siward left Rome much as he had Venice: confused and unhappy. He'd spent his last evening composing a long letter to Nikolas, telling him that the bank could now survive without help from the trading company, and asking him to watch out for Violetta's safety. He rode the Appian Way to Brindisi without speaking a sentence to Petros, and then took a ship to Modon, intending to ride east to Monemvasia and from there travel by sea to Constantinople.

But Plethon was waiting for him on the dock at Modon, his toga flapping high like the port was surrendering. He had new instructions from the Emperor.

'You're to stay here,' he said as Siward came down the gang-plank. They kissed on each cheek and Plethon led him to a carriage, Petros behind. 'Our despot thinks Mehmed might attack here first. He wants the Varangians to hold the Hexamilion Wall.'

Siward wasn't much disappointed. He'd done some thinking on the journey and found his spirits lifting with each mile of dis-tance. Rome, Burgundy, Venice . . . these were places of duplicity

231

and fear and hidden danger. Whether it was Constantinople or the Hexamilion Wall, at least he'd be able to see his enemy when he came at him. He was a soldier, after all.

They got into the carriage and Plethon closed the door.

'Tell me about Violetta Cavarse.'

Siward groaned. 'If you're asking about her, you know. She is a courtesan, a spy and friend of Zoe Mamonas, who has been helpful. We came together to Rome.'

'From Burgundy. Was the ride pleasant?'

Siward stared at the philosopher. 'Yes. It was springtime. Now, can we talk about something else? What news from Mistra?'

Plethon tidied his toga. 'We've had Minotto here, on his way to Constantinople. He will promise Constantine cannon and a fleet before the siege begins.'

'Cannon from where?'

'From Orban the Hungarian. Minotto himself will deliver them to Constantinople after Christmas. The fleet will come later.'

'The Grand Council has met?'

'Met and deplored the sinking of its ship and murder of its subjects. Venice's treaty with Mehmed is no more. She will certainly come to Constantinople's aid.'

Siward frowned. 'Perhaps. Who else promises to come?'

'No one for free, it would seem,' said Plethon. 'Hunyadi wants Mesembria for his pains, and Alfonso of Spain the island of Lemnos. There'll be nothing left after their help.' He gave a short laugh. 'And the Emperor Frederick has written to Mehmed threatening another crusade. Empty words.'

'The Pope?'

'He'll send three boatloads of food and Cardinal Isidore with two hundred bowmen from Crete. We both know what he'll want in return.'

It had been the subject of the Council of Florence thirteen years ago and the reason for Cleope's marriage to Theodore.

'A union of the Churches with the Pope in charge,' murmured Siward. 'But we know by now the people won't have it. They rioted last time.' He looked out of the window at a place far from riots, a place of peace and plenty. *My home. For now.* 'So when does Constantine think it'll begin?'

'In the spring, so he has some months still to prepare. He's brought in food, strengthened the walls and put the chain across the mouth of the Horn. What else should he be doing?'

'Getting more men,' said Siward. 'We've about six thousand soldiers in the city, including all civilian volunteers, manning walls twenty miles long. We need more men.'

'What about mercenaries?'

'The money I've raised will pay for the Venetians and Genoese to fight, but we need more. Zoe Mamonas says she'll pay for an army from Chios.'

Plethon nodded. 'What about Giovanni? Did you talk to him in Rome?'

Siward grunted. 'I'm surprised you don't know. He won't come. He says that it's not his fight.'

Plethon sighed. 'Not with his son in the enemy camp, I suppose. Still, he would be invaluable there.' He turned to him. 'So tell me about Violetta Cavarse.'

Siward raised his hands. 'Again? I don't know any more about her than you do, old man. She has returned to Venice, I imagine, to continue her profitable work.'

But Plethon wasn't smiling. 'I have heard from Nikolas,' he said. 'She has returned, yes, but she's also disappeared. Not even Zoe knows where she has gone.'

CHAPTER TWENTY-ONE

VENICE

It seemed long ago that Violetta Cavarse had rejected the advances of Girolamo Minotto, but some men never forget.

Violetta was considering this fact as she lay on her bed in a house empty of anyone but her, with soldiers at its doors. Minotto had believed the rejection because of his rank but in truth, she'd just not liked him. Here, she'd thought, was a man not to trust to any degree.

She'd been proved right. Quite soon she was to stand trial as a traitor to Venice, accused of spying for the Turk. She would be led into one of those cavernous panelled rooms in the Doge's palace where the council, all in black, would sentence her to death. And Minotto would be there watching it all, enjoying himself.

Violetta was propped against pillows in the same bed where she'd nursed Siward. She looked down at the white sheet and remembered his arm resting on it, the fair down against his skin, the way his hand had stroked it when he'd talked. Where was he now? Constantinople?

She shook her head slowly. That had been the biggest lie. He'd told her he'd have to go there and she'd feigned indifference.

Was she frightened? Of course, although they'd not burn her as they did the witches. No, she'd probably hang from the Rialto Bridge: a lesson to the meaner whores who plied their trade there. She was as frightened as she'd been when the Sultan's men had come to the village, yes, but there was another, more overwhelming sensation that required all her strength to overcome: *I'll not see him again.*

She looked up at the windows, remembering them smeared with rain when he'd first lain there. Had she felt love from that moment? Probably. But she'd not known the feeling for what it was then. That had taken time. And another, mistaken love.

She thought back to the conversation in the Colonna garden. She remembered the look of disbelief, then pain, as she'd told Makkim the truth. She'd heard that he'd left Rome soon afterwards, that someone had come to collect him to take him back to Edirne. Was he accused of treating with the enemy too? It seemed unlikely. He was Mehmed's favourite.

She glanced down at her arms. She was too thin. She'd not eaten properly since she'd come back, first because she'd no appetite, then because there'd been no one to fetch food from the market, even if she'd wanted it. She'd been imprisoned in her own house by the Doge's men. They'd dismissed all her servants and she'd seen no one for weeks. Zoe's messengers had been turned away and Nikolas's too, all told she was elsewhere. The Doge wanted her dead and, until then, hidden.

And Siward. Did he even know what had happened to her?

She forced herself to think about something else. Fra Mauro's map would do. It must be on its way to Portugal by now, to tell Prince Henry that he should stick with what he'd found and go no further. A terrible lie, but to what more terrible end? She wanted so much to talk to Zoe.

She thought of her lovers, the great men of Venice, not one of whom had tried to visit her, so far as she knew. Perhaps they'd been talking to the Doge, persuading him to drop these ludicrous charges. How could someone be condemned to death for a *conversation*? Perhaps, without her lovers, she'd be dead already.

She was glad of her lovers' desertion in one way: it meant she'd not have to sleep with anyone but herself; she'd not have to feel the same shame she'd felt when she and Siward had ridden away from Dijon. Was that the priest's fault or Siward's?

Makkim had vowed to find the priest in Constantinople but she didn't really care, except that it would give him another reason to attack the city where Siward was. It was strange how alike they were, Makkim and Siward. They were cousins and rivals and only one of them did she want to spend the rest of her life with. What life? In two months' time, she'd be dead.

She closed her eyes again. *Was there a heaven for courtesans?*

In another part of Venice, behind a high wall with broken glass at its top, the bailo Minotto was walking with Zaganos bey. The wall was patrolled by *arsenalotti,* men who lived among the shipyards and kept their secrets. Within them were rows of long sheds that held galleys in various stages of production. In the spaces between were piles of tree-trunks, planking, ropes and barrels. Tall chimneys belched smoke into a grey sky and cranes looked over the water like giant crows.

While waiting for Zaganos to arrive, Minotto had been thinking with satisfaction about Violetta Cavarse. It hadn't been hard to convince the Doge of her guilt. When he'd got back from Rome, he'd gone straight to the palace and told Foscari about what had happened at the Colonna Palace. That afternoon, Violetta had been arrested.

Now to spread the harm to someone he hated almost as much for years of humiliation. He'd heard that Makkim's star was fading. He had the means to extinguish it altogether.

'Makkim Pasha behaved strangely in Rome,' he said to Zaganos as they walked past the sheds. 'Were you there?'

The two men had met often before to refine a plan known only to them, the Sultan and the Doge. It was, however, the first time they'd met at the arsenale to discuss it.

The vizier shook his head. 'No, but I brought him home.'

Minotto glanced up at the man. He was dressed in a single tunic that hung well from the magnificent body beneath. He smelt of lilac.

'Did he explain himself?'

'He claimed to be taken by her charms. It seems unlikely.'

Minotto stopped and turned to his companion. 'You may like to know that we have arrested the courtesan,' he said in a low voice, 'for spying.'

Zaganos looked interested. 'Spying? For us?'

The bailo dipped his head. 'We considered her explanation to be a lie. We felt that she and Makkim already knew each other when they met at the ball.' He paused. 'Your sultan may take a similar view.'

Zaganos was nodding slowly. 'He may, although Makkim has been greatly loved by him in the past. Is there anything else you can tell me?'

Minotto nodded. 'He has asked me to secure him the embassy of Venice after Constantinople falls. Why would the Sultan's most brilliant general want to come here, do you think?'

Zaganos had a smile gathering along the whole line of his mouth. 'Why indeed?'

Minotto walked on, the man beside him silent in

contemplation. It was the right time to change the subject. He pointed to the shed they were passing.

'You see here a revolution in ship-building,' he said. 'For the first time, the ship is brought to the man, rather than the man to the ship. They come through canals to these sheds where they undergo three stages of production: framing, planking, and final assembly. We use standardised, interchangeable parts. The process is cheaper, quicker, and more efficient. Soon we'll be making one a day.'

Zaganos was amazed. 'One a day? That is miraculous.'

'And necessary when you have a whole sea to protect. Our navy has more than three thousand vessels in it. Imagine the work to maintain it, quite apart from building it. We devote ten percent of our revenues to the task.'

Few foreigners had seen inside the arsenale and Zaganos understood the message. He asked, 'What of our cannon?'

'Being cast in Zara,' said the bailo. 'They will be loaded onto ships, and taken to Thessaloniki where we expect them to be intercepted by pirates. How you get them to Constantinople is up to you.'

'When do they sail?'

'By the end of the year. They'll be available at Constantinople soon afterwards, as you requested.'

'And the fleet?'

'A Venetian fleet will be seen to leave for Constantinople in the spring. After the Erizzo business, the council was unanimous in going to the city's aid.' He smiled. 'As I told you they would be.'

'As you did.'

Minotto stopped. 'And I am to assume that only you and Mehmed know of our ... *other* plan? Makkim has no idea?'

'None. And when he learns of what Makkim's done, Mehmed will be thankful he was never told.'

They had arrived at some gates where arsenalotti stood guard with handguns. They were strong and bolted and had spikes at their tops. The walls either side of them were higher than any they'd seen so far.

'Open them,' said Minotto to the guards.

The bolts were slid back and the gates swung apart. They walked into a new basin with its own sheds and crane. In a dry dock to one side, held in a cradle of wood, sat a caravel.

'Not just the Portuguese now,' said Minotto. He gestured. 'Please.'

They walked over to a group of shipwrights bent over a table covered with paper. They looked up as Minotto and Zaganos approached. They were all in shirts and had their doublets piled on a single chair. One of them came up to them, buttoning his chemise as he drew closer.

'Androtti,' said the bailo, putting his hand on the man's shoulder. 'Please tell the vizier what we have here.'

The shipwright was a small man who seemed permanently windswept, though there was no hint of a breeze. His hair was tangled and his cheeks ruddy. He smelt of salt and oil. He turned to the caravel.

'Well, we've followed the Portuguese design to the letter and you can see it's almost finished. Next, we take it apart.'

Zaganos hadn't spoken since coming through the gates. Now he strode over to the caravel and put his hand on the wood. 'It's perfect.'

Minotto joined him. 'Only fifty feet long and no more than fifty tons in weight, yet it can do what no other ship has done yet.' He pointed up to the three masts. 'With its lateen sails, it can sail into the wind.'

'Down Africa and back,' said the vizier.

'We will witness the end of coastal navigation,' said Minotto. 'Up until now, no one has been able to overcome the strong winds and ocean currents of southward exploration. Now we can. Come, I have something more to show you.'

The shipwright excused himself back to his work as Minotto began to walk towards a building next to the dry dock. They came into a room bare of anything but a large map of the world. It was crudely drawn. Minotto walked up to it and pointed at its bottom where there was blue ocean beneath a landmass.

'Africa and the way to the East,' he said, tapping the blue. 'This map is a clumsy copy of Fra Mauro's true masterpiece. But it shows what it needs to show.' He gestured. 'What the Portuguese do not know.'

Zaganos looked down. 'Indeed. When do you expect to hear from Prince Henry? At some point, he'll find out that his map is a lie.'

'Ah, but that's the point, isn't it? By the time he finds out, it won't matter any more.'

CHAPTER TWENTY-TWO

EDIRNE

Makkim led the army out of Edirne with more horsetails than he'd have liked. Some belonged to the man beside him: the veteran general, Turakhan Bey, whose two sons rode behind. He was not, after all, to be the sole commander of the army that would march south to break the Hexamilion Wall and take Mistra.

It had been a week ago that Candarli Halil had confirmed to him what he already feared.

'The Sultan no longer trusts you.'

They'd been talking alone after a meeting of the *divan* during which Mehmed had not once met Makkim's eye. They'd been standing in the vizier's office, a room of thick panel, inlaid with mother-of-pearl, and thicker carpet – all sound absorbed to a whisper, which was how Candarli liked it. 'He doesn't trust you to conquer Mistra alone. Turakhan is to be released from prison to come with you.'

The news had not been so startling to Makkim. Ever since his return from Rome, he'd felt the change. Mehmed had stopped visiting him and they'd not spoken alone for weeks. He'd known the reason: his meeting with Violetta had been reported and, quite possibly, his meeting with Minotto too. What had surprised him, though, was that no explanation had been demanded.

'He is turning to Zaganos.' Candarli had looked apologetic. 'He heard from Minotto that the woman you'd talked to, this Venetian courtesan, has been arrested and is awaiting trial for spying. They mean to execute her.' He'd shaken his head. 'And he knows that you want to retire to Venice.'

So Minotto had betrayed him. They said that Venetians were the first to smell the rot of decay. Was that what was happening to him?

His mind, already numbed by rejection, had been slow to come to terms with what Mehmed's withdrawal might mean. Makkim was a pasha: he was rich and powerful but he was also a slave. His position came from the whim of one dangerous man. Displease him, and it would all disappear, as might his life. So he needed to please him again, and quickly. The task he'd been given, to subdue Mistra, offered him the chance. He would bring back a great victory.

But there was something else, too. Two months from now, someone he loved would die for a crime she was innocent of, because of him. She needed his help now as she'd always done. He had to find a way to go to Venice.

She didn't want him there – she'd made that clear. He knew the business of diplomacy, the nuance of language, and there was no mistaking her meaning: she had loved him as a brother, but only as a brother. It wasn't because she loved another but because she valued her freedom above all else. What had she said?

'I have no master, as you have Mehmed. I can do as I please.'

No longer, though. He must get to Venice. But how?

Victory first. His army was twenty thousand strong, of which half were his janissaries, marching behind their giant aga Hasan, in perfect order, to the drum and cymbal of their *mehter* band. Their high white borks, plumes dancing to the step, made them into giants. Mehmed had wanted them properly tested before laying siege to Constantinople. The Hexamilion Wall at the Isthmus of Corinth, manned by Siward's Varangians, would be just that. The best would be pitted against the best, with considerable advantage to Hasan and his janissaries. After all, they had cannon.

Behind the janissaries and sipahi cavalry came the long tail of irregulars, the akinci light cavalry and the *bashibozouks* who would be the first to storm the wall after the cannon had done their work, clearing the path. These were unpaid peasants from the steppe who fought for God and plunder alone, and they would die in their hundreds with the name of Allah on their lips.

Testing the army. That had been the main reason that Mehmed had given for sending the army south: testing the army and convincing the Despot of Mistra not to send help to his brother when the time came. The second reason had been the better one, thought Makkim as he rode. The Varangians had to be destroyed before they could provide the nucleus for Constantinople's defence. And that was what he would do, so completely that Mehmed would never doubt his loyalty again.

Mehmed watched Makkim lead the army away from Edirne from the back of a white horse, Zaganos by his side, the old men of the *ulema* and his *silahder* bodyguard behind. First vizier Candarli Halil was elsewhere.

The Sultan was dressed in gold mail with an ostrich plume

243

rising from his turbaned helmet like flame. He turned to Zaganos. 'He will not come back.'

Zaganos looked solemn. 'No, master.'

Mehmed stared out at the view. He was very still. He said, 'We must watch the janissaries. They are loyal to him, Hasan especially.'

'Which is why this plan makes sense. He will die in battle.'

It was a good strategy. Let the hero die a hero's death, in full sight of men who would mind anything less. And there was irony too: the deed would be done by handgun, the weapon Makkim had fought so hard to be included in this new army of his. Along with the *topcu acagi* artillery corps, the handgunners had been those most derided by the gazi faction, led by the old general Turukhan bey. And it would be one of Turakhan's sons who would pull the trigger.

'He was always against taking Constantinople,' said Mehmed, almost to himself. 'Always. He and Candarli were my father's men, never mine. So what was the point in him building this army?' He looked at Zaganos. 'What good are his janissaries and guns if there's to be peace?'

Zaganos leant forward to pat his horse's neck. The mehter band had passed but the bashibozouks were a wild, undisciplined rabble. 'Who is to say he was not building up the janissaries for some other purpose?' he asked. 'As you say, majesty, he has made them especially loyal to him.'

Mehmed nodded. Once it had been an absurdity, then a possibility. Now it was a certainty. Makkim had made common ground with the faction in Venice opposed to the Doge. Why else the absence in Hungary? Why else the private talks in Rome with a notorious courtesan spy? And why else his request to be ambassador to Venice?

Mehmed had begun to feel the same fear that he'd felt on ascending the throne. He'd killed his brothers then. Now he'd have to kill someone he'd loved. He'd adored Makkim and believed that Makkim had felt the same. But it had all been a lie. He'd fallen for some whore the Venetians had sent to seduce him. The humiliation of it!

Zaganos continued, 'And of course there's King Lydislaw.' He spoke quietly. 'Some say that Makkim let him escape from Varna. Imagine it: your father rides into battle with the broken treaty nailed to his standard, and his general lets the man who broke it escape!'

Mehmed had imagined a lot of late, usually in the early hours when he couldn't sleep for his anger. He turned again to Zaganos. 'Do you worry that he might know of the bigger plan?'

The vizier shook his head. 'Minotto told me that no one knows of it but the Doge, himself and some shipwrights who are locked in the arsenale. And, of course, us. Not Makkim, not the courtesan.'

Mehmed nodded. 'Good. He must never know of that.'

Zaganos nodded. 'Well, majesty, he won't if he's dead.'

Makkim marched his army hard. It was six hundred miles to Corinth and he wanted to get there in three weeks. He wanted to win a decisive battle and then decide what to do about Venice.

So surprise was key. Every day, the akinci scouts would fan out ahead on their small, fast horses, looking for anyone who might take warning to Mistra. And the army marched in silence, even the bashibozouks persuaded to restrain themselves. It gave Makkim time to think.

The Ottoman conquests had been intended to bring peace and plenty to the conquered. But there was no plenty in Thrace, and little peace. The country was bare of crop and livestock. Even the forests had been felled.

As the army marched south, it got worse. Villages grew emptier and the beggars bolder. The janissaries marched in sullen anger behind Hasan. Many of them had been born into villages like these. They may have been brought to Islam but they'd not forgotten their roots. Nor had Makkim.

Was this the dar el-salaam?

Bulgaria was different, he told himself; he'd seen it for himself. But what would happen after Constantinople, when the army marched north to its next frontier?

He considered the danger he was in. Mehmed had always had his moods but they'd passed. He knew that Zaganos would be pouring poison into the Sultan's ear, but Makkim had been loved by Mehmed, surely. And he was indispensible. Wasn't it he who'd built up this army? Wasn't it he who'd organised the road-builders, the *derbenci* police corps to man the bridges and fords and crossroads on the march? Wasn't it he who'd overhauled the commissariat and created companies for tent-pitching, bread-making, medical support and everything else? Most of all, wasn't it he who'd studied the walls of Constantinople? No one knew them better than he did. No one else had disguised himself as a merchant to study them from inside. Only he, Makkim, could tell Mehmed where to launch the assault when the time arrived.

Giovanni Giustiniani Longo rode as if the gazis were behind, not ahead of him. He wanted to reach the Hexamilion Wall before Makkim's army got there. He was dressed as a merchant of Portugal.

Since leaving Rome, he had been in Edirne, trying, somehow,

to meet with his son. He'd followed Makkim's retinue through the streets when it rode out, loitered outside whatever house he'd gone into, waited at mosques and in gardens, desperate to talk to him but knowing it had to be the right place, the right time. Such was his concentration that he'd not noticed that an army was assembling outside the city. For three days he'd wondered where his quarry had disappeared to. Then he'd heard that Makkim was halfway to Mistra.

He'd ridden day and night, keeping to the roads that Makkim had ordered repaired. As he drew near to the Ottoman army, he branched off into the countryside and slept for the first time in days. He found an empty barn with a hayloft and lay down on hard wood, using his saddle for a pillow. In the morning, he tried to buy food from the farmer. There was none.

So he was hungry as he passed the Turks, watching their dust from a distance in the clear autumn air. He reached some hills and, from their top, saw the army: janissaries in front, irregulars fanning out to the rear. It was moving fast but made no more noise than the faint tread of boot and squeak of wheel. Below him was Armageddon on the march. The world should be more afraid than it was.

He saw the akinci light cavalry racing across the fields to either side, small groups of horsemen searching for forage and spies. He needed to move on. He turned his horse and trotted down the hill to a track that seemed to be going south. For the first time, he felt relieved. He'd get to the wall well ahead of Makkim. Would he stay there? Of course, now he knew what he knew.

He felt, rather than saw, his pursuers. Something warned him that he was not alone on the track, that horsemen were somewhere behind him. Was it a sound or the slight tremble in the ground? He looked over his shoulder, trying to see what had alerted him. Nothing.

He kicked his horse into a canter. He'd not take any chances. It was still three days' ride to the isthmus and he wanted some good space between him and the army.

He heard the jingle of harness first, then a neigh. Unmistakable. He was being followed. Had they seen him on the hill? He urged his horse to go faster, leaning forward over the mane. He glanced behind him.

Akincis.

There was no doubt. There were six of them and they rode with the easy grace of men born to the steppe. He should get off the track. He pulled on the reins and veered suddenly to the left, grateful for the field's hard earth. There were trees ahead, perhaps half a mile away. He had to reach them. He looked behind.

The akincis were closer now and riding low and hard. He watched them leave the track, using their reins to whip their horses' sides as they closed the distance. He wasn't going to make it. Should he surrender? Portugal was no enemy of the Ottomans but they might think him a spy. There'd be no quarter for a spy. He kicked his horse and loosened the reins. He'd have to out-ride them. Somehow.

Now he heard them. The gazis were closing in on their prey and the shouts of the hunt were in the air. He looked over his shoulder and saw the riders spread out across the field, ready to cut him off should he try to turn. The distance between them was half what it had been. It was hopeless.

The first arrow missed him by an arm's length. A warning. Akincis didn't miss at that range. They wanted him alive. He thought hard. He had a sword and they had bows.

I don't have a chance.

He reined in his horse and turned, raising his hands in the air.

On the Hexamilion Wall, Siward was inspecting longbows. It was late afternoon and the stone was still warm to the touch. He leant against it while his lieutenant talked to him.

'We have a thousand men here,' said Barnabus. 'Seven hundred Varangians and three hundred Albanians, hand-picked by myself. Enough to stop Makkim when he comes.'

'And our weapons?' Siward asked, flexing the Spanish yew against his knee. 'Have our cannon arrived?'

'A few small ones,' said the lieutenant. 'They'll fire shrapnel into the assault but nothing bigger.'

Siward was pulling the bowstring to his chest, pointing the longbow over the wall to the north, one eye closed. It was this weapon that had felled the chivalry of France at Agincourt, able to penetrate armour at two hundred paces. It was the English secret weapon and now it was their weapon too.

But against cannon? What kind of cannon had Makkim brought with him? These days, someone built a bigger gun every month and walls were falling all over the world. Was his lieutenant's optimism misplaced?

He put down his bow and looked along the wall. It appeared strong enough. It was thick and high and had towers every three hundred paces. There was no moat to its front but the land had been cleared for some distance for fields of fire. And in the evenings, when the sun dipped below the mountains and turned the Gulf of Corinth into liquid gold, you could see how it had been made. The shades of a thousand local monuments would merge as patchwork and Siward would remember that it had been built in just forty days, plundering half of Greece for its stone. But the question remained.

Is there any point to it any more?

Makkim reached the Hexamilion Wall in the evening and watched the sun go down over the Gulf of Corinth. He'd ridden the last part of the journey in silence, thinking of what lay ahead. Violetta's trial was closer by a week and it would take at least two for the fastest galley to get to Venice, assuming, of course, that a ship could take him. He still hadn't worked out what he'd do when he got there.

To the west, the sun melted into the sea, throwing a pathway of rippled fire across the water, turning the sky to amber. He was standing amidst trees on a hill far from the wall, but he thought he could see soldiers on its ramparts and the glint of small cannon on its towers. It was impossible to tell whether they were expected or not. He turned to the man by his side.

'Turakhan, should we attack now with the last of the light, or wait until dawn?' He looked back towards where the army was hidden behind hills. 'Do we rest the men and chance that they discover us, or do we go now? I think we should go now.'

The old gazi was small and tough, beaten by every kind of weather, and he was known for his caution. 'What do we lose by waiting until dawn?' he asked, shrugging. 'If they find out we're here in the night, they'll not have time to bring reinforcements. If they already know, what difference will it make?'

Makkim nodded slowly. So many of his decisions had been made on instinct and his hunches had usually been right. But he was not sole commander here and if he was wrong this time, and they lost the battle . . . It didn't bear thinking about.

Turakhan's two sons were standing behind their father,

as they always did. One said, 'We captured a man riding fast towards Mistra a week ago. He was using tracks, so perhaps trying to avoid us. He might know something.'

Makkim turned. 'What sort of man? A messenger?'

The man shook his head. 'Portuguese. A merchant, he says.'

Makkim considered this. The Sultan was not at war with the King of Portugal and would have no reason to detain his subjects. But Makkim had made clear that surprise was to be everything. And the man might know something. 'Bring him here.'

He went back to the view, shielding his eyes from the last of the sun's rays. He could see no catapults or arrow-throwers or Greek fire siphons on the walls, even in this uncertain light. His instinct told him now was the time to rush it. But then . . .

'When we do attack,' Turakhan was saying, 'the Sultan wishes for the full janissary corps to be deployed behind the irregulars. He wants Hasan and the men properly tested.'

Makkim was still staring at the wall. The light was fading fast and it was getting cold. He pulled his cloak around him. 'As the Sultan wishes,' he said. 'They will account for themselves well, I can promise you.'

'No doubt,' said Turakhan. 'So I would suggest leaving the Serbian handgunners in reserve. They can act as your bodyguard too, under one of my sons.' He hesitated. 'Their guns won't be needed until the wall is taken.'

Makkim had been only half-listening. It all seemed to make sense. The more janissaries used for the battle, the more likely a quick victory. And he'd like to see the full corps deployed. 'Yes,' he said. 'I agree.'

There was the sound of movement behind them. He turned to see a man standing between two janissaries. He was staring at him.

'Are you Portuguese?' Makkim asked.

The man was dressed in the dark, expensive clothes of the merchant. He looked rich. Familiar somehow. 'By what right do you hold me for a week?' he asked.

Makkim found the man's gaze disconcerting. 'Perhaps none, in which case you have my apology. May we know your name?'

'My name is Giovanni Giustiniani Longo.'

'Not a Portuguese name.'

The man glanced at the dragon sword at his side. 'Which is why I haven't claimed to be Portuguese,' he said. 'I am from Genoa but live on the island of Madeira.'

Which was where King Lydislaw was said to be hiding, thought Makkim. Why would someone from Portuguese Madeira be so far from home? There must be closer places to trade.

'I trade in Malvasie wine. We are trying the grapes,' said the man, as if reading his thoughts. He looked again at Makkim's sword.

'But why the side roads? Wouldn't it be easier to travel by the main route?'

'With your army in the way? Hardly.' The man tilted his head. 'I would speak with you. Alone.'

Turakhan had been following the conversation. The old man cleared his throat. 'I don't think so,' he said.

Makkim was annoyed. 'I am in danger from one man?'

'If the man wishes to give information, we should both hear it. No?'

It was difficult to argue. 'Very well,' said Makkim. 'Shall we go inside the tent?'

But the man was shaking his head. 'It can be said here,' he said. 'I wanted to say that I am a Portuguese subject and we are not at war with your master. I demand to be released.'

Makkim looked at him with curiosity. Something wasn't right.

'I will release you at dawn tomorrow,' he said firmly, 'and certainly not before that. We'd not like you to ruin a surprise.' He pointed. 'I would suggest that you ride east and wide of my army. That way, you'll arrive at Corinth unhurt.'

CHAPTER TWENTY-THREE

HEXAMILION WALL

Giovanni fell late into sleep. He'd been given a comfortable bed in his own tent and even wine, but his mind was too full. It was filled with Makkim, with every look and gesture that he'd made, with his voice.

When he did manage to sleep, it was to dream of someone else, someone he'd hoped buried too deep to rise again. He'd spent years forcing Cleope to the very depths of his consciousness but now she was back. They were sitting on a riverbank in the vale of Sparta and it was a warm summer evening. There were dragonflies and drowsy bees in the air, and the scent of harvest in the taking. He was lying next to her and she'd guided his hand to her breast.

'No.'

'Then I shall die.'

And she had. He had done what she'd asked him to and ten years later she'd died. She had gone forever, leaving a child he'd thought dead.

He woke from the dream to the feel of a hand on his shoulder. He opened his eyes to that child sitting on his bed. There was some light in the tent, the vague, silvery light of dawn. He was looking at him curiously.

'Get up. You're leaving. Your horse is outside.'

Makkim was dressed for battle. He wore mail and held a turbaned helmet on his knee. He looked tired.

Giovanni raised himself to his elbow. He looked around the tent. They were alone.

'I must talk with you,' he whispered, taking Makkim's forearm. 'I have been trying to for weeks.'

'Then talk,' said Makkim. 'We have a few moments.'

Giovanni leant forward. 'You were taken in the devshirme from parents who were Bulgarian. Except that they weren't your parents. Am I correct?'

Makkim frowned. 'Possibly.'

'And a sword was put in your cradle when you were sent away from your birthplace, the same dragon sword you now wear at your side. Is this also correct?'

He saw Makkim feel the first prick of unease. Revelation had its place, but perhaps not on the morning of battle.

'Who were my parents?' he asked softly.

There was a sound behind them, the sound of canvas drawn aside. Makkim turned to see one of Turakhan's sons silhouetted against the pale morning light.

'My father awaits you,' said the son, glancing at Giovanni.

Makkim nodded. 'A moment,' he said.

The son didn't move. He stood there, watching them both.

Makkim rose with a sigh. He said to Giovanni, 'Ride north to the end of the wall, towards Corinth. They'll let you through the gate there.'

*

On the Hexamilion Wall, they'd known Makkim was coming for a week. Long ago, Siward had introduced a system of messaging, farm to farm, hill to hill, using sun reflected from glass. He knew how big the Turk army was and who commanded it. He'd passed the message on to Mistra and got one back from the Despot: there were no more soldiers to spare. They were on their own.

They were outnumbered twenty to one. That didn't worry him overmuch. They'd faced worse odds than that in Constantine's campaigns. He'd gathered the Varangians from the rest of the wall and he'd hidden the catapults and siphons below so that the Turks would believe they had surprise.

No, what worried him was the cannon. The latest messages had been clear: Makkim had cannon.

'Here they come.'

Barnabus was pointing across the plain to where a low dust cloud had appeared. He could hear the faint sound of music.

'What have they got?'

'Janissaries, sipahi and akinci cavalry, wild irregulars. And a band by the sound of it.'

'Are we ready?'

He heard the sound of squeaking rope. The catapults were being winched up to the ramparts and men were carrying stones up the steps. 'We will be. We've plenty of arrows and the cannon are loaded.'

'We'll use our range advantage,' said Siward. 'We'll start firing at two hundred paces. Is the ground marked?'

The lieutenant nodded and moved away to give orders. Siward looked along the wall and saw men doing what they always did while waiting for battle. Some tested their bows, some counted arrows, some sharpened swords on the stone or polished handguns. Some had their eyes closed in prayer. It was the waiting that was hardest.

'Cannon!'

Siward looked out and saw that the Ottoman army had stopped about four hundred paces to their front. Out from the restless ranks of the bashibozouks came wagons pulled by horses. They cantered forward, halted and turned. Men jumped out with firing frames, then others emerged with cannon. In another minute, the first bang had echoed across the plain and stone had crashed into stone. Siward could see the impact quite clearly. It wouldn't take long to reduce this wall.

He looked forward again to see four puffs of smoke rise into the dry air. More debris flew from the wall below him. Every strike made the ramparts tremble.

'They're aiming for the same place,' shouted Barnabus.

It was true: the dents to the wall were becoming one.

'Can't our cannon shoot back?'

Barnabus shook his head. 'Too far.'

'What about the catapults? Are they ready? Will they work at this range?'

They were ready and being loaded with stones. Men were straining at pivot-wheels to tighten the ropes. Barnabus raised his hand. He said, 'Let's see.'

His arm came down and the stones arced into the air and fell harmlessly to earth. They heard jeering from across the plain.

Siward turned to the men at the catapult. 'That's the furthest you can throw?'

It was. And suddenly Siward saw how the world had changed forever. Walls could be thick, tall, double or triple-strength. It didn't matter any more. With the right size of cannon, fired in the right way, they were simply rubble. He thought of Constantinople with the greatest walls in the world. Their survival hinged on one question: would the Turks be able to get the right cannon?

Or did they have them already?

'Get down!' A man had flung himself at Siward, bringing him to the ground. A stray shot hit the battlements, sending stone flying in every direction. Siward got to his knees and looked over the top. The Ottoman army was beginning to move. The bashibozouks were fanning out over the plain in a huge crescent shape on either side of the cannon. There were more bangs and the wall trembled again. Siward looked over it. A whole section was sagging, stones breaking away from the top and front. Above it hung a cloud of dust.

Siward stood and raised his sword. 'Here they come!' He looked to left and right along the wall. 'Remember they're untrained and poorly armed. Cut them down and save yourselves for the janissaries!'

The Varangians rose with their longbows and put arrows to their strings. Each was a clothier's-yard long and could stop anything. But the bashibozouks were closing the distance fast. Siward kept his sword raised.

'On my command.'

The Varangians watched him over their bowstrings or shoulders, their arms trembling with the strain.

The Turks passed the two-hundred-yard marker. '*Now!*'

Three hundred arrows rose into the air and fell onto the bashibozouks like black rain. Men went down in their dozens, arrows in their faces, throats, shoulders, blood splashing over their neighbours. The men behind them stumbled, some picking up weapons. They slowed for a moment, then came on.

Another rank of Varangians had stepped forward to the

parapet. They drew their bows and fired. More rain, more death, but still the wild men of the steppe came on, screaming the will of Allah. It was a massacre but no one seemed to care.

Now the cannon roared from the towers, pouring shrapnel into the front ranks. More men fell, most without limbs. Perhaps a quarter of the bashibozouks had gone down but still the remaining charged. They were less than fifty paces from the wall and they were converging on the part that had been demolished.

Siward heard trumpets behind the bashibozouks and the steady beat of drum. The mehter band had struck up again and the janissaries were on the move, stepping forward with their aga Hasan in front of them brandishing his sword. They were as disciplined and silent as the bashibozouks were wild and loud. But, like them, they would stop for nothing. They were a remorseless fighting machine every bit as feared as the Varangians, and they would kill those left on the wall once the wild men had done their work.

By now, the bashibozouks were scrambling up the rubble that made an uneven ramp to the wall. The Varangians were there to meet them, some with handguns that they aimed and discharged. Soon, blood ran between the stones where the Turks' bodies lay piled in their rags and skins, their spears and clubs broken. But the bashibozouks didn't stop; they knew the janissaries were behind them and would kill them if they broke. So they came on and on, wave after wave, and the Varangians swung and slashed and grew tired, as Makkim had planned they would. Siward fought alongside them, roaring defiance into every face that challenged him. He was tiring too.

'Siward!'

It was a voice he recognised. He glanced behind him. Giovanni was there. He shouted to his neighbour, 'Close the gap!' He disengaged and turned to his uncle.

'What in God's name are you doing here?' he said, hands on his knees. 'I thought this wasn't your fight.'

'I followed Makkim here.' Giovanni looked out towards the Turkish army. 'You've got to retreat.'

Siward was breathing hard. He shook his head. 'No. We don't retreat.'

Giovanni came round to his front. 'Then you'll die, all of you.' He placed his hands on Siward's shoulders. 'The wall is breached, Siward, and I know about walls. They're tiring you out with the wild men so that the janissaries can finish you off.' He shook him. 'They want to destroy the Varangians before you can take them to defend Constantinople, don't you see?'

Siward wiped sweat from his brow. He glanced back at the line he'd just left. It seemed to be holding. 'We have joined battle,' he said between breaths. 'If we fall back, it will be a massacre.'

'So fall back in stages,' said Giovannni. 'But do it quickly before the janissaries get here.' He glanced at the fighting to their front. 'You may need to sacrifice a few but at least you'll live to fight another day.'

'Fight where? We'll have lost the wall.'

'You lost the wall the minute cannon came over that horizon.' Giovanni gestured. 'There must be somewhere else you can hold them?'

Siward looked at his uncle for a long time. Then he nodded. 'Yes. There may be.' He turned to find his lieutenant, then ran over to him, staying behind him as he fought. He said, 'Barnabus, there is something I need to ask of you.'

*

260

A hundred and twenty Varangians lost their lives on the wall, Barnabus among them. The rearguard fought with a courage that ensured their comrades got away.

That evening, Giovanni sat with Siward in a cave twenty miles away, and their mood was sombre. They were overlooking a valley with caves dug deep into its sides, some used for ancient burial. A road ran along the valley bottom.

'You are sure they will come this way?' Giovanni asked. 'It's an obvious place for an ambush.'

The two of them were leaning against their saddles on either side of a fire. They'd been sitting in silence for some time, watching the flames make dancers on the walls. Siward was thinking about Barnabus and what he'd done. He'd miss his optimism, his faith. So would the men.

'There's no other way to go,' he said. 'It's the only route through these mountains. But they'll send out scouts before they attempt it.'

Giovanni frowned. He held a stick that he used to prod the embers. 'So how do we fool them?'

'There are tombs on the high ground,' said Siward, 'big tombs from ancient times where the Mycenae put their kings. They look like hills from the outside. We can hide in them.'

Giovanni nodded slowly. 'It might work.'

They fell silent again. They heard the murmur of men outside, sitting around fires in other caves in the valley, perhaps talking about Barnabus and the friends they'd lost. An owl hooted and was answered by another.

Siward reached over to the pile of wood and threw a log onto the fire. Sparks flew into the air and he waved them away with his hand. Giovanni saw that it had blood on it. 'Were you hurt today?' he asked.

Siward shook his head. 'No, not hurt.' He looked up from the fire. 'You were right. If we'd engaged with the janissaries, I doubt we'd have got away. Especially with Makkim there.' He looked down at his hands. 'We owe you our lives. Thank you.'

Except that Makkim hadn't been there until the last moment, thought Giovanni. After the order had been given, Giovanni had stayed with Siward to ensure that the disengagement happened before the janissaries joined battle. He'd stayed long enough to see Makkim leave his bodyguard and run up behind the janissaries to urge more speed. Makkim had seen what the Varangians were going to do.

'Did you tell him?' asked Siward.

'Who he is? No, we were disturbed.' He prodded the fire. 'Perhaps it's better to capture him first.'

'How do you think he'll react?'

Giovanni had considered this question again and again. He had no idea of the answer because he didn't know his son. 'It depends on so many things,' he said.

'Like what?'

'Like how much of his inherited nature still exists after all that janissary training. Like how much Mehmed still favours him.' He added, 'You'll have seen that there were two generals in that army today. Strange.'

Siward had noticed it too. 'Perhaps he is slipping from favour,' he said. 'But why?'

Giovanni thought he knew why. He still remembered Makkim's meeting with Violetta at the ball, in full view of everyone. He also remembered how Siward had taken it.

'Violetta Cavarse had an effect on him – you saw that.'

Siward frowned. 'Which means that he might be more attracted to the idea of taking his fortune and settling in the west?' A thought came to him: had Giovanni *arranged* Violetta's seduction of Makkim? He dismissed it. 'Well, you want him for a son and I don't want him at Constantinople. So we should work out how we're going to capture him.'

Giovanni leant back against the saddle. 'Do you have a plan?'

Siward looked up. 'Yes. I do.'

CHAPTER TWENTY-FOUR

PELOPONNESE

Makkim, it seemed, was in a hurry. Ottoman armies always marched at dawn and stopped to camp at midday, or had until now. Makkim had reached the wall as quickly as he had by marching all day. Now he was marching at night.

Admittedly, it felt like day. Siward sat in his tree and watched the moon through a cobweb of branches. It was full and sharp and every feature of its surface seemed close enough to pinch. A giant eye was watching him, sometimes wiped by scudding clouds.

The night was warm for the end of the year and Siward was using his cloak for a cushion. He would put it on when the Turks arrived, which was sometime soon, he hoped. They'd had the message that Makkim was on the march flashed to them at sunset, and that was four hours ago.

All five hundred and eighty of the Varangians were entombed in three separate vaults in the field next to the wood where Siward was hiding. From a distance, the chamber tombs looked like grassy mounds and would be treated as such by anyone unacquainted with Mycenaean burials.

The plan was simple: wait until the akinci scouting party had come and gone, then come out and move back into the caves. Siward couldn't see the valley bottom from his tree. He could see its closest edge and half of the opposite slope, sandstone glowing in the moonlight, the black holes of the caves. He thought about the speed of this Turkish army. Why was Makkim in such a hurry?

He closed his eyes and saw Violetta talking to Makkim on the window seat, saw his look and hers. Why was that so preposterous? He was Giovanni's son and Luke's grandson. Of course she'd be attracted to him. But was Makkim to her?

Assuming he was, he wondered if it would be enough to extract him from the Sultan's service. Possibly, given the fortune that went with it. He thought of what he knew about janissaries. They were only allowed to marry when they retired. So was that the plan? He would take over the trading company, then retire to Venice to be with Violetta. But how easy would that be? He was, after all, the Sultan's slave, for all his rank.

He heard a sound from the valley and sat up, straining to hear. He could see shadows moving along its side, going from cave to cave. He heard the fall of hoof and looked down the path that ran along the valley edge. There were six shapes on it, riding slowly and quietly, looking from side to side. They were approaching the wood.

Siward reached down and slowly wrapped his cloak around him, sinking back into the shadows of the tree. He'd be invisible from the ground. He could hear whispered conversation as the men approached, the clink of harness. He kept very still.

The riders came into the wood and rode between the trees, prodding bushes with their spears. Occasionally they looked up, shielding their eyes from the moon. An owl hooted and they laughed.

Then they moved on, one of them riding over to the valley's edge to signal to the men searching below. All clear.

When they'd left, Siward remained in place for a long while. Then, very carefully, he began to climb down from the tree. At the bottom, he listened for some time before walking over to the valley's edge, where he dropped onto his stomach. After a long look, he turned, brought his hand to his mouth and whistled.

Soon there were shadows moving across the field towards him, giant shadows stooped low. Some were carrying something long between them: cannon. They climbed down the valley's side and went back into the caves, some crossing to the other side to do the same. It was just in time. There was the sound of hooves approaching. The riders were coming back.

But they didn't stop. They rode along the track, fast and silent, their little horn bows shining under the moon. Siward was crouched below the valley's edge and felt them pass within inches of him. He held his breath until they'd gone. Then he crept down to join Giovanni in his cave, where a man with a bow knelt by his side.

'Are you Fergal?' he asked, squatting down beside the archer. Even in the half-light of the cave he could see that the man was powerful. Barnabus had recommended him, Barnabus who'd given his life so that they could live on. He pushed aside the guilt. 'You're our best shot?'

The man nodded. 'So I'm told.'

'Good. Then I have a target for you. One you mustn't miss.'

Makkim had halted the army at the entrance to the valley. He was in a hurry, but it would be madness to go further without hearing from the scouts. He was standing next to Turakhan bey and in front of his two sons, as always these days. Behind him stood the silent ranks of the janissaries.

The two generals hadn't spoken much on the march, which had given Makkim time to consider his predicament. He had wondered if he was in danger, now he was certain.

At first, Mehmed's wish for the janissaries to be tested on their own had seemed sensible, but the attack on the wall had made him see things differently. He had sent in the bashibozouks, then the janissaries, but when he'd tried to follow them, Turakhan had taken his arm.

'No. The Sultan wishes you to observe, not join.'

'Why?' He'd frowned. 'I'll be safe enough behind them.'

'Because they must be led by Hasan, not you. You are their general, he is their aga. You must not risk your life.' He gestured behind him. 'If you insist on going forward, then take the hand-gunners for your protection. My son will go too.'

So Makkim had gone forward flanked by six Serbian handgunners and Turakhan's son. He'd watched the wave of bashibozouks crash against the Varangian rock and fall back, then crash again. He'd watched the Varangians tiring. He'd judged it well. The janissaries would hit them when they were too exhausted to lift their weapons.

But then he'd heard a trumpet blast and things had begun to happen that shouldn't happen. The Varangians were disengaging. Men were falling back from the line, the gaps closing fast behind them. They were getting away.

Makkim had tried to run forward but found his arm held.

'No, sir.'

It had been Turakhan's son. His other hand was holding a handgun. The Serbs had stopped and were all looking at him, their own guns levelled.

'What is this?' he'd said, staring at the young man. 'Who do you think you are?' He'd looked around him. 'Are you threatening me?'

He'd shaken himself free and pushed his way through and run to join his janissaries. It was too late. The Varangians were escaping.

Now he was staying with his men. He'd simply ridden to their front and remained there, riding ahead of Hasan, willing Turakhan or his sons to remove him. They'd not tried to.

He had to escape this army somehow.

The scouts were approaching at the gallop. They halted and gave their report. The valley was clear – they could advance.

Further down the road, Siward was waiting with his archer. He'd given Giovanni his orders an hour ago and watched him disappear to the cave furthest up the valley. His uncle's task was vital. As soon as the ambush was sprung, he and nine others were to run down to the wagons and spike the Turks' cannon. Siward had concluded that without their cannon and commander, the Turks would go home.

The more difficult task was to capture Makkim, and that very much depended on the skill of the man beside him.

An owl hooted once, twice. The Turks were on their way. Another hoot. Makkim was at their head. Siward put his hand on the archer's shoulder. 'He's coming.' He watched the man move to the front of the cave and lay six arrows carefully on the ground, licking his fingers to smooth their flights, each in turn. Siward turned to the other men. 'Are you ready?'

He went to kneel next to the bowman at the front of the cave. He looked down the road, twisting its way like silver thread down the valley. He could see shapes on it and hear the tread of men on the march. He lay down to wait, watching the shapes grow bigger. As the column drew near, Siward saw Makkim's giant shadow climb the whole side of the valley and beyond. With relief, he saw that there was distance between him and Hasan and the men behind. He tapped the bowman on the shoulder. He turned and nodded to the others. Any moment now.

The cave was only thirty paces from the road, but that distance was everything. Siward waited until Makkim had passed and the first of the janissaries was level with them.

'Now!' he hissed.

The horse screamed as it went down, the arrow through its gaskin. Makkim threw himself clear, landing on his back. He got up, drawing his sword, then fell to his knees, a second arrow in his thigh.

Hasan and the janissaries didn't see what had happened because they themselves were under attack. A hundred arrows drove into their ranks like hail. They reeled back, some kneeling to find cover. They didn't notice the men running towards their general.

Siward reached Makkim first. He found him lying on his side with his hand round the arrow shaft. He knelt. 'Don't pull it. We'll get it out.'

Makkim lifted his dragon sword, pointing it at Siward. 'Try.'

Siward stared at the sword. He'd dreamt for so long of seeing it again, but not like this. He looked up. 'How will you stop me?' he asked. 'You can't move and your men can't either.' He nodded to the Varangians, who surrounded Makkim with arrows pointed at his heart. 'Don't be a fool.'

Makkim looked around him. He seemed to think for a moment. Then he offered his sword. 'I am your prisoner,' he said.

He let his arms be pinned to his sides as he was lifted and carried up the valley. He turned his head to Hasan and his janissaries below, cowering before the rain of arrows. Turakhan's sons were running through their ranks.

Siward stayed and lifted the sword and stared into the dragon's eyes. They were redder than he'd remembered them: the colour of rubies, of blood. *At last.*

He walked up to the cave where Fergal was giving Makkim something to drink and something to chew on and warning him that pain was on its way. 'I put it in, I'll pull it out. Hold tight.'

Siward watched it all. He saw Makkim grit his teeth as the arrow was pulled out. He saw the bandage applied and Makkim shifted onto a stretcher and hauled further up the valley side. He saw Hasan and the janissaries in full retreat below. They'd lost their general and too many men, and their cannon had been rendered useless. It was as he'd hoped: they were on their way home to Edirne.

He reached the top, where Giovanni and a horse were waiting. He saw Giovanni go up to the stretcher and lean down to the man in it. He heard what was said.

'You, Makkim, are my son.'

CHAPTER TWENTY-FIVE

VENICE

It was as if the lagoon had been turned upside down. For three consecutive weeks it had rained, and each island turned into its own ark, campanile for mast. Venice became a place of recluse as melancholy spread its dark wings and took back the city for its own. Only the churches were full.

Violetta hadn't seen the inside of a church for over two months. She knew that because she marked the passage of time on her bedroom wall. She was counting the days to her trial and execution for being the Sultan's spy. It didn't occur to her that there'd be any other outcome. Where she'd once been afraid, now she was impatient.

She spent every day in her bedroom, and most of them in bed – at first for warmth, then because she was too weak to rise. She'd not eaten in days. She had a mirror tucked beneath her pillow that she brought out for horror. In its reflection she saw wild hair above a ravaged face of pallid skin and shadowed eyes. She saw a woman dying of starvation.

She saw no one else. Not Nikolas, Loredan . . . even Minotto. The guards had insulted, then robbed her; now they ignored her. The people who passed in the street sometimes stopped to spit on her windows or scrawl the many words for whore and traitor on her walls.

Her mood changed daily, from despair to defiance to all the feelings between. On good days, she felt her life had been better than most women's. She'd not suffered childbirth or violence; she'd been nobody's slave. Until now, she'd not felt the joy of love, but then she'd not felt the pain of loss. She'd found a version of happiness in the space between extremes. Only now did that version seem wanting.

The torture of the mirror was nothing to the torture of regret. It hollowed her out like a lightning-struck tree. She thought of every moment when she might have said something – anything – that would have told him that she considered him more than a friend.

'It doesn't matter what I think. You'll go anyway.'

She'd said it, but why hadn't she had the courage, at least, to test it? Had the priest so deadened her feelings that they were beyond repair? Might they have woken to Siward's miracle, if he'd only been allowed to perform it? When she thought like this, she screwed her eyes shut and rocked from side to side, her head lost in the pillow. She'd cry through her eyes and nose and, for once, not smell her own filth.

But then her mood would change suddenly. She'd drag herself out of despair to find hope somewhere. She'd sit up and dry her eyes. She'd tell herself that however deranged Doge Foscari was, due process of law must be carried out and she was innocent of the charge. She'd not plotted against Venice, only the workings of its leader.

And what of her friends? She'd not heard from them but then they didn't know she was there. Were they working for her release? Zoe could certainly help. Everyone owed her money, even the Doge.

At least she knew Siward was still alive. Her last ducat had bought news from one of her guards. Makkim had been defeated and was Siward's prisoner. They were both alive and they were together.

She slept little and, when she did, she woke to the slightest sound. So the knock on her bedroom door early one evening was like gunshot. She answered immediately. 'Come in.'

It was a man from the Doge's palace, all tabard and lions. He looked concerned. 'You are to present yourself to the Council of Ten. Can you walk?'

She sat up. 'Now?'

The hour first seemed strange, then it didn't. As she was rowed out into the lagoon, a setting sun blinding her, she thought she understood. If you want to do something wrong, then do it at night. She looked over at the channel that led to the arsenale.

Like building ships for the Turk.

She came to the Doge's palace by sea gate. The evening was still and the flames of the torches unaltered by wind. They were held by cloaked men who didn't speak as she came alongside but took her bony elbow and helped her onto the landing. They led her up steps into a passage that smelt of rot and along to more steps. She climbed them and was shown into a panelled room with sconced candles that left most of it in shadow. The men left and she heard the murmur of voices through the wall. She found herself frightened for the first time.

She was also hungry. There was a bowl of apples on a table that she supposed were there for eating. She was biting into her third when a door she'd not seen opened and Loredan stepped into the room. He stared at her, too shocked to speak.

'Don't come near me,' she said through apple, her hand raised. 'I haven't bathed in weeks.'

Loredan looked her up and down. 'I had no idea . . .'

She swallowed the apple. She felt faint and put her hand to the table. 'You didn't know where I was, I know. I heard the guards turn you away.' She straightened. 'Well, I'm here tonight, a little thinner than you've known me, but alive. Am I now to die?'

Loredan continued to stare at her. Disgust was the prominent feature in his face, but for whom? 'You're to be tried, Violetta.'

'I'm to be killed,' she said flatly. 'This Doge won't have it any other way. You know that.'

'Can you prove that you've not consorted with the Turk?'

'It wouldn't matter if I could. It's not for that that I'm here.'

She was wondering what more she should say when the door in the panel opened again and another man came in. 'They're ready.' He turned and walked out.

Loredan still stared at her. 'There is hope,' he said softly. 'Just be careful what you say. Curb your wit.'

She walked past him into a much bigger room. It was a confusing mix of the real and unreal. Lit by tall candlesticks, the walls were full of divine intervention: God, in all His versions, answering the calls of past Doges who knelt before Venice, sometimes with a lion. At one end, twelve real men with beards, dressed in purple, sat in individual stalls, all perfectly still. Above them, the Trinity looked down. It might have been another picture.

Loredan walked over to the empty stall and sat. Violetta went to the centre of the room. There was no chair. She wondered if she'd manage to stay upright for very long. Thank God for the apples. She saw movement to her side and turned her head. Minotto had stepped out of a picture.

A man in front of her said something. It was the Doge and he spoke without moving his head, as if justice was a formality. 'You are the courtesan Violetta Cavarse, of this city of Venice,' he said, staring at her without apparent interest. 'You are charged with spying for the Turk, who is our enemy. The bailo Minotto will summarise the charges.'

Minotto was dressed in black, which was why she'd not seen him when she came in. Now, he stood next to a candlestick, leaning into its light to read his notes. He looked up. 'It is reported that you had two meetings with Makkim Pasha in Rome, one in full public view during the celebrations to honour the new Emperor and Empress, then one, three days later, in the garden of the Colonna Palace which I myself witnessed. In both meetings, it was clear that you knew the man well.'

The Doge asked, 'What was the nature of these meetings?'

Violetta had expected this question. She'd concluded that telling the truth about her and Makkim wouldn't save her and might endanger him, so better to lie. 'I am a courtesan,' she said. 'My profession obliges me to meet men from all over the world. I saw no reason to make an exception in Rome. Are we at war with the Turk?'

It was the right question. Despite Erizzo's impalement and the decision to send a fleet to Constantinople, there'd been no formal declaration of war between Venice and the Ottoman Empire. The Doge said, 'The Turk is preparing to besiege Constantinople, which is our ally. He sank our galley in the Bosporos and executed its crew. These are not the actions of a friend.'

'But I know of no edict banning us from talking to them. We

see men in turbans all over Venice.' Violetta studied the men in front of her. Some of them had shared her bed and the rest had enjoyed her wit and beauty outside it. Beneath their reserve, she could see deep shock at what she'd become: shock and unease. Good. If her appearance forced them to consider how cruel their republic had become, then good. But would they dare oppose their Doge? Probably not.

Minotto was speaking, addressing the council. 'Your eminences will want to understand how this courtesan's actions have betrayed our city. It is our estimation that, during the month he stayed at the courtesan's house, the Greek Magoris told her of the dispositions at the Hexamilion Wall, which he commanded. These she passed on to Makkim. The result has been the recent attack, and breach of the wall, thus putting our ports of Modon, Coron and Nauplion in direct danger.'

What he said was plausible, she saw that, particularly given the fear and suspicion that now gripped this city. In such a climate, people would believe what they wanted to believe, leaving logic at the door and insults scrawled on the walls. In the soft light of the candles she could see some men nodding. After all, she was a courtesan and a known spy. And she wasn't even Venetian.

But one of them had risen. Loredan.

'Is the lady to be allowed a proper defence?' he asked.

The Doge turned to him. His mitre threw a long shadow across the ecstasy behind, almost smothering it. 'Do you wish to speak on her behalf?'

Loredan shook his head. He looked composed. 'No, because I have nothing to offer on the subject. But there is a man outside who can. I have asked him to attend. May he be summoned?'

For the first time, Foscari showed some feeling. It was anger and it was fleeting. He stared at Loredan from beneath a pulpit of heavy eyebrows, then nodded. 'Of course. Call him.'

Loredan left his stall and walked past Violetta. He opened the door behind her and she felt a draught. She was dizzy for a moment and closed her eyes, swaying. She remembered that she was wearing little more than her night-clothes. Then she heard footsteps. She opened her eyes to a man standing beside her whom she knew.

'Nikolas.'

He smiled and took off his cloak. He put it around her shoulders and drew her into him, hugging her. She felt relief rise within her like a tide, washing tears up into her eyes that she fought to hold back.

Loredan walked back to his seat and turned to the Doge. 'May we hear what this man has to say?'

The Doge could only acquiesce. Nikolas turned, his arm still around Violetta, supporting her in her weakness. He looked along the line of men in front of him. Some shifted in their seats, some inspected their shoes. He knew them all.

'The charge against this woman rests on her relationship with two men. You are asked to believe that she used her courtesan charms to elicit information from an ally, which she passed on to an enemy. But what if Makkim wasn't that? What if he was, in fact, her *brother*?'

The room fell quiet. All fidgeting stopped and Violetta became rigid. This was not how she'd planned it. She looked up, but Nikolas was already speaking again.

'There is a woman in Bulgaria who will tell you that she is Violetta Cavarse's mother, and that she acted as mother to Makkim from the time she brought him to her village as a child, to when he was taken away as the Sultan's slave.' Nikolas produced papers from a pocket that he lifted for the room to see. 'I have here the parish records of the village where Makkim grew up with his sister,' he looked down at Violetta, 'who became the Violetta Cavarse you see before you tonight.'

Minotto walked forward, snatched the papers from Nikolas's hand and took them over to the Doge. There was silence while he read them. He looked up. 'I am not sure why this information changes anything,' he said. 'If they had known each other so well, all the more reason to exchange information.'

'It may be,' Nikolas continued, 'that your grace believes the lady to know certain . . . state secrets valuable to our enemies.' He was choosing his words with care. 'It may also be that you have been misinformed in this matter,' he glanced at Minotto, 'and that she has no such information.'

Foscari was frowning, his lips working beneath his beard. He joined his hands in his lap, tapping together fingers corded by rings.

'I am not persuaded,' he said at last. 'Venice is under threat and our most famous courtesan consorts with the enemy general. She can be tried as traitor or witch – I don't mind. She is culpable and should die.'

Violetta clutched Nikolas's arm. She wanted to be strong, defiant, but she felt weak. This was finally the end of it all. She wanted it to be over soon.

But there was discomfort in the room. The men of the council looked at each other, then at their Doge. This was not how it was supposed to happen. Loredan rose again.

'Can we at least see if Ser Nikolas, who we all know to be an honourable man, has any further defence?'

Foscari's frown grew. This hearing should be over by now. She was a courtesan, for God's sake. Her life was not worth this much discussion. And he was *Doge*. He composed himself. 'If you insist.' He turned to Nikolas, 'Have you?'

Nikolas had. He held Violetta hard to him. He said, 'I call the banker Zoe Mamonas.'

There was general murmur. In a city of recluse, Zoe was its greatest exponent. None of the council had seen her in years. Some wondered if she was still alive. But Nikolas had left Violetta and gone to a door that led to another waiting room. He opened it and disappeared into darkness. There was silence, then the squeak of wheels.

A wheelchair appeared, Nikolas pushing it. In the tentative light of the candles, Violetta saw that Zoe wore black from head to toe, including veil, so that she was almost invisible. She looked even smaller than when she'd seen her last.

Violetta watched Nikolas push Zoe next to her. She looked down and saw a tiny gloved hand appear from beneath the folds of black cloth. She took it and felt a squeeze.

The Doge stared at Zoe. For the first time, he looked uncertain. He said, 'You have something to say to us. Please do so.'

Zoe spoke from behind the veil. 'Foscari, you know this woman is innocent. What you think she knows, she doesn't. You have abused this city's laws for long enough. This time, see sense.'

It was all said with the minimum of words in a tired voice. Foscari glared at her. 'How are we to know that you are Zoe Mamonas?'

'You know, Francesco,' she replied carefully. 'If you want me to show you my face, I will. But you won't enjoy it.'

Loredan dared to ask the question everyone else wanted to. 'What do we think Violetta Cavarse knows?'

Zoe waited for Foscari to answer. When he didn't, she said,

'That is something you must ask your Doge. Meanwhile, I can tell you this: yes, Violetta has spied. Yes, she is good at it. But she has only ever done it for Venice.'

Zoe moved her head slowly along the line of men seated to her front. 'So the question is this: how has our city managed to inspire such loyalty in this intelligent peasant girl from Bulgaria? How in me? How in you? Because we are all refugees, whether we flee from barbarians, priests or tyrants, whether today, yesterday or a thousand years ago. Because we find in Venice a home we cannot find anywhere else. Because we find freedom here and, for all the city's sins, some fairness in a world without it.'

There was silence as the men absorbed her words. They knew them to be quiet slivers of truth in a room still shadowed with lies.

'Until now,' she continued. 'What you are doing you know to be unfair. And St Mark is the patron saint of lawyers. Now there is irony.'

Violetta felt her hand squeezed again. She was feeling fainter. There was a sharp pain in her empty stomach, perhaps the apples. She tried to focus on the men to her front.

The Doge was leaning forward. 'All very pretty,' he said, 'but still unconvincing. Have you more to offer?'

Zoe let go of Violetta's hand. She placed hers on the arms of her wheelchair and slowly rose. There was the sound of silk rustling on silk. Then she stood and lifted her veil. Violetta saw Foscari's eyes widen.

'I have this,' she said, standing quite still. 'If this woman is executed, then I will move my bank to Florence. Every loan I have made to this republic will be recalled. Every creditor – whatsoever his rank – will be required to repay his debt within a week. I will assume that Venice no longer wishes to be my home.' She moved her head slowly along the line of men watching her in silence. She came back to Foscari. 'That is what I offer.'

Violetta heard the words but not how they were answered. The faintness that had afflicted her throughout suddenly rose in her like boiled milk. She felt drumming in her temples and saw lights dance before her eyes. Then she fell.

CHAPTER TWENTY-SIX

MISTRA

For Makkim, the ride was a mix of agony and dream. It was a hundred miles to Mistra and the wagon could cover no more than twenty in a day. They packed it full of straw and fur and made a cover against the rain, but the winds from the north gained entry at every join. Giovanni sat with his son throughout, shielding him as best he could.

The first day, they talked. There was a lifetime to discover and neither of them knew where to begin. So they decided to work backwards, starting with the battle that had just been. But one question rose above all others.

'How did you know?'

'The sword,' said Giovanni, rocking to the motion of the wagon. He was leaning against its side, still staring at the miracle of his son. 'Your grandfather put it in your cradle when you went away with the wet-nurse. He wanted it to lead us to you. It did.'

The sword was lying next to him. Giovanni picked it up and looked into the dragon's eyes. 'It is the Varangian sword,' he murmured.

'It was,' said Makkim. 'But it has been used against Varangians now, and it will be again, if I can find a way.'

Giovanni smiled. 'Can we forget who we are for this journey? Can we just get to know each other, father and son?'

So they did. But as they talked, Makkim's pain increased. Something was wrong with the wound in his leg, something that made every jolt an earthquake. He began to lose his thread, then his consciousness. At last, he lapsed into coma, sweating and mumbling and jerking his head from side to side. Giovanni held his hand throughout.

The fever set in and Giovanni urged the wagon driver to more speed, despite the winter ruts. The wind whined outside and the rain drummed on the canvas and Giovanni did his best to soothe his son, who was talking of nothing sensible. He needed medicine.

At last they came to Mistra and Makkim was put onto a stretcher and gently carried to the Peribletos Monastery where the monks knew about healing. They brought herbs from their garden: sage and garlic for antiseptic, ginger for sickness, thyme for his lungs and fennel for sour breath. And Giovanni sat beside him every moment, cooling him with water, massaging his limbs, loving him for the helpless child he'd never known.

It took a month, but, slowly, Makkim recovered. The wound lost its infection, the lungs their water, and Giovanni saw the fever loosen its grip, then slink away to find a less stubborn victim.

One morning Makkim awoke. 'Venice,' he said, gripping his father's arm.

By now Giovanni knew why his son might want to talk about Venice; he'd heard much in his fever. He patted his hand. 'She is free,' he said gently. 'She is coming here.'

Makkim slumped back on his pillows and closed his eyes, letting out a long sigh. Giovanni watched relief creep over him like a cat, to curl up and sleep. Sleep without dream.

Bit by bit, they took up their conversation where they'd left off. Except that now Giovanni did most of the talking. He started from the beginning, describing his first meeting with Cleope in Florence, their elopement to Mistra, and then his final, unspoken arrangement with the Despot when a marriage was decreed for the cause of Church union.

'Have you heard of Platonic love?' he asked one day, pouring water for his son. 'Plethon told me about it. It's where you love each other in the mind only.' He handed the water to Makkim who was propped up in bed. 'Your existence is proof that it doesn't work.'

Makkim smiled.

'We managed abstinence for two years. Then there was an evening in the valley when we were alone . . . well, you won't want the details. Cleope hid the bump as best she could, but when it was obvious to everyone . . .' Giovanni shrugged. 'Your grandfather did what was right. He had to banish me.' He walked to the window and looked out. 'I had broken the agreement.'

'But you blamed him.'

'For not letting Cleope come with me into exile, yes. But how could he? She was married to the Despot.' He leant on the sill. 'I regret many things in my life, Makkim,' he continued quietly, 'but none more than my estrangement from my father.' He turned. 'Perhaps that is why I have been so desperate to find you.'

'To kidnap me,' corrected his son. 'So what happens now?'

Giovanni came and sat down on the bed. He worried it was too soon to tell him, but to delay further was to risk Makkim

284

finding out from the wrong person. 'There is something you must know,' he said. 'Your grandfather left a will that divides his fortune between his two grandsons: you and Siward Magoris. You are to get the more valuable part: the trading company that owns businesses all over the world. You'll also get my estates on Madeira and Chios when I die, a considerable fortune. You will be one of the richest men in Europe.'

Makkim stared at him for a long time. He seemed neither pleased nor displeased by the news.

'You've not told me of Siward Magoris,' he said eventually, lowering his eyes, 'beyond the fact that he is son of your legitimate half-brother Hilarion. What sort of a man is he?'

Giovanni considered this. What did he know of his nephew? Not much. 'He is a good man,' he said carefully. 'He is a soldier and now a banker as well, a skilled one.' He tilted his head to study his son. 'He looks like you: shorter, without the scar.'

'But he can't be happy with what's happened.'

'The banking side was in trouble, but now he's mended it. Is he happy? I don't know. There's some anger there, certainly.'

Makkim nodded slowly. 'Anger about me, I don't doubt.' He looked away. 'I suppose I can do what I wish with the trading company? Including turning it all into gold?'

Giovanni frowned. 'It's yours. But why would you do that?'

Makkim looked up, surprised. 'I am a Muslim,' he said, 'a slave. What I have belongs to God or my sultan.'

Now Giovanni stared at him. He'd thought from all their conversations that there was some place where their minds might have met, but Makkim's education seemed to have taken him somewhere very strange. 'Didn't Mehmed try to have you killed?'

'As was his right, if he thought me disloyal.'

285

'But you must question the whole *system* now, don't you? How can you feel any loyalty to it?'

'My loyalty is to the Koran. Mehmed is just a man.'

Giovanni became exasperated. 'Mehmed is a tyrant, not so different from Tamerlane or Genghis Khan. He uses the Koran to enslave the world.'

Makkim shook his head. 'And your priests don't use the Bible to enslave?' He hadn't told his father about the one he'd nearly killed. 'At least our *system* allows men to rise by merit.'

Giovanni said nothing. His son had all the stubbornness of the Magoris dynasty. It would take time to draw him away from the clutches of Islam. He'd try another way.

'Your mother,' he said. 'We should visit her grave.'

Three days later, they went together to see Cleope's grave at the Church of Holy Wisdom above the Despot's palace. The day was cold, and Giovanni wrapped his son in the pelts of a dozen animals before they set forth.

They walked up in silence, hunched in their furs, Makkim pausing every few steps to rest. As they passed the palace, Makkim stopped to look for the place where he'd been born, while Giovanni went on. There were countless windows overlooking the square. Which was the room?

He sat and rubbed his leg. People passed him carrying things. A woman stopped to offer him water. There was comfort, familiarity, in it all.

He thought of what his father had said of Mehmed's monstrous deceit. He was right: Mehmed must have told Turakhan to kill him because he no longer trusted him. He closed his eyes and put his fingers to his temples.

He'd have died if he'd stayed, as Mehmed's brothers had

died and Candarli Halil would one day. Despair wrapped him in another cloak. He looked up.

Which window?

'Makkim!'

Giovanni was calling. He got to his feet and joined him. Together, they walked up to the church, his hand on his father's shoulder. They found Cleope's grave in a side chapel, her husband's beside it. Giovanni lit a candle and they stood in silence, reading Plethon's elegant eulogy etched into the marble. Makkim looked across at his father and saw his chin buried in his chest.

He put his arm around his father's shoulders. 'Well, we found each other,' he said softly. 'She'd have been pleased at that.'

Giovanni nodded slowly.

Makkim glanced at him. 'You must have been lonely on Madeira, living on your own.'

Giovanni looked at him. 'I thought a lot,' he said. 'About you, mostly. I wondered what you'd have been like had you lived, how I'd have taught you.' He smiled. 'I didn't imagine someone else would do it so thoroughly.'

Not long afterwards, Siward was on the quayside at Monemvasia watching a Venetian galley ship its oars. It was on its way to Constantinople and had valuable cargo in its hold: the cannon for its defence.

But Siward was more interested in the ship's human cargo.

'Disappeared?' He'd just embraced Nikolas on the jetty and was standing apart, staring at him. He felt stricken, bereft.

'Completely,' said Nikolas. 'It happened at Ragusa.'

He mastered himself, brushing dust from his shoulders. 'Do you know where she's gone?'

Nikolas was shaking his head. 'I delayed our departure for several days looking for her. Then I discovered she'd taken another ship.'

'Where to?'

'Nowhere good, I'm afraid. Constantinople.'

'Constantinople? Why in God's name would she go there?'

Nikolas put a hand on his shoulder. 'Forget her, Siward,' he said gently, patting. 'You've got to. There are other things to think about now.'

So they'd ridden on to Mistra, muffled against a cold wind from the north, passing through a landscape reduced by winter. The trees were skeletal, the vines cut back to the trunk, the rivers low and sluggish. The animals they saw were thin things, the birds few. Even the smoke rising from hearths was spare and mean.

Siward was mainly silent. Nikolas had recommended that he forget Violetta, but that was impossible. He'd heard about her trial and its revelation that she was Makkim's sister and found himself, at first, overjoyed by the news. But then the joy had turned to confusion. Of course they'd never been brother and sister. So what had they been? What were they now?

'The bank staff think you should be canonised,' Nikolas was saying through fur. 'St Siward, Patron Saint of Bankers. You can take over from St Matthew.'

Siward came back to the present. 'Things are going well?'

'The money pours in, even from misty England. What did you do?'

A bit, he thought, but perhaps not as much as others. Isabella of Burgundy, Zoe, Giovanni had all helped him. And Violetta, of course, though never claiming to. Had that always been her way? *Why Constantinople?* 'So you can retire at last. I'm glad. Who is to run things?'

'Someone you met at the Medici bank in Germany,' said Nikolas. 'A Levantino has jumped ship. You clearly impressed him.' The old man lifted his hood over his head as the first snowflakes drifted towards them on the wind. 'How are things in Constantinople, do you know?'

'It's still open to the south. Mehmed's fleet is gathering at Thessaloniki, so the blockade will begin in the spring.' He looked at Nikolas. 'Will Venice actually send a fleet?'

The old man shrugged. 'The council has voted unanimously to do so.' He leant forward to flick snow from the horse's mane. 'Perhaps we were wrong about this Doge.' He patted the animal. 'Will you go to Constantinople?'

Siward nodded. 'After Christmas, with my Varangians.'

'So you can get Violetta out, if she's there.' He paused. 'How is Makkim?'

Siward looked away. 'Recovering at the Peribletos Monastery. The arrow went deeper than I'd planned. Giovanni is with him.'

Nikolas stayed silent awhile, his eyes straight ahead. At last he said, 'You know they grew up together as brother and sister, don't you?'

'Yes, I know,' he said.

Nikolas watched him for a while, frowning. 'What do you think he'll do with his fortune?'

He shrugged. 'I have no idea. We don't need it, anyway.'

They rode on without speaking and when the snow stopped, made faster progress. They arrived in Mistra in the evening to the lights of a thousand hearths climbing the hill like glow-worms. The faintest were at the top: the citadel. Nikolas stopped his horse outside the gate.

'It's good to be back,' he said, looking up at the city. 'I've missed it.'

Siward saw the old man dab a finger to each eye. He waited, then kicked his horse. 'We'll go to the monastery first. Giovanni has been impatient to see you.'

Leaving their horses at the stables, they walked up through the narrow streets, Nikolas stopping every ten paces to stare. Even in the poor evening light, it was clear that the city had changed much in the time he'd been absent, filling the space between its walls with new palaces and churches as the rich had fled Constantinople to find safety there.

They arrived late at the monastery. They found Giovanni and Makkim seated around a fire in the bedroom reserved for visitors with money. It smelt of herbs.

Giovanni rose when he saw them. 'Nikolas.'

The embrace was tight and long and Siward watched it. They held each other hard, rocking in the clasp, neither wanting to part. At last they did.

Giovanni turned. 'This is my son.'

Makkim had risen too. He was dressed in a long silk day-gown that had once been his grandfather's. He came over to Nikolas. 'I've heard much about you.'

Nikolas took his hands. 'And I you. Are you mended?'

Makkim patted his thigh. 'The leg is healing. I took a fever, but I'm better.'

'Which is how I've managed to keep him to myself for so long,' said Giovanni. 'We've talked for two months.' He put his arm around Makkim's shoulders. 'Father and son.'

Siward had not greeted either Giovanni or Makkim. Now he turned to Nikolas. 'I'll leave you,' he said. 'You'll have much to catch up on.'

He closed the door quietly as he went out, not wanting to draw attention to his departure. He'd gone five paces down the corridor when he heard it open again. He stopped and looked round. Makkim was closing the door behind him.

Makkim turned to face him. 'You do not speak to me.'

Siward saw how calm he was. He felt sudden irritation. 'You are my enemy,' he said. 'We fight on different sides.'

'As did Saladin and the Lionheart, but there was respect too. And we share a grandfather.' He looked intently at him. 'Is it the inheritance?'

'Why should it be that?' Siward replied. 'Have you decided what to do with yours yet?'

Makkim placed his hands in sleeves that almost reached the floor. Siward saw that Luke's gown fitted him as if it was his own. 'Assuming I want any part of it and am not in prison? My religion encourages acts of piety and charity.'

Siward grunted. 'So you'll build mosques. You don't deserve it. There are livelihoods all over the world that depend on that trading company.' He shifted his feet. 'Why did you want to speak to me?'

Makkim breathed in. 'Violetta. She is not coming here, choosing Constantinople instead. A siege is no place for a woman. You know that.' He hesitated. 'Why has she gone there?'

Siward shrugged. 'I don't know. Why is it my business?'

'You came to Rome together. I assumed you knew her.'

'You know her better than I. She is your sister.'

Makkim shook his head. 'You know she's not that.' He studied Siward for a while. 'But whatever she is, I must protect her. You are going to Constantinople.'

Siward turned. 'I am going to Constantinople to fight, Makkim. I don't suppose I'll have time for much else.'

CHAPTER TWENTY-SEVEN

MISTRA

Siward sailed out of Monemvasia for Constantinople in the cold, dark days that follow the turn of the year, when the world lurches to its feet to start again the exhausting business of evolution. He sailed with four hundred Varangians in three round ships. They were going to stop at the island of Chios to pick up three hundred Genoese mercenaries, armour and cannon, all paid for by the Mamonas Bank.

It was a morning of brittle sunshine and keen, ice-cold wind that cut to the bone. An eagle, riding the currents above the coastline, might have seen as far as the treacherous waters of Cape Malea to the south. Pennants streamed from the masts like bunting, and the Giustiniani and Palaiologoi emblems raised cheers from the battlements as the big sails caught the wind. Giovanni, Plethon and Nikolas, together with most of the city's population, saw him off from the city square. Most assumed it was for the last time.

All of them would remember that Christmas as the best of times. They would store its memory for as long as they were permitted to live. It had been a time of careful, measured celebration, when people had blessed every minute, hoarding them before the coming of Armageddon. It had been a time of reserve set aside for candour, of appreciation for the priceless gift of *now*. It had been a time of present joy made better by a hazardous future. It had been a time of reconciliation and fragile happiness.

Except for Siward and Makkim.

For Siward, there was the very presence of Makkim in Mistra. Whatever his parentage, he was a janissary, indoctrinated by Islam, seemingly unchanged. Worse, he was Violetta'a brother and probably something else as well.

For both of them, there was the unspoken worry about where she'd gone, a worry that gnawed its way into every moment of the day.

Then had come news of the cannon. The galley taking them to Constantinople had been attacked off the coast of Thessaly and its cargo stolen by corsairs. Reports had arrived of huge burdens being pulled by sixty oxen up the coast road to the Maritsa River, where they'd been put on a barge for Edirne.

Nikolas had asked the question no one else dared to: were they ever meant for Constantinople?

It seemed too shocking to be true. Giovanni had decided to ask his son what he knew. He'd found him reading in his room.

'Did you know that the cannon were going to Mehmed?'

And Makkim, who'd expected the question for some time, had answered simply.

'Yes.'

'And you didn't think to tell us?'

'Because you never asked. Because I am not on your side.'

Makkim was kneeling towards Mecca, his head to the prayer mat, when Giovanni visited him two weeks later. It was his first submission of the day and the sun shone low from the east, blinding him. He'd finished his *sura* and stood, rolled up the mat and placed it against the wall. Then he'd sat on the bed.

His bedroom was high up in the Despot's palace. It was a comfortable room, reserved for visiting kings and princes, with tall windows that overlooked the city and the vale of Sparta. Outside was a scene of peace and prosperity, a picture of wise and stable government. In certain moods, Makkim kept the curtains closed.

He looked around the room, seeing again the objects that had become so familiar over the past months: the map on the wall with the Empire of Justinian sprawled across a Roman world, the icons of Christ and his Virgin Mother, the prie-dieu with the book of hours on its lectern. There was a message in everything, he knew, carefully selected, not subtle. He admired and ignored it all in equal measure.

He thought often about Violetta. When he'd first heard that she was coming to Mistra, he'd been overjoyed, but not completely. Some part of him had wanted to go to Venice to rescue her, to show her that Ilya was still alive. She had been delivered and he was glad, but it had not been done by him.

She'd be in Constantinople by now. If the city was taken, it would mean three days of pillage and he'd not be there to protect her. No one would be spared the vengeance of the bashi-bozouks, least of all a woman of beauty and no standing. There'd be no secret tunnel to the harbour to take her out. She would die.

And he remembered another thing. *The priest is there.*

Could he save her still? He had to. Siward seemed disinclined to help her.

He rose from the bed and went to the window. The scene

below was of people talking, laughing, obeying the little cour-
tesies that made life tolerable in a city of steep, narrow streets.
It seemed a scene worth preserving, familiar to him somewhere
deep within.

There was a knock on the door, but not that of the servant
bringing food.

'Come in.'

His father entered. He looked tired. 'We should speak,' he
said. He went over to the bed and sat.

'Yes, we should.' Makkim drew up a chair facing him. He was
wearing the loose gown he used for praying. It wasn't thick
enough for the cold but he didn't mind; he wanted to be alert.
He waited.

Giovanni joined his hands and brought them to his chin, his
elbows on his knees. He looked at the floor for a time, then
back up. 'You've been here four months,' he said. 'At times I've
thought us friends, at others strangers. I have loved you as my
son, but you've not always made it easy.'

Makkim said nothing.

'I had hoped that this great fortune that's been given to you,'
Giovanni continued, 'combined with Mehmed's treachery,
might persuade you to consider another life. One that we could
live out together.' He hesitated. 'I am not so young, after all.'

Makkim couldn't speak. There was nothing he could find to
say.

His father went on. 'There are Muslim merchants in the West.
They understand the laws of eastern trade and are trusted by
other Muslim merchants. You could keep your religion, but
trade in the West. Just change enough things to stop Mehmed
finding you.' He leant in. 'Have you even considered it?'

Makkim shook his head. 'I am a soldier, not a merchant. And

I won't hide.' He asked, 'Father, do you believe in the prophesy that the fall of Rome means the end of time?'

Giovanni shook his head. 'No, but it may mean the end of Christian Europe. Not much will stop Mehmed should Constantinople fall.'

'Exactly. The end of time is the beginning of the age of Islam. So where would I hide? Why would I *want* to hide?'

Giovanni leant further forward, his joined fingers pointing. 'Because now there is an alternative: better than Islam, better than Rome. Europe is entering a new age, an enlightened age of curiosity and discovery. Its future – perhaps the world's future – depends on it. I have seen it, Makkim. In Portugal, in Prince Henry the Navigator's court. It's where new thinking prevails over old, where reason conquers superstition, where religion knows its place.' He sat back. 'That is the future and it is a good one. Men are daring to dream, and they dream of commerce rather than war.'

Makkim stared at him. How could a world distancing itself from the word of God be a better one?

Giovanni was frowning at him, shaking his head. 'What do you want?' he asked. 'Now, after everything, what do you want, Makkim?'

What did he want? He had no idea what he wanted, except one thing.

'Violetta,' he said. 'My sister is in Constantinople, which will be attacked in the spring. I want to get her out.'

Giovanni nodded slowly. 'And if I was to help you?'

Makkim looked into his father eyes. *What are you thinking of?* He looked away. 'If you were to help me,' he said carefully, ' – if you were to help me get into the city and get her out – then I would consider almost anything.'

He looked back at his father. The scales were so finely balanced. On one side was the life of a son he'd just found, on the other, that son's only remaining reason for existence. Would Giovanni deny him that?

'And if you can't get out? If Mehmed finds you there?'

Makkim had considered this. No, he might not live, but she would because he'd make sure it was the janissaries who found her. And a certain priest would die before discovering who she was, before hurting her again. He said, 'I'll get out.'

'You've given your oath not to escape. Would you break it?'

'As Lydislaw did, yes.'

CHAPTER TWENTY-EIGHT

CHIOS

Violetta admired Nikolas. In the absence of a father, he had come closest to the role but his intervention in her trial had been better than his advice afterwards. He'd suggested she go to Mistra, but Mistra was where Siward and Makkim were, and only one of them would stay there. The other would go to Constantinople and probably die. She knew where she wanted to go.

Zoe had agreed with her. Before leaving Venice, Violetta had gone to say goodbye to her, travelling in disguise, for the city was no longer safe for courtesans who'd spied.

'He is going to Constantinople and probably won't come back,' she'd said. 'You love him and you want to be with him. That's where you should be.'

So she'd taken ship with Nikolas but had not stayed on it.

It was on the first evening, after she'd changed ship at Ragusa to one going to Chios then Constantinople, that she'd met Johannes Grant. She'd been so lost to her thoughts that she'd not noticed him come up to stand beside her.

'You don't have a cabin.'

She'd glanced at him. He was short and old but looked fit

and alert. His face was weather-beaten beneath white hair, cut short. He smiled to reveal all his teeth.

'Don't I?' She'd not really considered it, but it didn't surprise her. She'd taken the first ship she could find.

'No. You can have mine.'

She'd frowned. 'Where will you sleep?'

'On the floor. Don't worry, I'm too old for any adventures.'

She'd doubted this but the man seemed sincere.

They'd turned back to the view and Violetta had felt spray on her face. They were sailing fast. She'd turned. 'I am Violetta Cavarse, once a courtesan of Venice. And you?'

'Johannes Grant, once of Scotland,' he replied, bowing. 'I am an engineer and I'm on my way to Constantinople to save it.'

She'd laughed. 'All by yourself?'

'I am an expert on sieges. With Giustiniani Longo, I built the great defences at Ceuta.' He'd looked out at the sea, wiping salt from his eyes. 'Where are you going to?'

'Constantinople as well.'

He'd stared at her, frowning. Then his eyebrows had lifted. 'I know you. The courtesan, yes. The one who was tried.'

Her mistake had been telling him her name. News of her trial had travelled furthest by sea, often warped by distance. The version heard by Grant had been of spying and Turks. Now she was imprisoned on Chios. The engineer had clearly decided that Constantinople was no place for someone suspected of spying for the enemy. He'd asked the Genoese governor of Chios to keep her there when they'd landed.

She found herself inside a gilded cage. The Adorno Palace was opulent, as befitted the man who governed one of the richest islands on earth. It had marble enough for ten temples and carpets deeper than lawns. Her balcony looked out over the harbour where, all day, ships came and went, low in the water, groaning under the weight of mastic, alum, salt and everything else that served the cause of enriching the Genoese *signoria*.

She felt like a goose before Christmas. Food was served at the start, middle and end of each day, all of it delicious. She'd been measured for new dresses and now could barely fit into them. Soon, she'd regained most of her beauty.

She knew what was happening, of course. Vito Gabrielle Adorno was middle-aged but sprightly. His wife was plain and devout and spent most of her time visiting the island's convents. The governor had learnt the name of his prisoner and recognised it.

Violetta decided to turn events to her advantage, however unwelcome the process. She would seduce her way off the island. She chose a dinner when Adorno's wife was away and eight of the signoria were being entertained. She was the only woman present and sat next to him at the end of the table.

The company ate pheasant and pasta, with wine from the *kambos*, laying wagers as to whose estate it had come from. As they drank, the conversation got louder and the pressure from Adorno's leg firmer. When his hand came to her thigh, she let it stay.

As they drank, the signoria enjoyed themselves more and more. It was late when Adorno pushed the last of them out the door.

He closed it, turned and sprang immediately. He put one hand on her bottom and the other to her breast, pressing himself against her. They kissed and his palm explored her restored curves like a dog following scent, darting here and there. His other hand started to unbutton his hose. He let go of her lips and breathed into her ear.

'Upstairs, quickly. My bedroom.'

But Violetta had never entertained a man in his wife's bed and wouldn't now.

'No,' she said, 'mine.'

He stopped and drew back, staring at her. 'I want to do it in my bed, not yours.' He was breathing heavily. 'You are in my palace, eating my food, wearing my clothes. My bedroom, if you please.'

'No,' she said.

'No? What do you mean "no"?'

'I mean that I will not do what you want in your wife's bed. In fact,' she said, stepping back and smoothing her dress to her sides, 'I will not do what you want at all.'

Adorno looked bewildered. 'But you're a whore, damn you. Do you demand payment?'

She turned and began to walk away. 'No payment. I'll go. I'm sorry.'

'But you're a whore!' he shouted again, his hose open, the poise of generations vanished.

Violetta walked out of Adorno's palace even as the threats turned to entreaty: they could do it wherever she wanted; she could keep the clothes; he'd pay whatever sum she asked for. But she was not to be swayed.

Much later, she found herself on the seafront, this time alone and cold. Her dress was made for the drawing room, not the port. She cursed her pride. She cursed Siward.

The night was clear of cloud and held a moon full enough to read by. The stars were as bright as ice and looking up, she wondered if tonight they were. It was cold enough to die. What had she been thinking of? Should she go back?

She heard a shout from above. It came from the deck of a round ship tied up to the quay.

'I'd hardly know you!'

She looked up. Minotto was leaning over the side with his doublet undone and a wine skin in his hand. There was no mistaking him in the moonlight. He was gripping the rail to keep himself standing.

'You'd thought yourself rid of me,' he shouted, raising his hands. 'But here I am.' He lifted the wine skin and drank, the wine dripping from his chin. He wiped his mouth and belched. 'What are you doing here?'

She'd last seen him in a room full of inquisitors when he'd tried hard to kill her. He could do so now, she thought, though his aim might be wild.

But then he'd also played suit to her for many years, might even have loved her in his strange way. Perhaps he still did. She decided.

'You are on your way to Constantinople. Will you take me?'

He threw back his head and laughed. He drank again and wiped. 'So you finally want something from me. Not so proud now.'

She could have walked on, though she had no idea where she would go. Instead, she stood and looked up at him. She was suddenly aware of her clothes. She felt a burning humiliation.

'Well, are you coming aboard?' he asked, leaning out from the rail. 'It's not the night for sleeping outdoors.'

Violetta stared up at him. There was no one in the world she would rather share a boat with less than Minotto, but it was a ship bound for Constantinople. She walked over to the gangplank.

He helped her on board, bowing unsteadily. She saw there was food on his clothes and, even from a distance, smelt the wine on his breath. She felt revulsion.

'Will you take me to Constantinople?'

'If we come to an arrangement, yes.' He straightened. 'Let's talk about it in the warmth.'

He led her towards a door beneath the upper deck. She walked into a cabin lit by candles and heated by an open stove at the back. There was a table with another wine skin and the remains of a meal on it, a cup up-ended. There were two cots either side of the table, one with a satchel leaning against it. A small chart-table stood next to the stove. The room smelt of food and sweat but it was warm.

'There,' he said, closing the door. 'Not so cold in here.'

Warmth and compromise; she'd made up her mind. She'd do it to get to Constantinople. She decided to make things easier.

'Would you like me to undress?' she asked, turning to him. 'Or do you prefer me as I am?'

He was taken aback. For a moment, the snide, mocking reserve vanished. His eyes widened, then narrowed again. He sat down on a cot. 'Do you know what happens to attractive women when a city falls to the Turk?' he asked, leaning back. 'It's not pretty.'

She didn't reply.

He put his head to one side, curious. 'Why are you so desperate to die, Violetta Cavarse?' he asked quietly. 'Surely the world is not that bad?' His eyes travelled over her body. 'After all, you're back to what you were.'

She noticed that his breathing had quickened and that sweat had gathered below his hairline.

'It doesn't matter why I want to go,' she said carefully. 'The bargain is a simple one: my body for a berth on your ship. It's up to you.'

*

303

Later, when it was finished and she'd gone to the spare cot and laid her bruised body down, she remained awake. At least he'd been quick. Now his spent form was asleep and snoring loud enough to wake the port.

She turned onto her side, staring at the hull and listening to the creak of wood, the slap of water outside. Did she feel shame? Yes, but not of the same type she'd felt with the Duke. This time, it had been a sensible transaction.

She looked across at Minotto. Lying next to his cot, she saw the dark shape of the satchel. Might it contain anything of interest? Money perhaps? She'd need it if he turned her off the ship tomorrow as he probably would. He was lying on his back, his chest rising and falling with noisy sleep. If she reached out . . .

She moved to the edge of the cot and stretched out her arm. A little further, yes . . . there. She had hold of it. With great care, she pulled the satchel towards her and lifted it onto her bed. It was heavy.

She glanced at Minotto. His snoring hadn't missed a beat, his thin lips quivering with each exhalation. The cabin was a fug of wood smoke and wine.

She sat up, untied the straps and opened it. Inside was a map. She took it out and carefully opened it, shutting her eyes each time the parchment rustled. She laid it on the bed, smoothing it flat with her fingers. She reached behind her to the table and brought the candle over. Slowly, slowly, she raised it above the paper.

It was the map of a city, or at least a city's defences. There were notations scrawled beside the walls, all in a language she didn't recognise. They seemed to list the height and width of every wall and tower, the nature of the ground beneath and in front of them. Cannon emplacements were shown with the bore of every gun. At each gate was a scribble of words and numbers.

It was the blueprint for a city's defence. But which? She searched the corners of the map where the legend might be. None. She glanced at the sleeping Minotto.

Which city are you planning to attack?

She looked at the plan more closely. It was too small for Constantinople. Milan, perhaps? After all, the Sforzas were perennial enemies of Venice. But no, too small again. And anyway, there were pictures of ships in a harbour. This city was on the sea.

She was thinking hard. She couldn't take it with her because he'd miss it and be alerted. She looked around the cabin, lifting the candle to do so. There were more maps on the chart-table. She rose and went over to them.

'Whore.'

A grunt and the smacking together of dry lips. The snoring resumed. Minotto was talking in his sleep.

She took a deep breath. She looked down and saw a blank parchment and a pen. She lifted the pen and drew the paper out slowly. She carried them back to the bed and sat.

She would make a copy as well as she was able, then take it to Constantinople. Perhaps someone else might make sense of it.

PART FOUR

1453
THE SIEGE

CHAPTER TWENTY-NINE

CONSTANTINOPLE, APRIL 1453

Siward was standing in a large room, high in the Blachernae Palace, looking out to the west where the sun was setting among clouds moored like islands in a copper sea. Arched windows surrounded him, addressing all points of the compass, flooding the room with light and shadow and fine gold dust between. The first candles had been lit to no effect.

On one side, the room had views over the Golden Horn where the remnants of the Roman fleet lay at anchor, protected by their floating chain. On the other was a plain with tents that hadn't been there yesterday: small tents surrounding a pavilion big enough to house a village. Beside it, a pole had been thrust into the ground with five horsetails tied to it.

Mehmed had come to Constantinople.

Siward had arrived a month ago. He'd ridden through the Golden Gate with Petros at his side and seen the weeds growing from its cracks. He'd ridden through fields that had once been streets, past rubble that had once been palaces. It was five years since he'd last seen the city but it was worse, much worse.

He'd spent the month inspecting the city's defences with

Petros and often felt close to tears. Constantinople: capital of the greatest empire the world had ever known, bridge of continents, city of seven hills and seven hundred churches, home to half a million with walls twenty miles around . . . this glory was all in the past.

Now, barely fifty thousand lived in the city. Its wealth had fled to Mistra. Its walls were crumbling, its fields were bare, and its orchards and ruins were stripped to make ramparts. Constantinople was an empty shell. No wonder Constantine had chosen Mistra for his coronation.

Petros, having never seen the city before, had been more shocked. On the first day, he'd hardly spoken at all, just ridden through the city in a daze.

'They said it was made of gold,' he'd said at last.

Siward had felt his friend's disillusionment. The myth of Constantinople had been part of Plethon's teaching: a deliberate lie. Now the lie was exposed.

'The Venetians did most of it,' he'd explained. 'Two hundred and fifty years ago they captured the city on their way to the crusades. They took most of it back to Venice. You remember the horses above St Mark's Cathedral? They came from the hippodrome.'

Petros had shaken his head and said nothing.

'But there are good people here still,' Siward had said.

Now one of them was speaking to him.

'Looking at him won't make Mehmed disappear.'

Constantine was leaning against a pillar, his face as pale as the veined marble behind. Beyond was a blue spring sky flecked by tiny clouds and swifts that darted in and out of tall columns. There was no sound but the sigh of breeze through stone. 'Try this view instead.'

Siward came over. Beneath the swifts, the Golden Horn was alive with silent, faraway ships: merchantmen bringing food in from the south, galleys being loaded from wharves, skiffs taking passengers from bank to bank. Between them all, the water sparkled and shimmered like distant snow.

The Emperor put his hand on his shoulder. 'So peaceful,' he murmured.

If Siward had been shocked by how much the city had changed, he was more so by Constantine. The Emperor was forty-eight but his hair was grey, his face gaunt. Siward wondered when he'd last slept.

A throat cleared behind them and they turned. Men were standing around a table, looking at them. Most of them he knew: Notaras the Megas Doux, Cardinal Isidore the Papal Legate and Johannes Grant from Scotland. Minotto was there too, the hero who'd slipped past the Sultan's fleet – the last man into Constantinople. There'd been regret about the cannon, but understanding too – at least from the Emperor. And there was one he didn't know: Gennadius the Patriarch. Siward had asked for him to be present.

Constantine and Siward walked over to the table. On it was a model of Constantinople, its buildings and fields set between a triangle of walls: two to the sea, one to the land. The sea had boats on it: merchant ships and galleys, some with crescent moons over their masts. The land had a line of fine earth for the siege works and a tiny tent for the Sultan.

The Emperor looked up, his gaze moving from face to face, pausing on each. 'My friends,' he said. 'Our enemy is outside.'

He pointed to the land walls. 'This is where they'll attack,' he said, 'where their siege lines have already been prepared. These walls are the mightiest in the world. They've withstood

Arab, Avar, Bulgar, Rus and Turk. They've been impregnable to every army and every kind of siege engine. But this time they'll have cannon aimed at them, big cannon that were meant for us.'

Siward watched Minotto stare down at the model, his look one of solemn concentration. How could a guilty man arrange his face into such open innocence? Was every bailo taught to lie so well? He thought suddenly of Minotto's fury at the masque in Venice. He thought of Luke, of a map that was also a lie. He felt sudden anger. *Was it you who killed him?*

He looked back to the Emperor, who was pointing now at water. 'Here is our harbour of the Golden Horn, where we have fifty-six fighting ships – ours, Venice's, Genoa's – all safe behind the chain that was put out this morning. And here,' he pointed north into the Bosporos, 'are the one hundred and twenty ships of the Sultan's fleet that have taken up position in Diplokionon harbour under Admiral Baltaoğlu.'

He looked up at the Genoese contingent. 'A second army under Zaganos bey lies on the other side of the Golden Horn overlooking your colony of Pera, which you've decided to make neutral, though many of you have chosen to fight with us.'

He smiled. No blame, but some sadness. He straightened and looked around. 'Mehmed will move his army into position over the next few days, his cannon with it. From then on, we will be besieged and blockaded, cut off from the outside world. We can expect an offer of clemency if we surrender. If we choose not to . . .' He released his breath. 'Well, you know what happens then.'

Siward had thought of little else on his journey up from Monemvasia. He'd been so convinced that Violetta was in Constantinople that he'd not even stopped at Chios, instead sending two of his ships to pick the mercenaries up. When he'd arrived to find that Grant had left her there, he'd nearly kissed the old engineer.

'So, we have to face the question,' Constantine continued. 'Are we to fight or surrender?'

There were growls around the table and the Emperor raised his hand. 'Please. The question must be addressed. And its answer must lie in whether we think we can win this siege.'

Minotto said, 'Venice is sending a fleet. It will destroy Baltaoğ-lu's and put another two thousand men ashore. We can win.'

Constantine dipped his head. 'And we are grateful beyond measure, Signor Minotto. But it won't stop Mehmed attacking.' He looked down at the table and pointed back to the land walls. 'So the answer must lie here.' He looked up. 'Engineer Grant, if you please.'

Grant had not protested with the others, loyal only to the cause of engineering. He would go where he was paid and where he could achieve success. The fact that he was in Constantinople at all was cause for optimism. He bent low over the model.

'I designed the defences of Ceuta for the Portuguese to withstand cannon, and its walls are nothing to yours.' He tapped them each in turn. 'Look at them. The inner wall is forty feet high and fifteen thick, the outer only a third lower. Then there's the moat with another wall on its inside bank. But it's not the thickness that matters, it's what they're made of. Watch.' He banged the table hard: one, two, three. The walls jumped up and down. 'Imagine an earthquake. That's what it's like when cannon balls hit stone. It's the shock that brings them down.'

Minotto asked, 'Which means what, exactly?'

'Which means,' said Grant, 'that at some point, they'll fall.'

There was an uncomfortable silence that Grant quickly filled.

'And that's not such a bad thing,' he said. 'Because rubble is better than wall against cannon.'

'How so?' This was Notaras, always cautious, always curious.

'Because,' said Grant, in the deliberate way of explaining something really simple, 'we can rebuild them every time they fall. If we have the people to do it.'

'Which we don't,' said Notaras. 'The consuls took the census in every parish. Six thousand soldiers, including fighting monks, eight thousand when the fleet from Venice gets here. Hardly enough to man the walls, let alone rebuild them after every cannon-shot.'

'Ah, but I said people, not soldiers,' said Grant. 'When Attila the Hun came after there'd been an earthquake, it was the people of Constantinople who rebuilt the walls while the soldiers rested. They did it in sixty days.' He turned to Constantine. 'Isn't it so?'

The Emperor nodded.

'So,' Grant went on, 'we need the people to come to the walls.' He looked at Siward. 'Your turn.'

Siward had positioned himself opposite Gennadius. He wanted there to be no misunderstanding with the Patriarch.

'The people are frightened and they're confused,' he said. 'They've seen omens in the sky and they don't believe that God is with them any more. Tell us, Gennadius, what will it take for them to rally behind their emperor?'

The Patriarch looked uncomfortable. He cleared his throat, glancing at Constantine. 'The people believe that God has abandoned them because of the union with the Latin Church.'

Siward turned to Constantine. 'The people's faith lies deep within their souls, their consciences. Let us put aside any more talk of Church union and let the citizens fight for their faith.' He looked at the Papal Legate. 'Am I right?'

Cardinal Isidore had arrived from Rome last November. He'd held a solemn service to celebrate Church union to which no one had come. He was tall, with long white hair and beard: an old snowdrift of a man with enough fire inside to melt it all. He nodded slowly. 'Yes, you are right.' He made the sign of the cross. 'Although I wish with all my heart that you weren't.'

Looking round, Siward could see most men nodding.

Not Minotto. He turned to Constantine. 'Majesty, the Venetian fleet is on its way. It is a Catholic fleet. My men are Catholic. They fight for one Church.'

Constantine smiled. 'Then let them fight here on the Catholic walls of my palace. We emperors have accepted union even if our people haven't.' He put his hand on Minotto's shoulder. 'My dear bailo, we have such faith in you that we'll even give you the keys to its gate.'

Siward tried hard to remain calm. He'd warned Constantine about Minotto, had been politely listened to, then diverted to another subject. *Now this.*

'Majesty, I . . .' He looked into eyes that needed so badly to close in sleep. He felt sudden pity for his emperor. He nodded, then turned to Minotto. 'My Varangians will be hard by you, Minotto,' he said, 'be sure of it. You can show us how to fight.'

Makkim and Giovanni had watched the Ottoman camp for two days before they went into it. They were waiting for Mehmed to leave.

'He always goes ahead of the army,' Makkim had said as they'd lain down between the trees. 'He likes to reconnoitre alone.'

They'd talked a lot about Mehmed as they'd ridden up through Thrace. They'd crept out of Mistra at night, Giovanni getting them through the guards at the city gates. He'd insisted on coming. If his new-found son was going into danger, he'd not let him go alone.

'He has prepared all his life for this moment,' Makkim had said as they'd walked their horses side by side through trees that sighed. 'He's read every book on the art of the siege, every campaign of Alexander's, Caesar's Gallic Wars. He sent me into Constantinople once, disguised as a merchant.'

'And what did you think?'

What had he thought? Decadence and greed. But now? What would he think when he got there? He'd become a merchant, after all. He didn't know.

He said, 'Mehmed knows he needs this victory to make his throne secure. His last rule was not a success.'

'It's still a gamble.'

'Yes, but he's lessened the odds. He's built a castle at the straits and he's neutralised his enemies by talking of peace.' He pointed ahead. 'You see this road? Every bridge from Edirne to Constantinople has been strengthened to bear the weight of the cannon.' He frowned. 'And he's studied Constantinople.'

'With your help.'

'Certainly. I walked around its walls dressed as an Armenian, mapping all the way.'

They both knew how crucial Makkim could be to the siege. He knew Mehmed's mind after all. But he'd still not betray his old master, his religion. Their plan was to get into Constantinople, find Violetta, then get out. They'd also tell Constantine about Minotto's cannon, if they could.

Now it was evening and they'd just seen Mehmed leave with Zaganos. It was time to put Makkim's part of the plan into practice. They changed into new clothes and walked forward towards the camp. Makkim wore his aventail high to cover his face.

The sentries did nothing to prevent two janissary officers from entering the camp. It wasn't long before they found the tent they were looking for.

'I wish to speak to the vizier Candarli Halil,' said Makkim to the guards at its entrance. 'Tell him it's an old friend.'

One of the men went into the tent and came out. They were ushered into an anteroom of silk and candle where herbs smoked in braziers. There were low sofas with carpets between. They heard voices from behind the silk. Then it drew apart and Candarli appeared. He looked from one to the other of them.

'You wish to speak with me?'

Makkim lowered his aventail. 'I do, Halil.'

Candarli was his family's third generation of vizier, schooled in reserve, but this was a surprise too great. 'Makkim!' He came forward and embraced his old friend, pulling him to his chest and kissing him. 'I'd thought you gone forever.'

Makkim smiled. 'Well, there wasn't much to come back to.'

Candarli nodded. 'You're declared a traitor.' He glanced at Giovanni. 'Who is this?'

'My father. My true father, Giovanni Giustiniani Longo of Genoa.'

Candarli came up to Giovanni, put his hands in his own. 'Then you are most welcome in my tent. Your son is loved by me.' He gestured to the next room. 'Come.'

He led them through. It had a bed and a big table with food on it and a man bowing between them. Candarli turned. 'Will you eat?'

They would. The man brought food and they ate well and fast. Candarli watched them in silence.

'You'll know that Mehmed has left, and taken Zaganos with him,' he said at last. 'I'm not included, of course.' He leaned in. 'Did you know they would go together into the streets of Edirne at night in disguise? They wanted to know what the people thought.'

Makkim felt a stab of jealousy, despite himself. 'And what do they think?'

'That Mehmed is a hothead, as we all do; that Constantinople may not fall. He pretends not to care, but he does.' Candarli took a peach from the bowl. 'He is worried, Makkim. All the planning, all the preparation. Now he's finally here and he might fail.' He bit into the peach. 'And he misses you.'

Makkim put down a chicken bone and wiped his mouth with his hand. 'Still?'

'More than ever, though he'll not say it. He won't have your name mentioned in his presence. He loved you, you know that – probably still does.' He took another bite. 'Why are you here?'

'I want you to get me into Constantinople.'

The vizier frowned. 'Why?'

'To bring out a sister who will die if I don't. And perhaps to help Mehmed. Are you still in contact with the Patriarch Gennadius?'

Candarli dipped his head. 'I have been in the past, as you know. To talk of peace. Not recently.'

'Could you arrange to meet with him in Pera, in secret?'

'I suppose so.' His frown deepened. 'I won't betray Mehmed, though.'

Makkim put his hand onto Candarli's arm. 'And I wouldn't ask you to, old friend. But I have learnt that the people of Constantinople are unhappy about the union of their Church to the Latin one and Gennadius has emerged as the one they listen to most. They do what he says.'

'Which means?'

'Which means that he might be persuaded to tell them to lay down their arms if their religious freedom can be guaranteed.' He squeezed his arm. 'Imagine: you can present Mehmed with his prize without all the risk, all the bloodshed.'

Candarli was silent for a while, thinking. 'But will Mehmed do that?'

'If it gives him a population to fill his new capital, yes. He wants it to work, after all.'

'And you would tell Gennadius this?'

'Not I, you. We would come as your guards, then disappear into the city.'

It took a further hour to convince Candarli and a day to arrange the meeting with Gennadius, a letter for Constantine being the pretext. Under cover of night, Candarli, Giovanni and Makkim, all disguised as monks, were let into neutral Pera across the Golden Horn. Gennadius was in a church to meet them. He'd brought his own monk, a true one, to stand guard outside.

They found the Patriarch praying. He was kneeling in a pew, a single candle the only light in the church. He was also dressed as a monk and his hood was raised. He didn't move when they entered. Candarli went to the pew behind him and sat, his two monk-guards either side of him, their heads lowered.

Gennadius made the sign of the cross, got slowly to his feet and sat down, his head close to theirs. He did not lower his hood. He did not turn.

'Candarli,' he whispered. 'You have something for the Emperor.'

'I have something for you.'

'Me?'

Candarli leant forward. 'Gennadius, you know me.' His voice was low. 'You know that I have tried to keep the peace between our peoples. Well, I have failed and now Mehmed is here with a hundred thousand men.' He waited for the number to be absorbed. 'Mehmed has cannon of a size not dreamt of and, this time, Constantinople will fall.' He was whispering, but his voice sounded loud in the empty church. 'The Koran forbids the sacking of a city if it surrenders. Think of all those lives saved.'

'And all those martyrs denied,' whispered Gennadius. 'They would die in the faith.'

'Ruled by Mehmed, they can keep their faith and live,' said Candarli. 'And you can live with them as Patriarch, leading them in their faith.'

The Patriarch half-turned. 'Mehmed has said this?'

'Yes.'

Silence. Gennadius shifted in his pew. He sighed. Then he said what Giovanni had expected him to say.

'You're too late. The Emperor has chosen not to force the union of the Churches. His people are with him. I am with him.' He rose. 'I am sorry but we fight.'

Outside the little church, the Patriarch's monk stood guard. He also wore his hood raised and knelt behind a gravestone so as not to be seen. When Candarli emerged from the church with his two guards, the moon appeared suddenly from behind a cloud. He watched the three men as they stopped to talk. One of them drew back his hood. His face was scarred, a long wound that ran from eye to chin, made deeper by the shadow. He frowned. *Familiar.*

The other monk also lowered his hood and it was not a Turkish face that the moon revealed. The three were whispering now, heads almost joined. He saw Candarli lean forward and kiss one of them, then leave. The other two lifted their hoods again and walked away towards the Golden Horn. They were going into the city.

320

CHAPTER THIRTY

CONSTANTINOPLE

The monk's name was Eugenius. Many years ago, he'd come to Constantinople on a Venetian ship, penniless and desperate. The ship's captain had seen his desperation and sensed opportunity for Venice. He'd persuaded him to convert to the Orthodox faith and find work with the Patriarch. The captain had been Minotto and Eugenius had reported Gennadius's movements to him ever since.

Now he went straight from the church to the ferry, not waiting for Gennadius to appear. He kept the two monks in sight, saw them board a ferry and waited for the next. He was its only passenger and stood alone at the prow, watching the chain float by, looking up at the city on the other shore. The night was wet and everything shone like porphyry, as if valuable. He wondered if this was, perhaps, how the Turks saw it.

The scar. Who had a scar on his face, was famed for it? But he was captured in Mistra. *Unless . . .*

He arrived at the Gate of Horaria and was let through by a guard who asked for a blessing. He knew this quarter well. He'd entered its warren of narrow streets often enough on his way to the slave market. He knew it for its smell of stale money and fresh fear. He could follow that fear, delicious and exotic, with his eyes shut, all the way to the child slaves.

The streets were empty of everything but dogs that stood under the dripping eaves, suffering and stupid. He heard the murmur of prayer as he passed doors: people praying to the Holy Virgin for their deliverance. He saw the smear of candle-light and people gathered around it, talking quietly because they knew how fear spread. He heard the sound of children crying. Always the children.

Children. Once he'd felt shame, but habit wears down shame, washes it away.

Tonight the slave market was empty. He heard the call of a sentry and the answer of another. He heard the rattle of rain on stone and the gurgle of water in gutter. He kicked out at a dog that strayed into his path.

He came to the door and knocked. It was opened by the usual servant.

'Is he here?'

The man nodded and stepped to one side, looking up and down the street. Eugenius went in. The servant followed him and shut the door. He left the room.

The monk lowered his hood and shook his head. He felt the trace of water on his neck. Cold. He looked around. The room was a kitchen with a range at one end with piles of wood beside it. Above was a rail from which hung copper pans of different sizes. There was a long, bare table in the middle with benches either side.

Minotto came in. He had a small bag of coin in his hand. 'Well?'

'Gennadius met with Candarli tonight,' he said. 'In Pera.'

322

The bailo went to a bench and sat. He didn't offer a place to his visitor. 'What did they talk about?'

He shrugged. 'I wasn't with them, but I can guess. Candarli will have tried to persuade him to use his influence with the people, to get them to refuse to fight.'

Minotto nodded. 'Well, it's too late for that. The Emperor won't push the union so the people are on his side.' He yawned and swung a leg over the bench. 'Was that it?'

Eugenius looked down. He watched the water pool on the stone beneath him. He hated this Venetian as much as any other man of privilege. 'There's more. It will be expensive.'

Minotto frowned. 'It will have to be good to be expensive. How much?'

'What you have in that bag.'

The bailo leant back against the table. He studied the monk for a while, then glanced at the bag of coin. 'Alright. What is it?'

'Makkim is inside the city.'

Minotto shook his head. 'Makkim is in Mistra.'

'I have seen him.'

Minotto looked away, still frowning. 'How do you know it was him?'

The monk shifted on his feet. 'He is said to be tall and have a scar on one cheek that runs from eye to chin. I saw such a man with Candarli tonight.'

'You're sure?'

'I'm sure. And there was another with him, also tall but older, fair. They looked alike.'

Minotto had risen. He picked up the bag of coin and tossed it to the monk. He went over to the door and opened it. As Eugenius passed him, he took his arm. 'Tell no one what you've told me, monk. And another thing: Makkim has a sister whom I've just seen on Chios. I want you to watch every ship that arrives; there won't be many. If there is a woman on one, it'll be her. I want you to hold her and come to me. Is that understood?'

Minotto rode fast to the Blachernae Palace. He took the main *mese* towards the Gate of Charisius, passing the black hulk of the aqueduct on his right. It was two miles to the gate and the rain had made the cratered road treacherous. His head was bent low to his horse's mane, his cloak flapping behind like chasing bats. How would he explain waking the Emperor at this hour?

He'd think of something. He just had to see him before Makkim did.

The horse stumbled and he nearly fell. He righted his cap and wiped rain from his eyes. He kicked harder.

Who was this other man who'd come with Makkim? He could guess. His spies at Mistra had told him that he'd spent hours shut up with the Genoese Longo, who'd come to Rome as part of the Portuguese party. He'd been with Siward Magoris when he'd tried to kill him in the Colonna garden.

He saw the Charisius Gate ahead of him and turned right along the walls, passing tents, horse pens and wagons. At the Blachernae Gate, the guards recognised him and waved him through. He galloped up the winding road to the palace and entered the courtyard. A man approached to take his horse.

'Is the Emperor awake?' he asked, reining in and jumping to the gound.

The man pointed up. 'He has visitors.'

Minotto looked up at the lighted window. 'How many?'

The groom was patting the sides of the horse, calming it. 'Two men. They arrived just before you.'

Minotto pushed past him. He opened big doors and mounted

the staircase two steps at a time. At the top, he saw light coming from the room where the model city lay. There were guards outside who would know him. He stopped and took a deep breath, wiping his brow and smoothing his hair and clothes. He walked down the landing and the guards let him pass. He opened the door and walked into the room.

Constantine was sitting in his nightgown, Makkim and Giovanni before him, still wet from the rain. They all turned as he entered.

'Bailo,' Constantine frowned. 'So late. Is there an alarm?'

Minotto came over to the Emperor and bowed. 'No more, apparently, majesty. I came to tell you that Makkim was inside the city, but I find him here.' He put his hand to his sword. 'Are you safe?'

Constantine was calm. 'Safe enough, I think. He's not armed.'

Minotto glanced at Makkim, his hand still on his sword hilt. 'Does he say why he's here?'

Giovanni said, 'We are here to warn the Emperor about you, Minotto. Makkim was telling him about the cannon.'

'Cannon?'

'The ones you bought for the Turk, yes.'

Minotto forced a laugh. 'And we are asked to believe the word of Mehmed's favourite general? I've just met a courtesan in Chios who was trying to join him here, the same one we tried in Venice for spying for the Turk.'

Makkim spoke before he should, his eyes wide with relief. 'She's not here?'

'No. I left her behind, but not before she'd admitted to her purpose.' His hand tightened around the sword grip. 'If I could draw in front of the Emperor, I'd arrest you.' He turned to Constantine. 'Majesty, the guards.'

325

The Emperor raised his hand. 'There's no need for that. I have two of you to defend me.' He looked at Makkim. 'I'd heard about you and the courtesan in Rome. Is it true she's on Chios?'

Makkim was smiling, the relief still with him. 'I hope so. I had thought her here.'

'So you came to find her?'

'To find her and bring her out, yes. She is my sister.'

Constantine considered this, his fingers stroking the beard at his cheek. He turned to Giovanni. 'And you, Giovanni? Why are you here?'

'Because I am his father, majesty.'

Constantine stared at him. 'I had hoped you had come to help us. You are an expert at the siege, after all. There was a time when you were loyal to our cause.'

Giovanni didn't answer.

The Emperor rose. 'I see.' He walked to the door, opened it and signalled to guards who came in. He turned to Makkim. 'I have your word against Minotto's. You were the Sultan's friend and Minotto has five hundred men ready to defend my city and a fleet on its way. I am inclined to take his word.'

Giovanni stepped forward. 'But majesty . . .'

Constantine swung round to him. 'Enough. I will not listen to a man skilled at defending cities who will not help me defend mine.' He motioned to the guards who had formed up on either side of Makkim. He said to Giovanni, 'You are, of course, free to go. But not your son. He is a janissary general and will be confined.'

CHAPTER THIRTY-ONE

CONSTANTINOPLE

Siward stood with Petros on the battlements above the Fifth Military Gate. Below them, spread out from the shores of the Propontis to the Golden Horn, was the largest army either of them had ever seen.

It had arrived at dawn. First had come the drums, faint to start with, then louder, a dark heartbeat from deep in the earth's core that silenced every man that stood on the walls. Then, little by little, they'd heard the shuffle of many feet, the shouts of men heaving things in unison, the crack of whip, the roar of oxen.

They'd seen the mangonels first, their tops rising in jerks as they were pulled over the hill. Then had come the trebuchets and the flags, then the army, turning the landscape black from end to end, the stain washing slowly towards them.

'How many,' asked Petros, his voice not quite level, 'would you say are down there?'

Siward looked over the landscape from beneath his hand. 'A hundred thousand?'

'Twenty to one. That's not so bad,' said Petros. 'After all, one

Varangian counts for ten Turks. Will the Venetians come, do you think?'

'Well, they have a fleet prepared, so yes, they might.' Siward shrugged. 'But it's Venice we're talking about, and their Doge is mad.'

'And they've betrayed us before,' said Petros gloomily, remembering. 'So six thousand men have got to defend twenty miles of walls.' He glanced at Siward. 'I suppose Giovanni would know where to put them if he was here.'

'Well, he's not,' said Siward irritably. 'The Emperor can't compel a man to fight, Petros.' He'd not seen Giovanni but he was still angry with him and Makkim for escaping from Mistra. It seemed they'd come to release Violetta. Well, they needn't have bothered. She was still at Chios, thank God. He pointed. 'Here come the cannon.'

The shouts were louder now and they could see row upon row of oxen, whips flying above them, inching their way over the horizon.

'*My God.*' Petros had put his hand to the battlement. He was leaning forward, his mouth slightly open. There they were: two colossal tubes of black wrought iron, each the length of a galley and the height of a man. Half-naked slaves pulled ropes on either side of them and the squeak of wheels could be heard over the sound of man and cattle.

Siward looked back at the Ottoman army. The stain covered most of the landscape now and there was music too: the swirl of bagpipe, the blast of horn, the clash of cymbal from the mehter band. He wondered what Giovanni would do now.

Then his world exploded. He'd not seen the oxen stopping and their loads rolled onto cradles dug into the ground. They'd not seen a man step forward with a lighted fuse.

*

Giovanni looked up. The sound had crashed through the silent library like a wrecking ball. He gripped the side of the table with both hands, his knuckles white to the bone. The cannon must be two miles away but his ears were ringing. He heard screams from the street outside.

He was alone in the library, sitting with a folder in front of him full of maps of the city walls. He'd not fight in this battle, especially when his son was imprisoned in the Blachernae Palace, but he couldn't stop himself taking an interest in it. Beside the folder lay the dragon sword.

The library was next to the Gate of St Barbara overlooking the mouth of the Golden Horn. Earlier, he'd watched the Ottoman admiral Baltaoğlu sail his ninety *galiots* and *fustae* over to the great chain to test if it might somehow be broken. Then he'd watched them sail away again, knowing that it couldn't. The Golden Horn, and all its shipping, would remain safe from the Ottoman navy. For now.

Then this explosion. The bombardment of the land walls had begun.

He returned to the folder, but it was no use. The cannon had blown away his concentration. He was in a city under siege, perhaps the most important siege in history. What was it that Constantine had said?

I will not listen to a man skilled in defending cities who will not help me defend mine.

Well, Johannes Grant was helping him. He would be advising where to place the cannon, the Greek fire. It didn't need two of them.

'Ah, that's where you've got to.'

He looked up to see the engineer in front of him.

'Aren't you needed elsewhere?' he asked.

'I've sited everything I need to site and it's about to get dangerous,' said Grant, dusting his shoulders. 'Better a library.'

Giovanni smiled. He'd missed seeing his old siege companion. He'd have sought him out if he hadn't thought it would lead to an awkward conversation. Like they were about to have now.

'You've been sent to persuade me,' he said. 'Don't bother.'

The engineer shook his head. 'I don't understand. We can win this siege. It can be like Ceuta again.'

Giovanni closed the folder in front of him. 'No, it can't, Johannes,' he said. 'Constantinople is the old world's fight, the one that sent me into exile. I'm part of the new world now. That's where I'll put my energies.'

Grant glanced down at the dragon sword. 'And your son has nothing to do with this?'

Before he could answer, there was another explosion, louder than the first. The door of the library opened and a flood of people poured in.

'Where else can we talk?' asked Grant.

Giovanni rose and picked up the folder, then the sword. 'We'll find somewhere. Come.'

They left the building and went down the steps into the street. It was crowded with people asking questions, women holding crying children, all wishing that someone were there to explain it all. The murmur of panic was everywhere.

'What about the Varangian church?' said Grant. 'It's around here somewhere.'

They set off, people running all around them. A man came up to Grant and said something in his ear.

He turned. 'I have to go,' he said. 'There's a big hole in one of the walls. Find the church so we know where to meet next time.'

Giovanni watched him push his way through the crowd. He

330

glanced up to see the Column of Constantine. Yes. That way. He turned into a side street, then another. He hurried down a less busy alley, then one that was deserted. He came into a little square with a sparse market in the middle, gathered around a dry fountain. All the traders were standing apart from their stalls, staring towards where the explosion had come from, waiting for the next one. A woman was lying on the ground, her eyes closed, an old man fanning her with his hands.

He passed through the square, his head down. He came to streets that were deserted, then streets that were falling down. At the end of one, he saw the church. It was half in ruins, its belfry decapitated, part of its roof collapsed with beams jutting out like teeth. As he approached, he saw that the rest was intact. He found the door and went inside.

He'd expected to find it empty. At first he thought it was.

He walked down the aisle, past stone and cracked mosaic, the light from the open roof scything the gloom, dust misting the distance. He thought he could make out tombs, big tombs, behind the altar dais.

Luke had spoken often of this place, the ancient church of the Varangian Guard. Once it had been splendid, made so from the wealth gathered by guarding generations of Roman emperors. Now it was ruined like everything else. He approached the altar and knelt down, placing the sword across his knees.

What to do? He'd vowed not to fight. He was Portuguese now and such allegiance as he felt was to that country. And they'd imprisoned his son. Constantinople was not his battle.

He heard a sound behind him, from where the tombs lay. He turned. There was a shadow standing between them, tall, unmoving. He grasped the sword and rose, slowly, narrowing his eyes to see better.

'Who's there? Show yourself.'

The shadow moved towards the shaft of light and became a man, old and tall, with long white hair and beard. He wore a simple tunic with a belt at his middle and leggings beneath. He was staring at the sword in Giovanni's hand.

'Your sword,' said the man.

Giovanni glanced down at the dragon. 'Not mine. My son's.'

The man looked up at him, frowning. 'But yours once, yes?'

'Mine once. Do you know it?'

'It was Luke's.'

Giovanni nodded. 'My father. Did you know him?'

'He came here once. He summoned all the Varangians to this church. He wanted to present us with a chalice and plate.' He smiled. 'You're Hilarion, then.'

'No. Hilarion died.'

The man nodded. 'The bastard then.' He dipped his head. 'Begging your pardon.'

Giovanni smiled. 'No need. I'm proud of it.' He looked down again at the dragon head. 'He gave it to me.'

'And now you've brought it to defend Constantinople.' The man was gazing at him now, taller than he had been. Were those tears in his eyes?

'Well . . .' He hesitated, sheathing the sword.

The man stepped forward and took his hand. His handshake was firm. 'I am Theogrid. Have you brought others?'

Others? Giovanni was puzzled, then understood. 'Varangians, yes. At the land wall. But brought from Mistra by Hilarion's son, Siward, not me.'

Theogrid squeezed his hand. 'Siward. Yes, of course. Well, there are more like me. We are old but we can still fight. Now that we have someone to lead us.'

Giovanni began to shake his head. He released the hand and stepped back. 'I . . .'

Theogrid frowned. 'You think us too old.' He stepped forward. 'But we are *Varangians*, son-of-Luke. You should know what that means.' He began to move towards the door. 'At present, we are spread amongst the militia, mainly on the sea walls.' He turned. 'Now I will call them all together.'

'Together?'

'Yes. A hundred at least. All old Varangians. It will take some time to muster them. I will meet you here at midday the day after tomorrow.'

He left the church and Giovanni stared after him.

CHAPTER THIRTY-TWO

CONSTANTINOPLE

The storm had raged all week and the Varangians were wet to the bone. The rain had marched in from the west like another army, turning the landscape to mud, filling the fosse below them with brown, foaming water, penetrating even the tightest join of their armour. Men had slipped on the walls, and at night, stone had slipped from the hands of the men rebuilding them. Like Petros.

From dawn until dusk, cannon of every size had vomited flame. The outer wall had partly collapsed at the Mesoteichon section, where the biggest had been aimed, where Siward was. A wooden stockade, packed with earth, now stood atop rubble that had been piled up overnight by the citizens of the city. Behind it stood Siward, his Varangians and the engineer Johannes Grant. Petros was sitting with his back to it, resting from his exertions. It was dark and had just stopped raining.

'No banging,' said Siward.

It had happened every night. As the guns had fallen silent, the banging had begun, the beating of fists on wooden shields to the rhythm of a hundred *kos* drums, the trumpets blasting horrid cacophony, the cries from a hundred thousand throats: 'God is Great! *Mehmed Caesar!*'

Grant had seen it before. 'In '22 they did the same,' he said quietly. 'Through the night. It's supposed to stop us from sleeping.'

The darkness before them suddenly lifted. The moon had emerged from behind a cloud and they could see a mass of silent bashibozouks behind the palisade. There were men passing ladders over their heads to the front, others holding big stacks of wood bound with rope. Archers, their bows slung over their shoulders, were pushing their way forward to the firing step.

Siward stepped back. 'They're coming.'

The Varangians were three deep behind the stockade, their bows at the ready. Further along, where the wall was still standing, they were in single rank. He double-checked the inner wall where there were archers and crossbowmen and machines ready to throw missiles over their heads when the time came. He looked out. Now the men were bringing forward a pole from which a huge banner was unfurling. On it was the Prophet's symbol, his *tugra,* shining silver in the moonlight. He examined the killing zone to their front. To get to the wall, the Turks must cross two hundred yards of open ground, then the fosse and its breastwork behind. It would be a massacre.

'They'll not stop 'til the walls,' said Grant, 'especially with the janissaries behind, ready to kill them if they so much as turn.' He wore a quilted jerkin that still had mud at its elbows, having spent much of the week prodding the ground around the Blachernae walls where he thought Mehmed would dig his mines.

Siward looked along the walls where giant bales of wool and leather sheets had been hung to absorb the impact of the cannon: Grant's idea. He heard the creak of rope from the Turkish lines and turned. The firing doors were opening for the cannon. 'One more volley to come,' he said. 'You should get behind.'

A moment later, the night exploded as the cannon all fired together. The wall shook as stone hurled into stone and a cloud of dust fogged the moon. Siward had blocked his ears, held his breath and closed his eyes. Now he opened them to stars. He put his fingers to his temples and shook his head, then jumped to his feet.

'Get ready!'

He looked out and saw the palisade gates open. A roar of 'Allahu akbar!' filled the night as the bashibozouks rushed through them.

Both walls erupted with fire. From behind came a hail of arrows, then rocks flung from catapults, some alight. There were the bangs of handguns, the crash of cannon and more arrows took to the air. The bashibozouks fell in their hundreds as arrows and shrapnel tore into them, hurling them off their feet, tossing their heads into the air, blood arcing. It was carnage.

Now the Turks had reached the fosse and bundles of wood were being thrown into the water. Some didn't wait but jumped in, splashing their way up to the breastwork. Ladders were passed forward, vanishing when a man went down, picked up by another. The low wall seemed to stop them for a while, but the bodies soon rose above the waterline, making bridges for the living. Then they were over the breastwork and streaming across the open ground, the Prophet's *tugra* leading them.

'Swords!' yelled Siward, and the Varangians threw aside their bows and drew their blades.

'Hold the line, no gaps, steady now . . .'

The bashibozouks were climbing the rubble, tripping and slipping on rain and blood, the arrows still falling on their heads and backs. The Prophet's flag went down, then came up again, raised by a giant of a man dressed in skins.

'Allahu akbar!'

Siward sent the first head that came over the stockade far into the night. The second got the point of his sword between its eyes. Heads came up and went down and still they came on. The stockade had been driven deep into the rubble but the press of men was too great. It began to concertina, then tip backwards.

'Step back!'

They moved just in time. The stockade collapsed, sending Turks falling to the ground like skittles, men over men: fresh necks for slaughter. But new warriors climbed over the backs of their comrades, grabbing their hair for support, seizing their weapons, pushed forward by the thousands behind.

'Hold!'

Siward smashed his sword hilt into the face of an enemy, saw rage turn to blood, felt the soft crack of bone beneath his fingers. He did it again, and again, and again. But he was tiring.

He glanced around. The line had to hold. This was all there was. He saw Johannes Grant behind, loading a handgun. 'Grant!' he yelled. 'What are you *doing* here?'

'Blow the recall!'

'Disengage? *Now?*' Siward looked around for the trumpeter. He was behind him.

'Do it!'

The trumpeter blew three notes. The Varangians raised their shields and stepped back. Then came another trumpet blast, this time from the Turks. It was the retreat.

Siward watched in amazement as the bashibozouks fell back. He turned to Grant. 'Is it over?'

The engineer shook his head. 'It's the janissaries' turn now. Listen.'

Above the moans of the dying could be heard the swirl of bagpipes and the tramp of men marching in time. The janissaries were on their way. Siward looked at his men and saw what the Turks must see: men bent forward with their hands on their knees; men hunched over on the stones; men who needed to rest. Some were shaking their heads. They'd heard the bagpipes too.

Not far away, Giovanni was being rattled to death in a wagon that was rolling towards the walls. They should have been there earlier and it was his fault. He'd not really believed that Theogrid would muster a hundred Varangian veterans or that they'd come to the Varangian church at the appointed time. Anyway, as he'd said to himself repeatedly, it was not his fight.

He'd been at the top of a ladder in the city record office when the Varangian had come in.

'Begging your pardon, lord, but the men are outside.'

Giovanni had looked down to see Theogrid wearing the armour of yesterday. It was the ceremonial uniform of the Varangian Guard: all blues and golds. He carried an axe in one hand and helmet in the other. He'd glanced towards the door. 'The men?'

'Just eighty, sir. The others weren't permitted to leave their militias.'

He'd leant over the side of the ladder. 'You have eighty Varangians as old as you waiting outside?'

Theogrid had looked offended. 'Old but bold, sir. Old but bold.' He was standing to attention. 'Just awaiting your command.'

Not long afterwards had come the miracle of the wagons: six of them, tethered to horses, right in their line of march.

'Well, there's a stroke of luck, sir,' Theogrid had said. 'Who'd have thought?'

Now Giovanni was sitting opposite Theogrid, wondering how his old bones were liking the ruts below. Half an hour ago, they'd heard the distant roar of fifty thousand men released into the charge. Suddenly he was desperate to be there.

Then they could go no further. The stones from mangonels were falling all around them and the horses were rearing and trying to turn.

Giovanni jumped from the wagon and raised his sword and they followed him to the walls, passing the tents where the night-workers had emerged to watch. They were cheered as they went. The Gate of Romanus was ahead, where they could enter the peribelos and reach the outer wall.

'Open the gate!' Giovanni yelled as they approached.

The guards looked at each other. Those hadn't been their orders.

Giovanni came up to them. He'd not yet put on his helmet and was panting. 'Open it or answer to Constantine.'

'But the Emperor said . . .'

'*Open it!*'

'Open it.'

The request, more reasonably made, came from behind him. He swung round and there was Constantine, dressed in armour of dazzling white. He was flanked by men of his household guard, Notaras among them. They had their swords drawn.

'You came,' said Constantine.

Then Giovanni saw it all. He looked at Theogrid, then back at Constantine. 'I think, majesty,' he said, 'that I was meant to come.'

On the wall, the Varangians were awaiting the onslaught. They'd had a short respite after the bashibozouks had been driven back, long enough to wipe swords and tighten bandages. But then the janissaries had emerged through the rabble, their aga at their front.

Siward had looked along the line on either side of him. Men were kneeling or leaning against stone, not speaking but breathing deeply. They'd fought for an hour and would not be able to fight much longer. 'Once again, lads,' he'd yelled. 'These are the tough ones.' The men rose and edged closer together, locking their shields.

Now the janissaries were crossing the fosse, stumbling sometimes on the bodies, but keeping formation. They were well-armed and they were fresh. Hasan raised his sword and they charged.

This time it was shield that smashed into shield, without stockade to intervene. The Varangians tried to hold, digging their heels into the stone, leaning into them, but the pressure was too great. After ten minutes of pushing and stabbing, they began to inch backwards.

'Hold!' Siward yelled. But they couldn't hold. There were just too many. The line only had to break once . . .

'Siward!'

It was Grant. He was behind and he was shouting. 'You'll not hold them! We've the mantelets prepared, and I have the Brochiardi brothers ready to fire shrapnel as you disengage!'

Siward nodded. He stepped back. 'Retreat on the horn-blast!'

The retreat was so sudden that the janissaries were left off-balance. They were readying themselves to pursue when the cannon roared from the side. Janissary fell on janissary, their mail pumping blood.

Siward and his men stumbled back down the rubble towards the *peribelos* where the mobile palisades stood. 'Close up!' he shouted. 'Torches!' All down the line, Varangians came forward with flame.

The janissaries were reforming on the rubble, Hasan hauling his men into position, yelling for shields to be raised as more arrows rained down on them from the inner wall. At any moment, they'd renew the attack.

Siward stepped back to be heard. 'Varangians! The outer wall is lost. You know what to do. Light the mantelets, then run for the gates!'

Siward glanced back. The gates were slowly opening. The mantelets, doused in Greek fire, might give them time to get through, but it was risky. Would the Turks get in as well? The Varangians lowered their torches and the mantelets burst into flame.

'Go!'

The men turned but didn't move.

Siward swung round. More Varangians were coming through the gates, old Varangians. At their head was Giovanni Giustiniani Longo brandishing a sword that he recognised.

However old, they fell upon the janissaries like young wolves. They fought with axe and sword and the savagery of long hatred for this enemy, many of whom were on fire, twisting and writhing in agony, throwing themselves against the men behind.

Siward lifted his own sword. 'Are we going to give our grandfathers this victory?' he yelled. 'Who'll follow me?'

341

All of them would. The Varangians summoned their last energy and charged. The janissaries turned and ran.

Later, Constantine joined them on the outer wall. Dawn was breaking in the east and the sky over Constantinople was streaked with yellow. Beneath it, all along the great walls of Theodosius, men and women worked to repair the damage, Petros somewhere among them, piling rubble on rubble, while tall columns of smoke reached into the air like old men's fingers. In the peribelos lay the ashes of mantelets and a million arrows. Everywhere, from the siege works to the base of the inner wall, lay Turkish bodies.

Constantine was standing facing Siward, Giovanni and Johannes Grant. 'I don't know which of you to thank more.'

Siward was wiping his blade. 'What of the rest of the wall, majesty?'

'The Venetians held at the Blachernae, and other parts were not so troubled. You got the full weight of the attack here at the Mesoteichon.' He gestured. 'It was close.'

Siward looked out at the landscape. The Ottoman siege works were almost deserted. The big cannon still had its guards around it, but it was silent. There were men with stretchers walking towards the fosse under white flags. There would be a lot of burial over the coming days. Then they'd come again. It had been close. *Too close.*

He looked back at Constantine. The Emperor held his hands together but the shaking was obvious. He went over to him, drew him away, whispered into his ear. 'You should rest.'

Constantine looked at him. 'And who commands then?'

Siward took a deep breath. 'You know who should.' He held his gaze. 'And we both know what it will take.'

The Emperor stared at him. Then he nodded slowly. He turned and went over to Giovanni. 'If I release your son, will you serve me?'

Giovanni glanced at Siward and back. 'How would you have me do so, majesty?'

'I would have you command the defence of this city.' Constantine gestured to the engineer. 'You and Grant organised the defence of Ceuta. I would have you do the same here.' He lowered his voice. 'Look at me. I am nearly spent, Giovanni. It is time for someone else to lead.'

CHAPTER THIRTY-THREE

CONSTANTINOPLE

The day after the Turkish assault, Giovanni summoned the leaders of the men defending Constantinople to the Romanus Gate. It was early morning and the day was already warm and the men had their helmets off and faces turned to the heat like sunflowers. They'd forgotten how good it felt to be alive.

Siward was watching steam rise from the city of tents below the walls. Their number had doubled since the night of the attack, with whole families arriving every hour to help rebuild the wall. He watched women putting out clothes to dry, chatting through the corner of their mouths because pegs filled the rest. The siege was two weeks old but life had to be lived. He watched Petros emerge from a tent and limp his way to a bucket of water to wash. He'd hardly seen him since he'd been put to work on the walls, but last night they'd managed to share a flagon. They'd even dared a toast to victory.

Constantine came to stand next to him. 'That was clever, bringing the women to the walls. Now they can be with their men.'

'The men will fight harder with their women behind them,'

said Siward. He felt well. Giovanni's first order had been to send him off to the palace to rest. Despite last night's wine, he felt better than he had in weeks. Violetta was safe in Chios and they might just win this siege.

'Gennadius has kept his word,' said Constantine, watching two boys sitting outside the tents sharpening arrowheads. 'The people want to fight.'

They heard voices behind them and turned to see Giovanni greeting the first of the arrivals. Not long afterwards, the space was full of men standing in groups, quietly grumbling. Giovanni was standing in front of a big map of the city set on an easel. He called for silence.

At last it came and he turned to the map. 'Behold, the dog's head,' he said. The city was indeed a dog's head, its nose the Acropolis Point, its thick neck the land walls, the triple defences its collar. 'But this dog is muzzled.'

Venetian, Genoese and Catalan looked up. Muzzled? They'd fought hard for this city that wasn't theirs.

'Why so?' asked Doria of the Genoese. He'd held the Rhegium Gate with great bravery the night before last.

'Well,' said Giovanni, smiling as if he was with his dearest friends, 'because its bark is so much less than it could be.'

Don Francesco de Toledo, the old Spaniard commanding the Castilian contingent, frowned. 'Castile's bark was loud enough. I'm sorry you didn't hear it, general.'

Giovanni turned to him. 'I'm sorry too, Francesco. But it wasn't the same bark as the Catalans' next to you at the Third Military Gate.' He swung round to face Doria. 'And yours was very different from Minotto's up at the Blachernae.' He waved all around him. 'This dog barks in a hundred different voices and our enemy hears it and is glad.'

Minotto was leaning against the battlement, using his beret to fan himself. 'It may have escaped your notice that we are all from different nations, Longo. We're different breeds of dog.'

Everyone laughed except Giovanni. 'Genoa, Venice, Florence?' He pointed out to the Turks. 'Not so far away as Anatolia is from Rumelia, I fancy. Yet our enemy doesn't quarrel.' No one said anything so Giovanni continued. 'I have seen Genoese draw on Venetian. I've heard Catalonia challenge Castile because a flag fell over in the wind. It must stop.'

Minotto said, 'These are long-standing quarrels, Longo. They won't prevent us fighting the Turk.'

'No, but will you fight best with one eye on your neighbour? Gentlemen, are we not all knights of Christendom? Is it not time to drop our enmities and unite behind our emperor?'

He walked over to Minotto and stretched out his hand. 'I am Genoese and you, Minotto, are Venetian. So we were born to be enemies. But I will ask you to take my hand.'

It was brilliantly done. There was little Minotto could do but agree. He slowly proffered his hand. Giovanni grasped it and pulled him close to his chest. 'Nobly done,' he said. He turned. 'Now will you all follow the bailo?'

They had no choice. Castilian shook with Catalan, Tuscany with Umbria. It was done with little grace, but it was done.

But Minotto wanted some small revenge. 'Longo,' he said, drawing away. 'It's said that the price of your service was the release of your son. Is it so?'

Giovanni nodded. 'The Emperor received Makkim's oath, yes. He'll not help the Turk. He is at the walls looking out for your fleet.'

'But did he not break his oath to escape Mistra? And wasn't he Mehmed's friend once? Who is to say that he's not been sent here to let him into the city?' He turned and spoke to Constantine. 'Majesty, might it not be prudent to have someone with Makkim? One of my men would oblige.'

It was a Greek, not Makkim, who saw them first. The man had been made lookout on the Golden Gate because he had the gift of long sight. While others stared all day at the Turkish palisade, he passed his watch looking out to sea. Beside him was a bell to ring.

Makkim had been sent there by his father, he supposed, because it would afford him the best view of the siege. They weren't to leave the city after all, and such a vantage point might save his life. He'd arrived that morning from his Blachernae prison dressed as a Byzantine soldier. He'd come through the streets and seen how worn the city had become. Last time he'd seen a place full of merchants and money-lenders: flies on a decaying corpse, detestable. Now he was surprised how much he pitied it, and admired it too. But Giovanni had said it himself: this was not his fight – not this side of the wall, anyway. Did he want to be on the other? *No, not any more.*

He looked out. To the north, the mighty Theodosian Walls ran all the way to the Golden Horn, the Turkish lines two hundred paces to their front. To the east, the sea walls followed the shoreline up to Acropolis Point and beyond. To the south, the vast spread of the Propontis lay blue and empty. In better times, it would have been busy with traffic. Now it was dolphins that caused the Greek lookout to reach for his bell.

He thought of the freedom Constantine had given him. The Emperor must know he'd broken his oath before and Siward would've argued hard for him not to be released. Was it just the inheritance that drove his cousin's hatred, or something else?

It was ironic, really, since he'd hardly thought of the trading company. But now? Violetta had lost everything. She'd need his money.

He shielded his eyes to see the far shore where some of the Ottoman fleet had been placed. He supposed they were there to intercept any help coming from the south. Such as a fleet from Venice. He saw the lookout lean out to the view, his hand up to the sun, still as a hunting dog.

'Do you see anything?' he asked.

'I thought . . .'

He'd heard the man had rung the bell before for seabirds. He'd not be mistaken again.

'You saw sails?'

The man remained silent. Two other guards joined him on his other side and looked for a while. 'Nothing,' said one, turning away.

But the man stayed there, cocking his head slightly and blinking.

'Yes,' he said. 'There.' He was pointing.

Makkim leant as far out as he dared, his hands to the ramparts. He saw empty sea dappled by tiny cloud, gulls swooping down for fish. He saw the single Turkish galley riding close to the shore that had been there all day.

Then he saw something else. A sail. A square-rigged sail, a sail with a cross on its front.

'By Allah,' he whispered. 'They've come.' He turned to the man. 'How many do you count?'

'Three. No, four.' He was young and breathless with excitement. This sighting might change his life forever. 'Four ships so far. Should I ring the bell, sir?'

Makkim nodded. 'Yes. Ring it.'

The man rang it and rang it and shouted as loud as he was able, 'Sails to the south! Venice is come!'

Officers arrived and stared out and saw the sails and clapped him on the back and messengers were dispatched to all parts of the city. Meanwhile, the churches passed on the message. First came the bells of St John Studius, then St Diomedes, then the queen of them all: Hagia Sophia, whose deep voice drowned them all.

And all the while, Makkim looked over at the far shore. Yes, the Turks had seen them too. And if they hadn't, then they'd heard the bells. The galleys would be making ready to cast off; messengers would be riding north to signal to the main fleet lying at Diplokionon harbour. He thought of his friend Baltaoğlu, Mehmed's *kapudan pasha*, whose task it would be to stop this fleet. He'd be summoning his galley captains, urging them to row like they'd never rowed.

He heard a shout behind him and turned. It was Siward and he was running towards him. Beside him was a Venetian soldier.

'Sails, I heard,' he said coming up, breathless. 'Venice?'

Makkim shrugged. 'Only four, so far,' he said, looking out again. 'Three are roundships, by their shape.'

Siward stood next to him and looked out. 'Then not Venice,' he said.

Makkim nodded. 'I would keep that to yourself for now,' he said quietly. 'The people want good news.'

Siward looked at him. 'Do you think I can't work that out for myself?' He looked away. 'And they're not your people.'

Makkim bridled. 'Are you here to insult me?'

Siward began to speak, then stopped himself. He said, 'Violetta is still in Chios but we know that she wants to come

349

here. If those are Genoese sails, they might have come from Chios.' He glanced back at the guards. 'They may have her on board.'

Makkim looked out to sea. Twelve galleys had detached themselves from the far shore and were rowing hard to intercept the ships. He glanced north. Still no sign of Baltaoğlu's fleet, but it would be on its way.

He looked back at Siward. 'We must hope she's not aboard.'

Salazar was confident.

'We've a brisk south-westerly behind us and a hull made of hardest oak,' he said, puffing out his chest like the sails above him. 'They'll not stop us.'

Violetta wanted to believe him, but there were twelve Turkish galleys blocking their path. They were strung out in the shape of a bull's head, triremes and biremes massed in the middle, smaller fustae at the horns. They had shipped their oars and were rocking in the swell, bows facing them. They were close enough for her to see cannon on their rembatas.

'But they've got guns,' she said. 'I can see them pointing at us.'

'Small bore,' said Salazar. 'They'll not hurt us.'

Violetta liked Salazar, had done since their first meeting on Chios. He had a bluff confidence and a frame to fill it. He stood with his hands on his hips and legs apart like he was about to laugh out loud, which he quite often did.

She'd met him on the same quayside where she'd met Minotto, two weeks after the dawn when she'd been ejected from the bailo's cabin. She'd not been surprised by Minotto breaking his word, just angry with herself for ever thinking he wouldn't. It must have been the cold that had muddled her judgement. Anyway, she'd escaped with the map she'd spent half the night copying stuffed inside her bosom, and a hefty amount of gold coin, some of which she'd spent on clothes.

Thank God, then, for her bright yellow dress. Salazar had spotted it in the crowd watching his ships come in. He'd sought her out the minute he'd set foot on land.

'Violetta Cavarse, I think,' he'd said, bowing low. 'I've a message for you.'

He'd handed her a letter from Zoe. It was short and to the point.

If you are reading this, you are at Chios, not Constantinople. The Portuguese Salazar is to be trusted. He carries my cargo of weapons and food for the city. Go with him. You will only be happy when you are with Siward.

She'd read it again and felt waves of happiness break over her. She'd looked up to find Salazar offering her an orange, quartered on a plate, as someone else had a long time ago. 'From Portugal, like me,' he'd said. 'Very sweet.'

Now the captain was standing, feet splayed, hands on hips, looking up at the pennants streaming from the tops of the masts. He was laughing.

'It's a good wind, this. It'll sweep us right into the Golden Horn.' He looked behind him at their companions: three round ships from Genoa and a Byzantine carrack full of grain.

They were passing Lighthouse Point and above, the walls of the Bucoleon Palace and great dome of the Hagia Sophia shimmered in the early light. They were pitted and broken but it didn't matter. This was Constantinople, greatest city in the world. This was where Siward was.

On the sea walls were hundreds of people. She saw a flare go up, then another. She saw soldiers on the towers, their armour glinting in the sunshine. Was he among them? Was he watching her even now? She looked down the length of the ship. Men with crossbows and handguns crowded the sides, some holding axes. They were almost on top of the galleys.

'Brace yourselves!' shouted Salazar.

She heard the crash of cannon to their front. The Turks were firing at point blank range and Violetta felt the ship shudder as the shot bounced off the hull. It was as strong as Salazar had boasted.

She could hear the beat of the kos drum now and see fat men on the galleys' *histodokes* cracking their whips above the heads of slaves, desperately trying to row out of the way of the leviathan bearing down on them. The galleys disappeared below the round ship's prow and Violetta held the deck rail hard. She heard the sound of fifty crossbows released.

The collision bent her double over the rail, winding her despite the breastplate. She opened her eyes to see the Genoese firing down into the galleys that clustered around their sides like termites. She saw grappling irons being tossed up and thrown back, ladders pushed away, blazing torches picked up and hurled over the side. The Turks were twenty feet below them, unable to climb the round ship's sides. They were hacking at the hull, trying to dig footholds, dying by the dozen from the hail of missiles above.

And the ship below her was still moving. The wind still filled its sails and it had the momentum of size. The Turks were being slowly pushed aside.

She heard a trumpet blast over the shouts and screams and the groan of timber. She looked up to see another, much larger fleet bearing down on them. Salazar came to stand at her side. He held a crossbow. 'Baltaoğlu,' he whispered. '*Diavolo.*'

There were perhaps seventy galleys rowing towards them, their kos drums beating out triple time, their oars rising and splashing to the fevered rhythm. Surely they'd not push their way through such a fleet.

'What will they do?' she asked.

'Do? Oh, everything, I imagine.' Salazar looked up at the pennants, then over to shore. 'They'll try and ram us, burn us, board us. If they can get here in time.' He glanced at her. 'You must go below.'

'No,' she said. 'I'll not sit down there and wait for my fate. Give me a weapon.'

He shook his head. 'Zoe Mamonas has paid me to take you into Constantinople. Alive.'

'Zoe Mamonas is in Venice. If I'm to die, let me die fighting.'

Salazar looked down the deck. So far, it had been safe enough. The height and strength of the round ship made it invulnerable. No Turk had yet reached halfway up its sides. He glanced behind. The other ships were the same: giant floating castles, lumbering war-elephants swarmed by jackals.

'Alright,' he said. 'But stay near me.' He gave her his crossbow. It had a quarrel in its flight groove.

There was a crash from below and the ship rail exploded into splinters. A man staggered back, half his face torn away. Two more lay dead on the deck.

'Culverin!' shouted Salazar.

Violetta watched one, then two grappling irons appear over the ship's side, their ropes snapping taut as they gripped. She heard the whine of old timber as the big ship slowed down. A moment later, two turbans appeared over the side.

Salazar ran over to one of the dead men and picked up his axe. He smashed it into a Turk's face, then hacked at the rope.

The other Turk had one hand on the rail and a scimitar in the other. He was raising it. Violetta brought the crossbow into the aim. She took a deep breath and closed one eye. She pulled the trigger.

A fountain of blood sprayed from the man's head and she wondered who else had fired. But the quarrel had left the groove. She felt elated.

Salazar turned and bowed. 'My compliments.'

She had no idea how to reload. She looked over at the ship's bow. Baltaoğlu's fleet was much closer now. She glanced up at the city walls to her left. She saw the ruins of the Acropolis and the tower of St Demetrius Church. The Golden Horn was just around the corner. They were so close. If the garrison were ready to raise the floating boom, then they'd make it. But would the ships behind?

She turned. The other three ships were surrounded by Turkish galleys but their sails were filled and they were still moving. She saw ladders and hooks and climbing nets being cut from their sides, the water full of Turks and splintered oars. The galleys were firing their culverins but the shots were flying high above the heads of the defenders. She heard the sound of cheering from their decks.

Then, quite suddenly, the wind died. It was as if God had held His breath. Violetta looked up and saw the sails luff, then droop. The ship slowed and came to a standstill, rocking gently in the swell. Now the cheers came from the Turks, both from behind and in front. Baltaoğlu's fleet was almost on top of them.

'Holy Mary, Mother of God,' she whispered, but the Virgin wasn't listening. The sails flapped and the ship began to move sideways, drifting with the current, away from the city and towards the shore where the Turks were waiting, where a figure on a white horse stood half in the sea. He was raised high in his stirrups, waving his arms, shouting, and a bodyguard in gold mail stood on the shore behind him. Mehmed.

She looked over towards the boom, no more than two hundred paces away. There were ships lined up on its other side, waiting to lift it.

'Can't they pull us in?'

But Salazar was concentrating on the approaching armada. It was moving fast and bronze beasts rose and fell in the waves with each pull of the oars. They were going to ram them.

The Turks drove into them and the ship shuddered as every beam collided with another. She saw men thrown across the deck. From all around them came drums and trumpets and the shouts of men scenting victory at last.

'*Allahu akbar!*'

Grappling irons were flying everywhere now. As soon as one was cut away, another landed. The air was thick with arrows. Violetta looked up at the sails. Men were furling them in case of fire. She looked over the side. There was no sea any more, only wood and men surrounding the ships in a chaos of interlocking oars. Turks were scrambling from galley to galley to join the assault.

Then she heard trumpets sounding in unison. Some of the galleys were pulling away from the round ships, making way for smaller fustae. She saw smoke coming from their decks.

Salazar was beside her. 'They're going to ram, then throw fire.' He rose and yelled down the deck, 'Get the buckets!'

Violetta felt another jolt run the length of the ship. She ran to the rail and looked down. The galley below had pots of fire all along its deck. Archers were dipping arrows into them, swathed in oiled cloth. Soon the arrows were landing on the ship's deck.

'Water!' yelled Salazar.

Men with buckets stepped forward. As soon as an arrow landed, it was extinguished. But the men were tiring fast. Violetta saw a crossbowman kneel to reload his weapon. She saw him fall back, clawing at the arrow sunk deep in his throat, blood swelling through his fingers. She turned away. She needed a sword. She wanted to fight and she wasn't afraid. *Where is a sword?* There. On the deck: a falchion. She picked it up.

She heard a shout. A man was pointing over the stern at the ship behind. It was floundering and Turks were nearly over its sides. Salazar ran over to the tiller and started to pull on it. Two men joined him. She felt the ship begin to turn. Slowly, slowly.

'Rope!' yelled Salazar as he pulled. Two more men came with it. 'Bind us to the next ship,' he yelled. 'Tell the others to do the same.'

Violetta watched the big ships slowly come together, everything between them crushed as the ropes were thrown that would bind them into a fortress afloat. But it was only delaying the inevitable. Bit by bit, they were nearing the shore where Mehmed was now up to his knees in the water, yelling at Baltaoğlu.

Then, another miracle.

Unnoticed by the battle, afternoon had turned into evening and with it had come another wind. Salazar ordered the sails unfurled and, looking up, Violetta saw them slowly fill. Timber shrieked as the ship began to move. Violetta saw the other ships' sails drop, one by one. The same wind filled them too and bound together, the ships lurched forward. Once more, they were heading towards the boom.

'A miracle!' yelled Salazar, grinning from the tiller. 'God knows His own after all!'

She ran to the side and saw the Turkish galleys being pushed aside as the ships edged towards the Golden Horn. She looked up. The sails were snapping, getting fatter every moment. She felt a thud and saw that a grappling iron had embedded itself inside the rail. Another landed beside it. Both ropes tautened and she felt the ship shudder as it slowed. She began hacking at the rope with her falchion. She heard a shout from below and felt an arrow part her hair. On her third hack, she cut the rope.

The next rope was thicker and she had to hit it again and again. She looked down to see a man crawling up it, knife between his teeth. She leant out to get into a better position. One more would do it.

She swiped, the rope broke and her blade struck air. She lost her balance and tried to hold onto the rail but her fingers couldn't find it. She was falling.

She landed on the water badly. A searing pain shot up her arm and her head nearly came away from her shoulders. She grabbed at a spar but it slipped from her hand. She was sinking fast in a cloud of bubbles, desperately kicking to stop her descent. She tried to undo her breastplate but one of her arms didn't seem to be working. Her lungs were bursting and her head pounding. She had to breathe.

She closed her eyes to commit herself to God. But it wasn't God who she wanted to commit herself to.

Siward.

CHAPTER THIRTY-FOUR

CONSTANTINOPLE

The slaves rowing the kapudan pasha's trireme back to Diplokionion harbour did so more slowly than on the journey out. Bataoğlu was in no hurry to see Mehmed again.

He sat beneath the awning on the aft deck with his bandaged head in his hands, the memory of Christian mockery still fresh in his mind. As they'd rowed away from the floating chain, having failed to slip in behind the four ships, he'd watched the walls of Constantinople erupt in jeering.

Well, at least he'd not have to suffer the humiliation for long. He just hoped Mehmed would allow him an honourable death.

He looked out at the rest of the fleet. They'd lost a dozen galleys and at least that many fustae, and were leaving behind a sea scattered with the limbs of ship and man. It had been a very public disaster, one witnessed by both armies and much of the citizenry of Constantinople. They'd seen Allah favour the besieger first, then change His mind. He felt sick. Perhaps he should kill himself now.

No. That was the Roman way but also the coward's way. He was a slave, the property of his sultan. It was for Mehmed to

358

decide how he should die. He thought of Makkim. They'd been friends once. He'd often wondered if he'd sought another way out: capture by the enemy. But surely that was the least honourable of all. Well, it was too late anyway.

Worse, though, was not being part of the great enterprise that would follow Constantinople's fall. Since being sworn to secrecy by Mehmed, he'd planned every detail, tested every assumption. It would be the greatest adventure ever undertaken by man, but he'd not lead it now. He put his head back in his hands and closed his eyes. Very quietly, he began to cry.

Not much later, after Baltaoğlu had stepped from his flagship to face the full fury of Mehmed, after he'd been spat on and slapped and seen his horsetails ripped from their spear and stamped into the ground, he sat in a cage with three other slaves.

Two were young Genoese sailors who'd been somehow captured during the battle. They were frightened men who remembered the fate of Venetians who'd tried to run the guns of Rumelihisar. The third was someone as amazed as Baltaoğlu that she was still alive.

Violetta Cavarse had committed herself to God, then Siward, not caring much about the blasphemy involved. An afterlife without him would not be an afterlife she could commit to. Now she lay very still and thought what a fool she'd been. Her vanity had brought her to Constantinople and now she found herself Mehmed's prisoner. At least Siward wouldn't know she was there.

She examined what she could see of the world around her. She was there with three men, two young and one older, with the moustaches of a janissary. He wore simple clothes but

359

looked like he was used to something better. He had a rope around his neck that also tied his hands. He sat with his head lowered between elbows resting on his knees. As far as she could tell, she wasn't bound at all. But she'd lost her breastplate.

One of the young men was whispering, leaning in to the other. 'They were *impaled*. Do you know what that means?'

The other let out a little wail. He had his back to the bars and was clutching his legs as if they might try to escape without him.

Violetta moved her head slightly to see where she was. It was late in the evening and everything was washed with orange. The cage seemed to be in the middle of an army camp, although there was little noise. She saw soldiers sitting around cauldrons between the tents, either silent or talking in low voices. The smell of cooking was in the air.

She slowly raised herself to sit, feeling her hair pressed cold to her neck by the bars. She glanced down at her tunic and trousers. Did they know she was a woman? The two Italians had stopped talking and were looking at her.

'What are you doing here?' asked the one who wasn't crying. 'You're a woman.'

'I don't know where I am,' she said.

She saw the older man raise his head from his elbows. His face was badly bruised and his spirits seemed the same. He spoke in Italian. 'You are in the camp of Zaganos bey,' he said, 'the Sultan's second vizier.' He smiled at her. 'You are here because the captain of my galley rescued you on my instruction. I saw you fall into the water.'

So that was how she was still alive. 'Thank you,' she said. 'And please thank your captain.'

'That is unlikely,' said Baltaoğlu. 'I have been relieved of my command.'

Violetta remembered something. 'You are Baltaoğlu?'

The older man nodded. 'I was Baltaoğlu. Now, I'm not so sure.' He turned to the men. 'You won't be impaled. The Sultan's anger will pass. You'll be sold as slaves, I expect.'

Violetta asked, 'And me?'

Baltaoğlu appraised her. 'Well, beneath the disguise I can see beauty. So you'll go to someone's harem, I suppose.' He smiled again. 'It might have been mine, once.'

Harem. The irony almost made her laugh. She'd just escaped her profession to find herself back in it. But no, she'd not go. Not if she could possibly help it. She heard the faint sound of banging and turned her head. Men were building something far away. Siege towers?

'Where is this camp?' she asked.

'Across the Golden Horn, facing the sea walls. Not where the fighting is.' The man shifted his body to better face her. 'The main assaults have been made against the land walls. The Varangians have beaten us back every time.'

The Varangians. That would be where he was, fighting where it was fiercest. She closed her eyes. *Siward.*

'So why are you here?' asked Baltaoğlu gently, watching her. 'Armageddon is hardly the place for a woman.' His head tilted. 'Is it a man?'

She so wanted to tell him, this stranger who seemed to have lost all hope, who might be thankful for some of hers. *Yes. It's a man. It's someone I'd rather die with than live without.* But she had to be careful; no one must know who she was. She had to escape. Somehow. She asked, 'Who are the Christian commanders, do you know?'

Baltaoğlu scratched the bandage at each temple with his joined thumbs. There was dried blood on it and it didn't look

361

as if it had been changed since the wound had been inflicted. 'Well, there's the Emperor Constantine and Minotto, the Venetian bailo,' he said. 'And now they have Giustiniani Longo, we hear, who's been reunited with Johannes Grant, the engineer.'

So Giovanni was in Constantinople. But why? Had he come with Siward? 'Have your cannon done much harm?'

'They've pounded the walls for three weeks. There are big holes in the outer wall but every night they rebuild it. The citizens of Constantinople are defending their city bravely.'

She felt some small relief. 'Will they win?' she asked.

Baltaoğlu shrugged. 'They might.' He glanced through the bars. 'Look at this camp. Morale is low, especially after today. Men think Allah has deserted Mehmed.' He frowned. 'And if the defenders were all to fight like the Varangians, well . . .' He let the sentence fade.

'Who commands the Varangians?' she asked.

Baltaoğlu shook his head. 'I don't know. They came up from Mistra, apparently. Perhaps the same man that took Makkim prisoner.'

Violetta looked away. She felt then a yearning for Siward stronger than it had ever been. How would she escape this cage? How would she get into Constantinople if she did? She glanced at the Genoese sailors, now staring blankly in front of them. She'd get no help from them.

She heard the banging again and the rumble of something being rolled. *What is it you're building out there?*

Eugenius was dressed as a monk but had the big wooden crucifix tucked inside his habit. The rain had turned the ground to a thick stew that oozed through his sandalled toes as he walked. Up ahead he could see the shapes of sentries huddled

362

around braziers in the rain, thankful perhaps that they were not facing the land walls.

He raised his hands as he approached them. He was more frightened than he'd ever been, but then no mission would ever again be so important. Opportunity like this wouldn't come twice in a lifetime.

Yesterday he'd stood on the walls at Acropolis Point and watched four transport ships fight their way into Constantinople. He'd seen their sails fill with wind and slowly pull away from the Turkish galleys. He'd cheered like everyone else. He'd watched Baltaoğlu make one desperate attempt to stop the last of the transports reaching sanctuary. He'd seen the kapudan pasha standing on the deck, shouting at the men throwing the grappling irons. He'd seen the hooks take hold, the round ship slow and someone fall into the water. He'd seen the person rescued and laid on the galley's deck, their breastplate and helmet removed. He'd seen long black hair spread out across the deck. He'd seen someone he'd been told to look out for. A sister. *Her.*

Then something had connected in his brain. He'd remembered Makkim's face that night outside the church. It had seemed somehow familiar behind the scar. Brother and sister, Minotto had said. *How had he got that scar?* Of course.

He'd felt some fear but it was all so long ago and they couldn't possibly know he was in the city. Then he'd seen opportunity.

Now, he was handing over a message.

'Zaganos bey,' he said, pointing into the camp.

The sentry looked at him, then the note. He turned and left through the mud. Eugenius waited and listened to the thump of his heart, the low murmur of the guards who stared at him and shook their heads.

The sentry returned and beckoned him to follow. He was led

through rows of tents. He passed a wagon full of stripped tree trunks and heard the sound of banging in the distance. He came to a piece of open ground with a cage and prisoners sitting inside it. He turned aside and crept closer, using the tents as cover. The cage had three men in it and a woman. He smiled. *Perfect.*

The sentry shouted something and he hurried back, nearly tripping on his habit. They came to a big pavilion and he was shown in. He waited.

A tall man entered from another room. He was drying his neck with a towel. He stopped and stared at the man before him for some time, then continued drying. He went over to a table and poured himself wine. He sat and drank and stretched out his legs.

'Your message said that you know where Makkim is and can bring him into this camp,' he said in Greek. 'Why would I believe you?'

A trickle of rain ran down the monk's back and he shivered. He took a deep breath. 'Why would I risk my life if the story was untrue?' he responded.

The man paused with his lips above the goblet. He lowered it. 'You are insolent, monk. Do you know who I am?'

'I hope you are Zaganos bey. If you are, you will take my message to your master.'

Zaganos studied him, running his eyes over the battered habit, the sandals, the muddy feet. He brushed imaginary dust from his sleeve. 'Makkim is imprisoned in Mistra.'

'No. He is here. In Constantinople.'

Zaganos put down his goblet. 'That is impossible.'

'I have seen him. He came with the vizier Candarli Halil to meet with Gennadius. Then he went into the city.'

Zaganos frowned. What was Candarli doing?

'Why?'

'To bring someone out. His sister.'

'The courtesan,' murmured Zaganos. He was nodding slowly now, turning this news over in his mind. He did not seem displeased.

There was a rustle behind the curtain to the other room. It was drawn back. Another man stood there, dressed in a thoub of patterned silk. He was staring at Eugenius.

'Makkim is in Constantinople?'

Eugenius knelt and put his head to the carpet. It smelt of wine. 'Yes, majesty. But I can bring him to you.'

Mehmed walked over to where the wine was. 'How? Sit up to speak.'

Eugenius rose and glanced at Zaganos. There was so much to play for. *Careful.*

'May I ask my reward?' he asked.

'What do you want? Name it.'

So much to play for. What did he want? Gold? *I could have everything.*

'Patriarch,' he said. 'I want to be Patriarch of Constantinople when the city falls.'

Mehmed poured two goblets and turned. He offered one. 'Will you take wine?'

Eugenius shook his head.

'A proper monk. Good.' He drank. 'A good Patriarch, in fact. So how will you deliver Makkim to me?'

'You have a valuable prisoner, lord.'

The Sultan went to a low table and sat before a game of chess. He picked up a piece and Eugenius saw that his hand was unsteady. Baltaoğlu's defeat had affected him as badly as it had his army. The eyes that met his had fear in them.

365

'Who?'

'Someone who will bring Makkim to you: his sister. She is outside in a cage.'

Zaganos bey intervened. 'How do you know this?'

The monk ignored him, continuing to address the Sultan. 'She was aboard one of the Genoese ships yesterday and fell into the water. She was coming to join Makkim in Constantinople. If you were to let it be known that you will kill her unless Makkim surrenders to you, he will give himself up.'

A light had appeared in Mehmed's eye. He was smiling for the first time in days. He said, 'Take me to this girl.'

Eugenius shook his head. 'I will point her out to you, master. Nothing more.'

CHAPTER THIRTY-FIVE

CONSTANTINOPLE

It was dawn. The rain had stopped and great blades of sunlight sliced through the dark clouds as if more Commandments were on their way. The bells were silent and the city held its breath. Two days ago, people had crowded onto the sea walls to watch Salazar's ships fight their way into the city. Now they looked over the Golden Horn to the hills behind. Something was happening there.

Siward and Makkim stood side by side in silence. It was Salazar who'd removed their power to speak. After watching the sea battle, they'd gone down to the harbour to see his four battered ships come in. They'd watched him helped onto the quay, his arm bandaged and his face caked with blood. Siward had gone up to him, Makkim behind.

'Do you have any passengers?' he'd asked. 'A woman?'

Salazar had looked at him through the eye that was not swollen. 'May I ask your name, sir?'

'I am Siward Magoris, commander of the Varangian Guard.'

Salazar shook his head. 'Then you must prepare yourself for bad news. We picked up Violetta Cavarse from Chios but she is no longer with us. She must have fallen overboard in the battle.'

Siward stared at the man. He shook his head. 'Why in the name of God would you bring her here?'

'Those were my orders.'

'Orders? From whom?'

'These ships belong to Zoe Mamonas of Venice.' He grimaced as he shifted a leg.

Makkim asked, 'Did any of the crew see her fall?'

'None.'

'So you don't know if she swam to the shore?'

Salazar shrugged slightly. 'It's possible, I suppose.'

It was hope, the merest sliver of it, but it was hope. They'd searched the city for two nights and a day, dividing it between them and looking in every place where a half-drowned woman might have sought refuge.

Now they were standing on the walls, as silent as everyone else, the only sounds the shouts that came from the other side of the hill. They were the shouts of men straining to pull something heavy. They'd first been heard two hours ago and were getting louder with every passing minute. More and more people had come up to see what was happening. Siward thought he knew.

'Cannon,' he said, his voice dry of feeling. 'They must have cast another of the monsters.' He'd turned to Makkim. 'Did you know anything about this?'

Makkim shook his head. 'Nothing.'

Siward grunted. Part of him didn't care any more. They'd not found Violetta and if she was dead, then it didn't much matter how many cannon had been cast. But was she dead?

He heard footsteps on the steps behind him. He looked round to see the Emperor coming up. With him were Giovanni and Grant.

'Minotto is not happy,' said Constantine, as he arrived on the battlements. 'He doesn't like your Varangians fighting beside his men.'

They'd had this conversation many times before but Siward didn't feel ready for it now. He dipped his head but remained silent.

The Emperor looked at him for a while, then out at the view. He'd been told about Violetta. 'Anyway, the city smells better this morning,' he said simply. 'Bread's being baked and people smile. They think the Venetians are coming.'

'The fleet should have arrived by now, highness,' he said. 'Salazar says he'd heard it left Venice in February, long before he sailed out of Genoa. Someone on Chios thought it was being held at Negroponte.'

'Does Salazar know to keep quiet?'

Siward nodded. 'He knows, though rumour runs like fire through this city these days.'

The Emperor returned to the view. He shielded his eyes. 'What are we looking at?'

The sounds of exertion were louder now. They could hear the roar of thousands of men pulling, pausing, pulling; the crack of whip, the heavy beat of drum. It was a raw, animal sound, and it ran up the walls and through the spine of every person who stood there.

Siward scanned the horizon. It was lit by a single shaft of sunlight and steam rose from the ground as a mist. He saw movement through the mist. He pointed. 'What's that?'

There was something coming over the hill. It was long and pointed and was, perhaps, the axle for a team of oxen. It shuddered as it moved, coming and going through the mist.

Constantine turned to Giovanni. 'Can we fetch the man who saw the ships? His long sight would be useful.'

But Giovanni knew what he was seeing. 'No need, majesty,' he said quietly. 'Those are more ships.'

Siward could see what it was now: the prow of a *fusta* and, on either side of it, lines of men pulling ropes. As he watched, the ship hovered on the crest of the hill, then began to drop. He saw men stagger forward on either side, carrying gigantic logs that they laid on the ground before it. Sufi holy men in long black skirts danced and wheeled around them, ululating and waving their arms in the air. The ship was sailing over the hill and down into the Golden Horn. And there would be others behind it.

'My God,' whispered Grant. 'The bastards have actually done it.'

'And they're rowing.'

The oars were quite visible now, a line of them on either side of the hull, rising and falling through the air, working to the beat of the drum, the deep chant of thousands of voices. The first ship was moving down the slope and the men on either side were straining at the ropes to slow its descent. Another had appeared behind it, a bigger ship with banners full of script. Two rows of oars paddled the air on either side in perfect unison. It balanced on the crest of the hill then began its own progress downhill.

'Look,' said Giovanni, pointing. 'At the back.'

The stern deck had a raised dais below an awning of different-coloured silks. Two people were sat beneath it, side by side, a man and a woman.

'Thank God,' whispered Siward. He glanced at Makkim, then, unthinking, reached for his arm. 'Thank God.'

Violetta and Mehmed were sitting side by side on two thrones. Mehmed was dressed in full armour as if he was riding his chariot to war. Violetta was wearing a simple white gown and her head was bare. She didn't move, just stared straight ahead.

The Turks' chant was louder now, a deep, rolling dirge that might have accompanied a funeral march. All along the walls, people were on their knees crossing themselves, their eyes closed and lips moving, the sound of wailing rising above the sound of prayer. They knew what this meant: Constantinople was now besieged on all sides. The sea walls would have to be manned. The exhausted defenders would be spread too thin.

The front ship had now reached the Golden Horn and the first of the oars splashed into the water. A cheer went up from the rowers and the men who could now release their ropes. The fat man on the histodoke waved his whip over the heads of the oarsman and delivered one last crack.

Constantine turned to Grant. 'Will our cannon reach them?'

The engineer was glowering at the ships in a way that was not entirely critical. He shook his head. 'Too far, majesty. We'll have to think of another way.'

The third ship was coming over the hill and down into the Valley of the Springs. This one had its sail spread and its oarsmen dressed in mail that winked in the sunlight. They sang as they rowed.

Mehmed's galley was being slid gently into the water, its oars like caterpillar legs. When the ship had settled, Mehmed rose from his throne and his gaze travelled along the walls. He raised his arms slowly and the singing and cheering of the rowers died. Bit by bit, the people on the walls fell silent too.

Siward hadn't taken his eyes from Violetta. He couldn't see her expression but her pose said everything he needed to know. She was rigid with the shame. She would be torturing herself for her folly in letting herself become Mehmed's most lethal weapon. And he? Now that the relief had run its course, was he angry? *No.*

'Constantine!'

Mehmed's voice carried across the Golden Horn.

'Constantine! Your city is doomed. I am behind you now, as well as in front. Venice is not coming to your aid. I will send you my terms of surrender tomorrow and perhaps you will decide that your people should not be put to the sword.'

There were murmurs along the wall but Mehmed had more to say.

'There is one called Makkim among you. He was once my slave.' He gestured to Violetta who had not moved beside him. 'I have here someone he knows. If he does not present himself at my camp by sundown, she will die.'

Siward felt Makkim stiffen. He looked at him, saw something new in his eyes. He asked, 'Will you go?'

Makkim turned to him. 'Do you even have to ask?'

CHAPTER THIRTY-SIX

CONSTANTINOPLE

Makkim steered his horse between the twisted bodies, holding a cloth to his face. The air was thick with flies and the stench was beyond any battlefield he'd smelt, even Varna. Birds rose before him with meat between their beaks – slowly, for the servings were large. He was approaching the Turkish palisade and he could feel a thousand eyes on him; eyes that saw the janissary armour, high white hat, scimitar by his side. He was dressed as Mehmed had once known him. Would it work?

The stockade gates opened and Makkim found himself in a sea of brown. He looked around him. The camp was well-ordered, despite the mud. There were wooden tracks to dry spaces where barrels were stacked and men sat making arrows and sharpening swords. The cannons had islands of their own with drainage trenches and stone-shot piled beside the guns. There were wicker fences built around mineshafts and wood piled high for props. A line of mangonels stood beyond with their long necks dipped to the ground like sleeping *jornuffa*.

Makkim looked ahead. Fanned out across the hill were his janissaries, ten thousand of them, watching their former general approach. At their centre was Mehmed – Violetta and Zaganos beside him, all staring at him. Mehmed was wearing mail and a simple crown that might have been laurel leaves.

Makkim's eyes moved from Mehmed to Violetta and stayed there. She wore the same white gown she'd worn that morning and stood with her hands to her front and her head erect. Her eyes held the dull misery of one who knew herself the cause of Mehmed's current victory. *Laurel leaves.*

He stopped and dismounted, lifting his reins and glancing to his right. A janissary officer came forward and led his horse away. He walked up to Mehmed and knelt.

There was silence. No one dared breathe. Nobody wanted to miss a word of this meeting. At last Mehmed spoke.

'You dare to wear that?'

Makkim looked up. He saw something new in Mehmed's eyes. He saw hate and rage and something much more terrible: madness. Here was a man who'd ruled too young, been disgraced and forced to give way to his father. Here was one who'd sought to prove himself through one triumphant deed. But it wasn't going according to plan. Constantinople hadn't fallen and it seemed that he, Makkim, might be to blame.

'They are the clothes of a fallen janissary, lord.'

'Of a better man than you. You have no right to them.' Mehmed stopped and Makkim saw the tremble of his lip beneath the beard. 'So you came back.'

Makkim said, 'I never left you, majesty. I was captured and have been held prisoner.'

Mehmed shook his head. 'My spies tell me you moved around quite freely in Mistra. Hardly imprisoned.'

The voice trembled with unsmothered fury. Mehmed was close to breaking.

'I gave my word not to escape, majesty,' Makkim said calmly. 'So they gave me some liberty.'

'Yet you broke your word and came to Constantinople. Then you met with Candarli. Why?'

'There was a plan meant to deliver the city to you.'

'Except that it had the opposite effect,' said Mehmed. 'It allowed Constantine to rally the people around him.' His hands were shaking and he pressed them together. 'But then perhaps you expected that? Just as you expected Lydislaw to escape from the field of Varna?'

Makkim stared at him. Did Mehmed think that he'd betrayed him from the start? He sat back on his heels. 'Majesty, what is this?' he asked softly. 'When did my loyalty to you become so doubted?'

Mehmed stepped forward and crouched down so that their heads were level. Makkim felt his hot, sour breath on his face.

'*When?*' he whispered. He gestured towards Violetta. 'Who is *this*? No, don't say it. I know who this is. This is Venice's greatest whore, whose beauty has entrapped more men than *Circe*. She entrapped you entirely, didn't she?'

Makkim recoiled. Surely he must know that Violetta was his sister? But Mehmed had taken hold of his mail and pulled him closer so that their faces almost touched. 'So you must tell me, Makkim Pasha,' he whispered. 'Have you betrayed me?'

'Lord . . .'

'Do you love this spy? *Do you love her?*'

Then Makkim looked at Violetta and saw there the girl he'd once known, the girl he'd loved more than any creature on God's earth, still loved. They'd lain together in fields of wheat and sworn themselves to each other. Then had come Siward. And, it seemed, Mehmed.

He looked at Violetta and his eyes stayed on hers, and hers on his.

'Yes,' he said quietly. 'I love her.'

Mehmed let go of his mail. His head fell to his chest and he sighed. Neither of them moved; neither spoke.

At last the Sultan rose. He brushed the dust from his knees, straightened and turned to Zaganos, his hands held tight behind his back. His voice was calm.

'We will make our proposals known to Constantine through Makkim Pasha, since he knows his way to the palace better than we. You will instruct him in our terms. You will tell him that he will leave with them this afternoon and return no later than midday tomorrow.' He turned now to Violetta. 'If he fails to return, we shall kill the girl as all spies must be killed.'

Makkim rode back into Constantinople as he'd come out: alone and dressed as a janissary. He had with him the terms for Constantinople's surrender. He entered through the Romanus Gate, the walls either side lined with men trying to gauge from his expression what the scroll in his hand might say. But Makkim neither smiled nor frowned. He just looked straight ahead.

Constantine met him at his tent with Notaras. They both read the terms, then the Emperor summoned Giovanni, Siward, Minotto and Gennadius to join them.

'They're very straightforward,' said Constantine when they'd assembled. 'I surrender Constantinople and go to rule in Mistra, which they'll leave in peace. No one gets slaughtered and no one is made to convert. Those are his terms.'

Constantine led them over to a table. On the way, Siward took Makkim's arm.

'Just tell me he hasn't harmed her,' he whispered.

Makkim stopped and turned. He brought his head close to Siward's, whispering too. 'Not yet. But he wants to hurt me, so may do it through her. We have to get her out.'

They went to place themselves around the table, no one questioning Makkim's right to be there. It was the same model of Constantinople, only now it had galleys in the Golden Horn. Constantine waved his hand over the scene.

'The siege is a month old and we are properly surrounded,' he said. 'Mehmed has offered us reasonable terms. Do we surrender or fight on?' He looked at Giovanni. 'Do we have any chance of winning this siege?'

Giovanni scratched his ribs. He'd removed the top half of his armour and the dried sweat pricked at his skin. 'That depends on two things, majesty: whether the people will go on fighting and whether a fleet comes from Venice.'

Gennadius was leaning with his palms in the Bosporos, the Turkish fleet between his forearms. He spoke to Constantine. 'The citizens are hungry and frightened but they are resolute: they are Romans and they will defend their city.'

Constantine turned to Minotto. 'And the Venetian fleet?'

The bailo didn't flinch. 'Is on its way, majesty,' he said.

Siward snorted.

Constantine turned to him. 'You don't believe the bailo, Varangopoulos?'

'No, majesty,' said Siward, staring at Minotto, 'any more than I believe Mehmed will leave you in peace in Mistra. Venice is helping Mehmed and their reward will be Mistra. That's why their fleet hasn't arrived. It's stuck at Negroponte, readying itself to strike the Peloponnese.'

Minotto put his hand to his sword. Constantine raised his arm.

'How do you know this?'

'It's obvious. The Peloponnese is vital to their trade route to the East. They've always wanted it.' He shook his head. 'Mehmed won't give you Mistra, he'll give it to Venice. It's the exchange they've agreed.'

'Exchange for what?' asked Minotto. He stepped forward, his hand still on his hilt. 'If my loyalty is so questioned, I'll take my men from the walls and sail away.' His voice was unsteady. 'And on the way I'll tell our fleet to turn back.'

Giovanni had taken Siward's arm. 'You will be silent,' he said. '*Now.*'

'This is not the time to question any man's loyalty,' said Constantine. 'We should be grateful that Lord Minotto is with us, not insult him. You will ask pardon of the bailo, then leave us.'

Siward stood very still.

'You will, Siward,' said Constantine softly. 'Without delay.'

And Siward felt the same rage he'd felt at the petty injustices of childhood. The years rolled back and he was defending Petros from bullies. He felt powerless but he knew what he had to do. He forced himself to look at Minotto. 'I ask your pardon.'

Giovanni led him quickly to the tent door and through it, Makkim following. On the other side was an antechamber with low couches and braziers. It was empty and smelt of lemon. All three stopped and faced each other, their faces dappled by flame, one grooved by a scar.

Giovanni said, 'That was stupid.'

'But irresistible,' said Makkim. He glanced at Siward who was still trying to control himself. 'We all know Minotto is lying.'

Siward took a deep breath. He'd not heard Makkim talk like that before. 'If only we knew what they're up to with this fleet,' he said. 'Is it bound for Mistra, or somewhere else?'

'Petros learnt nothing from the Venetian quarter?' asked Giovanni.

Siward shook his head. 'He went to all the taverns, got men drunk. Nothing. They all think the fleet is coming.'

'Minotto may try to open a gate,' said Makkim. 'It's what he once promised me he'd do.'

'Not with my Varangarians watching him,' said Siward. He stretched out his hands to the flame. He looked at Makkim. 'But how do we rescue Violetta?'

That night was the quietest Constantinople had experienced since the start of the siege. The cannon were silent and the city slept under an unclouded moon like it hadn't for weeks. Soldiers kept watch on the walls but hardly a dog stirred in the syrup of the Turkish camp. The terms of surrender had been offered and tomorrow they'd be answered. Until then, there'd be rest.

Rest for all except Siward, who couldn't sleep. Tomorrow, he would accompany Makkim as part of his Varangian escort. In a few hours, he might see Violetta.

Partly it was memory that kept him awake. He wanted to remember their time together in Venice. He wanted to summon a room of exotic scents and soft velvets. He wanted to conjure up spring landscapes in Burgundy and the jingle of harness. But what came to him instead was one single memory: Violetta's face when she'd first seen Makkim in Rome. It was the picture that wouldn't leave.

He lay on his back and tried to imagine Violetta lying beside him, breathing deeply in a sleep brought on by love. He turned onto his side. He'd not even kissed her. He didn't even know if she liked him.

He turned again. He thought about the earlier meeting in Makkim's bedroom when father and son had sat side by side on the bed, holding hands, aware that it might be their last night together. Siward had seen the new calm that had fallen on Makkim. He thought of the plan they'd agreed: not a good one but all they had.

With dawn came more rain. It pounded on the many roofs of the Blachernae Palace, filled the gutters and dripped onto the heads of emperors in their leaky alcoves. Siward rose as the first weak light crept its way into his room. He washed and put on his most splendid Varangian uniform. He'd not slept at all.

Downstairs in the hall he met Giovanni and Makkim talking in low voices. They'd probably talked through the night. They looked up as he approached.

'I'm going to keep this,' said Giovanni, lifting the dragon sword. He had dark shadows beneath his eyes. 'Neither of you will be allowed it where you're going. Better it's used.'

Siward nodded. 'Is the guard outside?'

It was. They were eight Varangians, all as tall as Makkim. They were formed up, wet to the bone and ready to march to the Romanus Gate.

'I'll leave you here,' said Giovanni. He was frowning at Makkim, his jaw set. 'Kiss me and go.'

The embrace was strong, made so by a love too recently found. They held each other for a long time and parted with a kiss. When Makkim walked away, he didn't look back.

At the gate, they were met by the Emperor.

'Buy us as much time as you are able. Minotto says the fleet is only days away.'

Siward saw in his eyes how much Constantine wanted to believe this fiction. His belief was the city's belief. It was a reason to hold out, but it was false. He nearly said something but stopped himself. He nodded and they clasped arms.

Siward, Makkim and their guard rode through the gate, past corpses spattered by rain, some half-submerged, some with sockets for eyes. The fat, sodden rats hardly stirred before them. As they came up to the Turkish lines, Siward turned in his saddle to look back. The city walls looked colossal, unending, their ruin veiled by rain.

They came to Mehmed's tent and dismounted. Janissaries stood guard but they didn't look at Makkim. Hasan approached them. He searched Makkim for weapons without meeting his eye, then opened the tent flap to let them pass. It was a tent bigger than anything Siward had ever imagined. It had rooms divided by canvas and silk, carpets stretching into the distance, couches, divans and low tables with flowers. There were stoves at the sides and the air was warm after the chill of dawn. Siward looked around it, hoping that Mehmed had included Violetta in this meeting.

He had. She was sitting on a raised wooden platform with cushions round its edges. He met her eye and felt sudden, unexpected joy. The doubts of the night melted away. *She feels it too.*

He and Makkim knelt.

'Why do you smile?' asked Mehmed.

Was he smiling? Yes, he must be. He looked again at Violetta, unable to prevent himself. Suddenly, anything and everything seemed possible. He felt exhilarated.

'I . . . I am overawed, highness.'

Mehmed turned to Makkim. 'Why is he here?'

Makkim was watching Violetta too, a little frown gathered above sad eyes. He said, 'Because the Emperor's answer will itself need an answer. Another must take it back, since I will remain.'

Mehmed grunted. 'And his response?'

'The Emperor says that the Roman Empire has stood for two thousand years and its fate will not be decided in a day. He would like a week to consider your offer and asks what assurances can be given should he decide to remove himself to the Peloponnese.'

Mehmed stared at Makkim. 'Assurances? He has my word. What more does he need?' He was restless, constantly pulling at his sleeves and twisting his rings. He looked at Siward. 'We'll not give you a week to repair your defences.'

Siward had recovered himself. He said, 'The Emperor does not believe the city will fall. He has reliable hopes of reinforcement.'

Mehmed shook his head. 'From Venice, perhaps? I'm afraid that fleet has other plans.'

Zaganos interrupted quickly. 'Lord, surely the issue is this delay. How long do we need to give the Emperor to consider our offer?'

Mehmed nodded. 'A further day, no more.'

Siward frowned. 'There is also the question of religion. Our citizens will need to be reassured that they can continue to pray as they wish. They will want a signal of your good intentions. I would recommend the release of a Christian prisoner.' He gestured towards Violetta. 'This lady we know to be Christian. If Makkim stays, she is of no importance to you but her release might send a powerful message to the women of Constantinople who so fear your army.' He paused. 'It is they who persuade their husbands.'

Mehmed pretended to consider this, nodding slowly with his elbows on his knees. 'No.'

'And if I offer to take the lady's place? I am Siward Magoris, commander of the Varangians who have done such harm to your men.'

Mehmed had risen. He came and stood before Siward. 'I am more interested in the courtesan than you, Varangopoulos,' he said softly. 'Makkim and she will stay with me and you will return to your foolish emperor. Together, you will watch your city die.'

CHAPTER THIRTY-SEVEN

CONSTANTINOPLE

Siward was standing on the ship's deck between Giovanni and Petros, pointing to where he wanted the faggots stowed. He wanted them stacked tightly up against the sides of the vessel so that the fire would be most intense where it struck. He looked up at the single pennant above the mast. He could just see it.

'Is there enough wind?'

Giovanni followed his gaze. Night had almost fallen over the Golden Horn and the breeze was gathering. 'Not yet. We'll let it build for another hour. Are you happy about hoisting the sail?'

Siward nodded. 'I'll be towed out to the middle where the wind will be strongest. I'm to raise it as late as I can.'

'You'll need someone to help you,' said Petros. He'd arrived earlier with breastplate and sword, expecting to be part of things.

Siward sighed. 'Petros, I'm going alone. I need to be fast and you'll slow me down.'

'I'll watch your back.'

Giovanni intervened. He put his hand on Petros's shoulder. 'You can come in one of the boats.'

'Alright.'

'No, Petros,' said Siward. 'You can't swim – have you forgotten that?'

Petros turned to him. 'It's not your decision,' he said. 'The generalissimo has spoken. I go with the boats.' He turned and hobbled away.

Giovanni said, 'I'll put him next to me.' He went back to the plan. 'Now, after the sail's gone up, and when you're near the Turk fleet, use the grenades and then jump. I'll be in the boat behind with Petros, ready to fish you out.'

Siward looked down at the sack of naphtha grenades by his feet. They were Grant's invention, small canisters of Greek fire with delay fuses. He looked over the side. In the gathering dusk he could just see the outlines of the skiffs lined up on the other side of the jetty. Each would carry a dozen men who'd follow the fireship in, board any galley that didn't ignite and finally land on the shore where the enemy guns were. If all went well, not one of them would be firing by tomorrow morning.

'So, while we do our work, you'll creep ashore,' Giovanni continued. 'You'll cross the Horn further up by the new pontoon bridge that Mehmed's built. You'll get into the Ottoman camp and then it's up to you. Do you have a plan?'

An hour later, Siward still didn't have a plan. But the wind was up and he was watching Giovanni put men into boats, Minotto beside him, both of them in long cloaks that covered their armour. There was no talking and no clink of arms. Everything was muffled, including the oars.

There'd been endless argument as to who would undertake the mission to destroy the Turkish fleet in the Golden Horn, the Venetians and Genoese almost breaking their truce over it. In the end, Constantine had appointed Minotto and the Venetians, perhaps to make up for Siward's insult.

Giovanni broke away and came up to the ship's side. 'Everyone's aboard. We're just attaching culverins to the prows.'

Siward nodded. 'You'll watch Petros?'

'And Minotto.' Giovanni glanced over to where the Venetian was standing, watching them. 'If he tries anything, I'll kill him.' He gave a little salute. 'Good luck and don't forget to jump.'

Siward moved to the stern to cast off from the jetty. He felt the first tug of the tow and walked up to the prow. He felt another and heard the ripple of water passing the hull. He was underway. He looked over at the other bank. A half-moon had scattered silver coin across the surface of the Horn and the wind made furrows in the sea and sang through the ship's rigging as if lyres were perched above. The joy he'd felt when Violetta had looked at him hadn't gone away. He could do anything, achieve anything. He could even – God willing – rescue her.

God willing.

They were making good progress and a mix of wind and current was taking them quickly out into the Horn. He thought he could see the black bulk of the Turkish fleet ahead. He saw the tow-ropes slacken as the ship began to outpace its tugs. It was time to raise the sails.

He walked back to where the rigging was clustered at the rail. He took the ropes that had been marked for him to pull. The slower it was done the better, for no sound must alert the Turk. He pulled.

Gradually, the big sail worked its way up the mast, the wind filling it as it went, Siward cursing every snap. He felt the ship gather speed beneath him, the wind moving through his hair.

He looked up and saw the sail spread out above him, its red cross thrust proud. Time for the fire.

But just then, another fire lit the sky. At the moment he was about to strike the flint, night became day as twenty flares exploded from the Turkish shore.

'God's mercy.'

There was a salvo of explosions as the Turkish cannon fired from the shore. They were aiming high and shot flew over the Ottoman fleet to splash amongst the Christian flotilla. He spun round.

Petros.

But nothing had been hit and only huge waves rocked the little ships. He heard Giovanni's shout.

'Row for your lives!'

He looked over the bow. More flares were aloft and he could see the Turkish fleet moving apart, the oarsmen working hard to separate the ships. There would be nothing for the fireship to hit. He ran up to the stern deck. He leant out into the night, shouting towards where he thought Giovanni's skiff was.

'I'm not going to fire the ship! Look after Petros!'

There might have been a reply but he didn't hear any. Instead he heard a crash and the screams of men. The boat beside Giovanni's was in splinters on the water.

'Sweet Jesus.'

Siward saw Giovanni's boat slow down to pick up survivors. He saw Giovanni and Minotto pulling a man on board between them. It was hopeless. Cannon shot was falling all around the skiffs. Siward saw another go down, then another. He looked towards the prow.

As he'd feared, the Turks were on their way. He saw three galleys racing towards them, well spaced out in case the

387

fireship should try and do its work. He heard the beat of drums and the crack of whips. There would be archers on their rembatas who'd show no mercy to the men in the water. He looked behind him. The surviving skiffs were turning for the shore. Which one was Giovanni's? He saw flares go up from the sea walls. He saw a cannon spit fire, then another. With luck Petros might make it.

He sat down on the deck to think. The ship was going too fast to be stopped or boarded, so he'd likely make the shore. He could do nothing for the poor wretches in the water behind him. He got to his knees. He was sailing straight for the beach, no galleys in his path. He saw the flash of cannon from the trees behind it. Perhaps he could fix that.

He felt the bump of the seabed beneath his hull, the sudden slowing throwing him forward. The ship came to a standstill. He was there.

He stood up, crept to the side and looked over. On the beach were rows of abandoned tents, fires still smoking between them. He smelt charcoal and burnt mutton. He picked up the sack of grenades, climbed down the side and dropped into the water. It came up to his waist and was cold. He waited a moment to see if the splash had alerted anyone but the bay seemed deserted. He waded ashore, holding the sack high above his head. Once on the shingle, he bent low and ran between the tents. He reached the tree line and fell to the ground. Voices, not Turkish. He listened. *Serbians.*

He didn't understand what they were saying and was sure that no one in the Turkish camp would either. He crept forward through the undergrowth. Two men were standing next to a stubby cannon, its smoking barrel aimed at the sky. He saw a wagon parked behind it with its horse tied to a tree, the moon pooling on its back. It had brought the gun to this place and it could take it away.

He studied the men. They were dressed in padded jerkins and had short swords tucked into their belts. He put down the grenades, found a long stick, rose and limped forward as if wounded, muttering what he thought might sound Turkish. The men stopped talking and looked at him. They came over to help.

He hit one, then the other, using both ends of the stick. After they'd fallen, he drew their daggers and stabbed them. He dragged their bodies over to the trees, choosing the bigger of the two to change clothes with. He took care to attach the grenades, flint box and spare fuses to his belt.

He emerged from the wood, tethered the horse to the wagon and backed it up to where the cannon sat on its bricks. He lifted it onto the back of the wagon, the horse starting as its harness jerked upwards. He loaded the bricks on either side to keep it secure, then closed up the back.

The road to the pontoon bridge was a temporary affair, a mix of rubble and mud. It was busy with soldiers and supplies travelling in both directions and no one paid attention to a Serbian gunner bringing his cannon in for repair. He crossed the bridge and followed the road up to the rear of the camp. He was waved past by sentries.

The shadow of Maltepe Hill rose up to his right, with the Sultan's tent at its top. He followed the traffic round until he came to the janissary tents that guarded the entrance, separated from the rest of the camp by gently sloping open ground. Then he saw the cage. It was situated among the tents and lit by their fires. It seemed full of people sitting or leaning against its sides. He left the horse and wagon and edged into the mass of people, working his way closer. At last he was at its bars. He dropped to his knees and whispered at the back of a man in a doublet.

'Are you Greek? Don't turn round.'

The man moved his face to the side. He had a beard and pockmarked skin above it, sallow. 'No, Genoese,' he said. 'Who are you?'

'Who has the keys to this cage?'

The man shifted round more. 'God's hairy balls, you're the Varangian.' He grinned. 'They're held by a janissary who sleeps in one of those tents. Are you going to get us out?'

'I'm going to try.' Siward went silent as two janissaries approached carrying a cauldron. He lowered his head as they passed, then watched them go. 'If I do, I'll need you to lead everyone away from the hill.' He pointed. 'I want a distraction. Can you do that?'

The man nodded.

'Good.' Siward put his hand through the bars and patted the man's shoulder. He rose, the sack of grenades heavy at his belt, and walked over to the other end of the cage. His heart lifted. Makkim was sitting next to the gate.

'Don't turn round.'

Makkim rested his head back on the bars. 'I heard explosions. What happened?'

'We sent a fireship against their fleet in the Horn. They knew we were coming. It was a massacre.'

'Giovanni?'

Giovanni. Had Giovanni survived? 'I don't know. I'm sorry.' He leant against the cage, pretending to take a piss. 'Where is she?'

'In Mehmed's tent.'

Siward looked up the hill. He saw commotion outside the

390

tent, janissaries falling into line, horses being led forward by men with torches.

'What will he have done with her?'

Makkim shifted position. 'You needn't worry. He doesn't incline to her sex.'

Siward saw two men emerge from the tent, talking: Mehmed and Zaganos bey. Men around him began to move in their direction.

Makkim said, 'He'll be going over to the Golden Horn to gloat over your failure. The janissaries will follow him. That will be your chance to get her.'

Siward shook his head. 'Not without you. I'll need your help. Where are the keys to this cage?'

Makkim stretched an arm through the bars to point. 'The one with the keys lives in that tent. I've not seen him come out.'

Siward took a grenade from his bag. 'Then we'll just have to persuade him.'

Siward waited until Mehmed and his janissary retinue had left the camp before creating chaos. Not until he'd seen the last white bork, lit by the last torch, disappear over the hill, did he light and throw a grenade.

The effect was as he'd hoped. The explosion brought the man with the keys out of his tent and straight onto Siward's out-stretched leg. The man fell and was stabbed and Siward rose with the keys. By the time other Turks had emerged, the cage door was open and men were escaping like wasps from a jar. The Genoese was as good as his word and led them away from the Sultan's hill.

Makkim was last to come out, waiting patiently until all of the prisoners had passed him. With him was Baltaoğlu, who looked unhappy.

'I'll not betray Mehmed,' he said as he lifted his arms for Siward to unlock his chains. 'You must leave me here.'

Makkim went up to him and took his hands in his. 'I know that, friend. But you can protect Mehmed from himself. My sister is innocent and doesn't deserve to die. Help me free her before our sultan does something he'll regret.'

The admiral glanced up at the tent on the hill. He was rubbing his wrists. 'How?'

Makkim bent and picked up a sword and put it in his waistband. 'The guards know me for a traitor. But you? They probably don't even know you've been put in that cage. You just need to distract them, that's all.'

There was further discussion while Siward exchanged clothes with the dead janissary. In the end, a plan was agreed. Baltaoğlu found a long cloak in one of the tents and donned it over his torn uniform. He picked up a torch, lit it from the fire and began to walk up the hill towards the tent, Siward and Makkim behind. The two janissary guards straightened when they saw him.

'I am to bring the girl to the Sultan,' Baltaoğlu said. 'Go and make her ready. My men will take your place.'

The men went into the tent. Baltaoğlu began to walk away. 'I'll do nothing more.'

Makkim stopped him, took his arm. 'Thank you. May Allah bless you.'

Baltaoğlu looked at him. 'It's as you said,' he remarked sadly. 'Mehmed is not himself.'

Then he turned and walked down the hill.

Siward drew his sword and walked over to one side of the tent door. Makkim went to the other. The two janissaries died quickly, pushing back the flaps and striding out onto the blades waiting for them. Behind came Violetta, nearly stumbling over

392

the bodies. When she saw Siward and Makkim, she stopped. Her eyes went from one to the other, then back to Siward. They stayed there.

Silence. Then Makkim spoke. His voice was uneven. 'We should go.'

Violetta looked at him. She walked over and took his face in her hands and kissed him so gently on his forehead that it might have been a breath. 'Thank you,' she said.

Makkim straightened and took a pace backwards, not looking at her. He nodded once, twice, as if to properly absorb some new information. 'You must change. I'll strip him.' He turned and dragged a guard into the tent by his armpits. The tent-flap fell behind them.

Siward went to Violetta and turned her face to him. He kissed her where she'd kissed Makkim but his lips stayed. A grumble of thunder came from the sky and the moonlight went and they looked up to see dark clouds massing. Lightning flickered at their edges, so quick that it might not have happened. A sudden sigh of wind came and went, as if rehearsing. Rain brushed their hair like fingers.

Violetta took Siward's hand and brought it to her upturned cheek. 'The world is strange tonight,' she whispered.

Siward's fingers stroked her skin. 'Everything is out of order. It's been like this since the siege began.' He gazed down at her. 'Perhaps it is the end of days.'

Makkim came out of the tent. He saw them and looked away. 'We need to try and cross the bridge with the janissaries. Violetta, you need to change.'

She went in and the two men watched the tent in silence. Thunder rumbled, louder this time, and Siward thanked God for the darkness.

'Makkim.'

'Don't.'

The tent opened and Violetta stepped out as a janissary. She looked from one to the other.

'Let's go.'

They followed the road out of the camp towards the Golden Horn, hurrying as fast as they could through the mud and darkness. It would be dawn soon but it seemed perpetual night above them now, a darkness sucked up from the earth that would stay forever. Siward felt apprehension prick every part of his body. Something terrible was about to happen, orchestrated by forces beyond the experience of men. The warnings were in the electric air.

The lightning flashed and in the distance Siward could see the bridge and a great multitude of men. He felt the tramp of their boots in the ground and heard the dirge of their chant through the darkness. Somewhere out there, a twenty-one-year-old man was leading the faithful to a terrible revelation. Mehmed was dragging the darkness behind him.

'We need to hurry,' said Makkim. 'They're nearly across the bridge.'

They quickened their pace. When the lightning struck next, they saw janissaries in their white hats fanned out at the approach to the bridge, like rice feeding a funnel.

Makkim turned. 'Pull up your aventails, both of you, and don't speak.'

They joined the back of the column. The men were jostling to get forward, none of them wanting to miss what would happen next. They'd heard about the ships coming over the hill.

Siward looked up. The dawn was trying hard to break through.

It shone briefly between vents in the clouds, only to be snatched away by darkness. The thunder was louder now and he felt the hair on his arms stiffen. He looked down into the wide eyes of Violetta, who was pressed hard against him. He felt her hand slide into his. He heard Makkim shout something in Turkish to the men in front.

'*Cabuk ol!*'

At last they came onto the bridge where men with torches were ushering them across. Looking down, Siward saw that barrels had been lashed to the planks and were moving up and down with the swell. There were ropes either side of the bridge for people to hold onto. He turned to Violetta.

'Get behind me and hold onto my waist.'

They crossed the bridge, step by step, until they reached the far bank, where they turned south to follow the shoreline. On their right were the lights of the Blachernae Palace, its roofs just visible in the early light. Up ahead was a long pebble beach with rising ground at its end. It was where the Golden Horn was narrowest.

Makkim fell back to walk beside them. He lowered his head and spoke softly. 'When we find a boat, we'll drop behind it and hide. When they've gone, we'll row across.'

Violetta tried to take his arm but he moved forward.

'There.'

He hadn't pointed but they could see the shape coming up to their right: an upturned boat. They slowed their pace. There was no one immediately behind them. They came level.

'Now.'

They broke away from the column and ducked down behind the small craft. They waited until the last crunch of shingle had died. Siward raised his head and saw the long line of torches snaking up the hill at the end of the bay. He looked around. They were alone on the beach.

'Violetta, go up behind that boulder and keep watch. Makkim and I will turn this thing over and push it out. Let's hope its oars are underneath.'

They were. The paddles had been stored beneath the benches and rattled to one side as the boat turned. When it was on its keel, they dragged it into the water. Violetta ran down to join them.

Makkim went to the back. 'Get in, both of you. I'll push.'

'You'll need me,' said Siward.

Makkim shook his head. 'No. It's easier this way. Push off with the oars.'

Siward helped Violetta aboard, then got in himself. He pulled out the oars and they used them to push away.

There was commotion among the trees above the beach. Soldiers emerged, running fast towards them.

Makkim glanced round. He was up to his waist in water and the boat was free of the shore. He drew his sword from his waistband.

'Get in,' shouted Siward. 'Quick!'

But Makkim didn't move. He glanced from the soldiers to the boat and back again. Then he raised his hand. 'I'm staying.'

Violetta scrambled to the back of the boat. She knelt on the bench, her hands clasped to the side. 'What are you talking about? He'll kill you!'

He shook his head. He had to shout now. 'No, he won't. He loves me.'

Makkim had turned and was walking up the beach. In a moment the soldiers would be upon him.

'Makkim!' yelled Siward. 'We're not going without you! Swim out to the boat!'

But it was too late. The soldiers surrounded him and there were too many of them.

Siward was at the back with Violetta now. The boat was drifting slowly out but was still within the range of arrows. He took her arm. 'We've got to get away. He's giving us our chance.'

She shook herself free and stood up. '*Makkim!*' she screamed.

But some of the torches were now moving towards the sea. The soldiers would be temporarily blinded by the light but the boat was only twenty paces away. Siward took her shoulders and forced her round to face him.

'We can't help him!' he shouted. 'We have to go.'

She was still staring back at the shore as he pushed her down onto the stern bench. He could hear her sobbing, see the heave of her shoulders. He hurried back to the middle of the boat and plunged the oars into the water. He pulled.

An arrow landed between them and bounced over the side. They heard others in the air and men in the water. He pulled with all his strength. Only a boat could stop them now, but theirs had been the only one on the bank.

He looked up. The soldiers were marching away, Makkim somewhere amongst them. Violetta was slumped forward, her head in her hands. He felt rain on his forehead and looked up. Black clouds were scudding before some wind unavailable to the ground. Where they parted, a weak light broke through that turned the rain silver and made the sea glow. He glanced over his shoulder. The walls of Constantinople were visible now. They'd be there soon.

'Do you think he's right?' She was looking at him, her face crumpled in misery. 'Will Mehmed spare him?'

Siward stopped rowing. He wiped his forehead with the back of his hand and looked at her. Makkim had loved her every bit as much as he and for much, much longer. And he'd chosen to stay to let them escape.

'I don't know,' he said simply. He took hold of the oars again and began to row. The light was gathering quickly now and the far shore becoming clearer. Something was happening on the high ground. Violetta saw him staring beyond her and turned.

'What are they doing?' She shielded her eyes. 'Are those *stakes* they're driving into the ground?'

Siward had started rowing faster. He too had seen the janissaries hammering the sharpened poles. 'Face me,' he said quietly. 'Violetta, do as I say.'

He saw her hand go to her mouth.

'My God. *No*.'

Siward looked over his shoulder. It wasn't so far now. How could he distract her?

'I need you to tell me where I'm going,' he said. 'There are ships ahead and we have to get between them.'

'*Oh my God*.'

He heard a shout from the hill and saw a naked man being dragged forward towards the stakes, begging and crying and struggling with every muscle in his body. Siward saw two giant janissaries lift him up.

'Violetta, look at me!'

But the horror was everywhere. Siward looked behind and saw the walls lined with people, silent and watching. He pulled harder at the oars.

Violetta let out a little cry just as the man's scream echoed across the Golden Horn.

'Violetta! *Look at me!*'

It was too late. She had seen what Mehmed wanted every inhabitant of the city to see: the fate of those who defied him, a fate so agonising that it was only reserved for the most heinous of crimes. Siward heard the wail that rose from the city's walls. He imagined women turning their children's heads away, then their own.

Violetta was facing him now, her face set in denial. They both knew that Makkim was being marched up that hill. The shock made her eyes wide as she stared out to sea. He wanted to row faster but he was at the limits of his strength. He heard calls behind him and glanced round to see men bent over the sides of ships, waving him on. He pushed through debris, planks that had once been a boat, and saw a hand float by on a tide of blood.

Then he felt the scrape of stone against the hull and there were men splashing into the sea to haul them ashore. Violetta was sitting as still as she could, looking down at her hands. He saw they were trembling. He reached forward to take one.

'Violetta,' he said gently, feeling how cold her skin was. 'Come into the city.'

She shook her head, went on shaking it slowly. Her mind was somewhere else.

'We can't help him like this. Please come in and rest.'

There were more screams and he saw her jaw tighten as her teeth set. She looked up at him. 'If he is to die, then I will watch it.'

He thought of saying something but stopped himself. He nodded and brought her gently to her feet. They stepped out of the boat and walked, hand in hand, through the Gate of the Phanar and up the steps to the ramparts. People watched them in silence and parted to make way. They stopped at the battlements and looked out. It was nearly light now. The black clouds were hurrying off to the west and the rain had stopped. The dawn was a bashful presence, but it was strong enough to see by.

There were six men impaled now, all naked, all writhing slowly in their torment. More stakes were being hammered in beside them.

Violetta cried out, her fist to her lips. Mehmed had walked up to the stakes with someone tall and fair beside him. He was stripped to the waist and his arms were held by janissaries. It was Makkim.

CHAPTER THIRTY-EIGHT

CONSTANTINOPLE

Makkim prayed for the clouds to return and, with them, the rain. He was stripped to his loincloth but would gladly suffer any discomfort if the rain would come back and mask this spectacle from the other bank.

In front of him, Mehmed was watching twelve men sink lower onto stakes that were being driven up their spines by the weight of their own bodies. Their screams told the horror of their suffering. It was the cruellest way to kill: the men's vital organs bypassed so that they would take days to die.

In the half-light of dawn, Makkim had watched the janissaries – his janissaries – hating what they did. But they hated even more what they were doing now. A Genoese had been brought forward, a fair man of Makkim's height and build. He'd been dressed in janissary clothes, then stripped to the waist and gagged. Now he was being dragged towards a stake that had been set forward from the others.

Mehmed was standing between Zaganos and Hasan. As the impalements had begun, the janissary aga had shaken his head and twice turned to look at Makkim, as he hadn't before. This wasn't how war should be. But Makkim was looking across at the walls of Constantinople. Somewhere on them would be Violetta. She'd be standing next to Siward and she'd be watching a man she thought was him being made to suffer the worst death imaginable. The agony of that thought had numbed him even more than the look she'd given Siward when coming from the tent, even more than the breath that she'd planted on his own forehead, the breath that had blown away the last trace of their childhood. It had numbed him even from the rage that had swept over Mehmed when he'd heard that Violetta had escaped.

'How will she like *this*?' the Sultan was yelling, his face to Makkim's, his madness distorting every feature. His eyes were bloodshot and spittle bubbled at the corners of his mouth. 'Will the whore throw herself from the walls, do you think?'

The man was being lifted onto the stake, his arms pinned to his sides, his ankles held apart. Mehmed watched him twist and jerk in his first moments of torture, all muffled by the gag. He brought his face even closer to Makkim's.

'You think you've set her free,' he whispered, his bloody eyes an inch away, 'but you've just sent her into another prison. I have a man inside who will find her and keep her for me to kill when I take the city.' He tossed his head towards the wretches on the stakes. 'Perhaps like that.'

Siward sat on the end of the bed where Violetta was lying on her front, her face pressed into the pillow. She'd not spoken since he'd led her gently from the walls more than an hour ago, guiding her down the narrow steps to the ground lest she fall. He'd found a wagon to take them to the Blachernae Palace, one that had carried bread once and still smelt of it. They'd driven through streets where word of what the Turks had done was travelling faster than they could ride. They'd seen people with eyes large with horror. They'd seen anger erupting everywhere, the anger of terror unleashed.

They'd passed a queue for bread where a noblewoman was being assaulted by a mob that tore loaves from her arms, then the clothes from her body. Monks were on their knees, arms outstretched, begging people to show mercy in their hunger. Violetta had stared straight ahead but Siward had looked back. He'd seen the woman lifted up in her plump nakedness and turned round and round by the mob. He'd put his arm around Violetta's shoulders and pulled her close to him.

Now she curled into a little ball of self-loathing. She'd watched Makkim die for her, for a love she'd not managed to share. She hated herself more completely that she did Mehmed. She wouldn't speak.

'It may have been someone else,' Siward said gently, stroking her shoulder through the sheet. 'It was too far to see.'

She didn't answer.

'Mehmed wants him alive,' he said, the words spare and useless in the silence between them. He felt her body rise and fall beneath his hand with each breath. He wanted more than anything to hold her but she held only herself, gripping her limbs, binding her body tight around her fractured soul.

He watched her for a while, listening to the rain on the palace roofs, hearing the deep murmur of wind through the trees and the distant shout of sentries. She looked fragile like he'd never seen her before, but soft too, soft enough to make herself into whatever shape might go unnoticed by the horror outside. But she'd be noticed by Mehmed when he came. Now that he knew who she was, he'd not let her escape when the city fell.

403

He looked out of the window at the grey, rain-pocked morning that seemed so like any other. Had he given up? He thought of the ruined walls, the Turks' ships in the Horn, the hungry citizens, the exhausted soldiers. He thought of the numberless army waiting outside. He thought of all the dead. *Petros.* He'd not heard from him.

He thought of Makkim impaled.

He felt her body stir beneath his hand and looked down. She had turned and was looking up at him with eyes so lost that he felt his heart would shatter.

'Hold me,' she said softly, taking his hand. 'Come in and hold me, Siward. Please.'

Much later, when it was evening, Siward still lay with her in his arms. He wasn't sure if she was awake. He was listening to how quiet it was.

The Blachernae Palace had always been a place of bustling ceremony. Now its halls and corridors were empty and silent. The cooks, the stewards, the gardeners, the men who wound the Emperor's many clocks: all had been sent to the walls.

Siward and Violetta were in a room big enough to hold a hundred clocks and their winders. Tall windows looked out over the palace orchards, felled now to plug the walls. They were lying on a bed with faded curtains that had once been luxurious. On one wall was a frayed tapestry of Neptune riding a shell through monstrous seas.

He'd held her for most of the day, neither of them speaking. He'd only left the room when a gentle knock at the door had summoned him to a meeting. Constantine, Giovanni and Grant had been waiting in the throne room.

He'd entered to six eyes that told him that Petros was dead.

Giovanni had risen. 'I tried to reach him when our boat was hit, but he sank too quickly. His armour.'

Siward had closed his eyes. *He couldn't swim.* He saw the breast-plate, too large for him, the sword in his belt that he could barely use. Why hadn't he stopped him from going? *Useless friend, I'll miss you.*

He'd remembered something else. He'd opened his eyes and looked into Giovanni's and seen the fear in them. *Makkim.*

'It was too far to see,' he'd said, as he had before. 'It could have been someone else.'

The Emperor had come over to Giovanni. 'The time to mourn is not now, friend,' he'd said gently. 'We don't know for sure and we need you for the siege.'

And Giovanni Giustiniani Longo had straightened and rubbed his tired eyes between his thumb and forefinger and said, 'Yes. Of course, majesty.'

Then the Emperor had addressed all of them. 'Mehmed is planning an attack all along the land walls, judging by what we've seen. It could be tonight or tomorrow.'

Johannes Grant had spoken next. 'They've dug a mine right next to the Blachernae wall. Tonight they plan to go under but we'll intercept them with our counter-mine.' He'd turned to Siward. 'I'll need your help.'

Then they'd gone through the plan. It involved Grant's miners digging right up to the enemy and Siward being down there, ready with the Greek fire. It would be dangerous and he'd known that the chances of him surviving would be slight. But he'd listened and asked the right questions. Then he'd risen to leave. If these were to be his last hours on earth, he'd spend them somewhere else.

Giovanni had left the room with him. Outside, Siward had

taken his shoulders and looked into a face hung with worry. 'It may not have been him.'

'Perhaps.' Giovanni had nodded slowly. 'Anyway, there's nothing we can do for him now.' He'd halted, then undone his sword belt. 'Take the dragon sword. If he is dead, he'll need avenging.'

Siward had hesitated, then nodded. He'd drawn the sword.

Giovanni had taken a deep breath. 'Has Violetta said anything? Did she hear things while she was with Mehmed?'

He'd forgotten to ask. 'I'll find out.'

Now Violetta was lying silent beside him, lost in her own hellish maze of reproach. She seemed not to hear anything but the voices inside her head telling her what might have been.

He held her tighter, pulling her into him so that his lips were pressed to the back of her neck. He felt the muscles of her arm relax a little, heard her breathe in deeply, then exhale in little blows. He closed his eyes and smelt the salt misery of her tears. He remembered the smell he'd always associated with her: the scent of artifice, the many scents of the courtesan. Now there was just the untempered smell of her tragedy.

She turned her head so that one cheek was shown to him, the first offer of any part of herself that she'd made. He saw the dried riverbed of old tears and the glisten of new ones gathering above. He drew back his arm and cupped her eye with his finger, tilting it to collect the tear.

'We have life, Violetta,' he said gently, watching the tear course down his finger. 'We have a life in front of us.'

She turned a little more to him. 'Do we?' she whispered. 'Will there be life after this siege, Siward? Will there even be a world?'

She had spoken in a voice so faint that it might have been the breeze.

He kissed her neck and kept his lips there. 'Yes. There will be life and love. Our love.'

She was silent for a while. Then she turned slowly onto her back, taking his arm and bringing his hand to her lips. She kept it there and stared at the ceiling and they both listened to the patter of infinite rain, a shield of comfort against whatever terror lay beyond. His elbow was touching her side and he felt the beat of her heart against his skin. It was quicker than it had been.

She turned her head to him. 'Love me, Siward. Love me now.'

Their joining was as unhurried and gentle as the rain. There was a wilderness of unspoken, complicated desire to be broken through and it had to be done with care. Only in the last stages, as Siward wanted more than anything to cast out the demon of her despair, did he make it more urgent.

Afterwards they slept and Siward, his eyelids closing on Neptune riding his colossal shell, fell into a dream of storm-tossed ocean. He was clinging to a raft on which Violetta lay, a raft that might have been made from Mehmed's pontoon bridge. All around were enormous waves, sometimes lifting the raft, sometimes plunging it down into deep valleys. It was night and the wind howled around them.

He was trying to climb onto the raft but kept slipping off, his hands unable to find purchase on the sodden wood. And Violetta was at its other end, reaching out for him, her mouth open but no sound emerging above the wind. A huge wave raised them higher than all the others: up, up towards a sky livid with lightning. He heard the crack of the raft breaking but couldn't see her. For a moment he thought he touched her hand, heard her voice. But no. She was gone and he was alone.

'Siward.'

He opened his eyes and saw her face and nothing else. She was staring at him beneath a little frown of worry. Relief washed over him.

'I'm here,' she said softly. She lifted his hand to her lips and kissed his fingers each in turn, her eyes always on his. 'Where were you?'

Siward found that he was trembling all over his body. He was sweating. 'I don't know. Some sea in a storm. You were on a raft . . .'

She brought her palm to his cheek and stroked his beard. 'Shhh. I thought you were here to comfort me.' She was smiling. 'I'm glad you need it too. You must be so tired.'

She was right: he was so very tired. He felt his eyelids closing again but her finger had moved to stop them.

'Not yet.'

This time they loved each other with more earnestness, both knowing that they might never do it again. Each explored the other's body with measured deliberation, pressing every touch, every caress into its own folder of memory to be opened, if necessary, in a future life without the other. When the moment came, they held each other hard enough to break bones, forcing their bodies to merge and never part. For a long time afterwards, they lay on their backs and didn't speak.

When they eventually did, it was because Siward remembered where they were: besieged Constantinople with a mine perhaps already reaching beneath its walls. What time was it? He looked at the window and saw night. How long had he been asleep? Giovanni might come at any moment to take him away. He turned his head to her.

'Violetta?'

His whisper sounded enormous. The rain had stopped and the only sounds were the drips from the eaves. She looked at him.

'Have you got to go?'

'How did you know?'

She gathered herself into his arms so that her cheek was pressed against his heart. 'It was in your every move. As if each had to be eternal.' She held him close. 'Is it dangerous?'

For a moment he considered lying, but there was no horror she hadn't imagined or lived through the past few days. He said instead, 'The Turks have dug a tunnel under the Blachernae wall. We have to intercept it.'

She looked up. 'Don't we have miners?'

Siward saw the fear in her eyes. He lifted her hair with his fingers and placed it behind her ear. 'It's not worth discussing,' he murmured gently. 'I have to go, you know that.'

She looked at him a while longer, then nodded slowly. There was too little time to waste with unnecessary words.

'When you were with Mehmed, I need to know whether you heard or saw anything,' he said. 'Anything that might be useful.'

There was a knock on the door. *So soon?* He'd hoped for longer. He called, 'One minute!'

She was sitting up now, her long ringlets cascading over her breasts like oil. She was looking away, remembering. 'No, but there were things I found out from Minotto on Chios.'

'Minotto? Why . . . ?'

She brought her finger to his lips. 'As you say, it's not worth discussing. Not now, anyway.' She frowned. 'But there was a drawing.'

'Wait. Cover yourself.' He rose from the bed and pulled on his tunic as she reached for her dress. He gave her a second then went to the door and opened it. Giovanni was standing there, Grant beside him. He stood to one side. 'Come in.'

They glanced at each other. Siward gestured to the bed. 'Come in and sit. We all have to hear something.'

'We must be quick,' said Grant, entering. 'The Turk mine is under the wall.'

Violetta said, 'I found a map in Minotto's satchel on Chios. I copied it but it was lost when I fell into the water. I can remember it though.' She went to a table where there was parchment and pencil. She drew for a while then picked up the paper and brought it to Giovanni. 'Do you know where this is?'

Giovanni looked at it. Then he passed it to Grant. 'It's Ceuta.'

Grant looked at the drawing. 'Yes, it is. But what does it mean?'

Giovanni stared at the bed below him, one finger resting on his beard. He spoke quietly to himself. 'The Venetian fleet is being held at Negroponte. Why? To sail to Ceuta and attack it?' He shook his head. 'But Venice and Portugal are allies.' He looked up. 'Unless . . .' He turned to Grant. 'What do you remember about Ceuta's defences?'

'I remember everything; I designed them with you. The best in the world.'

'But they're all facing landward, no? Because the attack would always have come from the Moors inland – not from the sea, because the Moors didn't have much of a navy. The sea walls are completely vulnerable.'

Grant nodded slowly. 'Yes. But why would Venice want to attack Ceuta?'

Siward had seen it. 'Not just Venice,' he said, 'Mehmed as well.'

'But Mehmed's galleys would have no idea how to get there.'

'Venice's would though, wouldn't they?' Siward was nodding. 'They're going to carry the Turks.'

'And I think I know why,' said Giovanni. He turned to Siward. 'Do you remember when I told you about the Portuguese caravel designs that had been stolen from Prince Henry's palace at Sagres?'

Then Grant finally understood. 'They're going to beat Portugal to India,' he whispered. 'Mehmed will take Ceuta for them and they'll launch their own caravels south and Portugal won't be able to stop them.'

Siward nodded. 'That's why they changed Fra Mauro's map, so that Prince Henry would still think the way round Africa closed. They just needed to buy enough time to take Ceuta.'

And Violetta, who understood Venetians better than any of them, shook her head in wonder at it all. 'It's so obvious. When Constantinople falls, the trade route to the East will be closed. Whoever finds another one will rule the world. Venice has no plans for anyone to rule the world but her. She has made Mehmed her pawn.'

They were all silent, reflecting.

Grant was the first to rise. 'Well, we know what we have to do. We have to get out of this city and warn Portugal. And we have to survive to escape.'

An hour ago, Violetta had watched Siward go. He'd been the last to leave the room and he'd stopped at the door and turned.

'I'll do it and I'll come back,' he'd said. 'Don't leave this room. Wait for me.'

Wait for me. All the years of waiting and it had come to this moment. She'd run forward and held his face between her hands and kissed him so hard that her lips were still numb.

411

She was lying on the bed now, waiting for her heartbeat to fade and thinking of what had been. She'd had a lifetime of love in Venice. She'd loved old men and fat men and men of no skill who'd thought themselves otherwise when she'd finished with them. She'd enjoyed giving pleasure without needing to take any in return. That night she'd known what she'd missed.

She turned onto her side and breathed in deeply, trying to steady her heart. He would come back – his kind always did, favoured by whatever god smiled on the brave. He'd come back and he'd love her for the rest of their long lives together.

So why did she feel that everything was spiralling out of control? Why did the world suddenly seem so disordered, so arbitrary on its axis? Chaos was all around: in the sky and the terrible deeds of men.

Makkim is dead.

She heard a crash, then another. She sat up. The cannon had started and the attack would begin soon. What should she do? She rose and went to the window. The Blachernae walls were lit by gunfire and she could see the silhouettes of running men. She wanted to go to them, help them in any way she could. But he'd been specific. *Wait for me.*

Now she heard the sound of battle. At the ramparts, there were men fighting, the unmistakeable clash of weapons. She heard the cries of death and survival, the shrill shouts of encouragement. The fighting was fiercest on the tower. There the struggle was so intense that it was hard to know who had the advantage. But above it all, the Lion of St Mark still flew undisturbed. Minotto, and Venice, were holding the Blachernae wall.

She'd thought of Minotto. He'd be keeping himself alive for when the moment came to leave: to run down to whichever harbour held the galley manned and rigged for his escape. But it must be a dangerous business, this staying alive, this double-game. She'd heard he'd even led the attack with the fireship. He was nothing if not brave.

Then she heard the whump of imploding earth. She gripped the window frame and saw a great cloud reach into the sky beyond the walls. Siward had done it. He'd blown up the Turks' mine and they'd not be able to get into the city. She only had to stay there and he'd be back for her. She sat down on the bed to wait.

But then she heard something new outside the window. She rose and walked over. It was the tower. There were more men on it than before and the shouts were not all Italian. She saw a turban and, above it, a flag that was not the Lion of St Mark. It dipped down, came up again, was lifted higher: a crescent moon.

She recoiled as if cold water had been thrown at her. She put her hand to her mouth. Yes, the flag was there next to Venice's. It could mean only one, terrible thing. The Turks had got into the city. Their mine had worked.

So where was Siward?

The answer came to her as ice to the veins. His mine had collapsed, not the Turks'. He must have been trapped in it, suffocating beneath a ton of earth. She couldn't stay there a moment longer.

She dressed fully, went to the door and opened it. Outside, the corridor was empty. Which way would he be? She'd hardly been conscious when he'd carried her there last night. She looked to the right. That was the direction of the walls, yes. She could hear the distant sound of fighting. She ran.

She turned a corner, then another. Was this right? The sounds didn't seem to be getting any closer. Where was everybody? Surely a single servant . . .

She rounded a third corner and nearly tripped over the legs of a man leaning out of the window. They were the bare legs of a monk.

'Please . . .'

The man turned from the window and her heart stopped. Someone she'd not forgotten, would never forget, was standing in front of her, a cloth in his hand.

Suddenly, she felt a fury like she'd never felt before. This man . . . *this perverted reptile* . . . was daring to keep her from Siward. She lunged at him, pushing him back against the wall. She'd claw out the eyes that had devoured her, rip the tongue from the mouth that had . . . '*No!*'

The monk was cowering now, his back sliding down the wall. One hand was shielding his face, but the other still held onto the cloth. She was screaming at him, tearing at his eyes, his hair. She would slow soon. He'd wait for it.

When it happened, he brought the cloth up to her mouth and clamped it on, holding it there until she fell.

CHAPTER THIRTY-NINE

CONSTANTINOPLE

The wagons had been coming in all day from Edirne and beyond with whole carcasses of sheep and goats piled high. As soon as they arrived, the cooks skinned the animals and impaled them on a hundred spits and the scent of roasting meat filled the noses of countless hungry men. Mehmed's army would feast well before the final battle. The bashibozouks would eat last, as was the custom, but be allowed to take away the skins for clothing. They would eat last, but die first. It had always been the way.

Makkim had never been amongst them before. Like every janissary, he'd seen them as creatures from another world, savages of the steppe only good for unfocussed violence, for preparing the way for the more elegant butchery of the janissaries. He'd seen them as expendable.

Now he was one of them.

It had been Mehmed's final command. They'd been in his tent and he'd made it in a whisper, crouched in front of him, both hands on his shoulders as if he was passing on a confidence.

'You will be the one to plant the flag,' he'd said into eyes that held his without the fear he so wanted to see in them. 'You will attack with the bashibozouks and you will carry the flag and you will plant it in front of Constantine to show him that *no one* deserts Mehmed *Fatih*.'

Makkim had remained silent, wondering why Mehmed thought he'd obey such a command.

Then he'd told him, his face so close that their noses almost touched. 'I have her, you see,' he'd said slowly, enjoying every word that passed his lips. 'I have her somewhere in Constantinople where she won't be found until we get to her.' He'd pulled his head back, searching Makkim's face for the reaction he so craved. 'And do you know where she was when she was taken? In the Blachernae Palace, fresh from bed with another man! She is a whore, Makkim – a dirty Venetian whore.'

Now he was watching a line of men gnawing food that was almost raw, the cooks knowing how the bashibozouks liked their meat. None of them spoke; their concentration was total. They were sitting with their backs to a gigantic siege tower lying on its side. It had been built by Mehmed's carpenters in secret, section by section, before being assembled that afternoon. When it was hauled to its feet, it would stand slightly taller than the Romanus Gate. It was from the top of this tower that a bridge would be lowered, above the outer wall and peribelos below, to reach over to the gate. And across that bridge Makkim would go with the flag.

It was suicide. He knew it, and every man across from him, their beards filthy with animal juices, knew it too. None of them much minded. The bashibozouks lived short, brutish lives that might as well end at Constantinople as anywhere else. And for Makkim, life had ceased to have any purpose. He'd lost everything.

He'd spent the afternoon with these men, pulling forward the siege engines and giant battering rams that would be needed for the final attack. He'd hauled on ropes until his palms were raw, looking into the faces of the bronze devils that would break down the gates of Constantinople. It had been done beneath a merciless sun and his back was an agony of sunburn.

The leader of these bashibozouks was called Yadik. He was a giant of a man into whose maw almost a whole goat had already disappeared. He had no idea who Makkim was, only that he'd been chosen to plant the flag on the Romanus tower. From Makkim's appearance, he'd guessed that he'd once been a janissary. He set aside his bone and stared at him.

'Janissary,' he growled, 'you don't share food with us because you think yourself better. We will see.' He wiped his lips with bearskin. 'All men die the same.'

A younger man, unbearded and with the face of a weasel, joined in. 'The first over that bridge is not a good place to be.' His voice was high, almost a eunuch's. Makkim noticed that one of his eyes permanently looked away. 'You must be being offered a lot of gold.'

Makkim stayed silent. He'd not been offered gold, just the life of a woman who may or may not be held somewhere in Constantinople. It didn't matter if it was true. He had no choice. He knew he'd have to cross that bridge. But who would he meet at its other side?

He fought the thought away and dropped to his haunches so that he was at the same level as Yadik and the rest of them. 'I'll share my gold with you if you'll help me,' he said. 'I can't do it on my own.'

Yadik growled again. 'So we'll all die. What good is gold to a dead man?'

But the weasel was more interested. He got up and went over to squat beside Makkim. He was dressed in new sheep-skins that left blood trails all over his bare arms and legs. He stank so badly that Makkim put his hands to his mouth. The man said, 'How?'

Makkim rose and went over to the siege tower behind them. He patted its sides. 'First, we have to get to the wall,' he said. 'These leather hides will be doused with water but they won't stop the fire the Greeks will shoot from the walls. The tower will burn and we'll burn inside it.'

Yadik was nodding. 'I've seen this Greek fire. It does burn everything. It burns on water.'

Makkim had raised his finger. 'But there is one thing that can put it out. Piss. Lots of piss.'

The weasel laughed. 'You want us to go forward with our cocks out?'

The others joined the laughter, some of them choking on their meat, spitting it out to the ground. It was Yadik who raised his hand. 'Let him speak.'

'No, not that,' said Makkim, smiling too. 'But I do want us to gather every drop of piss we can tomorrow and spray it over the hides just before we go forward. Can we do that?'

The men exchanged glances. Yadik said, 'Yes, we can do that. What else?'

'We must also find and fill pots with it and have them ready on every storey of the tower to put out other fires.'

The men were quiet now. Yadik nodded. 'We can do that too.'

The weasel was watching Makkim carefully. 'If we do this, you'll share the gold?'

Makkim walked back to squat beside the weasel again, trying to ignore his smell. He seemed the most intelligent of the men so he spoke directly to him. 'No, that will get you to the walls. You have to do more to share my gold.'

Yadik asked, 'How much gold is there?'

Makkim thought fast. How much was a lot of gold to these men? He'd always had more than he knew how to spend. He turned towards where the janissaries were feasting around their fires. 'You have seen the janissary cauldrons? Enough gold coin to fill one of those.'

Yadik whistled through his teeth. This janissary had somehow disgraced himself and was seeking redemption by being the first over the walls. It was fitting that his reward would be a cauldron of coin. Yadik had come to this siege from a village far out on the steppe where he fought a daily battle to survive. He had five children and his wife was pregnant with a sixth. If any man in the world needed gold, it was him.

'What more must we do?'

Makkim turned to him, then looked slowly down the line of men, seeing faces aged and torn by suffering. He felt a sudden surge of pity.

'You must charge with me,' he said. 'When the bridge goes down, we must all charge together. Some may die, yes, but those who don't will have a better chance of living through the night.' He paused. 'And of sharing the Sultan's reward.'

There was silence and the men all looked at each other, then at the ground. It wasn't what they'd wanted to hear.

But the weasel had seen the logic of what Makkim proposed. 'He's right,' he said. He spat on the ground and turned to Yadik. 'If he goes alone, he gets killed. Then we go next and get killed. We must go together.'

CHAPTER FORTY

CONSTANTINOPLE

In the Blachernae Palace, along the land walls and in the scattered encampments behind, they heard the Turks feasting all through the night and understood what it meant. Soon every citizen knew as well.

The Day of Judgement had finally arrived. Tomorrow the Turks would gather every creature of their terrible army to make one last assault, and Constantinople would either hold or fall. People looked to the heavens to see which it would be.

The morning broke without omen of any kind, least of all from the Turkish camp, which was silent. After its feasting, Mehmed's army would rest until noon to conserve energy for the battle ahead. So, leaving only lookouts on the city walls, the people of Constantinople went into the Church of Holy Wisdom to pray and be shriven.

With a congregation of fifty thousand, they had to open the doors for the people who stood outside. Patriarch Gennadius led the liturgy, having gathered to the great altar every bishop, abbot and priest in the city, of whatever persuasion, to pray for a miracle. Some would pray for divine intervention, others for a more worldly kind. Venice's fleet hadn't come but there was still a little time.

Siward watched it all from a balcony. His Varangians were at the back of the church, ready, like he was, to hurry back to the walls should the Turks decide to come early. He looked round at the battered glory of Hagia Sofia, Justinian's masterpiece, this mother of all churches. He looked at its gilded saints and emperors who'd looked down on congregations for a thousand years. He doubted they'd ever seen one like this.

At the front was Constantine in his white armour with Giovanni beside him, Loukas Notaras on his other side. Behind were the soldiers of a score of different nations, each under their flag. He saw Hungary, Spain, Genoa, Naples, Pisa and the Papal States. He saw the Holy Roman Empire, with its upstart double-headed eagle, and France with its fleur-de-lys. And he saw the biggest group of all: Venice, all good men who'd fought with courage, whatever their leader's allegiance. Every man was in armour and carried his weapon, for this was a congregation to be blessed and sent off to fight.

Behind the soldiers were the dignitaries of Constantinople, many in armour too, and behind them the women and the old, the infirm and the young: the people who would stay behind. It was these Siward felt most pity for. They'd seen terrible things over the past weeks and now they just had to await their fate. He wondered at their calm. Did they still believe Venice would come?

He felt exhausted. Since coming back from the mine two nights earlier and finding Violetta gone, he'd scoured the city for her. First, he'd searched the palace, racing from room to room crying her name until he was hoarse. It was only when he'd found the cook, lying in the kitchens with his throat cut,

421

that he realised what had happened. Someone had broken in and learnt where she was. Later, he'd found a guard who'd seen a monk leave in a wagon, the same who'd arrived earlier with a cargo of bread.

So he'd gone to every monastery, every church, school and bakery ... anywhere that a monk might go. By the morning of the service, he was in despair. Giovanni had met him at the doors of the church.

'She may have decided to look out for herself,' Giovanni had said, his face more tired than Siward had ever seen it. 'Perhaps she didn't want to burden you with the extra worry.'

'But the murdered cook?' he'd asked. 'The monk with the wagon who had not, in fact, brought bread into the palace? How do you explain those?'

Giovanni had shrugged and placed his hand on his shoulder. 'Who knows? But we have a battle to fight and your Varangians will need you,' he'd said gently. 'I'll need you, Siward.'

Now he was praying for another kind of miracle. He'd make one last search, then go to the walls. He would at least die knowing that she'd loved him.

The service was drawing to an end and Gennadius was giving his blessing, incense rising all around his outstretched arms. Siward heard a commotion and saw the congregation look up, even Gennadius and the bishops. He looked up too. There was a big black bird inside the church, circling inside the massive dome, its screech echoing through the building as it gyred. He looked down at Constantine, who was standing as still as salt.

Are you remembering a coronation four years ago?

But this time Siward could do nothing but watch. He heard the murmurs below, the whispered worry passed from lip to lip. Legend had it that an angel would appear with a flaming sword to defend this Church of Holy Wisdom, and many had resolved to remain there after the service. There was no mention of ravens.

The bird dipped suddenly, its wings drawn in, its screech suspended. It swooped over the upturned heads, over the flags and the pooled incense, flapping its wings to keep the glide. It flew through the doors and out into the square. Siward looked down at Constantine again.

The Emperor was staring up at him, a small smile playing across his lips. He nodded.

Gennadius had raised his hands for silence. 'Citizens and soldiers! Our emperor wishes to speak.'

Constantine strode up to the altar and turned. He raised his arms.

'Behold! A bird has come into our holiest place, seen what it cannot have, and left.' He brought his hands together. 'A good omen by any reckoning.'

There was silence before him.

'Friends,' he said, turning his head slowly so that his voice would carry throughout the church and beyond, 'our time has come. This city, which has dazzled the world for a thousand years, whose walls have humbled our enemies for eleven centuries, faces its greatest challenge. And God has given to us the honour ... the glory ... of meeting that challenge. We must in no way fail Him. We have fought back this enemy for eight brave weeks. Tonight, either Mehmed triumphs or he departs like that bird. Tonight, we have it in our grasp to send him home to Edirne.'

Apart from the clink of shifted armour, the muffled cry of a baby, the sniff of those already overcome by the moment, there was no sound in the Church of Hagia Sofia, or outside it.

Siward looked down on a sea of faces: Greek, Italian, Catholic and Orthodox, looking up at an emperor only God could have sent them in their hour of peril. Surely, this was the miracle that really mattered. It was the only one Siward could believe in.

Constantine, once and future emperor.

'You knights from foreign lands,' Constantine continued, gesturing to them, 'brave Giustiniani of Genoa, Minotto of Venice, Don Francesco of Toledo, Diedo, Contarini and the rest . . . you have done everything expected of a Christian knight and more. I thank you from the bottom of an emperor's heart. I thank you on behalf of every citizen of Constantinople. If the odds have seemed sometimes too great, how much greater will be your victory to have vanquished them? And how much greater will be this city's gratitude when it knows that its children can grow up under the protection of the One True God and his Mother the Blessed Virgin Mary?'

The clink of armour was more general now as men tried to hide their emotion, many looking to the ground to conceal their tears. Mothers lifted their children, the better to see their emperor.

Constantine raised his hand. 'I will go from this church,' he said, a catch in his voice, 'to visit every one of you on your wall. Then I will go to my place at the Romanus Gate to fight and, if God wills it, die. But before I go, I will ask one last thing of you. There have been divisions among us, between Venetian and Genoan, between Catholic and Orthodox, between Greek and foreigner. We must face our judgement united, our quarrels forgotten, a true brotherhood of arms. I ask forgiveness of any man among you whom I have wronged. I would ask you to do likewise, to embrace each other in this Church of Holy Wisdom in the name of the One Lord Jesus Christ.'

It was a powerful call made in a voice cracked with fatigue and entreaty. Siward watched as Constantine walked down to embrace Giovanni, then Loukas Notaras. Then he saw Giovanni turn and walk over to the bailo Minotto. For a moment, the two men looked at each other, then they hugged. It was the signal that everyone else had needed. Catalan and Aragonese kissed, Florence fell into the arms of Milan, and even Venice and Genoa joined hands and wished God's blessing upon the other.

Siward found his eyes wet. He'd not thought to see such a thing in his lifetime. If Constantinople fell that night, perhaps this example might spread across the rest of fractious Christendom. He might wish it so. But more than anything, more than any other single thing, he wished that Violetta was beside him to see it all.

He should leave to carry out that last search for her. He should go before the congregation spilled out onto the streets. He turned.

Outside, something strange had happened. A dense fog had descended on the city, a sea of grey that swirled about his legs like ghost fishes, obscuring the ground, dismembering every person at the knee, every building at its foundations. There was a smell of sulphur in the air and birds, invisible and directionless, shrieked their alarm from above. It was an omen every bit as ominous as Constantine's speech had been uplifting. Siward hurried away.

He ran down streets, shouting her name into empty houses, tripping on the loose stones he couldn't see. The fog rolled up his voice and gave it back to him, muffled and smaller. He heard nothing but his footsteps and the birds above.

'Violetta. *Violetta!*'

He had come to the end of a street of dilapidated houses,

where the rich merchants of Amalfi had once had their quarter. He remembered that the old Varangian church was near here somewhere. He looked over wasteland and into the murk that hid everything beyond. He thought about miracles. He'd heard of a church way out across the fields where snakes had gathered. It was a week ago they'd started coming, they said: snakes of all sizes slithering over the fields to crawl up the steps and curl themselves around the foot of the Cross. Was it true? And if it was, what did it mean? That even the snakes were now seeking sanctuary?

A miracle. I need a miracle.

Then, perhaps, a small one. The fog lifted as suddenly as it had fallen. The birds went away. Sunshine broke through, shy at first, then with conviction. And there, in front of him, was a church.

The Varangian church?

He had no way of knowing. Only Giovanni had seen it. He walked forward shouting her name, louder now without the fog. He would look inside.

But the old church door, hung from only one hinge, creaked open as he approached it. An old Varangian appeared, holding his helmet and sword belt in one hand, stooping beneath the fissured lintel with the dragon carved onto it. It was Theogrid.

'Captain, I'm sorry,' he said. He put on his helmet and fastened his sword around his waist. 'The Liturgy in the Holy Wisdom was good enough, but it wasn't *our* liturgy. I came here for a last prayer.'

Siward nodded. He was bewildered and a little relieved. Perhaps this had been a miracle of sorts. Perhaps, without Theogrid here to guide him back to his duty, he'd have gone on with his pointless search. He was finished with it now. She was gone and he wouldn't find her.

Violetta rose from the bed and dressed. She had quite clearly heard Siward calling to her. She went over to the door and opened it. The corridor outside was washed in milk, the moonlight merging every colour into a sepia whey. The world was striped: either in shadow, or outside it. She walked between the stripes hearing no sound of her footsteps or breathing or even heart, waiting for the only sound that mattered, the one telling her where to go. She thought she saw something reflected through the windows and went over to them, glided really, to see the Grand Canal below full of busy, mute craft. She stopped to look at them all, wondering at their silence.

He called again and she turned and hurried on, past a courtier asleep at a window, past sleeping cats. Then she was in an orchard full of trees heavy with fruit that shone white beneath the moon. His voice came to her between the trees, calling her name in the way he had when they'd loved each other. When had that been? She saw Johannes Grant in the distance. He was with Giovanni and they were standing beside a hole in the ground, gesturing and smiling, silent as everything else. She went up to them.

Go down. He's there waiting for you. Buried in earth you just have to remove.

She went down into a tunnel. There was darkness and a tiny light far, far away. He called her name again and the light moved. She began to go towards it on her hands and knees. She wanted so much to touch him, knowing that his touch would restore colour and sound to the world, but he was buried and she didn't have a spade. And something was slowing her, making her limbs so heavy that she couldn't lift one in front of the other. She heard her name again but fainter. She was losing him . . .

She woke to confusion, then dread.

It had been a dream but his voice had seemed so real. She strained every nerve to hear it again but it didn't come. Instead she heard the hollow sound of footsteps on wood. Someone descending a staircase.

She shook her head. She was bound at her wrists and ankles with thick rope. She felt heavy with sleep and something else. She remembered another dream: much worse.

The sounds were closer now, someone shuffling down the corridor outside. She felt the inside of her mouth with her tongue. Yes, the same taste was with her still. Had he drugged her?

She looked around her. There was an oil lamp alight on the ground beside her, the only object in the room. She was in a small, earthen-floored space, only tall enough to kneel in, about three lengths of her body long and half as wide. She was underground, in a hidden place, a place of secrets. Its walls were half-stone, half-rock and had chains with manacles fastened to them. At both ends were wooden doors, the furthest with a grille through which she could feel air. She sniffed. Salt air. She must be somewhere near water.

She heard the sliding of bolts behind her and turned, crawling away from the door. Suddenly her head was clear. She felt sick with fear.

The priest.

The door inched open, a light flickering behind it. A hand appeared holding a lamp, then a frayed woollen sleeve, a monk's sleeve. She heard the wheeze of breath in a dry throat and smelt something she'd not smelt for twenty years: it was the sweet, rancid smell of a man who'd once come too close to her, who'd

428

touched and probed her and silenced her with hands wet with excitement.

'Get back from the door.'

His voice was the same: nasal and with that edge of whine. She felt bile rise from her stomach to replace the taste of whatever drug he'd fed to her. She couldn't feel anything but the thump of her heart against her ribcage.

Then he was crawling inside the room, his body thinner than she'd remembered. He was carrying a plate with food on it and a lamp. She stared at it, not him.

'I've brought you food.'

She said nothing, holding her knees to her chin between her tied wrists. She found she was shaking.

'You have nothing to fear from me,' he said softly, placing the plate on the ground. 'I have no plan to hurt you.'

She was sure she'd heard him say those words before. She hugged her knees tighter, feeling the rope dig into her wrists. She stared at the plate and tried to control her shaking, to fight down her nausea.

'I'm too old now, I suppose,' she said. She heard the tremor in her voice, hating it. 'No longer a child.'

He sighed. She heard him shift and the sound of creaking wood as he leant back against the door. She felt his eyes on her. She would not look into them, only at the plate. It was metal, perhaps gold.

'People change,' he said.

'And this room? The chains?' she asked. 'You've been here before. It stinks of you.' She looked away and noticed something. There were marks grooved into the stone by something sharp. They might have been numbers. Days perhaps. 'What are those scratchings on the wall?'

He didn't answer but she heard him look to where she looked.

'What are they?' She shook her head, anger rising. 'You haven't changed, have you? How young were *they*, you bastard?'

Silence. He might be about to strike her, but she heard him shift again. 'Did you hear him?' he asked.

'Who?'

'He was outside, shouting for you. He nearly came into the church.'

She felt despair break over her, then joy. She *had* heard him. It hadn't all been a dream. And if he was there, then he was alive.

'The old Varangian was praying here,' he said. 'The fool went out to meet him. Then they left.' He sighed again. 'He'd have found you if he'd come in. If only you'd shouted.'

She felt her face burn. So close! He'd only had to walk through a door. She felt tears well in her eyes and looked back at the plate.

'Why am I here?'

'Because a powerful prince wants you to be. He told me to bring you here.'

'Mehmed.'

The priest nodded. 'He must have hated your brother very much.' He pressed. 'Except that he wasn't your brother, was he? Did you love him, or the one who was looking for you?'

She continued to stare at the plate he'd brought. On it were scraps that a dog might have walked past. She closed her eyes.

He said, 'You will look at me.'

'No.'

'If you want answers,' he said, 'then you will look at me.'

She wanted to know so many things. The priest would probably lie, but what did she have to lose? She forced her head up and opened her eyes.

430

His face, like his body, was thinner, but his eyes were the same. Set within grey, pocked skin dissected by dirt, the stones he used for eyes looked back at her with infinite coldness. He was unshaven on his chin and at the top of his tonsured pate. She saw his tongue part his lips and then retreat, like a snake's.

'So. I will tell you. None of it is good, I'm afraid.'

She waited. She knew Siward was alive, at least. Was he about to tell her that it had been someone else? She steeled herself.

'You are here because Mehmed doesn't want you to escape the siege. I am to keep you here until his soldiers come.'

'Which they won't,' she said. 'Constantinople will hold.'

'Ah, well it might have done, yes. But do you see that door?' He pointed to the grille. 'That door leads to a tunnel which goes right out to the Golden Horn. Quite soon, I will leave here to meet Mehmed's soldiers and lead them all the way down it to find you here. Then they will enter the city.'

She glanced at the door, smelling the salt air that came through it. She couldn't think of anything to say.

'Though I don't understand why he wants you alive,' the priest continued, shaking his head at the mystery. 'After all, Makkim is dead. I saw him impaled.' He shrugged. 'I think perhaps he loved Makkim. Would you say that?'

She dug her fingernails into her knees to fight the waves of misery that assailed her from all sides. She would not let this man break her into pieces.

He sighed for a third time. 'I suppose I should go now. The Turks are all feasted and ready for battle. Two hours before dawn, that's when they'll attack the walls. But my Turks will come sooner.' He looked down at the plate. 'You should eat.'

But she wanted to know something else before he went. 'Is he giving you gold?'

431

'No, something much better than gold. You'll see.'

He pulled open the door and shuffled outside. She heard the bolts slide to, then his voice muffled by the wood. 'Eat something. It's not poisoned.'

She listened to him leaving, the sound of his breath coming in pants as he made his way back up the staircase and into the church. She heard his footsteps above. She felt the same as she had all those years ago in another room below another church: hatred like it was a searing, scalding torch pressed to her body. She clutched herself and closed her eyes.

Eat something.

It was good advice. She'd not eaten for two days. She opened her eyes and stared at the plate.

She picked up what looked like bread. It was stale and hard and unfit to eat but it was all there was. She looked down at the plate as she ate. It looked like it was made of gold. What were those markings on it? She held it up to see better in the lamplight. What *were* they?

Eugenius knew he would be early to meet the Turks but he'd take no chances. The streets were empty now except for the procession of some late relic, as if anything could help now. He heard the murmurs of prayer through windows he passed, saw the flicker of candles around shrines. Mothers would be hugging their children to them, searching their faces to remember every feature lest they be parted.

Children. No, that was the past. He was to be Patriarch of Constantinople or whatever they would call the city next. No more children.

He kept his head bowed beneath his hood, walking quickly. He did not want to be stopped for a blessing or to hear a confession. He must get to the sea walls and out through the gate to meet Zaganos. It would be almost deserted, Longo having hauled every last soldier away to the land walls. Good.

He turned a corner. Soldiers were coming his way. He'd bless them as they passed. But they stopped.

'Come with us,' said the man at their head. He was Greek, an officer.

'What? I am a monk.'

'And all monks are to go to the walls. Emperor's orders.'

'But I don't fight.'

'Then tend the wounded or give absolution, I don't care.' The officer had grabbed Eugenius's sleeve as he was trying to turn away. 'Whoa. You're not going that way, father, you're coming with us. To the land walls. Now.'

CHAPTER FORTY-ONE

CONSTANTINOPLE

It was as if a million fireflies had alighted on the plain. Since nightfall, and as far as the eye could see, torches had been moving in the darkness, some in long lines, some in formation, some rising into the sky as if climbing an invisible stairway to heaven.

It was this last phenomenon that had caught Siward's attention. From the top of the Romanus Gate, he could see both ways along the Turkish lines but it was only to his front that the torches climbed heavenward. Then, when a flare went up, he saw why. Some djinn had silently pulled a siege tower to its feet, a huge monster whose sides were covered by wet, gleaming hides. At its top, a bridge was suspended by chains.

'That is big.'

Johannes Grant was standing beside him holding the nozzle of a fire canister. They'd spent the last hour together, fixing ranges for the Greek fire.

'It's level with this tower,' said Siward, as more flares went up. 'They'll drop the bridge over the outer wall and come across.'

'Or we'll burn it to the ground before it gets here.' Grant tightened a nozzle. 'I pity the poor bastards inside.'

Siward thought of the hundreds of bashibozouk faces that he'd seen come at him over the past weeks. They'd been half-savages: wild men with no fear and no skill. For a big man in armour, they'd been too easy to kill. Tonight it would be the same. He and Giovanni would meet their charge and hurl it into the peribelos.

But then what? Would the city fall? Would he take ship for Portugal? It was what he should do but he'd not go without her. Violetta was somewhere in the city and he'd find her or die there. Someone else could go to warn Portugal.

He looked down at the space between the walls. There were men in a line passing stone from the open gate, others standing behind them with torches. He thought of Petros who should be down there with them.

Yet another barricade was being strengthened on the outer wall but the work had more dogged purpose tonight. People knew this might be the last act in the long tragedy that was the end of the Roman Empire. Some time before dawn would come the biggest, most ferocious attack any of them had ever faced and their city would either endure or fall.

Perhaps Giovanni was right. Perhaps Violetta had melted into the city and deliberately made herself lost to him. But she would have left word, surely. And how to explain the monk and murdered cook?

He heard cheers – tired, defiant – and the slow beat of swords against shields. He looked over the tower to see the Emperor approaching with Giovanni and Loukas Notaras. They walked through a group of Varangians and Constantine stopped to talk to a boy passing stones, then take the hand of an old man. His armour shone gold in the light of the torches. A man behind him held the Palaiologos flag in both hands. It would fly from

435

wherever the Emperor fought tonight. He saw Constantine enter the tower.

'Well, we've had our first victory of the night, Siward,' said Constantine as he emerged at the top. The smile he wore was an emperor's smile: calm and strong. 'Tell him, Giovanni.'

'We were visiting the sea walls,' said Giovanni. 'We saw five Turkish longboats rowing back across the Golden Horn. Apparently some men had landed on the shore and milled about until a sentry heard them and sent up a flare. Then the archers shot them to pieces. They couldn't miss.'

'Perhaps they'd heard the wall is defended by monks now,' said Notaras. 'We passed one on our way, coming here. He looked unhappy.'

Constantine walked to the front of the tower and looked out at the view for a long time. He turned.

'I know about the Venetian plan for Ceuta,' he said quietly. 'Giovanni has told me everything. We have agreed that nothing will be said to Minotto. His men fight bravely and he is needed to lead them, and your chances of getting away from the city will be improved if he doesn't know you're a danger to his plans. I know neither Giustiniani nor you will leave before you need to, and for that I am grateful. Men look to you both.' He looked resigned. 'What will you do?'

So the Emperor knew at last. He didn't seem surprised, or even horrified.

'There is a ship waiting at the harbour of Proshorianus,' said Siward, 'a round ship that should break through the blockade. We'll sail to the mainland and ride hard for Venice, then Portugal. We'll tell the Doge that his plan is known, then warn Prince Henry to turn round the guns at Ceuta.'

Constantine nodded and turned to look along the inner wall

where men stood beside catapults, cannons, siphons and every other killing machine that had been hoisted onto it. He looked at what had once been the outer wall and was now a series of stockades crowded by archers and men-at-arms. Every man was looking out into the night, waiting for the single cry that would hurl men forward to their deaths.

Not far away, Makkim was holding his nose. All afternoon his band of bashibozouks had been collecting the army's piss and now they had great barrels of it, frothing and stinking and keeping the rest of the army at bay. They'd already soaked the siege tower's hides once and would do so again. The army's prayers were done and it was three hours to dawn and soon it would be time.

He'd tried not to think of what he had to do with the flag. He'd listened to the giant Yadik and the weasel spending the gold they'd get many times over. Yadik's share had gone to sheep and goats and enough land for them to roam in. The weasel, not having a wife or children, had spent his on a lifetime of fornication in Edirne's brothels. Makkim had felt little guilt for the lie. The men would die anyway.

The army was very silent. The drums had stopped, the hurling machines were in place and the archers' bows poised. The siege tower to his front blocked out all sight of the walls, and much of the night. Each of its eight wheels was the size of a man. Very soon, those wheels would turn as they pushed it forward, across the levelled fosse, right up to the outer wall. Then he would climb to its top and hurl himself into the arms of . . . who? Siward? *Giovanni*?

He heard the whoosh of flares go up behind him and put his hands to his ears as the cannons roared all at once. He saw clouds of stone and dust as the shot exploded against the city walls and he heard the jeers of the men behind their barricades. He heard one clear voice not far away.

'Allahu akbar!'

Then a hundred thousand others.

'Allahu akbar!'

It had begun.

The kos drums started up, then the pipes, and the army surged forward as Makkim bent his shoulder to the back of the siege tower. Men either side of it, protected by shelters that moved as they moved, pulled on their ropes. The wheels began to turn, the timber groaned and the monster started to roll, swaying drunkenly as it travelled over the uneven ground. Makkim felt the frame shudder as a blizzard of arrows hit its sides and heard the crack of wood as a rock struck home. Soon would come fire. He looked behind and saw men dragging the barrels of piss forward, Yadik beating their backs with his *bastinado*.

The noise around him was beyond anything he'd ever heard. Wave after wave of half-shadowed men ran past, clutching every kind of weapon, skins on their backs and nothing on their feet. They screamed every one of the ninety-nine names for their God. By now, the first of them would be charging the barricades, dying beneath the blades of Varangian swords.

They had reached the fosse and the wheels were meeting resistance. Yadik ran up beside him to add his weight. The tower rose and fell and rose again, lurching and swaying as it did so.

'When will they shoot fire?' the giant yelled into Makkim's ear.

'Any moment . . .'

He heard a roar and saw flame arc through the night like a comet, saw it splash against hides that gleamed with the

438

contents of men's bladders. He saw stitches stiffen and break and the fire come and go, not taking hold. He heard the cheers of men all around him who'd seen it too.

He leant into the tower and pushed again and saw arrows fall around him, some aimed, some sprung from the hides above. A cannon boomed from the walls, then another.

'Push, devil's spawn!' Yadik was running from man to man, urging every ounce of effort from them. '*Push!*'

Makkim looked up again and saw the ripped hides, the gaping holes where the shot had passed through. He shouted to Yadik. 'The barrels! Bring them up here. Tell the men to fill the pots and take them up the tower!'

Yadik yelled to the men behind, each of them holding a pot. Makkim looked up to see a wooden strut catch fire.

'*Quick!*'

They had reached the outer wall and the defenders were spewing flame from every direction. But men were already climbing the steps inside the tower with pots in their hands, throwing liquid at every fire. It was time for Makkim to climb to the top. He took the flag from the boy who'd been carrying it and turned to Yadik.

'Ready?'

They were ready. Bashibozouks had gathered around the base, waiting to follow him to the top, then over the bridge. At their front were Yadik and the weasel. They looked at him as he'd once seen his janissaries look at him. He nodded as he'd nodded to them, as you'd nod to your children. He drew his sword.

'Follow me!'

'*Wait!*'

The shout had come from behind. A big man was pushing

439

his way through, the plumes of his helmet rising and falling beyond the turned heads. He wore the clothes of the janissary.

'Hasan.'

The Aga stopped and looked at Makkim, then at the flag. 'I'm coming with you.'

'To make sure I do it? You can spare yourself the trouble, old friend.' He smiled. 'Tell Mehmed this: if it saves her, I'll do it or die trying.'

Hasan shook his head. 'It's not why I am here. You know that.'

The bashibozouks had backed away, forming a little circle around the two men, lost in wonder at this turn of events, not sure what it meant for their gold.

Makkim studied him. There had been other times when Hasan might have helped him, repaid the debt of Varna. Perhaps he'd been waiting for this one. 'You won't save me, Hasan,' he said. 'You'll just die with me. Go.'

But Hasan stayed where he was.

'Alright.' Makkim nodded, then turned and pushed his way through the hides and into the tower, Hasan close behind. He looked up at the steps winding their way to the first platform where men were standing with pots. Bits of charred wood lay on the ground all around, smoking. It was furnace-hot and he felt sweat course down his neck and chest. He gripped the flag.

'Follow me.'

They mounted the steps as arrows broke through the hides above them, passing over their heads, some trailing fire. Makkim reached the first platform. 'Bring up the shields!'

They were passed up, each man taking one to hold over his head. Makkim started up to the next platform, step by step, going as fast as he dared, feeling the thump of arrows against his shield, feeling the heat of new flames licking the sides around him, hearing Hasan's breathing on his heels. It would be a miracle if they reached the top. Halfway up, he heard Greek shouts outside. They must be at the height of the outer wall. He felt a jolt, saw the claws of a grappling iron take hold of a thick beam below him. Hasan was closest.

'Cut it!'

The Aga lifted his sword and slashed open the hide, then waited for the rope to go taut. When it did, he brought his sword down hard. The rope disappeared.

Makkim passed his shield back to the men behind him and looked up, fighting back the horror of what was to come, clutching the flag to his chest to remind him of why he was doing it. Then he was on the top platform where men were lying all around, pierced with arrows, scorched by fire, some with reeking pots still in their hands. He stepped over them and looked up to see the bridge perched above like some colossal bird of prey. His eyes followed the chains holding it, down to where they were looped around a ratcheted lever. One pull and it would fall. Then what?

Hasan came up beside him. They looked through a gap in the hides towards the Romanus tower opposite, still with the double-headed eagle flying over it. They saw archers lined up, waiting for them, handgunners between them. Behind, through the smoke, they saw men in armour shoulder to shoulder, their swords ready. Makkim gripped the flagpole tightly in a hand barely steady.

He turned to Hasan. 'Ready?'

Siward had watched the tower approach and thought of the Trojan Horse. He imagined the men waiting inside, huddled together, looking for their courage in another's eyes. He looked at the fire canisters on the outer wall, their nozzles all aimed, waiting for the range to close.

So far he'd yet to lift the dragon sword. He'd watched the bashibozouks erupt from the enemy lines, pour across the fosse and fall in their thousands to the hail of arrows. He'd seen the sky fill with fireballs that exploded in showers of flame as the bashibozouks reached the outer walls, hurling themselves at the barricades. He'd seen his Varangians behind their shield-wall, grimly throwing back everything that came at them, young and old fighting side by side. He should be with them.

He looked to his left and right. All along the wall, the hideous wave was crashing and rising in a surf of scaling ladders. He'd never imagined the world held so many ladders. The fireballs had turned the night sky red, washing the violence below with fresh blood. Beyond the sea of bashibozouks he could see the janissaries lined up in their ordered ranks, their flags before them, waiting to cut down any man that dared retreat. They were gathered in the Lycus Valley and would attack the walls to their front, where the Romanus Gate was. They were what the Varangians would face next.

He felt a hand on each of his shoulders and found Giovanni on one side of him and Grant on the other, just returned from the Emperor.

'You'd rather be down there, I know,' said Giovanni. 'But I need you here to throw back whatever comes over that bridge.' He turned to Grant. 'The tower must soon be in range.'

It was. Flame leapt out from the inner wall and swept up its height but didn't hold.

'Clever,' said the engineer. 'They must have pissed on the hides.'

A grappling iron was thrown from the outer wall. They saw

its rope curl, then straighten. A sword came through the hides and cut it.

'Damnation!' Grant was shaking his head. 'They're good. We'll have to face them.'

The siege tower was now hard against the outer wall. Siward looked up at the bridge. It was coming down in jerks, its underside a forest of arrows. In front of him was a line of archers and handgunners, weapons raised, waiting for the onslaught. Behind them were Varangians with their swords drawn and their shields lowered. Giovanni turned to Grant. 'Go. I don't want you here.'

The engineer grunted and left and another took his place. Theogrid. But he should be somewhere else. 'Why aren't you down at the outer wall?' Siward asked, his eyes still on the bridge lurching ever closer on its chains.

'The Emperor sent me up here,' said the old man. 'He wants me to make sure you get away when you have to.' He nodded towards Giovanni. 'You and the general.'

'You saw the Emperor?'

'Just prayed with him and the monk.' He laughed. 'He looked scared enough.'

Siward was shocked. 'The Emperor looked scared?'

'No, no, sir. The monk! I hauled him off the walls to bless us Varangians and he nearly ran away. But I wanted him to do it, no one else.'

The bridge was almost down. Siward was puzzled by something. *A monk.*

'Why could only he do it?'

Theogrid shrugged. 'I've seen him around the Varangian church sometimes. He was there when I found you today. I thought he might bring us some Varangian luck, I suppose.'

Something almost connected in Siward's mind, but the bridge was down and a big bashibozouk holding the flag of the Prophet was standing across it, a janissary giant by his side.

Giovanni gasped and took his arm. A moment later, he'd pushed through the line of archers and turned to face them, his arm raised, his face shining with joy.

'Hold your fire!'

Makkim knew it was Giovanni as soon as he'd raised his arm. He turned to Hasan. 'If you want to help me, stay here.'

The Aga had his scimitar drawn, his nose-guard down. He looked ready to sweep the bridge of anything in his way.

Makkim looked back at the man across the bridge. He saw someone else come forward to stand next to him, someone with a flag. *Siward*. He was thinking fast. What were they doing?

He began to walk forward. He had no plan. He hoped they did.

'Wait,' called Hasan.

Makkim didn't answer. He kept walking, flag in one hand, sword in the other. He heard the furious clash of arms below. The battle for the outer wall was in the balance and whichever flag flew from this tower would decide it.

Giovanni and Siward were only ten paces away.

He shouted in Greek. 'I am forced to do this. Violetta is held somewhere in Constantinople. If I don't plant this flag, Mehmed will kill her.'

'I know where she is,' shouted Siward.

He felt the bridge shake and glanced back. Hasan was coming to join him.

Giovanni shouted, 'Run back to our tower with Siward! I'll hold the janissary off.'

'No, he . . .'

444

Hasan ran past him. Makkim swung the flagpole and struck him on the back. Yelling with rage, the Aga fell to his knees. Makkim grabbed his sword and threw it into the night.

He knelt. 'I'm sorry, old friend. Get back to the tower.'

The bridge shook again and he looked back to see the bashi-bozouks coming. He rose and went to his father.

'Thank God!' said Giovanni, embracing him. 'Now go with Siward.'

Makkim glanced back to where Hasan still knelt. 'Don't hurt the Aga. He is unarmed.'

Giovanni nodded. He went past them, took up position, legs astride. 'Go!' he shouted. 'I'll join you when the Varangians get here.'

Makkim allowed himself to be pulled away, staring back as he went. The Varangians had stopped behind Giovanni, as the bashibozouks had done behind the Aga. But Hasan had been given a sword.

Makkim saw it. '*No!*'

Giovanni and Hasan were going to fight and it would be impossible to interrupt them in such a space. Others could only stand and watch.

The two men joined battle. At first, Giovanni seemed to be winning, but Hasan was the bigger of the two and his reach was longer. Soon, he was forcing Giovanni back towards where the helpless Varangians looked on. The bashibozouks had crept up behind the Aga, ready for the final rush when he won.

The two big men stamped backwards and forwards, the wood shaking with every tread. The bridge was barely the width of three men abreast and one wrong move would mean a fall of sixty feet. So they chopped and thrust and kept their feet apart.

Makkim had been pulled as far as the line of archers and

Siward was shouting into his ear, 'I know where she is. We need to get there.'

'Not yet.'

Hasan had twisted to his side to avoid a thrust. Now he pushed Giovanni's sword away with his own. Giovanni threw an arm out for balance, then a leg, but the bridge was wet and his foot slipped. It was Hasan's chance and he took it. He lifted his leg and kicked Giovanni hard in the side.

For a moment, it looked as if Giovanni might recover. If he dropped onto his arm, he might even gain advantage. But Hasan kicked again.

Giovanni fell.

'No!'

'*NO!*'

Constantinople's hero had fallen. The city must surely be lost. Hasan looked down, swaying as he breathed. Then he raised his fist into the air.

'*Allahu akbar!*'

The bashibozouks shouted as one. Then they charged past him and the Varangians fell back before them. They were backing onto the archers, who could do nothing to help them. Makkim ran over to the edge of the tower and leant over. Giovanni had landed on a pile of bodies. Four Varangians had dropped back from the outer wall and were kneeling around him, a stretcher on the ground beside them.

'He's moving,' shouted Makkim. 'Siward!'

But Siward was busy getting the rest of the Varangians into line.

A shout came from the other side of the tower. 'Is he alive?'

It was Constantine striding towards them. His helmet was off and his long hair clung to his face.

'He lives, lord,' said Makkim. 'We must bring him into the city.'

'No!' shouted Siward, running up to them. 'Open the gate and the front will collapse.'

It was too late. The gates were already being opened by some other command. They heard the groan of the great Romanus doors being pulled apart on their battered hinges, as did every man at the barricades. First one, then another, looked back. They saw it as the signal to retreat.

'No,' shouted Siward from the tower. '*NO!*'

But it was happening and he and Theogrid were too far away to stop it. First the retreat was slow and precise, because the Varangians were doing it. But others further down the walls saw and were less ordered. Men began leaving their posts in their dozens, racing for the opening. Soon it was a rout.

And the Turks were following.

The Emperor lifted his helmet onto his head. 'I will fight here with your Varangians,' he said. 'But you two must leave. We can hold them while you get away.'

'But my father,' said Makkim.

'He'll be taken to the ship. Follow him. Tell the world what you know. Go.'

Makkim turned but Siward didn't. He took Constantine's hand. It was the hand of the last Roman Emperor and would become as immortal as the man himself. He pulled his friend to him and they hugged as hard as armour allowed. At last Siward pulled away. He straightened, then bowed. Then he turned and ran for the stairs.

CHAPTER FORTY-TWO

CONSTANTINOPLE

Siward and Makkim hadn't yet left the Romanus Tower. Siward needed to speak to Theogrid but the old Varangian was holding back the bashibozouks on the bridge. Sounds of fierce battle were coming up from the peribelos below where the Turks were fighting their way slowly to the open gate. Soon they would be inside the city.

He saw his chance and pulled Theogrid from the line. He put his hands on his shoulders as the old man bent to catch his breath, waiting until he straightened. There was blood on every part of his face.

'Stay with the Emperor until there's no longer any reason to,' he said. 'Then bring every Varangian you can find to the harbour where our ship is.'

'I'll do that, sir, but us old ones will stay. This is our city.'

Siward nodded. He glanced at the bridge where Constantine had joined the Varangians. There were more Turks coming out of the tower every second. He turned back. 'The Emperor may wish to die,' he said, 'but you needn't. Fall back as soon as you are able.'

Theogrid dipped his head. 'And you look after the general. Pray that he lives.'

Siward heard Makkim's shout from below. He had to go.

A moment later, he emerged from the bottom of the tower into a scene of panic. The tent village was full of people climbing onto wagons or mounting horses or already running through the fields towards the city centre. Fireballs were landing everywhere and mothers were screaming for their children, husbands for their wives. Siward saw monks running too, every one of them Violetta's abductor.

He'll have got away.

There were horses tied to a rail that looked on in bewilderment, shrieking their fear as another fireball landed. 'The horses!'

They untied two and mounted them. They weaved their way through the tents until they came to the road. It was packed with people and they'd not make much speed on it. Siward pulled on his rein.

'The fields! We'll keep as close to the road as we can and look for a wagon with Varangians on it. That will be Giovanni.'

They kicked their horses and rode on, searching the road to their right for the wagon. They spotted it and turned in, pulling up on either side.

Giovanni was lying on thick straw, his face pale above the armour. Every sway of the wagon, every jolt, was causing him agony. His eyes were shut.

Two Varangians were at the front, one driving, and another walked at the rear. He said to Makkim, 'His back's broken, I think, sir. He fell a long way.'

Makkim got off his horse. He walked beside the wagon, one hand on its side to steady it. People pushed past him, swearing at him for his slowness, but Makkim didn't notice. One man tried to grab his horse's reins, then saw the Varangians and moved on.

Siward glanced behind. There were no signs of greater panic, no terrified shouts of the pursued. The Turks were being held back for now. He turned to Makkim. 'I've got to go. I'm going to get Violetta. I'll meet you at the ship. If I'm not there when the Turks arrive, go without me.'

Makkim took his arm. 'Find her, Siward.'

Siward nodded and steered his horse away from the road. He broke into a trot, then a canter. People made way for the Varangian with fire in his eyes. He navigated his way through the fleeing mass to reach open ground and the sound of distant bells. The terrible message was being passed from tower to tower.

Constantinople had fallen.

At the old wall of Constantine, two men tried to stop him. They were young noblemen who thought their birth entitled them to another man's horse. They rushed him from the ruins and the horse reared and he nearly fell. But he beat one back with the flat of the dragon sword and kicked the other to the ground. He rode into the forum of Arcadius where people were kneeling around a man holding a casket aloft: the finger or toe of some saint. He saw a woman sitting on the ground with shorn hair all around her, another shaving her young son's scalp, a hungry dog circling them both, sniffing at the hair. They said the Turks made no distinction in rape.

At the Forum of Theodosius, there was panic. The Church of St Agnes had people fighting at its doors, trying to get inside. He wanted to shout to them: *they won't respect your sanctuary,* but where else could they go? Mehmed would have declared three days of plunder and they'd be dragged from every hole and cellar they had found. Anyway, he had another church to get to. He kicked his horse and turned north for the Venetian quarter.

There he saw his first Turk. The sea wall must have been abandoned. The Turks were inside the city here, running from house to house, kicking in doors, pulling out the old and young, killing anyone who showed the faintest will to resist, killing just for killing's sake. There were screams and there were prayers shouted loud enough to block out the horror all around. He passed a church in flames, Turks on its steps passing out angels and apostles in frames, gouging the silver from icons with their knives. He rode through it all, slashing at any Turk in his path. None tried to stop him for that might mean forgoing plunder. He reached the Amalfi quarter and passed dogs tugging at a corpse. One looked up, teeth bared, snarling. He passed a child with an arrow in her back and a toy in her hand and heard the screams of her mother being raped indoors. He shut his eyes and rode on.

Another needs me more.

Then the streets were full of ruined houses and empty of Turks. He sped through them and saw the church standing alone in its field, the ribs of its shattered roof stark against the first glimmer of dawn. Soon the sun would rise over Constantinople and its shame would be there for all to see. Soon the sun would rise over a world in which the Roman Empire was no more.

He dismounted and ran into the church, stopping to listen for any sound. He shouted her name once, twice. No answer. He vaulted the benches, looking for a door. He saw one open, the key still in its lock. He went through it and down some steps and found an open trapdoor that led him into a long corridor. He shouted her name again and heard it come back to him alone, his own voice and no other's. He came to a little room with a lamp on its earthen floor, still alight, with a piece of bread lying nearby. He picked up the lamp and, crouching, made his way to the open door at the other end, feeling faint wind on his face and smelling the salt of sea. He entered the tunnel.

Eugenius was on the bank of the Golden Horn and the bundle at his feet was stirring. He'd given her only what was left of the drug that had brought her from the palace, and she was already waking up. She was tied at her wrists and feet and was lying curled up on the ground, clutching her stomach. Was she in pain?

He looked up at the city's walls. They were deserted, abandoned scaling ladders propped against their battlements. There was fire and smoke beyond, and the sounds of greed and terror and sudden death. He looked along the shoreline to where the galleys were beached. Every Turk who could walk was inside Constantinople getting his share of the plunder. Would they be venting their fury on the citizens when they realised how little there was? He looked down. She was lucky to be with him.

Violetta had opened her eyes and was looking up at him.

'What are you doing?' she asked.

The monk studied her. Even dirty and bound, she was beautiful. She would surely have been raped by now if he hadn't brought her here. She should be grateful, not looking at him like that.

'I am saving you,' he said. 'From that.'

He nodded towards the walls. It seemed every sort of horror was stalking the narrow streets beyond. Soon the Horn would be washed with blood.

'I'd rather take my chances there,' she said. 'I'll only slow you down.'

How little she understood, he thought. He saw a younger version of her who'd lain where she lay not so long ago, dead and wrapped, waiting for the boat that would let him send her to the bottom. She'd been a slave, of course, missed by no one, but Violetta was his path to a world where any amount of sin was possible because absolution would be within his gift. He looked around for a boat to take them across to safety. There was one tied to a galley. He rose and looked back down the shore; it was still empty. He bent and tied a gag around Violetta's mouth then shuffled over towards the ship.

He looked over the side. There were men still chained, three to a bench, most with their heads sunk in their folded arms, oars suspended above them. A man looked up. He was a wretched, skeletal thing who looked unlikely to pull the oars for much longer. 'Are you Greek?' he asked. 'Can you free us?'

Eugenius turned away. He untied the boat and pulled it along the shore. He looked up and saw a figure on his knees beside Violetta: tall, fair.

He leant back on the boat and cursed. He looked down and picked up the biggest stone at his feet. Crouching low, he crept up the beach, his eyes never leaving the man's back. The noise from the city was so loud that he could have danced on the shingle and not been heard. Ten paces, five, three.

He rose up and brought the stone down on the man's head, hearing the crack, pitching him forward onto her. He lifted it again, but Siward was still. Eugenius looked at Violetta's hands. They were still tied. He looked at her face. There was more agony there than he ever could have dreamt of.

*

Makkim had left the road and followed the old wall of Constantine north towards the Golden Horn, watching the dawn steal out to reveal the horror of an empire in its death throes. He walked in front of the wagon with two of the Varangians, his sword drawn, ready to clear a path if need be. It had all been agonisingly slow.

They came to the sea wall and turned right, following smaller streets that ran parallel, hoping to avoid the Turks. They heard them all around: arguing, laughing, murdering. A woman ran from a house and fell to her knees before a Varangian, pleading to join them. The man looked at Makkim.

No.

But it wasn't that easy. A sipahi knight came out of the house to find what he'd lost. He saw the Varangians and shouted back through the door for help. Three men emerged to join him and the Varangians turned to face them. The Turks glanced at each other. They'd done their fighting and now it was time for plunder. They backed away, went back inside.

The woman rose, pulling her tunic together, then went to the side of the wagon and looked over.

'I am a nurse,' she said. 'I can help. Take me with you.'

Makkim looked at her. She was pretty. She'd not last long. He nodded. 'Look after him in the wagon. Cover both of you with straw.'

They went on, through more streets and alleys, horror all around them. They passed the Horaia Gate and came to the little harbour of Proshorianus, the chain still strung across its entrance. The Genoese round ship was tied to the quay, its gangplank down. Two Varangians lay dead on the ground.

A voice addressed them from the ship. It spoke in Italian.

'We've had to commandeer your ship, I'm afraid,' said

454

Minotto. He was leaning over the rail and had two men with crossbows either side of him. He was wearing armour spattered with gore and his face was almost black. 'Ours was burnt, you see.'

Makkim looked up at the round ship. It was Salazar's, the same that had brought Violetta into Constantinople. He could see a dozen Venetian soldiers, and at least that many Genoese sailors, but no Salazar. He must be locked in some cabin, or dead. Whichever it was, the ship was about to set sail. No one wanted to stay a moment longer.

'Do you have Longo in that wagon?' asked Minotto, this time in Greek. 'I'd heard he fell before the Emperor did.'

Constantine had fallen? The last Emperor of Rome had died? It should be shouted from the heavens, not spoken like this. Makkim glanced at the Varangian next to him who was slowly shaking his head in disbelief. There was the sound of a crossbow released and the man staggered backwards. Then two more Varangians fell behind him.

Makkim backed towards the wagon, waiting for the bolt. He said, 'Longo needs to get away. He is very hurt. He has a nurse with him.'

Minotto gestured. 'Then they can come aboard. You too. My men will carry Longo up.'

Makkim knew he had no choice. They'd not make it to another boat. He had planned to leave Giovanni at the round ship, then go in search of Violetta, but the ship was setting sail and he couldn't leave his father alone with Minotto.

He followed the stretcher up the gangplank. At the top, they lifted Giovanni gently onto the aft-deck. Makkim knelt and took his hand. Minotto crouched at his other side. Giovanni opened his eyes and turned his head slowly to his son.

455

'Is it true?' he whispered. Makkim could feel no pressure from his hand. 'Is it true that the Emperor has fallen?'

When Makkim didn't reply, Giovanni let out a long groan and closed his eyes. It was true. It had all been in vain. The last Emperor of Rome was dead.

'God help us,' he whispered. He looked at Minotto. 'The reptiles will take over the world.'

The ship was moving. Two giant paddles were being worked by three men on each side of the aft-deck, steering it slowly towards the harbour entrance where the chain had been released.

There were more explosions from the city and a sheet of flame leapt up, then another. The air was filled with the sounds of ecstasy and agony. Constantinople was dying.

Violetta had held the plate fast to her body throughout every part of her ordeal. She'd clutched its cold metal to her flesh under her clothes, feeling the sharpness of its rim with her fingers, holding it there beneath her folded arms.

She'd wanted to tell Siward about it but he had to untie her gag first. She'd wanted to warn him about the monk, too, who would be back soon. She'd wanted to tell him that she loved him more than any creature on this earth. Her eyes had been fixed to his as he'd stretched round to untie the gag and her head had swum with the miracle of him being there.

Then horror. She'd seen the monk rise up suddenly behind him, both hands raised above his head. She'd heard the crack and felt the full weight of his body fall onto hers. Beneath the gag she'd screamed out her fury.

At first she'd thought him dead. He'd lain there so still, the blood pooling in the folds of her tunic. But then she'd felt warm

456

breath on her arm and his heart's solid beat against her body. *Thank God.*

The monk had seen that he lived too, so he'd taken his dragon sword and tied him as he'd tied her. Then he'd risen and begun to drag Siward's body towards the boat. It had taken him a long time, for Siward was big. He'd returned breathing heavily.

Then it had been her turn. She'd held the plate flat to her breasts as he'd heaved her over the pebbles, bruising her heels and bottom, stopping to rest, mumbling all the while. Then he'd lifted her onto the boat and the plate had dug into her and she'd bitten her lip hard beneath her gag.

The priest had begun to row, Siward unconscious at the back and she on her knees at the front. She watched his back as he pulled on the oars, and very slowly, very carefully, she began to rub the side of the plate against the ropes binding her wrists. She felt one strand break, then another. And she began to chew aside the gag.

Violetta heard movement on the other side of Eugenius. Siward was stirring, coughing out the dried blood in his mouth. He wasn't gagged and he spoke.

'Where is she?'

'Behind me,' said the monk. 'Can't you see her?'

She saw Siward shuffle his body to a place where he could see her. Their eyes met.

'Where are you taking us?'

'To Zaganos bey's tent, to await his return. Then Mehmed.'

Siward coughed again, spat out more blood. 'Why does Mehmed want us?'

The monk paused in his rowing, rubbing his arms. There was a mist on the water that shimmered in the first sunshine and he looked out at it. 'You, I don't know if he does want. We shall see. But he wants her, certainly.' He tilted his head. 'He can't hurt Makkim any more but he can hurt her.'

Siward frowned. He realised something. 'But Makkim lives, priest,' he said. 'He lives to kill you.'

'No. I saw him impaled.'

'It was someone else.' He sat up, his tied hands before him. 'Makkim lives and he has made his peace with Mehmed. He is waiting for you.'

Violetta felt giddy. Could it be true? She met his eye. *It is true.* She finally broke through the gag and found herself smiling. She had to distract the priest.

'And you have another problem,' she said. 'This boat is leaking.'

The priest turned and Siward lunged. He was tied at the wrists and ankles but he was a missile in bondage. He struck the monk's side with his head, sending him to the bottom of the boat. But the monk was not badly hurt, and he was quick. He reached for the oar.

Violetta had the plate's sides between her thighs, its rim up. She sawed frantically and felt the last strands give way. Her hands came apart. She took the plate and rose to her knees, then her feet. The monk had his back to her. *This time.*

She swung the plate down, felt its rim, sharp as any blade, slice into his neck. She drove it in again and again, blinded by the blood that splashed across her face. Only when the neck was half-severed did she stop.

She slumped across his body, the bloodied plate still in her hands. Then, finally, she wept.

Like a child.

CHAPTER FORTY-THREE

CONSTANTINOPLE

Makkim knelt beside his father watching another siege reach its conclusion. For the past three hours, death's army had battered at the walls of Giovanni's mind and now was inside it. Makkim was watching his father die.

Minotto had gone to the prow, leaving him, Giovanni and the nurse on the aft-deck with the men pulling the paddles. They'd brought a mattress up from a cabin and laid him on it, his head propped up against a stanchion. His face was the texture of wet calfskin, his eyes sunk deep in shadow. He yearned for water but couldn't swallow it through his swollen throat. Whatever the pain, he wished to speak.

'What of the city?' he whispered, his eyes on his son's.

Makkim looked out across the morning mist, watching the sunlight gather in its many folds. They said Venice's lagoon was like this, but beyond this mist was the city Venice had once aspired to be. Now, what was left of its palaces and churches, its baths and markets, its libraries and universities, was being torn apart by a barbarian army he'd once commanded. Thank God he no longer did. He looked down at Giovanni.

'The city is taken, Father,' he said softly. 'Mehmed will be riding his horse into Hagia Sophia soon.'

Giovanni closed his eyes. 'The slaughter will be very great.'

It was probably true. He thought of Siward and Violetta caught somewhere within the chaos, whom he couldn't save now. 'You held out for two months with old men and monks against the best army in the world. You have nothing to reproach yourself for.'

Giovanni grimaced as he sipped at the water they offered. He tried to take Makkim's hand, touching his son's fingers so gently that they hardly connected. 'I abandoned them, Makkim,' he said. 'I left the walls and the men saw it and they fled.'

'You had no choice. Others took you away.'

Giovanni waited for the nurse to massage the water down his neck before speaking again. 'What of Siward?'

'He'll have found a boat, be sure of it.'

Makkim looked back at the city, suspended above the mist beneath its tonsure of smoke. He scanned the shoreline. He saw the top halves of galleys beached all along it with their oars in the air and sails still spread. He looked back down the Golden Horn and saw no other ships floating in the fog. Were Violetta and Siward waiting for him somewhere? He was surprised by how much he wanted both of them to be. *Both of them.*

Siward had just thrown the monk overboard, then watched him float into the mist in his inflated habit, a slick of blood following behind. Soon, he'd sink to the bottom to join his child victims.

He sat down on a plank and she sat opposite him. She still held the bloodied plate in her hands.

'What do we do now?' she asked. Her smile said that she didn't much care what they did. They had survived and were together under a new morning.

460

'Well,' he said, taking the plate from her and putting it down, 'we have two shores to choose from.' He pointed. 'I suggest Pera. We might pick up a Genoese ship to take us out.'

'But will that be quick enough? Minotto will be on his way to join the Venetian fleet by now.'

Siward took up the oars. 'It's our only choice.' He began to row, leaning forward so that their knees touched with each motion. She was silent and he knew she was thinking about Makkim, caught between joy that he was alive and the agony of guilt and fear. He looked at her over his knees and said gently, 'Makkim will be alright. He'll take Giovanni to Chios and we'll all meet up again.'

She picked up the plate and dipped it in the sea. It caught the morning sun as it emerged, making a sister sun.

'What's that?'

He'd seen a ship. It was Salazar's and it was coming their way, riding the mist like an apparition, its sails stretched out to gather every breath of wind.

She rose and climbed past him to the front, still holding the plate. 'That's Salazar's ship.' She looked round, her eyes bright with excitement. 'It must be Makkim and Giovanni. They made it!'

Siward stared. It wasn't Makkim at the prow but someone else, and the Lion of Venice was flying from its mast. He thought quickly. Minotto would want to join the fleet at Negroponte as quickly as possible, but he might stop for Violetta. He said, 'Stay where you are and don't turn round. I am going over the side. They'll take you aboard and tie the boat to the stern. Then I'll think of something.'

He picked up his sword and tucked it into his belt. He slipped over the side into the water. She waited a moment, then waved and shouted.

The round ship slowed and came about and as predicted, Violetta was brought aboard. The little boat was fed round to the stern and tied up while Siward clung unseen to its hull. He held his breath for what seemed an eternity.

When he could bear it no longer, he felt his way to the back and surfaced silently, his fingers over the stern rail. He watched men above working the paddles to get the ship underway again. He saw Violetta come to the rail with Makkim and look out. Makkim was tied at the wrists but the message was clear. *Hope.*

Much later, the hope had given way to reality. It was night and Siward was still in the water and colder than he could remember. He had a dragon sword in his belt but there were a score of Venetians aboard with crossbows and handguns. Makkim was up there but how was he to get to him?

First he had to get out of the water. He climbed as soundlessly as he could over the back of the skiff and lay there for a moment, shivering and looking up at the full moon. They were somewhere in the Sea of Marmara and he'd not seen any other sails all day. There was a cool breeze coming in from the north and the ship was moving quickly through the water. He crawled his way to the front of the boat, took hold of the rope and began to pull himself slowly towards the ship, grateful for the noise of its wake.

Once there, he used the rope to haul himself out of the boat, then walk up the back of the ship, arm over arm, foot over foot, pausing with every creak of its timbers. At the top he waited, then pulled himself up to peer over the side. There were two men at the tiller, talking quietly, looking up at the stars from time to time. They might be Genoese or Venetian, probably Genoese. Against the side lay a man on a mattress with two

462

women bent over him. Where was Makkim? He lifted himself onto the rail and dropped silently onto the deck.

Makkim was beside him. He was seated with his back to the ship's side, his tied hands in his lap. He nodded at the men on the tiller. 'They're Genoese,' he whispered. 'Following orders.'

Siward pulled his sword from his belt and cut Makkim's ropes. Together, they crept over to the tiller. 'Just keep steering, don't look back,' Siward said to the men in a low voice. He glanced over to where Giovanni lay. Violetta was signalling for him to lie down. He dropped to his stomach and Makkim sat down in front of him and joined his hands together as if still tied.

Minotto came onto the upper deck. With him were two men in armour carrying crossbows. He looked around for Makkim.

'I'm over here. Learning how to navigate.'

Minotto nodded and walked over to where Violetta knelt beside Giovanni. Siward could just hear their conversation.

'How is he?'

'Unconscious,' Violetta murmured. 'He'll not last the night.'

Minotto was silent after that. Whatever his allegiance, he was first a soldier and he knew what the man below him had done.

She asked, 'When will we get to Negroponte?'

'Negroponte? What makes you think we're going there?'

'Because,' she said , 'that is where your fleet is. The one that is going to Ceuta.' She looked squarely at him. 'We know the plan.'

Minotto sighed. 'Well, it's too late now, courtesan.'

'Not so,' she said. 'Others have been told and are on their way to Portugal. You'll not take Ceuta.'

Minotto laughed. 'I think we will. No other ship can get out of Constantinople, I promise you. The city is surrounded. As I said, it's too late.'

'Will you be leading the fleet to Ceuta?'

463

Minotto put his head to one side. 'I have that honour, yes. Why?'

Giovanni spoke then. His voice was faint. 'Because it's mad,' he said. 'You'll need Portuguese navigators to take you down Africa, Portuguese maps.'

Minotto looked down. 'We have the only map that matters,' he said, 'the one your father so generously helped with.'

'You murdered him,' said Giovanni.

Minotto dropped into a crouch. 'Perhaps,' he said, 'but think of what will come of it.'

'You will let Islam take over the world.' Giovanni was trying to speak louder but his voice was breaking.

Minotto shrugged. 'Islam and trade combine well enough. They can do the religion, we'll do the commerce. Everyone is happy.'

Minotto rose. He walked towards the steps down to the main deck, the men with crossbows following him. He stopped and looked up. 'Ah, the wind is freshening. Good.'

Siward slowly raised his head from the deck. He could see the lion stretching its claws away from the masthead. He looked at the men on the tiller. He had to judge it right.

'Step away from the tiller,' he whispered.

He rolled over onto his back and gauged the distance. He sprang to his feet and threw all his weight against the tiller arm. The ship let forth a groan and turned aside. The sails filled and it lurched, sending barrels, buckets and men spinning across the deck.

'Now, Makkim, *now*!'

They both ran to the edge of the aft-deck and leapt over. As Siward had guessed, the two crossbowmen had dropped their loaded weapons. He picked up one, Makkim the other. They both fired and the two Venetians went down. Makkim bent and pulled a sword from its scabbard.

464

The fight was unequal. As more Venetians came running across the deck, Makkim and Siward were outnumbered ten to one, but they were many times more skilled than the men they fought. They were light and agile, the Venetians armoured and cumbersome. And they fought on a deck that was plunging.

Two more Venetians went down, then a third, fourth and fifth. But Siward had seen something from the corner of his eye.

'Handgun!' he yelled.

They threw themselves back with the explosion, the shot missing them by inches. But they were on their backs now and too far from their enemy for their swords to reach. Another handgunner was taking aim.

There was an explosion, this time from behind them. They turned to see Salazar standing in his cabin doorway, its splintered door hanging from its hinges. He had a gun in each hand, one of them smoking. He swung round and fired again and the man taking aim dropped his gun.

'Beneath my bed in case of mutiny,' Salazar shouted. He dropped the guns to the floor. 'Give me a sword.'

They'd not seen Minotto climb to the upper deck.

'Put down your weapons or she dies.'

Minotto was standing holding Violetta to his front, one arm around her neck, one hand pointing a dagger to her ribs. 'You know I'll do it.'

Siward and Makkim slowly laid their swords on the deck. Out of the corner of his eye, Siward saw Salazar inching away from his cabin. He was invisible to the upper deck.

'Release her, Minotto,' said Siward. 'You've won.' He'd lost sight of Salazar but it seemed right to keep the conversation going. 'What will you do with us?'

'Nothing too dreadful,' said Minotto. He tightened his hold on

Violetta's throat. 'Just tie you up and drop you off at Negroponte.'

Makkim said, 'You know my father won't last that long. He needs to be put ashore at Chios.'

Minotto shook his head. 'You have a nurse. Let her do her calling.'

At that moment, Salazar intervened again. He was standing behind a ribaudkin this time. It was pointing downwards at the deck.

'Enough! *Enough!*' he shouted. 'I don't care if the courtesan lives or dies, but I'm not going to let Venice rule the world. Tell your men to drop their weapons or I'll sink this ship.'

Minotto couldn't see him. 'You'd sink your own ship?'

'If I have to. And at this range, it would only take a matter of minutes. Not long enough for your men to remove their armour.'

Siward saw the Venetians exchange glances. Drowning wasn't what they'd expected. One by one, they laid down their arms.

Minotto also watched them in silence. Then he started to drag Violetta towards the stern, the knife still at her chest. He reached the rail and pushed her away.

Then he made a deep bow, turned, and climbed onto the rail. He jumped.

By evening, Giovanni was very weak. They'd set up a canvas awning over him for shade but he was fading and Chios was still far away.

The wind had dropped and the sun they were sailing towards was low in the sky. They'd rolled back the canvas so he could see it set. The sea behind them was an unbroken wake of molten gold and somewhere on it Minotto was adrift in a boat, waiting for Hamza Bey's fleet to arrive and learn that Ceuta would be warned of their coming.

Makkim knelt on one side of Giovanni, Siward the other, Violetta at his head. They were a trinity as still as he, as calm as the sea around them, waiting on every word coaxed from his mouth. He spoke in short, whispered sentences, staring up at the evening sky through eyes already trained on a different world.

'He wanted us together,' he said, 'and we are here. That is good.'

'And we'll be together on Chios,' said Makkim, 'where you will rest and get better.'

They let the lie settle gently as a mayfly on water. There had been so many lies, though none so kindly meant. Its place was there, amongst them: comfortable and at home.

Giovanni breathed in slowly. 'What . . . ?'

Siward knew what he wanted to ask. 'We will put in at Chios, then I'll go to Venice. From there it'll take me three weeks to reach Portugal, which is a quarter of the time the fleet will take to row along the African coast to Ceuta. There will be time for a fleet out of Lagos to intercept it.' He considered. 'That is, if Hamza Bey doesn't turn back after he's picked up Minotto.'

'And Makkim?'

'I will stay with you on Chios,' said Makkim.

Giovanni moved his head. 'Not that. Have you decided?'

Makkim knew what he meant. He nodded very slowly. This could not be a lie, however kindly meant. 'Yes, we have spoken.' He looked up at Siward. He reached out and took his cousin's hand so that Giovanni could see them joined. 'We will work together, join the trading company with the bank.' He paused. 'As Luke wanted.'

'Ah, now that is good.' Giovanni closed his eyes and smiled. He was still smiling a minute later, when he released his final breath.

CHAPTER FORTY-FOUR

VENICE, THEN SAGRES PENINSULA

Coming fast behind Doge Foscari's impeachment, Violetta's marriage to the Varangopoulos Siward Magoris was a double celebration. If the preparations seemed hasty, it had more to do with Zoe's signs of leaving the world than Violetta's of bringing someone new into it.

The wedding was a watery affair, staged on the Grand Canal so that Zoe could watch it all from the balcony of her fondaco. A gondola had been consecrated and garlanded for the occasion and the bishop stood on a box at its prow to officiate. They waited until after the blessing before pushing him in, the Church being blamed for supporting the Doge. The Ceuta fiasco, stopped in its tracks once Minotto had been fished from the Sea of Marmara, was to be a State secret. Minotto had been exiled to Crete.

The wedding gondola contained Siward and Violetta, both dressed in white beneath an arch of blossom, with Makkim and Johannes Grant who'd sent the bishop over the side. Makkim wore the *thoub* of the Muslim, having put aside Mehmed and his empire, but not Islam. His hair was long, as was his beard, and he called himself Ilya.

In their wake came a fleet separated by gender: the cortigiane oneste to the left of the canal, the Varangians to the right. Then came the grandees of Venice, still shamed by Violetta's trial. Most didn't want to be there at all, but Loredan had warned of revolution were they to snub the courtesan. And anyway, Zoe Mamonas was paying for it all.

As the flotilla passed under the Rialto bridge, the cortigiane di lume, breasts put away for the occasion, showered the boats with petals and a few dropped, less lightly, into the laps of the Varangians. Theogrid had done what he'd said he'd do. After Constantine had fallen, he'd marched the Varangians to a harbour where they'd taken ship for Mistra. The Despot had not wanted them to go to Venice, but they'd set sail with Nikolas anyway. Not a single Varangian would miss Siward's wedding, nor the entertainments of this city.

So, by the time it reached Zoe's balcony, the party was noisy and the bishop amongst company in the canal. The cortigiane oneste, provoked by their lume sisters, had stripped down to their petticoats and were jousting with the Varangian boats, using oars for lances, to the drummed tempo of the musicians' barge.

Meanwhile, Siward and Violetta, sober and happy, slipped ashore to bid farewell to Zoe. They climbed the stairs of the fondaco hand in hand, not wanting to speak into the sudden gloom. They found Zoe propped up in bed, shaded beneath a giant awning, with Nikolas by her side.

She was dying fast. Somewhere among its foul airs, the rot of Venice had finally entered her tired marrow. She'd succumbed to a cold that she'd have sneezed off in any other year. She'd lingered on, wrapped and leeched on her gigantic bed, for the sole purpose of seeing Siward and Violetta one more time. Now she held out her hand to Violetta.

469

'Good. You've come. Nikolas tells me Giovanni's dead.'

The sheets were scented but the smell of decay rose from the bed like old food. She was unveiled and her wasted face looked like charcoal, but her eyes were still bright as comets. Violetta sat down on the bed and took her hand. 'Giovanni died a hero's death,' she said gently. 'We buried him on Chios, next to Luke.'

'Makkim?'

'Is downstairs. He is coming with us to Chios.'

'That's close to Mehmed's lands.'

'He has grown hair and a beard that almost covers his scar. And he's changed his name back to what it was: Ilya. Makkim died at Constantinople. Mehmed won't look for him.'

Zoe nodded slowly, her mouth open, her tongue resting on her lower lip as she absorbed this information. Then she turned to Siward. 'You are married now, which is good. And you've some money.'

'Thanks to you, the bank is now solvent. We'll operate it from Chios where Ilya will also run his trading company.'

Zoe moved her head slightly. 'With the map, Prince Henry can do great things now.' There was a rattle to her breathing. 'But he'll need money, lots of it. I am leaving my fortune to you and Violetta. Spend it on that.'

They stared at her. The Mamonas bank was second only to the Medici in wealth. Combined with the Magoris, it would be greater. They would be the richest couple in Europe.

Zoe smiled. She closed her eyes and let out a long breath. 'Good. Now I can die.'

On the Sagres peninsula, it was a day of bluster and big white animals that chased each other across the blue plains of the sky, or so thought Siward as he stood between Violetta and Ilya. They were there to see their combined fortunes put to work.

It was half a year since Constantinople had fallen to a man they now called Fatih – conqueror. His fame would echo through the ages of man. He might have ruled the world.

Siward was watching a boy who was part of a group that stood a little away from them. It included Prince Henry of Portugal, Fra Mauro and the boy's father, King Lydislaw. Siward had been watching the boy for some time. He'd seen him look at the adults holding hats to their heads, at the grass that made patterns as it turned, sometimes at the ships in the sea below: three caravels out of Lagos, each with a cross on its lateen sail, each flying the flags of Portugal and the Magoris Company of Chios. But always, he noticed, he looked back to the west.

He pointed this out to Violetta who stood next to him and held his hand. Her condition made her into a sail at full stretch and the wind wrapped her cloak round her legs like rigging. She glanced at the boy.

'Christopher? It's because he speaks to Fra Mauro. Isn't that so, Ilya?'

Ilya looked over at the boy. He smiled. 'He's done little else since arriving from Madeira. He almost sleeps in his office.'

'And what does Fra Mauro tell him?'

'That it's not only to the east we should look.'

'Ah, that would explain it.'

Siward looked down at the marbled landscape of the sea, turning his face to the wind. The three caravels looked tiny in its enormity, even though they rode the waves with grace. He thought of Fra Mauro, now safe in Portugal with the correct map, the one that showed a world open to the East.

He turned to Violetta. 'Our son will grow up in a world

471

without the Roman Empire. He'll know that we three were in Constantinople when Rome fell, when the world changed forever. I hope he'll make sense of it.'

Violetta drew herself into him, pressing the life inside her to another she loved more than her own.

'You assume it's a boy,' she said.

HISTORICAL NOTE

In the 15th century, the world was both changing and enlarging. The Renaissance had brought new scientific thinking and, more than anyone, the Portuguese had embraced it to promote discovery. Locked out of Mediterranean trade by their geography, they were determined to find a way around Africa to the rich Indies. In 1415, they took the North African fortress of Ceuta from the Arabs and in 1421 discovered the island of Madeira, which became a rich sugar producer. In the 1440s they reached the Guinea coast of West Africa and began trading gold up the Niger delta. But it wouldn't be until the end of the century that Bartolomeu Dias would round the Cape of Good Hope.

All of this was made possible by the extraordinarily talented House of Aviz that came to the throne in 1385. They were the children and grandchildren of Philippa of Lancaster who'd married King John I of Portugal. Known to this day as 'The Illustrious Generation', they included Prince Henry the Navigator (1394-1460), brother to the king, who assembled a court of astronomers, map-makers, navigators and other men of science. Among other initiatives, they invented the first ship able to sail into the wind, the Caravel, thus allowing expeditions to take advantage of the trade winds.

This was bad news to the Venetians who, in the first half of the 15th century, were at the height of their power and wealth. The fall of Constantinople would matter much to them, as the city was the main western entrepot for the Silk Road. Moreover, with a monopoly of trade with Alexandria and virtual control of the sea-lanes of the eastern Mediterranean, they had much to lose by Portugal opening up the Indian Ocean. In particular, they minded the loss of the gold trade, most of which came to them from the African empire of Mali via Alexandria. It had made them the bullion centre of Europe.

The Doges who ruled the Venetian republic were elderly, elected and usually wise, but at the time of Constantinople's fall, Doge Francesco Foscari (1373–1457) was a bitter and reclusive man, made so by the exile of his son Jacopo to Crete for corruption.

A consequence of this changing world was a new fascination in maps. Fra Mauro of the Camaldolese monastery on Murano in Venice was commissioned by Venice and Portugal to make the definitive map of the world. Most maps at this time still adhered to those of Ptolemy of Alexandria (100–170 AD), which showed the Indian Ocean closed to the west. The map was finished around 1460 (so rather later than described in the book) and is now in the Correr Museum in Venice. As Siward saw, it indeed describes how Chinese junks had already sailed round Africa from the east, nearly a century before Bartolomeu Dias. These were the fleets of the Ming Emperors who sent the eunuch admiral Zheng He out to dominate the Indian Ocean in seven great expeditions between 1405 and 1433. Their abrupt cessation in the mid-15th century meant that the Portuguese would meet much less resistance in their eastern conquests.

The book's story is set against one of the most momentous events of history. The fall of Constantinople in 1453 was the fall of the two-thousand-year-old Roman Empire. It is often assumed that Rome fell to German barbarians in the 5th century, but in actuality, the eastern half went on for another one thousand years. We call it the Byzantine Empire, perhaps because all emperors after Justinian (482–565 AD) spoke Greek. But they, and everyone else, called themselves Roman.

Such an event had been prophesied to herald the end of days, a catastrophe so great that Christendom would never recover. But the fall of Constantinople, like so many catastrophes, turned out to be the start of a golden age for the West. The passage of time demonstrates that it was, in fact, one of history's great turning points.

Once a city of six hundred thousand, Constantinople had always been the gateway to Europe, the bridge between East and West, as it still is. It had been almost mythic in its greatness, in the wealth of its churches and palaces, the strength of its triple walls, the glory of its pomp and ritual. Indeed, it was the model for Tolkien's Minas Tirith that guarded Middle Earth from the hordes of Mordor.

The city had been besieged before. Arabs, Huns, Avars, Bulgars – the Ottoman Sultans Bayezid and Murad – all had tried to breach its walls over the centuries. But only Venice and the Fourth Crusade had succeeded, leading to the disastrous sixty-year Latin Empire (1204–1261), from which it never recovered. The city was stripped of much of its wealth (for example, the four horses of its hippodrome were sent off to St Mark's in Venice) and most of its territory. By 1453, the city was a place of fields and ruins and patched-up churches where only fifty thousand lived. Meanwhile, beyond its battered walls, all that was left of the Roman Empire was the Greek Peloponnese where the Emperor's brothers ruled their tiny Despotate of Mistra amidst a late flowering of artistic genius.

For decades, Roman Emperors had appealed to the West for help against the growing Turkish menace. Since gaining a foothold in Europe in 1354, the Ottomans had conquered as far as the Danube but crusade after crusade had failed to stem the tide. The price of these crusades had always been Church union. Since 1054, the Catholic and Orthodox Churches had been in schism over matters of dogma and, at the Council of Florence in 1438, the Pope and Roman Emperor had finally reached agreement on union, although the people of Constantinople later rejected it. A last crusade was launched that ended in 1444 at the disaster of Varna.

Mehmed II became Sultan in 1451 at the age of nineteen and at first seemed conciliatory to Byzantium. But it was not only Christendom's fate that was linked to Constantinople's: for Mehmed, failure to take the city might cost him his throne and life. He had ruled once before, brought to power at the age of twelve by his father, Murad, who'd wanted to retire to a monastery. But the young Mehmed had been a disastrous ruler and had had to recall his father to meet a surprise attack from King Lydislaw of Hungary who'd broken a ten-year truce. Murad had won at Varna but Mehmed had been humiliated. For Mehmed, winning Constantinople meant everything.

The siege lasted only two months but it was hard-fought and, for a time, it looked like the Roman Emperor Constantine XI might throw back the Turks. But Mehmed had prepared well. He'd built a fleet to blockade Constantinople (or the Venetian *arsenale* had built one for him) and a castle on the Bosporos to close the city to the north, the aptly-named 'Throat-cutter'. He'd massively increased the ranks of the elite janissary corps – slave-soldiers taken from the villages of Eastern Europe – to build an army perhaps one-hundred-thousand-strong, and he'd commissioned huge cannon from the Hungarian gunsmith Orban, who'd first offered his services to the impoverished Constantine.

The Emperor Constantine XI was forty-eight when the siege began. He'd been crowned in Mistra in 1449 because Constantinople had been considered too dangerous. At Constantinople, he had a garrison of only six thousand, made up of Greeks, Venetians, Genoese and warriors of other nations drawn to the call of stopping Islam from conquering the world. His commander was the brilliant Genoese Giovanni Giustiniani Longo, who, in an act of reckless chivalry, had brought seven hundred men-at-arms from the Island of Chios to fight for the cause. It was he who persuaded the warring Christian factions to fight side by side, and the population to come out to rebuild the walls every night.

There's no evidence that the men he brought with him were Varangians. The Varangian Guard was an elite body mainly recruited from Scandinavia, then England, with large numbers arriving after the Norman conquest of 1066. They were the Emperor's Praetorian Guard, carried large axes and had their own church in Constantinople. It is likely that the guard had died out by the time of the siege.

The events of the siege are pretty much as I describe them in the book: the initial Ottoman bombardments and assaults on the walls, the arrival of the three Genoese roundships, Mehmed dragging his galleys over the hill into the Golden Horn, the doomed fireship response, the final assault when Constantine died on the walls and Giustiniani was mortally wounded. It was an exciting battle.

While the main characters are invented, the book also includes many people who really existed.

Cleope Malatesta was the Pope's niece. She came from Italy to Mistra to marry the Despot Theodore II Palaiologos as part of the plan to reunite the Churches of East and West. It was not a happy marriage. Theodore was serious and devotional and Cleope beautiful and fun-loving. She died young at the age of thirty-three.

A similarly bad marriage was that of the Infanta Eleanor of Portugal to the grim Holy Roman Emperor Frederick III (1415–1493). As described in the book, she made a perilous sea-journey from Portugal to Rome to marry him, during which she was attacked by pirates. There is no evidence that the Fra Mauro map was presented to her in Rome after her marriage.

Her aunt Isabella, Duchess of Burgundy (1397–1471), was another extraordinary woman. Married to Philip the Good, one of the richest princes in Europe, her astuteness in diplomacy and trade did much to enrich the kingdom. Her mother had been the redoubtable Philippa of Lancaster.

My heroine Violetta Cavarse is based on the great 16th century Venetian courtesan Veronica Franco, about whom the film 'A Dangerous Beauty' was made. There were two types of courtesan in 15th century Venice, the *cortigiane oneste* and the *cortigiane di lume*. The former were women of great influence who kept the company of princes. Like Violetta, Veronica Franco was tried for treason, but acquitted. There is no evidence of any courtesan spy ring being operated in Venice.

So far as the story's men are concerned, the philosopher Georgius Gemistus Plethon (1355–1452) lived most of his life in Mistra, advising the various despots and creating his own eccentric theories of how the Peloponnese should return to its Hellenic roots to protect itself from the Turks. He died just before the siege began.

Girolamo Minotto was the bailo of Constantinople who rallied the Venetians in defence of the city and died on its walls. There's no evidence that he conspired with the Turks or was anything other than heroic.

On the Ottoman side, the Vizier Candarli Halil tried hard to restrain the impetuous young Mehmed in his reckless ambition. He'd been his father Murad's vizier and instrumental in bringing him back after Mehmed's first attempt at ruling. He was executed soon after Constantinople fell.

Zaganos bey was Mehmed's young Second Vizier and Candarli's nemesis. He encouraged Mehmed to march on Constantinople and was instrumental in holding him to his purpose after Baltaoğlu's disaster with the fleet.

Finally, we come to the intriguing King Lydislaw of Poland (1424–1444), who broke a ten-year truce agreed between Sultan Murad and the Pope and paid the price on the field of Varna. Officially he is supposed to have fallen in the battle, leading a last, desperate charge of his knights, but Portuguese legend has it that he escaped to Madeira where King Alfonso V granted him lands in the Cabo Girao, and he called himself 'Henry the German'. The theory that he was Christopher Columbus's father has been put forward by the Spanish historian Manuel Rosa, to join the many other speculations over the origins of the great explorer.

By Blood Divided has been written as story in its own right, but it does make constant reference to events and people that appear in the trilogy of books that precede it, and which feature Byzantine history over the period 1395-1420 and the characters of Luke and Zoe in their younger years. This was a fascinating time of crusade, the Mongol invasion of Tamerlane, civil war and expanding trade. The story of how the Roman Empire managed to survive a few more decades in such turbulent times is compelling.